AMONG THE FORGOTTEN

THE TESINDREN CHRONICLES
BOOK I

J.R. molt

Copyright © 2025 J.R. Molt

All rights reserved.

ISBN:
ISBN-13: 978-107370585-9-5

For my sweet potato, my darling Aurelia.
I love you with all my heart and soul.
You are the best gift God has ever given me.

For myself, the world you dreamed of is real at last.

For my reader, Tesindren will always welcome you home.

PRONUNCIATION GUIDE

CHARACTERS

Evara	Ee-var-ah
Caturthirian	Cat-ur-thee-reean
Jera	Jeh-rah
Türe	Tooh-r
Ivrik	Ihv-rick
Patryk	Pat-reek
Noran	No-ran
Eivan	Eye-van
Ilithyia	Ill-ith-yah
Athene	Ah-theen
Tanth	Tan-th
Isos	Eye-sos
Ionel Vacos	Eye-oh-nell Vah-kos
Arne	Arn
Hira	Hee-rah
Ladir	Lay-der
Rhodie	Road-ee
Dakar	Dah-kar
Ygrette	E-gret

OTHER

Nefriti	Neh-free-tee
Tomyris	Tom-ih-rhis
Magnar	Mag-nar
Florenta	Flow-ren-tah
Ynyra	In-rah

PLACES

Tesindren	Te-sin-drehn
Mirinth	Meer-in-th
Telor	Teh-lor
Paith	Pay-th
Eri	Eh-re
Bethos	Beh-thos
Eludar	Eh-loh-dar
Dolunt	Doh-loont
Merga	Mare-gah
Zanda	Zan-da
Anopthe	Ah-nope-they
Grezon	Gray-son
Alessandra	Ah-less-ann-d:
Vante	Van-te
Erit	Eh-reet
Saroch	Sah-row-ch
Naro	Nah-row
Dulen	Doo-lehn
Charobi	Kah-robee
Dothsmerna	Dawth-smeer-r
Sobek	Soh-beck
Baol	Bay-oh-l

TESINDREN
Forest of Memory
Baol Range
GREZON
Telor
Keena River
The River Road
ANOPTHE
ELUDAR
Lake Muir
ALESSANDRA
DOLUNT
MERGA
Agreto River
Bethos
Tugene River
VANTE
Lake Naro
Glin Ford
NARO
Eri
ERIT
Paith
ZANDA
Lake Chine
SAROCH
The Cliffs
DULEN
CHAROBI
Field of Pilar
ISLE OF SOBEK
MIRINTH

BEFORE

The bright light streaming down from the full moon above only makes the shadows stretch out ominously, their dark tendrils seeming to reach for me.

I had once more made my decision. But this time, I had people to hurt. People to forget. I pace back and forth, trying to think of what to say as the weight of a painfully familiar set of eyes track me. I don't know if I should be offended or relieved at the realization that he doesn't look even remotely surprised to be called there. In fact, he looks expectant. Like I had been stressing over my decision worthlessly when it had been clear all along what I would choose. Again.

A fact that makes the struggle happening in my heart only worsen.

"You are going. Aren't you?" The usually bright, intelligent face looks weary and sad. He asks, mostly out of courtesy. It was clear he knew the answer already. Pain glints like splintered shards of glass in his eyes, turning them even more of a silvery green than normal. So potent is his sorrow, I can feel it radiating, thick and heavy, sweeping through and clouding the once pure garden air that we had whispered so many secrets in, and shared so many kisses among the flower beds.

My steps falter, stumbling over my want for indecision. My gossamer skirts swish gently as a slight spring breeze kicks up the fabric in a soft rustle. Taking a shaky breath, I try to still the wind before it can feed on my mood and turn into a raging storm. I can only nod, though I try to force the words.

I don't have to do this if you don't want me to.

I will remember you.

I am still unsure.

I don't even want to do this.

But I can't. Anyway, he would know it's a lie. I can feel his eyes continue to track me as I begin to pace back and forth again. All the things I should say are replaced with defensive biting words as I stifle the tears that spring into my eyes.

"I have a duty. To everyone. Too many people are counting on me." I run through it all, every argument I have been lecturing myself on for the past month—the final countdown to this ultimate decision.

I don't reveal the true deciding factor. One I don't even like to dwell on myself. As if just acknowledging the deadly path could be what would take me down, should I falter in my devotion to the Goddess Jera.

He probably knows my fear anyway.

Shivering as another gust of wind rushes past me, I cast a thought to the force that dances across my skin. I channel a sliver of my power, currently pooling with anticipation and nervousness in the pit of my stomach, as if it can tell its time is drawing short. Giving a tug lightly with my mind, I check the door that shuts the monster in its cage within my heart and suddenly my skin is aflame, granting me a barrier against the chill of my conscience, as well as the now rapidly cooling night air.

Unfazed by my second skin of fire, he closes the distance my steps had put between us. Disregarding the barrier, he reaches out to pull me into his chest. I let him, dousing the flames a mere breath before they could singe him.

His shaking hands, normally steady, cup my cheek.

"I will help you. Please let us help you."

I bite my lip, struggling to find the words to decline. It would be too hard to look into their faces each day and know that every memory and interaction that they had with me, would be gone forever. My payment for such a radiant power and cruel responsibility.

"My love is not going to vanish like yours overnight. I will not abandon you." He adds with a murmur before I can respond. His words hit like a slap and I shove him away, although regret rushes through me at the cold air that replaces his familiar warmth.

I spin back to face him, my anger spiraling.

"That is what you think I am doing, is it?" I snap, but don't wait for his reply. "That by doing this I am *abandoning* you?" I scoff and accidentally throw off a bit more of my power in my guilt. Waiting quietly, but always ready to come out to play when I need it, a ripple of my flame pulses outwards like a rushing wave. I can see, even at the good distance I put between us, a bead of sweat that blooms on his forehead from the sudden, intense rise in temperature. "How long do you think our peace would last if the kingdom's enemies were no longer held at bay by the memory of what I can do with a single thought?" I release a now purposeful bolt of lightning from above, though no clouds appear in the sky. It strikes four times, the bolt's echoing claps mimicking my pounding heart. I know I am yelling at him, and he doesn't deserve it. But my fury and despair have taken over.

The truth of why I have to do this.

"How long before the others across the sea would come back to reclaim us all, once word spread that the ground itself would not rise up against them?" I illustrate my point, digging back into the pit of power now surging with excitement at being released. With a stomp of my lace slippered feet, the dirt and stone around us ripple, tossing everything around. The movement beneath him is enough to knock him to the ground. Only the gift of his quick reflexes keep him on his feet. He stumbles but still he doesn't say anything. He knows it is safer, and better to just let me blow off the steam that had been suppressed deep inside, boiling for the entire star-cycle under the stress of my decision.

My breaths come in gulps and I am unable to fight the tears that begin to flow freely down my cheeks. I reach out for the water pooled nearby in the towering marble fountain I had shaped with my power, at the center of the large private garden. With my mind, mirrored by my hands, I throw the water up into the air and, hundreds of feet in the sky above, freeze it with a second thought.

Exhaustion hits me, and I release the weight of it all, my hands falling back to my sides, limp from the emotional and physical outpouring. I look upwards to see the result drifting back down towards us. The white cascade of snowflakes rests upon everything within a hundred paces for a breath before evaporating in the still hot air of my inner flames.

"Who would I *be* without my power?" I admit, my words barely above a whisper. I cast a last tendril of power out, calling back inwards the bubble of heat that still surrounds the perimeter of the garden, smoothing the upturned garden ground, healing the once green beds of grass that was scorched black by the lightning strikes, and sweeping the water that had pooled back into the gurgling fountain.

Turning back to face him, I don't see fear in his eyes. Only sadness and concern.

He has never been afraid of me.

Again, he closes the distance, then pulls me into his chest. I close my eyes, listening to his heartbeat, the familiar rhythm that is my favorite sound. I let myself linger, knowing this may be the last chance I have to hear it. I tuck that memory alongside my power, still purring with pleasure from its bit of fun as it returns to its cavernous cage.

"I don't expect you to wait for me." I say, spitting out the words, hating them the second I speak them. He just laughs, though not unkindly, and with a finger under my chin, he pulls my gaze up to meet his own.

"There is no chance of me doing anything *but* that." With a kiss, he silences my half hearted argument. He pulls back and runs his fingers gently through my tangle of curls that trails down to my waist. I close my eyes, wishing I could cement this moment in time. I try to stamp the feel of him lightly tracing his fingers up and down my back into my memory.

But that all will be gone soon.

I mourn its loss already.

Breaking the silence, he says at last, "Well, we should probably go tell the others."

I groan at the thought of having to endure the questions, the upset, the anger yet again. But when he takes my hand, leading me from the garden, I squeeze the grip tight. Despite his own reservations, I knew he would still stand by my side and support me against the outrage of the others.

I pull him to a stop in the shadows of the doorway before we can enter. Surprise blooms on his face until I pull him in for another kiss. My pulse goes wild and I feel his do the same as he crushes my compact frame into his own. An entirely different kiss than the one we had shared just moments ago. This one is filled with anger, understanding, longing, and sadness. All the things that were pointless to voice. The knowledge that these moments were quickly coming to an end makes my heart cry out, even if I dare not. He knows this is killing me.

He has to know, right?

"I will long for you. Even when I don't remember what exactly is gone, it will be you. Every time I feel as if I am missing something, know that it is you. It will *always* be you I am looking for." I whisper into his ear, my voice cracking under the weight of the words that don't do true justice to what I feel for him.

"I will make you fall in love with me again." He promises, voice thick with emotion.

I pull away from him with one last lingering look at his handsome face. Glimmering with fresh tears and struggling with his own conflict, he releases me. I know him well enough to guess he is memorizing these last moments with me as much as I am him. Before I can change my mind, I turn away and tug open the garden door, trying not to think of him standing there alone watching me walk away.

ONE

The world spins around me and I roll to my chest, pushing up just in time to avoid coating myself with the contents of my stomach. I continue to wretch as my abdomen cramps and my vision continues to whirl. Gasping for breath, I sob at the pain that fills every thought that rushes through my throbbing head. Flashes of people and places race through my mind even as they vanish. Like smoke being lifted away by a breeze. Suddenly, the pain releases its hold on me and I gasp in relief. Exhaustion fills my trembling body, and I open my eyes to look around in a panic. Violently bright sunlight assaults my sensitive gaze. I hiss at the sudden onslaught of color and light, slamming my eyes shut before slowly, cautiously, prying them open again. This time I see the rough-barked trunks and dappled specks of sunlight that glint through the leafy, velvet-green canopy of the trees that surround me. Confusion and terror are all that I know. However, I try to put together how I ended up here—wherever I am—and why. But there is nothing. And by nothing, I mean *nothing*. The pieces that should fill my mind about where I am—*who* I am—are gone. I am surrounded by what should be a peaceful scene, aside from my puddle of sick that fills the air with a sour stench. But panic chokes me as I slam my eyes shut again, trying to focus. My fingers tangle in some kind of plait that my hair is woven into, with the hopeful ferocity that I could possibly yank the memories free from wherever they have retreated.

Alright. Simple thing to focus on. Who braided my hair today? I cast my mind back into the dark abyss of memory that now sits empty. *Did I hit my head?* I can't help but move my fingers across my scalp, praying to feel a lump, a gaping wound, anything to give me some answers. Determining that sitting here would bring me none of those answers, I shove to standing, making sure to avoid the vomit pooled to my left. I sway as a wave of dizziness washes over me. Swallowing hard and gagging slightly, the forest around me tips. Catching myself on the immense trunk of the nearest tree, I take the much needed moment to steady myself.

In. Out.

I walk myself through my breathing paces. Trying to quell the ache in my chest and throat from gulping air too harshly. I fight against the fear and look around again. My surroundings give little away as to how I had gotten there. And by little, I mean not a single hint. There are no footprints or batted down grass, other than where I had lain. No horse waits in the open space that I can see surrounding the shaded center where I stand. My slippers that are barely more than lace aren't even dirty or torn, so I can rule out that I walked here. I grit my teeth in frustration. Taking a tentative step forward, my feet sinking a few inches into the pillow soft grass, I move out from underneath the massive tree that I had awoken beneath. Looking around it is clear to see that, whatever forest I am in, it is incredibly old. I furrow my brow as I realize that the tree was directly in the center of the perfect circle that was this clearing. Filled with flowers, and as picturesque as a dream, it has to be unnatural. It was then I notice a soft hum. A musical vibration that begins to rise in pitch, trilling like a wild unanswered song. Its tune fills the air and despite realizing that this was not normal tree behavior, my fear begins to recede. I even manage a smile as the birds begin to join in the song and fill the air with the flutter of their wings as dozens take flight from the surrounding trees. Their dancing flight is a beautiful distraction. They return to their perches as the last hummed note rings in the air before falling silent again. I take a few more steps forward before kneeling down among the wildflowers that surround me. I have to blink tears from my eyes every few moments. Not from emotion, but from the radiance of my surroundings that makes them water uncontrollably. Everywhere I look is so bright and electric that the colors border on painful. I trail my fingertips along a few of the petals, unable to stop myself, and gasp at the velvet texture. *Could this be a dream? Is that why I have no memory of anything like this? Or anything at all?*

I chew my lip, struggling with the overwhelming confusion and before I can change my mind, pinch myself hard enough the first signs of a bruise blooms across my skin.

But I don't wake up.

My thoughts race again at all of the implications swirling around my mind.

What happened to me? And who am I?

There is only one thing I know, simply by instinct. Something about myself has changed. I could feel it, the way you could feel a thunderstorm rolling in. The energy palpable and building. My racing thoughts are diverted once more at the pull of the hum that begins to pulse and grow around me again. I rub my forehead in frustration at the empty black that fills my mind. I return to the tree in the center of the glen and press my sensitive palm to its rough bark. The trunk is giant; it would take four of me standing around its base to encompass its girth fully. My touch confirms that the humming song is coming from the tree. The soft vibrations brush against the touch of my hand and tingle up my arm. When it suddenly stops, I nearly cry out at its absence. All signs of its ringing life vanishes. In its absence, I hear what I had missed up until now. From the ring of trees surrounding my sanctuary comes the sound of leaves crunching underfoot. From the shadows of the thick trees beyond I hear the soft tones of men's voices.

Holding my breath, I spin around, bracing my back against the tree, letting its trunk hide me. Waiting with bated breath, my mind races with worst-case scenarios of whoever was approaching. At last I hear the steps change from the crunch of leaves to the dampened sound of walking on grass. I was no longer alone. I risk a glance around the tree to examine the newcomers.

The first I see is an enormous speckled grey horse breaking through the line of trunks and out from under the leafy canopy into the sunshine. Following closely behind the first horse walks a solid ebony stallion, so black it shimmers like oil in my sensitive vision. Finally trailing just behind those two are a pair of equally large copper mares. A trio of young men in friendly conversation sway atop them, leaving only the dappled grey horse saddled but without a rider. As they all enter fully into the open sun and sky of the meadow, I catch part of the animated conversation. They are hunting for someone. *Is it me? No—I don't recognize them at all.* But then again, I don't recognize anything at the moment. I contemplate stepping out from where I crouch hidden, but rethink when I realize my true vulnerability. *Not a great situation to be in.*

I stay hidden behind the thick trunk. Watching as the group gets closer, I decide I will just follow them from a distance until they lead me out of this forest as I examine their clothing. Light, colored tunics decorated with fine embroidery and polished leather saddles and boots; I am confident, despite my limited knowledge, that these gentlemen were of status and following them would be my best chance at finding safety and help. I feel the tickle of a pulse suddenly thrum from the tree yet again. I freeze, unsure of what it could mean. The distinct feeling that the tree was calling to someone, like it had called to me, fills me with apprehension. I glance back at the men who have pulled their horses to a stop at the noise. Only then do I notice the wolf.

Deep brown and the size of a pony, the wolf enters the clearing behind the group of horses and their riders. Its large pink tongue hangs lazily, thanks to its steady trot in the warm morning before it slams to a stop. Sniffing the air, its ears twitch as it too catches the low tone ringing from the tree. The fearsome beast's sharp eyes suddenly lock on the tree where I still am crouched. I plead with the tree to stop. Hoping that the group will just be on its way, taking the terrifying wolf with them before it can expose where I kneel, hidden and very afraid. The animal is intelligent however. That much I can tell even from this far. Its gaze catches on my own as I dare to peek out again. Leaping into sudden action, the wolf darts towards me. I have mere breaths to decide what to do. I flick my eyes up to the lowest branches that seem miles above me, then back to the bow and arrows strapped across the three men's backs. All of whom have begun to dismount. *No. Climbing the tree would only trap me and they could shoot me down if they so desire.*

This leaves the woods. Shoving to my feet with no time to spare, I hear a shout of surprise when I suddenly appear, running away from the wolf who chuffs an excited howl. I manage to make three hopeful steps towards the tree line and the dark shadows beyond.

Unsurprisingly—the wolf is faster.

It cuts me off. Its large form darting in front and blocking my path to the shadowy trees. I trip over my own feet, all sense of grace and poise that I had felt earlier vanish in the blink of an eye due to my terror. I scramble backwards in an awkward, useless crawl. I curse, and dare a look over my shoulder for anything I can use. Only to see the three men are now cautiously approaching me from behind. I am trapped as they encircle me completely. I bite my lip and try not to cry in frustration and fear. I return my focus to what I feel is the most imminent threat. The wolf that paces back and forth a few steps, watching me as closely as I do her.

"Ladir." One of the men calls out in a sharp low voice and the wolf lunges at me.

I scream, a ringing bell of pure terror as the wolf falls on me. Throwing up my hands in a last feeble attempt to protect myself, I feel warm wet liquid as it covers my face. I take a shuddering breath and wait for the pain to hit me. Suddenly the pressure of the wolf vanishes and, after a few hesitant breaths, I pry open an eye to find it sitting a few steps away. Tail wagging, tongue hanging, I reach up and wipe the hot, sticky slobber from my face. Too afraid to blink or look away from the beast in front of me, I slowly reach a shaking hand out and stroke the wolf's soft fur. This only excites it further. The wolf leaps into action again. Bouncing around me with clear ecstasy before returning back for more sloppy kisses. Unable to help myself, I laugh aloud watching the unexpectedly sweet animal, astounded at how I could have been so terrified just moments before. At last, the wolf settles on its haunches by my side, its intimidating demeanor returns. Her tail still sweeping back and forth the only thing that betrays her true glee. I hear a variety of rough male laughter and only then do I remember the three men that had been accompanying the wolf. I spin around to face them. Hoping that my fear of them is as misplaced as it was for my new furry friend.

I carefully roll back to my feet and find them all still standing a few feet away. I glance around, spotting their horses grazing freely nearby. I relax, though only slightly, when I see the smiles they all wear. The man who spoke before once again calls out. This time I can tell his voice is kind, though tinged with hesitation.

"Ladir! Be careful. You scare people." He is the tallest of the three, standing relaxed with one hand on his hip, the other on the pommel of a dagger sheathed at his waist. His long onyx hair catches slightly in the breeze, pulling a few strands free of where it was tethered back with an embellished leather strap. Everything about the man radiates darkness, aside from the fact that he stands directly in a patch of sun, face tilted up and clearly enjoying the beautiful warmth of its rays. I realize he matches almost exactly with the ebony stallion he had been riding. The other two men, one with cropped white-blond hair and the other with shoulder-length curly bright auburn, stand in the shade of a nearby tree. With a slight whine and a sideways glance toward me, the wolf, apparently named Ladir, trots towards the speaking man before flopping down to lay at his feet with a grumbled huff.

All four look at me expectantly now. I clear my throat and try to brush off the grass and leaves that stick to my once beautiful lavender-colored skirt, thanks to my panicked scurrying on the ground. Momentarily distracted, my fingers linger over the delicate fabric I hadn't even noticed until now, soft and smooth beneath my caress. I look back at them, unsure how to even begin this conversation.

I don't know who I am. How am I supposed to know what to ask? Do they even know me?

My question receives an answer before I can even ask it.

"You really don't recognize us, do you?" The blond speaks first, his tone thick with irritation. The other men shoot daggers in his direction, but he ignores them.

"Damn, Jera." He mutters through gritted teeth.

Is that my name? No. That doesn't seem right.

I don't know what that means—*Jera*—but a spike of tension ripples through the once calm surroundings.

I straighten up, holding my head high, and do my best to conceal my weakness and uncertainty.

"And why should I recognize you?" I ask with a snip, returning the attitude the stranger had directed at me.

His dark-haired companion, who seemed to be the leader, steps in between us. A beam of sunlight filtering through the leaves above catches his raven hair, transforming it into a shimmering shadow that distracts me as I try to memorize the variety of colors that are revealed in its strands.

A calming presence presses out and my tension regresses slightly. I glance curiously at the tree where the feeling had seemed to originate, but it falls silent, other than the rustle of leaves as a breeze rushes through them, making them dance.

"You wouldn't recognize us." The man speaks again, his voice soothing. "But this—" he gestures to the blond, "is Ivrik. That devil there is Patryk." He points now to the auburn-haired male, who gives a tentative wave. "And *this* devil is Ladir." He reaches down to scratch the wolf behind her ears and she rolls onto her back. I laugh at the strange sight, and the still unnamed leader looks up at me with surprised satisfaction. I stop, suddenly shy. Despite these men claiming to know me, I don't know them.

"And who are you?" I ask the black-haired man after an awkward moment of silence, still wary to engage too much with these strangers. Ladir rolls back to her paws, letting out another soft whine while looking up at the man with her gentle eyes.

I catch a glint of sharp pain mixed with sadness before he looks away, dodging my gaze.

"I am Türë," He answers after a breath of hesitation. I feel a soft caress of something down my neck and my heartbeat quickens of its own accord.

That name.

My brain tries to grasp at the thread of memory, like tendril of spider silk caught in a river current. It vanishes before I can catch it, the trickle of familiarity at the name disappears as quickly as it popped up.

I stand in silent contemplation at what to do next, then take a deep breath to try and settle my nerves. My eyes dart to the other two men, Ivrik and Patryk, who still stand a few feet away watching me carefully.

They don't seem malicious. Or even like they want to cause trouble. Returning my gaze to Türë, I examine him closer too, though I know I have already decided to trust them. At least a little.

If the wolf trusts him so implacably, I feel sure I can as well.

"And… who am I?" I finally seize my courage to ask after fighting my internal struggle of self-preservation.

At this, all three men seem to light up. Each of their eyes welling with a sudden pride that startles me.

"You are our Queen." Türë responds with a gentle whisper.

two

A bubble of laughter bursts out at this statement before I can stop it. Surely he was taking the opportunity of my obvious confusion to play a sick joke. That is until I see the look of reverence shining in his bright eyes, as well as in the eyes of the other two men. I feel myself straighten up, the invisible weight of a crown settling on my head. Like my body knew it should be there.

Queen.

Like a piece of a puzzle clicking perfectly into place. I have nothing but blackness filling the space of my mind, an empty cavern where everything in my life should be.

But this feels right somehow.

"Queen." I murmur. "Queen of where? I—" Hesitant to share too much with these people, I pause, trying to find the words. From my left I feel a trickle of warmth pushing out towards me, as if the tree was giving me a gentle nudge forward and encouraging me to speak. "I seem to be missing—well—everything... I don't even know my name." I admit at last. My words rush out in a stammer. I stare at the grass, examining each of the emerald strands that tickle my feet as I swallow, forcing back the tears that burn my eyes. This time it is the flame-haired male, Patryk, that answers my question.

Taking a few strides forward, he then drops to a knee in front of me. After a hesitant smile, he carefully takes my left hand in his own, moving slowly enough so to avoid startling me and also giving me time to pull away from his touch if I wished. "You are Queen Evara of Alessandra, High Queen of Tesindren and Protector of the Nefriti." He says this with a rhythm that lets me know that he has said this dozens, if not hundreds, of times. His eyes glint with obvious respect and reverence, but hidden beneath that...

There is something else there. A silent plea to remember.

It is clear he, and the others who watch me just as closely, are hoping that these words will magically unlock whatever is holding my memories from me.

I blink hard, trying to force my brain to snap into action and remember something.

Anything.

Türe must see the panic starting to well up inside, because he steps in to save me. Gripping Patryk's shoulder, his message is clear. Patryk stands, letting my hand fall from his own before turning to hide his face from me. Too slowly, however. I still see the disappointment that washes over his features. His shoulders dropping as he retreats back to Ivrik's side.

Unable to think of anything to say, I turn and walk until I am close enough to the tree to brace my forehead against it. Needing its quiet solace and its barely discernible hum. I lean against its trunk, pressing my palms against my eyes as I try to force back the tears that threaten to spill.

Barely audible, the soft tread of footsteps approach and I know without looking that it is Türë. Like the tree, I find a strange comfort in his calm presence. Even though I know nothing about him, other than a name. He leans against the tree beside me with his back against the trunk. I sneak a peek and take the opportunity to examine him more closely as he gazes up into the massive leafy canopy that blesses us with its shade. I wonder why I feel comfortable with him, when there is no memory to tie to this complete stranger. *Maybe my soul recognizes what my mind cannot?* Though it was possible that was solely because the wolf trusted him. I glance over my shoulder and see the two other men walking away from us. Giving me a moment, no doubt. Now out of earshot of the other two, I find the courage to speak again.

"I don't understand why don't I have any memories." I whisper. My lip quivers from both fear and frustration, and I huff aloud, pressing my palms back to my eyes hard enough to see bursts of light. My racing and already exhausted mind snags on the first thing Ivrik said. *You really don't recognize us, do you* he had asked. I spin around to face Türë. "Do you know why? None of you seemed to be surprised when I didn't recognize you. It was like you all were expecting it." Türë doesn't answer right away. He only watches me, clearly contemplating what to say. Immediately, my defenses rise up, and I take a step away from him. A few feet away, Ladir rises back to all fours. Her hackles rise along with a terrifying snarl that rumbles from her before she darts quickly to my side, placing herself between the two of us. Again, a flicker of something like regret or sadness sparks in Türë's eyes and he takes a step back, away from Ladir and me. He raises his hands in an attempt to calm us both as Ladir shows her teeth. The other two men are not so subtle from where they watch, pausing mid-bite of the apples they were snacking on to shuffle backwards another few steps. If the situation wasn't so confusing and frightening, their reaction would be comical. My eyes and throat suddenly feel like they are burning as I hack a cough. The scent of smoke fills my nose and mouth and I look around in panic. Then their fear makes sense. Looking down, I see that what had been a soft, luscious green patch of grass is now a smoking black circle of charred ash. I gape at the ground, trying to understand why the ground was burning, then I notice the trail of blue flames swirling up my fingers, down the face of my palms and up my forearms to my elbows. Gasping out a scream of panic, I wave them erratically in the air in a feeble attempt to rid myself of the fire. Ladir paces in a worried circle around me, whining and barking, but even she is wary to get closer.

Türë doesn't flee however. He instead steps forward now. Coming within arms reach, he speaks softly even as the scorched grass crumbles to ash with each step he takes.

"Breathe." He instructs in a level voice. "Imagine each breath extinguishing a little bit of the flames every time until it finally is gone." I close my eyes and do everything I can to obey. Turning my complete focus onto my breath, I tug my mind away from trying to understand what was happening. For now. After what feels like an eternity, I feel something warm and wet touch my fingers. I snap my eyes open to find Ladir sitting beside me. Her nose, the source of what had startled me, rests gently against my hand as her tail once again whips back and forth.

My eyes dart back towards the others who now dare to approach again. I shuffle shyly and begin to apologize. Türë standing closely, shakes my apology off, giving a hesitant nod of acceptance. My smile widens and seems to be what they were all waiting for. The three males perceptibly relax and Türë's smile grows too, lighting up his face. I stare a moment, before blushing and looking away, tugging on a piece of lace decorating the waist of my dress.

"If you are ready, Ladir has something for you." Patryk clicks his tongue, beckoning Ladir over to him. After a moment of hesitation and a side glance at me, she trots over to him, her mouth open from the ever-growing heat of the day. He pets her thick fur for a moment before making a covert move to untie something from around the wolf's neck. This apparently was not a good idea. The easygoing wolf once again shows her wild side. Snapping in warning at his fingers, he yanks backwards before getting close enough to remove the strand of rope I now notice loops around her neck in a sort of collar. Patryk loses his balance with a shouted curse, and scuffles back on his hands a few paces. But it isn't necessary. After the warning, and resulting reaction, Ladir sits watching the event with disinterest. Apparently content that her message had been fully received.

"Bloody wolf. You really need to train her better before she takes someone's head off." Ivrik mutters with impatience as he helps his friend back to his feet.

I bristle at the insulting tone.

"I believe she is trained just fine. A wolf knows a frightened sheep when she sees one." The rebuttal comes quick off my tongue as if it had done so a million times. Türë, who had also opened his mouth to respond, snaps it shut with an audible clack of his teeth. All three men blink in surprise at this and it takes a moment to realize that a snippet of memory—muscle memory or something more, I didn't know—had been triggered. I try to grasp more at the strand that seems to dangle in my mind, but it is as blank and empty as before.

"I don't know how many times you two can have this same argument." Türë chimes in after a shocked pause.

Ivrik snorts loudly, then sighs dramatically before stepping forward to take his turn. Reaching out to Ladir, his tone changes, casting aside the sarcastic facade that I had gathered was his go-to reaction and shifts into more of a respectful demeanor. I watch this and put together another puzzle piece of who these men were, and whether they were a threat. Again, everything pointed to no.

Though Ladir had been kind to me up to this point, despite my first fear of her, the men's trepidation let me know that my initial reaction wasn't so far off. She could be dangerous.

"She seems to be special to me?" I say, though not sure if it was an observation or a question.

Türë nods. "It is true. You two have always had a special bond. She lives in this forest and has an uncanny ability of knowing when you step foot here. She just shows up, often enough that we believe she is a servant of Jera." He chuckles a bit, as another growl ripples through the meadow, followed by the snap of teeth, that pulls us from our discussion. I am still not sure who Jera is but for this moment, it wasn't a priority. Türë and I turn to see Ivrik had failed in his attempt to retrieve the item dangling from around Ladir's neck. This second time, Ladir had in fact drawn blood. Her patience quickly dwindles at the continued attempts. Cursing the wolf, Ivrik stomps away to his horse, where I watch him yank a spare cloth from his saddlebag and stubbornly tries to bind the wound with only the one uninjured hand. After watching the pathetic, yet amusing sight for a moment, Patryk takes pity on him and, with a resolved sigh, goes to help him with the wrap.

"Why doesn't she want anyone to untie that from her neck?" I ask him.

"Because it was something you gave her to protect. She will give it to no other." He glances at me and sees the look of *I absolutely will not try* that must have appeared on my face and he laughs, the sound sending a warm shiver up my spine. "But maybe I can try." He waves Ladir over and she completely melts in front of him. Rolling over, she lets him scratch her belly as her eyes fall shut in pure bliss.

Watching closely, I hold my breath in anticipation as he manages to dart out with his long nimble fingers, ignoring the warning snarl now directed at him. With a quick and easy tug, the knot comes loose, and the object attached and hanging below Ladir's chin, hidden in her thick fur, is finally pulled free. I actually cheer aloud at his victory, and he laughs again in surprise at my reaction. I can't help but smile wide, biting my lip to stop from laughing along. With a flourish, he rises again before dropping into a bow, holding out the object to me.

"This is for you, my Queen." He says in a low voice. My heart skips a beat and I swallow hard to hide the sudden rapid beat my pulse thrums at the words. I like the way he says *that* too much.

"What is it?" I ask, clearing my throat as I shove away those thoughts, plucking it from his outstretched palm. The object is some kind of tube, about the length of the dagger attached to Türe's hip, with the rope that had held it around Ladir's neck threaded through it. Simple, yet beautiful. The tube is carved and painted in vibrant colors, depicting the same symbol over and over across its entirety; some kind of crest.

"It is a letter." Türe answers simply.

"A letter? From whom?"

"From yourself." I raise my eyebrows in surprise, but can't find the words to put together to form any coherent response. Thankfully, Türe continues to help without further prompting. "It will explain everything it can. You wrote to yourself to explain who you are and why you have no memories. I—I don't want to say too much…" He trails off, glancing pointedly over at the others who wait, watching but out of listening range. His meaning becomes clear. What was in the letter, and what he knew, was not widespread knowledge. Even to be kept from who he claimed were my friends.

Except him? He knows.

He continues, like he could read my thoughts. "Honestly, I don't know what all the letter entails, but you did say that it would help you *understand.*" He flashes a grin before bending to give Ladir one last belly scratch. Turning away from me, he heads toward the two men who had wrangled the horses and stand waiting. He turns back to me, an unspoken nervousness clear in his eyes. "We are going to let you get to know yourself alone for a while and get started on making camp for the night." He nods at Ladir. "When you are ready to find us, just tell her and she will lead you to us, okay?" He takes another step back to the horses, then hesitates before returning to my side. Unlatching the belt strung with the bejeweled dagger I had noticed slung around his hips, he wraps it around my waist so suddenly I don't have time to be struck by its impropriety before his feather light touch is gone again. He joins the others and I catch a snarky comment from Ivrik, followed by a laugh from Patryk, that Türë brushes off. I watch in awe as he smoothly mounts the huge seventeen-hand onyx horse in a single leap. I try, but fail to not gape as his arm muscles flex beneath the tunic and can't help but compare the horse's flowing mane and the master's as the group rides swiftly out of the meadow. I look down when I hear a whine from my remaining companion and shake myself from that distracted train of thought. I swear Ladir watches me with disapproval, like she could read my thoughts.

"What? I can think he is impressive looking, right?" I say defensively. She only huffs in response. Drawn back to the center tree's comforting shade, I sink into the grass that I had not scorched and inhale the sweet, earthy scent of the forest that surrounds me. Though I had, thankfully, gotten many answers in the short time since I had awoken, the number of questions had also multiplied to a nearly suffocating and certainly overwhelming amount.

I look down at the sealed tube still in my hand and examine it more closely. "A letter." I repeat aloud to Ladir, who now has sprawled at my side. She watches me with her big black eyes and shuffles closer, offering comfort. On a hunch, I twist the bottom half of the tube and squeak with glee when it separates from the top, revealing a rolled scroll of paper.

three

I am sorry that there is no easier way to do this to you... to us.

I will not bore you with the entire history of our kingdom. The rascals who you named as your Underkings can explain that to you at whatever length you desire. (Be wary asking Noran. He will go on until you learn how each city was made brick by brick.) I will, however, tell you what I must in order to ensure you have the knowledge you need to rule and to know who you are. There are things that are kept secret from even your most trusted companions and that would be lost along with time if I did not tell you here. Those I trust, and you should too, I shall name here: Patryk, who rules the territory of Telor, Eivan, who rules the territory of Eri, Ivrik, who rules the territory of Paith, and finally Noran, who rules the territory of Bethos. They are your Underkings. They uphold your laws and guide your kingdom when you cannot. However, even above those—

our most trusted is Türë. (He has adamantly refused any sort of title and territory along with it, despite me asking a multitude of times and trying everything short of blackmail.) But I am getting ahead of myself. It is hard to know what to say without dumping a torrent of information on your poor brain. I remember how awful it was.

The best place to start, I suppose, is at the beginning. You were not born of this realm, but found it. Liberated it. You were born in a different land. Thankfully, one far enough away that they do not threaten us. But, what matters now, is your home here, Tesindren, where you were reborn into who and what you are today. You are not mortal, nor are you immortal. You are something more.

Four thousand and twenty-two star-cycles ago I wanted some adventure, a life more than what I had. I caught word of a boat setting sail across the Grey Sea to the north and, for the right price, they would smuggle a woman aboard. I hunted it down and bartered my way on to the crew. Oh, the freedom! I had never experienced anything like it. The women in my land were seen as breeding stock and little more than slaves. I had been fortunate enough that my grandfather had taken pity on me, seeing that I had a will stronger than my sisters and cousins. So he trained me in secret with both bow and dagger. Not enough to truly liberate me, but just enough that he thought would curb the edge of my restlessness. How wrong he was. After his death the little slack in my leash—my noose—was once again pulled tight. That was when I fled. Only myself and two other women had found the courage to board the boat. I was the only one of us to reach this land alive. My knowledge of the dagger that had once saved my sanity now saved my life. The males also aboard were not used to a fiery woman and had quickly abandoned their attempts to bed me once one got a blade in his belly. When we caught sight of the shore, I threw myself into the waves and vanished before we could rejoin the others that had sailed ahead and waited on the beach. It was easy enough to guess that their intentions were little better than that of their friends. After the long days on the sea, many moon-cycles, I had only grown more certain that they would not be any different from what I had left behind.

Dragging myself, soaking and cold to shore, I ran for the dark shadow in the distance that seemed to call to me and found myself in a thick wood. With tears of relief dripping down my sunburnt, sea-worn skin, I praised all the emerald shadows and earthy corners that I could disappear into and finally live my life in peace.

But this was not meant to be.

The following morning, I was awakened by a caravan traveling through the woods. I heard their approach and hid. I tried to stay strong in my resolve that I would keep to myself and determined to silently let them pass as I watched, hidden in the shadows. That was until I saw the 'product' they were transporting. Women in crates, enough to fill seven wagons. I couldn't leave them. I saw an opportunity to save them all and refused to turn my back. Following at a safe distance, I waited until nightfall, then stole a bow from a sleeping guard. In the dark, I put my ramshackle plan into action. I don't remember all the details. Not anymore. But I was able to free them all. Together, we vanished into the trees and banded together. We became the Nefriti, the Saviors of the Forest. Freeing all slaves that we came across, our group and renown grew quickly. It was the star-cycle I turned twenty-five that it at last came to a great battle. Our numbers had grown to now include men, women, and Creatures of the Forest. Immortals and humans. Past enemies and old friends. Together we fought without hesitation until we liberated this world from the tyranny of the last rulers. We then re-named the kingdom Tesindren, which means 'Land for All' in the old language.

That was also the star-cycle that I died.

It was in the light of the full moon when a single assassin struck. My closest ally, Cernunnos, had been walking with me in the village we had made our capital at the time. Dreaming and discussing the future for this land as we walked, mulling over all of the possibilities of the now open future. For you see, as a Sidhe, (what we are) we don't reach old age until we are over a thousand star-cycles old. So now free from the tether of servitude, my life was an open book with a million pages to fill as I chose. It was going to be beautiful. But that night I was too calm, too inattentive—too secure in the illusion of safety among my people. That is how I ended up with a poisoned sword thrust into my abdomen, a mortal wound. It is only because of Cernunnos's quick action I was kept alive long enough for yet another chance. He had been born in this land and knew something very few others did. To most it was a fairytale; a fable. But Cernunnos had seen the power with his own eyes and knew, if anything was going to be able to save me, it would be this one chance.

That is how I met the Goddess Jera. She had been watching me my whole life, even across the sea—preparing me—I would come to find out. Laying me in the grass at her feet, Cernunnos begged for my life to be spared. That was the last I heard before I passed into the void of darkness. It was darkness thicker than even the blackest, moon-free night at sea. Then I saw a flicker of soft beautiful light in the distance and sought its origin. A tree. But this tree could speak. It could sing, and it sang to me the knowledge of the universe and all of its magic and enchantment. This was the Goddess Jera. The Goddess told me I had done well, and she would let me pass and sleep for eternity in her warmth. But I begged for more. For life. I still had too much to do for Tesindren and I needed to see it, as I had dreamed, in all of its splendor. I needed to see what it could be.

That was when she paused, her singing turning to a hum as she thought. Then Jera offered me a choice. I could live as long as I desired, as her presence in the mortal land, and she would bless me with magic and true immortality. However, in order to prevent me from the temptation that would lead to the Darkness and evil that comes with too much time and power, every thousand star-cycles I would have to return to her and have all I was—my abilities, my memories, my heart—wiped clean. Each time it gets harder and more of our history is lost. But there is so much still to be done that when the deadline came up, I made the decision yet again.

This will be my third time. In the past I have done everything to distance myself so as to dull the ache of putting those closest to me through the grief of watching me forget them. This time, I have chosen differently. I found myself unable to cut the ties of the mortals around me and let them convince me to allow them into the secrets of my history, and what would happen when this day came.

There is so much more to say. It is hard to know what is most important and what you will need in the star-cycles to come. I can only hope that this time, allowing the others to assist in the transition and not being so alone, will help cushion the shock and confusion that I know first hand you are feeling.

My best guidance is to listen to Jera and follow where your

intuition takes you. It will remember what your mind cannot. The soul always remembers.

May Jera bless you and fill your next thousand star-cycles with happiness.

Queen Evara of Alessandra

    High Queen of Tesindren

    Protector of the Nefriti

I let the scroll slip through my fingers and it rolls back up with a soft shuffling. No matter how hard I try, I cannot seem to wrap my mind around all that I just learned. It is impossible. This has to be some intricate joke. *There is no way I could be over four thousand star-cycles old. But then... what else is there to explain the blackness where everything used to be?*

Because I could feel it, like a scooped out hollow. I could feel the places where all my thoughts and memories used to be. Only now it was bare. Like an egg shell—unbroken, yet somehow everything inside was gone.

I feel a pulse down my back and I lean more against the cool bark of the tree, the soft hum wrapping around me like a reassuring hug. My eyes fall shut as I try to absorb all that the letter had revealed. They fly open again as something from the letter rings with familiarity. I grab the discarded scroll and reread with my heart thumping in excitement. *Then I saw a flicker of soft, beautiful light in the distance and found its origin. A tree—but this tree could speak. It could sing. And it sang to me the knowledge of the universe and all of its magic and enchantment. This was the Goddess Jera.* Gazing up in wonder at the vast canopy rustling in the slight wind that does not reach the meadow, I realize this tree is more than it appears to be.

"Hello, Jera." I whisper. I turn and press my forehead again to the massive trunk with a soft smile, some of my fear easing away.

Ladir lets out a soft whine of complaint at being ignored for so long. With a laugh, I reach out to placate her. My fingertips quickly become lost in the thick, soft fur. Counting to one hundred, I struggle to take measured breaths, but finally, after a few minutes, I no longer feel like screaming or crying at the weight of all these new revelations opening up before me. My eyes flutter open again, landing immediately on the letter curled in my grip. With a sigh, I read it again. Then twice more.

By the end of my fourth read, the information, though still a lot to take in, doesn't seem as overwhelming and the feeling of suffocation has begun to subside. Slightly. I see a stick laying nearby and absentmindedly twirl it in the air before tossing it across the meadow. Ladir immediately scampers after it, her tongue flopping out of the side of her mouth, as carefree as a child. I can't help but laugh at the sight as she lopes back to me with the stick. Dropping it on my lap, she sits expectantly. Tail sweeping enthusiastically behind her, I oblige with another toss.

I only half watch Ladir run off again. My mind drifts to Patryk, Ivrik, and Türë. Underkings, the letter had called them. They seemed genuine and I must have truly trusted them if they were each in charge of parts of my kingdom. Well, aside from Türë and whatever role he took on. His position, other than apparently a friend, confused me.

This time when Ladir returns to me, I am on my feet and ready to know more. To seize this chance offered to me. It was clear from my letter that in my long star-cycles of being alive, I had possessed enough courage and conviction that Jera herself saw great opportunity in my ruling. So much so that she agreed to extend my life when it should have been extinguished a long, long time before now.

Now it was my turn to believe in myself.

I had ensured that I would not be alone this time, and could not turn my back on that gift she had given me. A gift paid for by her pain and her friends—my friends.

I brush off the loose grass and debris that clings to my skirt. I pause to tuck the letter into a pouch dangling from the dagger belt Türe had given me. My mind drifts and I feel warmth seep into my body at the thought of his strong hands. Even the memory of just his featherlight touch on my waist makes my toes curl in my slippers. I shove my thoughts away from that line of thinking. Clearly if there had been anything like that between us, it would have been in the letter.

Do not go there and ruin what is clearly your closest friendship. Especially when you barely know the man!

I heave a sigh and turn to pat the tree one last time. I stare at the space that once held the ancient, vast oak. A small sapling, barely taller than my hip, now stands in its place. Bewildered, a spark of what could only be a message appears in my minds-eye with a flash, and I stumble back a few steps in surprise. The surrounding forest, though still old, is clearly younger in the image, and I understand this is a glimpse into the past. Jumping back to the current time, I realize that, like this tree, my thousand star-cycles was beginning again. Rippling through the meadow on the wind, a gentle voice echos around me as I stride across the meadow in the direction the others had gone.

"I am with you."

four

The day grows hotter as the sun reaches its peak. I wander through the forest on the game trail, following Ladir's lead. To my surprise, I don't tire. Climbing over a fallen log with ease, I can't help but wonder what all my body is capable of. Then another thought hits me. Are there things that I could do just yesterday that I am no longer able to? The letter had referenced magic and then there was the episode where I had burst into flames. I shudder and swipe my hands down each of my arms, fearful that it might happen again, now that I was thinking about it. I move through the trees filled with birdsong and all the daily sounds of its inhabitants, growing more familiar with my body. There are things that begin to stand out that send me down a rabbit hole. I have no memory of what I was like before, yet I still have the ghost of what must be pains from my past. A twinge in my left ankle that I brace for in the back of my mind, yet never comes. A stiffness in my right elbow that manages now to bend with ease. It was as if every ache and pain that my body had gotten used to automatically adjusting for had been wiped clean. It was disconcerting, to say the least.

Hours pass before the trees give way to a small, bubbling creek. Neither Ladir or I can resist the allure of the fresh, cold water. Ladir stops, lapping up enough water to fill a barrel. With a squeak of glee, I take off the pale-lilac lace slippers that had spared my feet from the assorted twigs, roots, and small stones that decorated the forest floor trail. Now covered in the dirt and grass stains, I dunk them and my feet in the goosebump-inducing water and sigh at the relief that it provides. I swish the slippers around to rinse them as best I can before flopping the limp material on a rock in a patch of warm sunlight nearby. Leaning back, I turn my face up to the warm rays before my attention is drawn back to my surroundings. I look around and can't help but admire the beauty of this place. I watch the sunbeams dance on the rock-strewn creek bed as it rushes down the small waterfall and into the small pool that I rest beside. Basking in the sun, I let myself relax and smile while the sounds of the creatures and woods surround me. The steady current runs over my feet, washing away my worries and uncertainty at joining, or should I say *rejoining*, the world that I no longer remember.

Ladir pants heavily as she rests nearby, sprawled contentedly in her own beam of sunlight. Breaking me from my peace, she suddenly jumps to her feet. She gives a ferocious warning growl, to let both whoever was approaching, and me, know that she is aware of their presence. I stand slowly, wobbling a bit on a loose stone, as my hand drifts habitually to the dagger that was still slung around my hips. Again I wonder at how much my body remembers. Or does it simply come down to my own learned talents—which as of now were nonexistent. I glance nervously at Ladir who still stares with her hackles raised toward the oncoming stranger.

Thankfully, I don't have to find out what skills remain. Without any further warning, or sign of reassurance, she only huffs with annoyance before flopping onto her belly and sprawling back out in the patch of warmth that she had been roused from. I blink, surprised, until Türë appears through the trees. His returning smile is as bright as the sun on his tanned face and stupidly I feel my stomach flip.

"I found you!" He says, eyes lighting up. He lingers to scratch Ladir's ears and I realize my hand still rests on the dagger. I try to quickly remove it before he can see, but the movement only makes his eyes flick towards my waist.

"Yes, sorry. We were coming and got distracted." I blush and sit back down on the rock. "I just couldn't resist the beautifully cold water." Türë nods, bending down and beginning to unlace his own polished boots.

"I don't blame you. We were just starting to get worried that you maybe wouldn't be able to find us before dark. Plus the other two's bickering was driving me nuts. I was ready to find an excuse for a peaceful, and most importantly, *quiet* walk."

A laugh bubbles out of me before I can stop it. His laughter matches the radiance of his dark eyes and fills me with a naive satisfaction that I managed to make him laugh.

"Are they always like that?" I ask, averting my eyes, as I swish my toes back in forth in the refreshing water. Watching it ripple, my mind returns to the letter and the instructions to rely on these people that clearly cared about me.

Türë contemplates this before responding, seemingly careful. "You and all of your Underkings have a relationship matching what I have seen with siblings. You all bicker, and egg each other on, but also have each other's best interests at heart. You protect them and trust them above all others, and they you. So to answer your question, yes and no. They are not always like that. But often." He concludes with a shrug before squinting up at the bright sky. He seems to relax a bit in the sun's rays, then steps into the water. I join him, following deeper into the water this time rather than just rinsing my feet. I can't help but stare at the rainbow hues the rivulets and ripples cast on the stony creek bed that dance with light. My hem floats in the current and I slip again slightly on the water-worn stones. With a reflex quicker than my eyes can track, Türë's arm flicks out, catching me before I can fall entirely into the water. I burst into a giggle again. He cracks a smile, but doesn't laugh this time. His brow furrows and lips purse as an odd look dances in a shadow across his face. It vanishes before I can be sure of what it could mean, making me wonder if it had even been there to begin with.

Releasing his grip on my arms the second he is sure I am not about to slip again, Türë steps back, putting feet of distance between us.

The silence grows uncomfortably long before I do my best to try and break it. "I feel like an awkward newborn. You should have seen me trying to clamber over some of the fallen branches in the path." I fail to keep my groan of embarrassment from slipping out as I try to lighten the shudder mood shift.

He answers with an amused smirk. "From what you told me, your body just always takes time to adjust after the Awakening. Like your limbs have fallen asleep. After everything done to your mind it makes sense the rest of your body is just catching up to it all."

"The Awakening?" I ask. "Is that what it is called?"

"Well, that's what you always called it. I don't know if it is the *technical* term for it." He pauses, rolling up his sleeves to his elbows and bending over to splash the chilly spring water onto his face. "There is nothing in history, that we are aware of at least, that says anyone other than you has been blessed so highly by

Jera."

Against my better judgement—I can't help but feel my eyes wander, momentarily distracted. I look back up to find him watching me in return and blush furiously.

Get it together. He is your friend— which is something you desperately need right now. What you don't need is to be making crazy eyes at his muscles.

I cough in a hopeless attempt to pretend I wasn't ogling him. Suddenly the sky becomes incredibly interesting instead. Thankfully he chooses not to comment.

"You know you can ask me whatever you need to. I don't know what all the letter said or how much it was able to explain…" He turns to face me fully and, stepping closer, pulls my hand into his own. *Maybe not so crazy.* I swallow hard at the unexpected warmth that shoots through my body at the feel of his callused skin. I try to calm my heart that suddenly beats so loudly that he must be able to hear it. And there is nothing I can do to stop my fingers from shaking at his touch. The first touch I have had in this memory, I realize with a jolt of surprise. "I am here to help you in any way I can to make this all easier. Okay?" He continues, his voice soft and soothing. *Screw it.* I open my mouth to just do it— to just ask him if there was something between us. Something that I had neglected to put into the letter. But as if he just then realizes how close we were, Türë suddenly drops my hand and steps out of the water and back onto the dry grass.

Well, never mind then.

I follow him out onto the bank, trying to not feel so disappointed. Ignoring my rapidly beating heart that continues to pound its racing rhythm in my chest, I take the opportunity of his turned back to recenter myself. I sit on the large rock beside my now sun-dry slippers, tracing a nonsense pattern with my big toe in the loose earth as I try to run through all I have learned and debate what to ask him first.

There is so much. I feel my head begin to pound as I stop to slip back on my shoes. He pauses to pat Ladir as he heads for the tree line again, the soft sound of forest debris crunching beneath his feet.

"I don't even know where to begin." I admit aloud, unable to hide the distress that was beginning to resurface. I look up to find him watching me closely, though his careful mask doesn't give any hint to his own thoughts.

The corner of his mouth twitches up and a spark flashes in his eyes. "I bet." He comments sarcastically. I feel my jaw tighten with irritation.

"Well I am glad you think this is so funny." I snap, yanking my slipper on so hard that, with my unfamiliar strength, it rips the top strap clean off. I bite down on the sudden burn of tears in my eyes. *I will not cry.* I pause, my fingers tightening around the now unwearable shoe and feel my nails dig into my palm as I stare at it. I try to breathe through my frustration and feeling of hopelessness. Ladir, who had been watching silently from her patch of sun pads over to me. Concern clear in her wide brown eyes, she head butts me gently. I can't help but to give in to her attention and the hint of a grateful smile pulls at my lips as I scratch what seems to be her favorite spot behind her ears, each the size of my foot.

How am I supposed to be a Queen? I can't even put on a shoe without losing my head. Who would rely on me as a ruler of anything?

I rest my head against her soft bulk as she pauses to sit beside me. Reassured by her wordless agreement to stay here and pout with me as long as I need, I focus on breathing through each wave of fear, doubt, and anguish. Each retreating as quickly as they came, only to be replaced by sudden overwhelming exhaustion.

Out of the corner of my eye, I can see Türë shifting back and forth on his feet. He keeps his eyes lowered away from me, in clear discomfort. I sigh, but am unable to work up any anger towards him again now. We are all learning how to handle this.

Has it only been a few hours since waking up? And I thought I was in a dream. No, just a nightmare.

I shake that dark thought as another one hits me.

This is supposed to be a blessing, and here I am pouting. *How ungrateful can I be?* This jolts me from my selfish track and I plant a kiss on Ladir's furry cheek before removing the other slipper I had successfully pulled on first. I push off the rock and set the beautiful pair on the rock nearby, discarding the shoes, along with all of my negativity and doubt. Like the shoes, those thoughts were now useless and would get me nowhere. So I would leave them all behind. *Or I would at least do my best to try.* I promise myself. To Jera.

I look up to meet Türë's eyes and begin to apologize. But to my surprise, he beats me to it.

"I am so sorry, Evara. I can't imagine how difficult this is for you. I should not have laughed. Please believe it was not aimed *at* you." He looks at me beneath endless dark eyelashes, trying to explain.

I found I did believe him and was so grateful for that feeling that I smile in relief.

"Thank you, Türë. But I am the one who should apologize. You have been extraordinarily kind to me, and I lost it at the slightest thing." I sigh and run my fingers through my waist long hair, grimacing when I find a few leaves tangled there.

Jera help me. How long have those been there? I groan internally, knowing deep down that it has been a while.

I then realize Türë has been talking again, and I beg my brain to have caught what he had said.

"Sorry, what?" I ask at last, unable to come up with anything.

"It was a joke we used to have." He says again, ever graciously patient.

I am an idiot.

"Um… What was?" I fully expect his tentative laugh, only this time I smile at the sound.

He glances up at the sky and I follow his line of sight, surprised to find the sun had already drifted behind the tree line and the shadows of dusk were growing fast.

"I will explain on the way back to camp." We both spare a look at my limp shoes that still sit on the rock. I regret my temper that had rendered one, and by default, both unwearable. I shrug and take the first steps into the forest, deciding to just go the rest of the way barefoot. Thankfully, he doesn't comment, only shakes his head at me. He huffs a soft chuckle again, but this time I feel warmth course through me at the sound. He cuts it off quickly with a worried side-eyed glance of concern at me. Not that I can blame him for his hesitation after my last reaction to him laughing at me.

I smack him on the arm playfully and this time I join in, unable to fight the contagiousness of his hearty, robust laugh that silences the cacophony of animal chatter with its echo. Walking alongside each other now, Türe follows an invisible path. I have no choice but to follow his lead as blindly as I had followed Ladir. We fall into comfortable silence as the birds begin to sing again. I take the opportunity to soak in this gorgeous forest and marvel at the animals we start to come across.

They aren't even wary of us. I reach out more than once, unable to stop from trailing my fingers along the sides of a few of the various deer. Even a giant, fluffy black bear doesn't look twice when we pass.

"How are they not afraid?" I can't help but ask, breaking the peace the silence had brought down upon us. "And with a huge wolf. It doesn't stand to reason." I mutter, half to myself glancing back at Ladir who follows only a few steps behind us.

"It is because we are *Sidhe*." He explains, pronouncing the word I remember seeing in my letter as *shee*. I shake my head, only more confused by this. I admit this and he quirks an understanding smile. "Maybe this will explain a little more." He hums a short tune and a responding hiss comes from above us in the trees. To my astonishment, from a limb above, an emerald green snake the length of Ladir descends and curls its way up Türë's arm, tongue flickering as he rests his behemoth head on his shoulder. My mouth falls open, but I am unable to find the words. Amazing as that skill is, I am only more confused.

He smiles widely at my gaping mouth, understanding that he indeed had only brought about more questions. I watch in awe as he thanks the snake and passes him onto another low-hanging tree branch. I shake my head, bewildered, when the creature continues its path, slithering happily along, before vanishing again, into the viridescent and blue-grey speckled foliage spread above us. Only then do I notice the sky growing dark more quickly than I expected. Türë must realize the same thing, because he begins to walk again as he talks.

"They see us as one of their own; a creature of the forest. They know that, like Ladir, we would only hurt them out of necessity. For food, for example. But the rest of the time, we are like them. We are their kin, residing alongside them in this beautiful forest." I nearly trip over a large branch I miss, so distracted by this simple yet beautifully put explanation.

But what was that he said? We? Is he—?

My steps falter again, and he stops with a concerned frown, turning to look at me.

"We. You said we." I state. I don't know why this is a surprise.

Maybe because I had assumed from my letter that my kind, our kind apparently—had basically died out. Or at least blended into the mortal population over hundreds of star-cycles. Even something as little as this revelation makes me feel lighter somehow.

Maybe I am not so alone. Now that I am thinking about it, that actually makes a lot of sense. My letter did say he was my most trusted friend. It would stand to reason that we are the same.

I emerge from my own deep, winding cavern of thoughts to find Türë examining me, bemused, and stifling his laughter again. I groan, feeling an embarrassed blush blooming red hot on my cheeks.

"You were talking to me again, weren't you?" I ask, though I know the answer from the glint of humor in his dark gaze . "You can laugh." I say with an eye roll, more at myself than him.

He shakes his head, his expression shifting suddenly to serious. "I would not dare." But his eyes sparkle in an obvious tease. "Besides I'm used to you never listening to me."

I stick my tongue out and stomp away, only pausing a second to smile at him over my shoulder. Making sure he knows I am not truly upset. I now follow Ladir—who had apparently gotten tired of our lagging pace and taken the lead—moving a decent distance ahead of us. So silent are his footsteps, the only hint of Türë's approach is the rough chuckle that precedes him.

"You were going to tell me about that joke we used to have!" I suddenly remember. When he doesn't respond, I glance back over my shoulder to make sure he is still there. He is, but to my surprise, isn't wearing any look I had seen on him before. Or even the blank mask I saw briefly earlier. For just a second, I swear I catch a look of such sorrow that I can feel the pain myself. I inhale sharply, but the look is gone a half a breath later, and when he speaks again, he is his usual self.

"It was very long ago when we met," Türë begins, eyes glazing over with a wistful smile as he drifts through his memories. "You immediately disliked me, actually. You associated male *Sidhe* with the controlling horrible males that you had known all your life. Aside from your grandfather." He pauses, helping me over a fallen limb with steady hands before letting go more quickly than I wanted him to. I barely knew this man, and here he was, making my pulse jump and palms clammy.

"Go on." I say, my attempt to be encouraging falling flat with my true purpose. I wanted—needed—to know more about this man that I was already wanting to trust so infallibly.

Thankfully, he continues.

"Where I came from is a longer story for a different day, but I ended up on your shores many centuries ago. We met by coincidence and I was thrilled to find another of my kind here. Mortal lives are so fleeting, it is hard to have every single person you know die while you stay young. So when I found another with a similar long life, I made every effort to make myself known to you. It took a very long time, but the happy conclusion is that you finally got to know me and at last admitted that we were acquaintances. And even after that, it took decades, but you finally trusted me enough to sit me down and tell me most of your story. Not all—but enough to understand what made you, you. And to explain why you were so disagreeable in the beginning." He turns to look at me. "The letter did cover that at least, right?" Türë looks uneasy suddenly, wondering if he had revealed too much at once without any explanation. I couldn't help but appreciate his sensitivity to how easily I was going to be overwhelmed right now. I nod with a grateful smile.

He really didn't know what was in the letter then. That, or he is a fantastic fraud.

"Yes. Not into great detail," I admit, "but the general overview of what the first star-cycles of her—my—life were covered." I stumble over the words, realizing even as I said them how absurd they were.

"Well, when you at last filled me in on your history," Türë continues, "I didn't know what to even say. So I responded with, 'I don't even know where to begin.' To which you replied, 'I bet.'" His eyes drift past me into the growing darkness of the forest, lost in his memory. He smiles into the distance, the expression tangled with a hint of sadness. I take the opportunity of his distraction to really look at him. But I quickly divert my gaze when his eyes refocus on me and he continues his explanation. "After that, it became a running joke between us. One of us would explain something, even something as simple as what we had for lunch that day, or a boring meeting with the Captain of the Guard, the other would answer with the 'I don't know where to begin.' And then the other, 'I bet.'" Türë scratches the slight shadow of stubble beginning to show on his jaw and finally the smile grows until it crinkles the corners of his eyes. "It was an old habit that I answered that way this morning, and that was where the laughter came from. So not at current you, but laughter at past you." He concluded with a cautious smile.

I let my thoughts linger over this for the next few steps before answering.

"So we have been friends for a very long time?" I inquire.

He opens his mouth, but then shuts it promptly with a snap.

That was a curious response. I wait patiently, realizing how much I truly wanted this answer and deciding to wait until he would give it to me.

"Like I said, our relationship was rocky and complicated for a *very* long time, so I don't know exactly when it changed. But yes, we were friends for a very long time." I stare at him openly now, trying to decide how much I wanted to push him for further defining of what had been a very strange and somewhat carefully worded response.

Much to my frustration, our unspoken impasse is suddenly interrupted with a sharp buzzing sound to our left. I jolt to a stop, waving at my ear, certain that it was an insect or something flitting around rather loudly and close to my head.

What is that? I spin around trying to find the continuing noise.

I turn to ask Türë if he can see the bug assaulting me, but instead find him watching me with his head cocked to the side in confusion.

"Problem?" He asks.

"Yes! There is a weird bug or something buzzing in my ear!" I hiss in annoyance, and a little bit of pain at the ringing in my head from its loud vibration. Snatching at the air, I again connect with and see nothing. I squint around trying to spot the annoyance and to my chagrin still find nothing—though the buzzing does not relent.

Türë bites his lip, fighting a laugh again. "It isn't a bug. Or at least not a biological one."

I don't understand what that means.

He takes in my confusion shifting quickly to frustration, and hurries to explain that it is yet another long time friendly joke.

"This particular *bug* is Patryk." My eyebrows shoot upwards and I only become more lost. "He decided to take the rare opportunity of the free time provided by this trip to try a flute he found at the market." Türë shakes his head and we begin walking towards the sound. The volume grows with each step in its direction until it gets so bad that even Türë has to cover his ears.

With each step closer to the campsite and the sound that apparently was supposed to be considered *music,* I feel my nerves rising steadily again at the silent expectation that these men, my old friends, held for me. According to my letter, I was their leader.

Their Queen.

And now…

I see Türë glance sideways at me, as if he could feel my trepidation thick in the air around us. "There is no expectation of you here from us." He murmurs. And I straighten up taller, a bit of the weight lifting off my shoulders. I don't let my steps falter. Only my rapid heartbeat and my breath gives away any sign of my anxiety. Ladir suddenly launches into happy leaping bounds towards the voices. After a short surprised exclamation, laughter erupts. Türë pauses and beckons me to follow him as he heads for the dancing light of a campfire that illuminates the now shadow covered forest. With a final reassuring smile, he steps off the path and into a swept clear, dirt circle that has been filled with a row small tents. At its center Patryk and Ivrik sit on logs set around the flickering campfire that fills the middle of the clearing. I look to the west, towards the soft rosy glow of dusk and the setting sun that is now all but gone.

Day one. You can do this.

Behind me I hear different nighttime sounds of the forest beginning to wake in the darkness.

I take a steadying breath and follow after Türë.

five

Around the campfire, I watch the three friends interact with interest. A far cry from the tense, irritable group that I had encountered that first time in the forest clearing. But I also am a little less skittish. I can't help but observe, smiling to myself, sipping from the mug of tea Patryk had given me. Ivrik chases Ladir around, trying to save his left boot that dangles from her mouth. Patryk now sits on a log beside mine, staring morosely at the fire where Ivrik had, thankfully, chucked the flute in. Our group encircles the stone ring of the campfire, sitting with our backs to the darkness that seeps from the trees surrounding us. I realize I am staring when Patryk's eyes dart in my direction, before quickly shifting away again. I see his throat bob with a nervous swallow and I look at Türë for reassurance. It is hard for me to forget the person they had known just a few days ago was all but gone. For them, it was impossible.

Just try to be normal. Though I don't know what exactly my normal was, I just do what the others do, and try what feels natural. "Thank you for the tea. It is delicious." I smile at Patryk, who beams at the complement.

"It was your favorite. But you always made me make it for you. You have a horrible habit of boiling the water too hot and singeing the tea leaves." I am spared from answering when Ladir bounces up to me. Ivrik follows closely, huffing from exertion at chasing the light-footed wolf around the camp. I can't help but laugh at the sight and with a stern look, I chide Ladir, though I admit it lacks the correct tone. I set down my mug out of danger of the prancing paws.

"Now give that back, you stinker! No wonder he doesn't like you very much, you ornery beastie." I tease her, pulling apart her mouth to save the boot from further destruction from her gleaming teeth. Her tongue lolls out of the side of her mouth, tail sweeping the dirt beneath it back and forth. I hand the slobber covered shoe over to Ivrik with faint hope that he would return my shy smile. To my surprise, he does.

"It's never anyone else's boots! Only mine, the little shit." He exclaims, laughing to himself and bobbling as he balances, tugging it on his foot, pausing only to frown at his filthy, dust-covered sock.

"The reason is obvious." Patryk chimes in, moving further down the log to make room for Ivrik. "She goes after the pair with the most odious smell." Türë chokes on the water skein he had been drinking from, spluttering in a mixture of stifled laughter mixed with coughing. I can't help but laugh along. A look of pleased excitement blooms on Ladir's face. I notice a discarded branch nearby, too small for the fire and toss it into the woods. We all watch as she takes off to retrieve it at top speed.

I return my attention to the men who now sit around the fire with Patryk and I. All watch me closely, while doing their best to pretend not to.

Act normal. I tell myself again. So instead of blushing and looking away like I want to— I roll my eyes and stare them all down. "Alright, this is awkward enough without you all at least *pretending* that this isn't weird." Türë diverts his gaze to the fire crackling in cozy rhythm, trying to hide the smile that crosses his face at my blunt approach.

The other two shift uncomfortably on their respective seats as Patryk blushes a deep rouge.

"This is just so strange." Ivrik admits first. "I don't even know what to say, because it's not like you would remember anything that we would talk about."

Patryk doesn't speak, but nods along in agreement.

Can't argue with that.

Ladir returns to me with the found stick in her mouth, her eyes wide and excited. So I throw it again, taking the time to think of what to say.

"I know. Trust me. I get it. Everything is new to me, but I know you all are my friends." I press my hand to my chest and look around the circle. "In here. I may not remember you, but this feels familiar." I confess. They all stare at me again, though with less expectation, my confession driving them to silence. "So tell me— " I rack my brain for anything, then I remember the letter. "—Tell me about your territories. That is what they are called, right?" Türë nods once, subtly encouraging me. "And you are my... Underkings? Right?"

Patryk answers this time. "Yes, to both. Tesindren—your kingdom— has four territories."

"I am going to start on dinner while you explain. I am sure Evara is starving." Türë interjects quietly before standing up. Sure enough, not moments later, my stomach growls aloud and we all laugh at his foresight. Ivrik reaches out to stoke the fire, as Türë begins to take a stack of dishes and cookware out of a nearby pack leaning against the canvas side of one of the tents. Patryk begins to explain more as the peaceful sound of the snapping fire and clanging of dishes sound around us.

"The four territories are Telor, Paith, Eri, and Bethos. Ivrik and I won the coin toss to join you today. Noran and Eivan had to stay behind, so you will get to meet them when you get back."

Back where? I want to ask, but it is so low on the rank of questions beginning to slam through my brain, one right after another. The thought of everything I did not know about an entire kingdom who all relied on me—all the pressure and uncertainty came rushing back in a torrent. Ladir returns with the stick. But this time when I throw it, she watches it fly through the air before choosing to just sit down at my feet. Laying her head on my lap, she gives a contented huff and watches me with her intelligent amber eyes. I let my fingers sink themselves deep in her warm fur and listen to Patryk continue to tell me about my lands and people.

"Noran oversees Bethos, the western-most territory—" He pauses, looking around for something. Ivrik must understand because he unexpectedly stands, making me jump. Ivrik makes his way over to another tent, across from where Türë is busy preparing our meal, and grabs a leather bag sitting against a tent.

"Thanks, Iv." Patryk says.

Ivrik only responds with a grunt that I take to mean 'you're welcome' before sitting back down, prodding at the logs until the stick he uses catches fire and he tosses it into the now roaring blaze.

My attention is drawn back to Patryk, who locates what he needs from the bag's depths. Pulling out a large folded parchment, he slides down from the log to the ground to his knees, where he unfolds it carefully, flattening it against the grass. The last glow of the sun had long ago been lost, but the fire casts enough light that

I can see clearly what he shows me.

I gasp aloud and drop down on my knees beside him. I let my fingers softly glide over the beautifully drawn image depicted on the parchment. I marvel at the illustrations and feel tears prick my eyes.

"Is this it? This is my kingdom?" I ask, my voice low with excitement and awe. I look up at the three men, whose attentions are all focused on my reaction. Ivrik nods with a rare smile.

"This is Tesindren."

Patryk takes my hand and, using my finger, follows a dark line drawn on the map. "This is the border. Everything inside this line is your kingdom." He releases my hand, but I trace the line again.

My kingdom.

"Tell me more, please." I ask, breathless, with a glance up at his face, bent close to the parchment next to my own.

He obliges me and starts with the territory he had been speaking of initially.

"Here is Bethos, where Noran is the Underking." He points his chin toward the giant world, then circles a portion of land the furthest left on the page. "It has four major cities, Dolunt, Merga, Zanda, and its most important, the Port city of Eludar. That is where we get most of our imports from across the sea." He explains. "Other than the city, it is mostly farms and a few smaller villages along the rivers in this territory. It also holds the kingdom's archives and largest library."

His fingers drift now to the right, to a territory labeled *Eri.* "This is Eivan's territory. Saroch is a notable port, but Eri's biggest city is actually Vante." He taps a label in the center of the territory where two rivers converge.

"What is that?" I ask, pointing at an interesting illustration depicted in the lower part of the territory.

"The Cliffs." He answers with a grim look at Ivrik. "It is said they are cursed and a beacon of death. That is where the last battle of the first war happened. Where you and the Nefriti fought and freed this land while under your leadership." Patryk takes in my wide eyes and waves off the outpouring of questions he can clearly see beginning to come his way. "That is a whole other story and one you will have to ask the Head Librarian for. It was before our time. Way, way before." He shrugs this off and continues walking me through the map with his slim fingers. I have to bite down on the questions that threaten to throw me off course and direct my focus back to the map.

"Eri also has a smaller military base at Erit," Patryk gestures to a small, miss-able marking on the map. "But the fortress has been mostly abandoned in the last centuries, and everyone just lives in the city proper."

I try to absorb all of this information, but each thing I learn seems to add ten more questions on top of the rapidly mounting total.

Ivrik takes over now, shuffling over until he sits in the dirt right alongside Patryk and me, pointing at a territory to the right of Eri. "This is Paith, the territory you—oh so kindly—granted me. We have a mixture of forest and mountain lands, with our most notable landmark being Lake Naro, which conveniently is named after the closest city and largest in Paith." His eyes grow darker and more serious as his pointer finger moves south now to the border. "We also have two larger military installations, Charobi to the east and Dulen to the west. That is where a large portion of our trained military force is stationed."

"Is there a threat to the south? Is that why they are all there?" Ivrik nods, appearing slightly impressed by my deduction. He slides his finger slowly to the south of the border and the mass of land that had been blacked out on the map.

"Mirinth." He says with a sneer. "It has been a while—but they used to ally with your old country across the sea. They began a bad habit of testing our borders and your strength all the time, invading villages and taking slaves. Until you concealed yourself in a village that they were rumored to hit next." With a maniac guffaw, he laughs hard, even slapping his knee in his delight. "Boy, oh boy, were they shocked to find the Queen herself among the women taken that day. You made them pay dearly for that mistake and they promptly released all who they had captured in the hope you wouldn't burn their entire kingdom to the ground. You even stayed in a tent down at the border until both fortresses were built to ensure your people would be safe. The military has been there since."

"Do they still try?" I ask, awestruck and trying to fathom the amount of star-cycles into the past that these stories had happened.

"Not in my lifetime." Ivirk says, with a genuine smile. "Or my grandfather's. Or my great-grandfather's. Or my—" Patryk reaches around me and smacks him not so gently on the back of the head to get him to stop.

I snort a laugh at the two and pause to look at Ivrik more closely. Up until now, I hadn't been entirely sure *why* I had chosen the man. Patryk made sense. He appeared to be well educated and kind. Ivrik, while friendly and helpful enough, seemed course and harder to get along with. I suppose, upon explanation of his territory being more military leaning, the rough edges made a little more sense.

If he realizes that I am watching him intently, Ivrik doesn't let on. I glance up though and make eye contact with Türë. Before I can smile at him, he returns his attention to slicing the various vegetables spread out before him. I had been briefly distracted by my thoughts, so it takes a minute or two before the full understanding of what Ivrik had said suddenly hits me. I grab his arm, halting his explanation of the goods that his own territory provides.

"Sorry, you said not in your lifetime?" I shake my head, awestruck at the amount of star-cycles in the past these stories had happened. "So how long ago? I am just trying to get a timeline in my head of how old I *really* am." I know what the letter had said, but I wanted—needed—to hear it confirmed. Both Ivrik and Patryk exchange a look with Türë, who at last steps forward when it becomes clear neither knew how to answer me.

"The last real battle with another country was six hundred and seventy three star-cycles ago, in 350 of Third Tesria, but the one they are referring to was over twenty-five hundred star-cycles ago." He says, voice calm like he is trying to soothe a wounded animal. My jaw drops. "In 462 of First Tesria, right?" He glances at the others for confirmation.

"I know the letter said—but—how is that even possible?" I drop my head into my hands, trying to wrap my head around the span of my lifetime.

Patryk tries to help reassure me, putting his hand on my shoulder only to yank it back as a snap of electricity sparks through his touch. I look up at the noise with a jerk and my breath catches in surprise. He hisses and rubs the now tender skin.

"I'm so sorry! Sorry!" I scramble to my feet and take a few steps away from the others who side-eye me with concern again.

Türë approaches me, relatively calm despite the fact that in the last six hours I have both exploded into flames and singed someone as he tried to comfort me.

"This is how it was possible." He explains with a soothing voice. "You have power inside you, gifted by Jera herself to protect your people. But when you go through the Awakening part of the memories taken also takes your control. So you have to start all over with learning how to wield it each time." He steps away, seeing that I need a moment to myself. I wrap my arms around myself tightly and look up at the sky, counting the stars that have appeared as I breathe through the overwhelming feelings. Listening to the others talking among each other quietly, though about nothing important—mainly on the camp setup and the like, helps me feel less embarrassed at least. I could only imagine their disappointment in me. So I appreciate their willingness to pretend I wasn't, in fact, a mess. When Türë approaches the fire carrying a large pot that he sets up in the red hot coal bed, I finally gather enough will to break my silent self-depreciation.

"If I don't remember how to do anything, how am I supposed to protect anyone? How am I supposed to not *hurt* anyone?" I ask weakly, trying and failing to keep my voice from cracking too much with hopelessness.

This time, it is Ivrik that reassures me, much to my surprise.

"That is why you have us. We will help you get back on your feet and find yourself again." He holds a hand out to me. I stare at it a moment before taking a shaky breath. Reaching out, I take it at last and sigh heavily with relief when nothing happens to him. And, more to his credit, he doesn't flinch at my touch as I yank him towards me and wrap my arms around him. He even returns the hug, squeezing me tightly until I at last let him go. I give him a shy, grateful smile, unsure of how to thank him for such a simple yet exceptionally meaningful gesture. Before I can express this, he walks over to Türë with the offer of help and leaves me alone with Patryk, who offers me an apologetic grin that was more of a wince.

"Would you like to continue? Or do you need a break?" Patryk asks, no judgment coloring his tone. I take a bracing breath and give a nod and rejoin him. "Good! We have reached the best territory." His eyes flash with excitement. "Here is the Northern Territory, called Telor. My territory." He shines with pride now that he gets to speak about his own home. "Telor is the oldest territory and the first you liberated four thousand star-cycles ago. It is actually where we are right now, technically." He points to another illustrated part of the map, drawn in emerald ink and peppered with dense drawn trees, then gestures to the dark trunks around us that encircle the camp. "This is the Forest of Memory, which is actually where we are right now." He points vaguely at a spot among the drawn trees to the farthest point north depicted on the map. His lips quirk in a grin as unmistakable fondness fills his eyes. He encircles the sketched city just below the forest's edge. "Here is Alessandra, the capital and location of Yvonya Castle, your home." I try desperately to memorize all the various points on the map he marks. "Our only port is Grezon, but we also have Anopthe that connects the rest of the kingdom by river, so we use that mainly for trade between the territories." I nod enthusiastically, as if I understand all of this. But I can tell from the glint in his eye that he knows I am pretending. He glances to the other two, chatting about something on the other side of the roaring campfire, before whispering conspiratorially to me, "Don't worry, I can help you with late night study sessions when you are ready. Feel free to ask me anything anytime, okay? Please feel no pressure to know all of this right now." I squeeze his hand gratefully.

"Here to the right border of the kingdom is the Baol Range—" He starts again at normal volume, with a wink. Unable to stop myself, I break into a giggle, drawing curious glances from the other two.

"And what is past that?" My own fingers drift to where the map cuts off anything past that point to the north east.

Patryk shrugs, before reaching out to take the steaming bowl of stew handed to him by Ivrik. I take my own from Türë and the campsite falls silent, aside from the sounds coming from the surrounding forest and our own eating. From the first bite, I can't eat it fast enough. Though hot, it was the perfect temperature and the flavors were almost intoxicating.

I didn't realize how hungry I was. I accidentally give a moan of satisfaction before blushing in embarrassment.

Luckily they all laugh heartily, and only tease me a little.

"Türë is by far the best cook of all of us. But he's had centuries on us to perfect his recipes." Patryk chimes in, devouring his own helping, even faster than I am. Ivrik grabs my empty bowl and kindly refills it and his own from the large bubbling pot in the campfire.

Centuries?? Ugh... another thing to add to the list of things to ask about later. I don't let myself get distracted by this and focus back on what we were previously talking about.

"Do we really not know what is beyond—what was it called again?" I lean forward to look closely at the map spread at my feet, wiping my mouth on my already dirty sleeve.

"The Baol Range." Ivrik fills in for me, wiping his own mouth dry. Then answers the question with a solemn shake of his head. "There isn't anything past it. Just more mountains and trees. And the mountains are too tall to try and pass. Everyone who has attempted it has died."

No... That doesn't seem right.

I voice my disbelief, but neither Patryk or Ivrik answer me. Instead they look towards Türë for his help with explaining again.

"There *was* someone who survived the mountains," He responds after a moment's pause, staring into the fire, unable to meet my gaze. "And, well, if you don't remember what is beyond them now, then no. Nobody knows what is beyond."

As this information fully sinks in, I feel my heart drop into my stomach.

"It was me?" I ask, even though I can tell the answer from their faces, added to the fact none of them now will make eye contact with me.

"Oh." I stare down at the darkened area beyond the eastern border of the kingdom. "Why—?" I begin, but realize that there was nothing to do about the loss of knowledge and there was no point to asking the question.

Why didn't I tell anyone? The regret at my part in allowing such things to be lost forever fills me with anger. I force it down, setting my bowl aside, no longer hungry.

Well, I can find out. I can find someone to go, or even go myself! Yes. That would fix it.

"What we do know is that we are *never* supposed to go beyond the mountains." Türë's voice cuts into my thoughts with a knowing glance. I jolt in surprise, wondering for a moment if I had actually voiced my idea aloud.

For the first time since entering the campsite, he meets my gaze with such intensity that I am the one to look away first.

Maybe I *had* told someone, I realize.

He knows something. But I let it go, for now. Though I make sure to remember to push the matter further later on. Once I knew more about—well, everything.

SIX

"So…" I begin, quirking an eyebrow and watching Türë closely. "Centuries?" I let the rest of my question hang in the air unspoken, taking a long sip of my broth. He doesn't reply, humored at my struggling to find a way to finish my question. I catch Patryk and Ivrik sharing a bemused look. "How old are you all, really?" I ask finally.

Patryk sets his bowl down, stretching his legs out and rubbing his now full belly with a contented, slightly sleepy sigh. "Well, Grandpa over there—" he says, casting a smirk towards Türë, and flicks a bit of bread at him. "—is the only one who has a longevity closest to you."

"Yeah, you two have been close friends for what, six hundred, seven hundred star-cycles now?" Ivrik adds, stretching his arms up and setting his empty bowl aside.

I blink, my mind trying to wrap around what he just said. "You said *how many* star-cycles? Six hundred? Seven hundred?" In truth, it doesn't surprise me that much at this point. Not when considering my age, plus knowing now that he too was a Sidhe. Though he didn't have my extreme opportunity of total immortality, according to the letter, being a Sidhe meant Türe would still have a very long lifetime. Across from me, Türe silently stokes the fire and adds a few more logs before answering.

"We met around 250 of Third Tesria, but it took a good eighty or so star-cycles after that for us to actually be *friends*." He looks up at me with a smirk. "You thought I was a stuck up asshole who just lived to irritate you."

"Not that much has changed there..." Patryk says, pretending to block his mouth so only Ivrik and I can see it, but still speaking loudly enough for everyone to hear. We all laugh, even Türe, who seems to grow more comfortable than he had appeared all night. He brushes a hand through his hair, pulling it back with a leather strap, before he replies, launching another stray carrot at Patryk with his other hand. With startling accuracy, the carrot beams towards him and sticks with a squelch in the center of Patryk's forehead. We all burst into kind laughter as Patryk streams curses and wipes the carrot away with a glare at Türe.

"Well then, I used to be *more* of an asshole who lived to irritate you." He says, conceding the point, albeit with good humor. "Either way, it has been a long, long time that we have been a team." He glances at me before returning his attention to the fire pit, the light of the flames casting dancing shadows onto his face. Though he still appears to be the same age as the other two men, for the first time a grim weight of the long star-cycles shows in his eyes. It makes me wonder if I had possessed a similar look prior to the Awakening. How much weight did the long star-cycles wear down on me before they were now blessedly wiped free by my Goddess? Then with a blink, the look is gone, and the light of youth is back to glimmering in his eyes. As if whatever memory he had been lost in for that moment had returned to the vast space of his mind.

"Seven hundred and fifty two star-cycles…" I repeat slowly. "But how old are you now then?" I blurt out, leaning forward in my eagerness for more information from the most quiet of the group.

He laughs at my enthusiasm. "I am now one thousand and four." My jaw drops and I almost fall off the log. The following silence seems to echo around the campfire. "Well, you look *great!*" I manage meekly, and Türë grins.

Patryk grabs absentmindedly for a nearby stick. "Hence — Grandpa." He says, chucking it into the forest. Ladir, who had previously been fast asleep, sprawled across the bare dirt, suddenly flails to her feet and scrambles after it. In her haste, she collides with Ivrik who, taking extra cautious steps to avoid spilling his third, filled to the brim, helping of soup, was returning to his seat. Riotous laughter that has us all hunched over and gasping for breath fills the air. The sound echoes off the trees in the darkness and the forest around us stills for a moment to listen. Even Ivrik, with soup covering his entire chest, can't fight it and it is a good while before we all regain our self-control. I wipe the tears that had spilled out of my eyes and clench at my stomach, cramping from the extended bout of laughter—now replaced with gasping and complaining of each of our own sore muscles. Patryk manages to haul Ivrik back to his feet and hands him a dry, clean cloth that he tugs free from his nearby pack. Ladir only watches us, her tail sweeping the dirt back and forth from where she sits. I do notice the trouble-making stick clenched tightly in her mouth with pride, clearly unconcerned about the commotion she caused.

I remember a name that had been mentioned alongside theirs in the letter. *Cernunnos.* I mention it to the others. Türë answers, as I expected, though with a light in his eyes I had not yet seen. Adoration? Fondness? I can't quite place it.

"Cernunnos was one of your oldest friends. You two met when you first began to wreak havoc on the slaver's caravans and sought sanctuary in the Forest. This forest actually. Nobody, even you I think, knew exactly *what* he was, but he was beyond ancient." He laughs lightly. "You two were a pair. You used to call him the *Lord of Wild Things*."

"Was? What happened to him?"

"It was never said. He just one day vanished." Türë stares into the fire, eyes filled with a dark sadness. "There were those who said that after the Creatures of the Forest disappeared, he no longer had the heart to live." Only the sound of the popping fire can be heard as his words sink in. "I am just glad I got to meet him at least once." He adds.

"So what are you guys? A hundred? Two hundred?" I manage to ask after another few minutes have passed and the ability to speak has been regained.

Ivrik snorts, continuing his pointless attempt to scrub the stew clean from his drenched shirt. "No luck. I am twenty-eight and Patryk is thirty-three. But Noran is thirty-eight and Eivan is the oldest of our brotherhood at forty-eight."

I don't know what I expected, but it wasn't that. After learning the total lifetimes of myself and Türë, I guess a precedent had been set for what I could guess was the average age. It didn't help that out of the three of them, Türë looked the youngest. My fingertips tingle and my hand drifts up to touch my own silken cheek.

I wonder what I look like? It hadn't occurred to me before that I hadn't an inkling of my own appearance. Well, aside from the spirals of deep caramel and gold interlaced locks that tumble all down the length of my back. I suddenly wish I had thought of it while we had been next to the river and there was a chance that I could catch a glimpse of myself in the water.

Realizing how quiet the camp had fallen, I look back up from the fire from where my eyes had drifted in my thoughts. To my surprise, I find that only Türë still sits nearby. I spot Patryk and Ivrik walking into the thick forest, for what must be a need to empty their bladders, disappearing into the dark night, made darker in the shadows that have enveloped the aged trunks all around us.

"Do you—?" I start to ask about something, but the thought vanishes and I freeze when I realize Türë has his entire focus trained on me. I meet his piercing eyes for a second, swallowing hard as my stomach does a little flip at the strength of that attention. A second is all I can take before it becomes too much and I have to look away.

"What were you thinking before?" He asks, kindly enough that I tell him without hesitation. Though I blush at the obvious conceit and embarrassment of my vanity.

"I—I realized that I don't know what I look like."

Thankfully, understanding without judgement shines from him in a flash. I jump in surprise at his movement when he gracefully, but with unexpected suddenness, moves to another bag propped up against a different tent than Patryk's bag had been.

It must be his pack, I deduce, as he searches inside for the object he wanted. At last he finds what he is looking for, but it doesn't answer my question when he holds it out to me. Brow furrowed, my eyes dart back and forth, from the object to his face, and back again until he realizes that I need an explanation.

"It's a looking glass. It shows your reflection. We use it for shaving." He again scratches the stubble. Suddenly understanding, I carefully take it and pull it towards myself. I inhale and hold it at arm's length in anticipation.

I don't care if it makes me vain. Please don't let me be a hag. I wince and turn my gaze fully to the reflection now cast in the glass.

Though I don't have any memory of other women to compare myself to, I still feel a flood of relief at the image that looks back at me in the glass. In the background, I see the shape of Türe move into view behind me and our eyes meet briefly in the reflection.

"Well..?" He asks, slightly trepidatious.

My gaze shifts back to my reflection and the hand that isn't holding the glass up drifts towards my face. I let my fingers softly brush across my sharp cheekbones. Even in the dim light, I can see the crimson blush that paints them perfectly rosy. Large silvery-blue almond-shaped eyes look back at me, surrounded by long black, thick eyelashes that bat rapidly in shock. As I turn my head, I can see a slight shimmer from my skin, like it has been dusted with gold. The action draws my attention to the rest of what I can see in the glass. I could tell when I had first woken that I had waist length brown hair, not dark as the burning bark of the walnut logs that crackle in the fire. More akin to the rich hue of the leather saddles, now stacked beside one of the tents. Strands of gold soften the tone, making it a brighter shade than I first thought. I am reminded of how the beams of sunlight had appeared on the trunks of the trees we passed today.

What I could not tell immediately—or even thought about— was the set of elongated horns the length of my forearm, the deep rich hue of the acorns strewn across the forest floor that protrude delicately from the top of my head. I run the tip of my finger over them and can't help but feel awed by their velvety smooth texture. My lips, as pink as the wild peonies that were scattered along our walk to the campsite, twitch upwards in a smile. I let out a small giggle. I can't help it. And Türe's chuckle joins mine.

"I guess that is a good sign!" He comments, moving forward and sitting on the log beside me. Relief fills me and I pull up the mirror again for another look.

"Türë?" I start, running a finger over the horns protruding from my head, each a delicate arch. "Are these part of being a Sidhe?" I glance to his own scalp, absent of horns, and my brow furrows. "Or is it because of my deal with Jera?" After a moment he opens his mouth to explain, when a crunch of the forest debris signals the return of the other two, who immediately are obviously curious about what we are doing. He snaps his mouth shut before turning his attention to the men. Türë manages to wave them off without explanation of what I was doing, instead coercing them to clean the dishes, since he had cooked. But I do notice that he avoids answering me. Obviously, that was a topic for another day, though I can't help but wonder why.

The darkness grows as the campfire continues to dwindle down, but nobody moves to add any more logs or even stir it. Rather we all simply sit in comfortable conversation. I listen, but only with half of my attention, more just absorbing the comforting sound of voices rather than the actual topic.

I already have enough information swirling around my tired brain for one day. I yawn hard, and Türë leans closer in to me. I collect myself enough to not lean my heavy head against his shoulder like I ache to.

"The second tent on the left is yours, if you are ready for some well-deserved sleep." He says, voice soft compared to the loud, rowdy conversation happening across from us where the other two speak with animated gestures about people and places of which I had no recollection.

I nod with a grateful smile, my exhaustion hitting me fully now that he mentioned sleep.

"And—uh—which is your tent, Türë?" Ivrik adds loudly with a roguish wink. His words slur a bit before taking another long gulp of some foul smelling drink he had pulled out of his bag upon his return to the camp.

Türë ignores him, other than a muscle jumping wildly in his jaw. But I feel myself blush and decide to respond.

"Oh, are you needing some late night cuddles, Ivrik?" I ask with raised eyebrows.

A momentary pause, then surprised laughter echoes around us yet again. Even Ivrik slaps his thigh in good humor and I can accept it all suddenly.

My friends. I can see that now.

A wave of affection washes over me as I bid them good night and make my way over to the tent that had been set up for me. With a final smile and glance over my shoulder, I let myself absorb the image before me. Ivrik still laughing heartily with his cheeks a ruddy rouge, another result of the drink he and Patryk had been passing back and forth. The latter, having fallen off the log, was rolling in the dirt. Trying and failing to regain his footing without any of the regal coordination that I would expect from someone who calls himself a king. My eyes flick over to Türë, who has moved to sit in a nearby patch of grass, illuminated only by the moonlight, beside Ladir. His head rests on her side as he stares upward to view the glorious spattering of stars painting the thick black sky. It looks too wonderful—I debate staying up a little longer and watching the stars with him, but as another yawn hits me, I realize that I would only end up sleeping outside if I did that. So, with one last look and smile, I tug back the canvas flap and duck into the tent before any of them can catch me watching. I crawl into the padded bed roll and fall asleep listening to the night.

seven

I toss and turn in the bedroll. I had managed to fall asleep until everyone else had gone to bed and the camp had become silent. Too silent for all the thoughts that swirl through my mind. Listening to Ladir snoring away beside me makes me smile, at least. Unable to still the churning thoughts, I can't help replaying the conversations from earlier in the night. After just a single summary and general glimpse of my kingdom's history and its layout, I was exhausted from that alone. Everything considered, I probably had enough information dumped into my head for one day. Now, alone and listening to the soft sounds of the forest, I cannot pull myself away from my continually growing list of questions.

I sit up, wrapping a nearby blanket around myself against the unexpected chilly night air. Stepping carefully over the dreaming wolf curled up beside me, I push through the tent flap and emerge back out into the now vacant camp. Thanks to my heightened hearing, a Sidhe gift according to Türë, I can hear the faint sounds of steady breathing and thunderous snores of my companions in their tents set up next to my own. I scan the small circle where we had sat before and, thanks to my excellent vision, apparently another gift of my blood, easily find the object that I can't get out of my mind. My bare-feet glimmer with the clinging dew that has already gathered in the grass. I am excited to take the chance to examine the map at my own pace, but I still take a brief moment to enjoy the night's crisp, wet chill on my toes. The refreshing feeling makes me a smile, but my heart seems to skip a beat, faltering when I am suddenly awash with a strange overwhelming feeling. One that sends prickles of discomfort across my entire skin. I turn back to my tent, unable to shake the feeling that I was missing *something*. Shaking my head to dislodge the unexplained feeling, drag my attention back to my current mission. I mutter a prayer that they are all heavy sleepers as a set of tin cups and the now empty liquor bottle clang loudly as I accidentally kick them into each other on my way to the map Patryk had brought out earlier. Scooping it up, I shuffle as close as I dare to the barely glowing remains of the fire from earlier. I study the cinders a moment, before determining that its light wouldn't be enough for me to see much by.

What if..? My thoughts drift as I stare into the fire, thinking of the hot, tickling flames that had engulfed me earlier in the meadow. *Am I able to do that on purpose?* I set the yellowed paper down on a log nearby and step back, far enough that should I ignite entirely again, I won't catch the nearby tents, my dozing friends, or the map on fire accidentally.

I brace myself with a deep breath.

Okay, Fire. You can come now.

I wait a moment, holding my breath as I stretch my arms out in front of me. A minute passes.

Still, nothing.

I curse under my breath and shrug off the blanket, trying to shake off the frustration a bit, before turning all my focus back towards my goal.

"Okay, give me something. Anything." I mutter aloud as I wiggle my fingers, feeling slightly silly, and squinting my eyes closed. I shut out everything else, forcing all my thoughts on the image in my mind of the campfire from earlier.

I sneak a peek, before dropping my arms in disappointment. *Nothing.*

I sigh and turn to pick up the cast-aside blanket and map when a soft shuffling comes from behind me.

"Focus on the feeling." A kind voice says, making me jump, gasping as I spin to find Türë watching me from the open flap of his tent. I glare at him, my hand pressed to my chest where my heart beats wildly from the surprise.

"What?" I say, too startled to snap in anger. He takes a step forward, letting the flap to the tent fall shut behind him.

"Focus on the *feeling* of a flame instead of the *thought* of it." He explains.

"I—don't—" I struggle to find the words to convey my confusion. Türë hums and pulls his hair back again with a leather-band, holding it in place. His eyes dart back and forth and his jaw tightens in apparent concentration.

After a few breaths, his face lights up and he strides towards me, taking my hand without any hesitation as he leads me over to the coal remains of the campfire. He hesitates, then slowly, with his hand still grasping my own, moves it over the top of the glowing ash. I fight his tug as he nears the coals, freezing an inch or so above the pale orange coals when he feels my hesitation.

"That." He murmurs, so close I feel his breath tickle my left ear. "Think about that warmth. Not simply the image of fire."

I start, turning my face to meet his. Unbidden, the thought of closing the inch between our lips and kiss him rises. I manage to ask, my voice low as my body warms, and not from the fire. "How did you know that was what I was doing?"

He hesitates before responding. "I have known you for a very long time." My eyes drift up to meet his eyes, as dark and gleaming as the coals before us, and I know he could tell where my mind had gone. After all, I had been staring unabashed at his lips. I shiver slightly, and unable to help myself, I inhale his scent.

He smells like the woods.

"Try it." Türe says.

My eyes flash back up to his own from where they had drifted back to his lips.

"What?" I ask, incredulous.

"Try lighting the fire again." He answers with a light chuckle, releasing my hand so it floats alone over the ash.

He definitely thinks you are an idiot. I groan silently, wishing I had just stayed in my tent. I make myself focus back on the task at hand as his warmth vanishes from my side. Fully stepping away, he disappears into the dark for a minute before returning with a few smaller logs. He adds them to the pile before stepping back again. But instead of walking away like I expect, he sits nearby, pulling out a knife and begins to chip away at a piece of wood pulled from his pocket. He ignores my baffled gaze. With a huff of annoyance, I turn back to my goal.

I close my eyes again, and focus as hard as I possibly can on the feeling of heat that Türe had showed me that still radiated from the coals.

A memory of the flames.

If I could just pull that out of the cinders that are already there, maybe that will do something. I wait for minutes, focusing solely on the feeling of the heat. When I at last open my eyes to see if there had been any success — *Nothing. Again!*

I groan aloud, this time in frustration and clench my fists at my side until the piercing pain of my nails tearing into my palms overwhelms me. Tears prick my eyes, but I force them back. I realize the rhythmic sound of Türë's carving has stopped and I can feel his concern wash over me. I throw my head back and look up at the stars glittering brightly against the dark blue of the clear night sky, blinking back the burning tears that pool.

You aren't going to figure all of this out in a single day. I take a shaky breath and let myself fall back onto the log. A breeze rushes through the campsite and I reach behind me for the blanket I had discarded. Türë begins his work again as I wrap myself tightly into a soft cocoon, tilting my head back. I take deep breaths, doing my best to relax and be lost in the beauty of the night.

My thoughts eventually begin to drift as my breathing steadies again. I find those thoughts moving to the warmth of Türë's breath on my cheek and neck. Of its own accord, my breath quickens at the brief memory. Suddenly I hear the shuffling of his hands stop again. I stiffen, afraid that he had heard my thoughts or even that I had accidentally spoken aloud. My eyes snap open and I turn to find him.

To say what exactly? There is not a non-embarrassing explanation for my unreturned feelings.

But his focus is not even on me.

"Evara..." He says, astonishment filling his voice. I follow his bright eyes to where a roaring fire now crackles in front of me. "You did it!" His face glows with pride at my success.

"I don't know how." I admit, but cannot shake off the smile spread across my face. Maybe I know how, just a little bit, but there is no way I am going to tell him that!

I watch, awestruck, as the fire dances and pops for a while before remembering at last why I wanted it lit again in the first place.

I turn and grab the map from where I had set it aside safely. Carefully unrolling it, I spread it out in front of me. Letting my finger-tips trail across the various landmarks that my three companions had shown me. I try to picture them in my mind as I pass each notation on the map. Like everything else, all I can picture in my minds eye is the black backdrop of my eyelids. Unable to draw upon any memory, I decide to ingrain this information into my new brain.

This is your kingdom. Your people. It should be as familiar to you as your own soul.

The time passes quickly and peacefully, as I sit through the rest of the night in silence. The only sound that fills the camp is the repetitive *shuuck* of Türë's knife, carving away the wood chunk with expert hands.

Until, finally, instead of the utter blackness when my eyes are closed; I could see the very map I have resting in front of me.

My Tesindren.

eight

After staying up examining the map, probably far too long, I stumble back to my tent to get some more sleep. It feels like I just close my eyes when bright light suddenly streams on my face. I pry them open at the invasion. Hissing at the pain in my eyes, I squint at Türë holding open the tent flap, trying to hide a grin.

"Morning sleepyhead." He greets me and I mumble a response as I hide my face in the blanket. "If we want to make it home tonight, we need to get going." He says apologetically. That zaps me into action. Excitement tingles through my body and I push to my feet, my lips tugging upward in anticipation for everything to come today. I roll my shoulders and shake my arms loose as I follow Türë out into the camp. I blink a few times to adjust fully to the morning light. The others have already disassembled all of their tents and, to my surprise, have everything ready, aside from the horses saddled and my tent. I hear a shuffle and some clicks of wood against wood, and I turn to find Türë and Patryk already dismantling it with efficient teamwork. Embarrassment fills me as

I realize how late I had slept, even through the noise of them packing up.

"I am so sorry I didn't help!" I say to them all, shifting on my feet.

"Don't worry, next time we will let you do it all." Ivrik says with a wink, nudging me playfully with an elbow.

Patryk adds as he passes me with an armful of the cloth that had been the exterior of my tent, rolled up into a tight bundle. "You had a big day yesterday. The least we could do was let you sleep." I manage a smile and move to help them as they begin to load the saddles and few remaining items onto the horses. Unfortunately, I do not make much progress. My memory is unhelpfully missing everything I needed to know regarding how to actually maneuver and tie the straps of the saddle securely, but I do my best. After a few minutes of fumbling fingers and guesswork, a gentle tug to test my handiwork sends the whole thing careening to the ground with a solid thump. The horse eyes me warily and nickers to Türe, who doesn't manage to hide his smirk fast enough. I glare at him a moment before heaving a sigh and stepping aside as he comes to help me.

"Better me than Ivrik." He whispers to me with a soft smile, his breath warming my cheek as it passes my ear. Leaning in beside me, he grabs for the strap across the mare's stomach and secures the saddle with practiced hands. "You teased him for an entire season after he missed a loop and slid off *with* his saddle on one of our first trips together. He would find total euphoria in the opportunity to pay you back!" I laugh along with him, and roll my shoulders again, trying to relax.

Even after everything I had seen and experienced since I had woken up the day before in the meadow, the urge to feel wary of trusting these men— anyone— that I could not remember, had returned with the new day. In spite of doing my best to allow them in, it was like leaping off of a cliff and hoping that underneath the clouds, there would be water rather than rocks. Everything was foreign, though they all knew *me*. That actually made it even harder to handle. They had expectations, history, respect, and resentment, all for a person I wasn't sure I was anymore.

How can you be someone you don't remember?

The realization that someone is talking to me breaks me from my thoughts. My sight refocuses from where I had been staring blankly into the trees to find all three men studying me with a mixture of humor and concern.

"I'm sorry," I groan. "Were you speaking to me again?" I shake my head at myself and laugh along with the chuckles that answer.

"Did you want anything to eat before we pack that away?" Patryk asks, holding out a wrapped bundle of what smelled like fresh bread.

The twinge in my stomach answers before I do, loud enough that even Ivrik and Patryk could hear it with their human ears. "Does that answer your question?" I take the extended bundle, inhaling deeply, as I unwrap the cloth and inside find the warm crusted loaf.

With one breath, I see a scene of streaming sunlight illuminating a worn wooden table in some small cabin kitchen, where a ball of bread dough sits rising in the heat. I hear a familiar voice and the words, though I cannot grasp what is said, fill my heart with joy. Looking down I see my fingers tracing a carving atop the table.

In the next breath, the scene is gone, transformed from golden warmth to the dewey green of my surroundings. I blink hard and try to hold onto the memory. Feeling its importance—somehow. But nothing else follows and the only thing I see is the three men in the clearing with me, continuing to ready the horses and ensuring we left no sign of our visit. Only Patryk seems to pause at the look on my face, concern sparking in his eyes. I shake my head and smile warmly at him, trying to reassure both him and myself that everything was fine. Inside, however, I hold on to that image, despite the feeling of sadness that seems to well up in me at its memory.

I peel off a piece of the herb-crusted shell. The steam that rises from the moist loaf is so soothing that I can't fight the instinct to let its curling tendrils caress my face and chase away the crisp spring morning.

"Well, Your Majesty," Ivrik's voice snaps me from my thoughts. "Are you ready to return home?" I swallow the mouthful of bread and nod, though my pulse races in trepidation at everything that encompasses. "Don't worry. We will be with you all of the way." He extends a palm, a bright smile blooms revealing a dimple on one cheek that makes his eyes sparkle. I let him take my arm, helping me up onto my waiting horse. The others pull themselves up with ease, and with a final glance around at the now empty forest clearing, Patryk nudges his steed and together we set off. Türe starts to whistle and the others join in with the words to his tune, Ivrik boisterous and off-key, Patryk just above a shy hum.

A peculiar feeling sweeps through me, making my breath catch. I again draw up the memory that had somehow appeared, the only thing I had to hold on to from my past, letting the image fill me with its warmth. After all, I had these friends to help me, a kingdom to see blossom, and a thousand star-cycles ahead of me to learn what I needed too.

A flicker of unease butts into my hope, only for a second before I shove it out again. Ivrik's voice echoes through my head—'we will be with you all the way'. And again, the shadow of doubt retreats into the corners of my mind.

✻ ✻ ✻ ✻ ✻

"Our star-cycles are broken into quarters: Vernas, Aurá, Umna, and Frë. Each quarter has ninety days, and can be further broken down into three moon-cycles of thirty days. Each star-cycle, also sometimes called a year, has three hundred and sixty days, and each Tesria has one thousand star-cycles. As of yesterday, we have now begun Fourth Tesria, meaning it has been the four thousandth star-cycle since you liberated the kingdom and Tesindren was born. Obviously, the general public doesn't know that it also means it is time for the Awakening—they don't know about that part of you. They just know you are immortal thanks to Jera's goodness."

I yawn for what seems to be the millionth time since we had set off that morning and rub my aching temples. *Why did I stay up so late last night?* The horse's steps rock me gently as Ivrik's voice drones with important, but overwhelming, information. It all makes it even harder to stay awake as I follow the others down a path that is undetectable to my eyes. Every tree seems indistinguishable from the last, so all I can do is hope they know exactly where they are leading us. They obviously knew the forest, seeing as they had located me within minutes of waking yesterday deep in the forest. My eyes drift closed again, the combination of the bright, warm spring day making the woods come alive with chirping birds. The sound of my companion's playful chatter envelops me, and I listen distantly, not following who and what they were talking about anymore. I open my eyes after a few minutes, with yet another yawn, to find all three of them watching me with eager grins on their faces. I hadn't even realized Ivrik had stopped talking.

"What?" I ask, slightly startled.

"We may have taken wagers on if you would wake up before you fell off the horse." Ivrik admits with a loud laugh before tossing a coin behind him to Türë, who brings up the rear in our column. Moments later, a glint flies past my shoulder as Patryk follows suit with a sheepish look.

"Oh really? You thought that just because I couldn't even remember my name, I wouldn't be able to stay upright on a horse?" I place my hand on my chest in mock offense, but laugh along. "Honestly, that wasn't a worry until just now!" I add and realize they seem to be relieved that I was feeling comfortable enough with them now to play along. "Who would like to volunteer to pinch me every so often to ensure I do not become reconciled with the ground in such an un-queen-like manner?" Patryk and Ivrik clamor for the opportunity before I interrupt with a wink at Türë. "Seeing as he was the only one with enough faith in me in the first place, I believe that he is the winner of such a pleasure." To my surprise, he blushes and looks away without answering. I wince and turn away, facing again to the front in the hopes of hiding my own blush. *Way to go. That was way too flirty, apparently.* I groan internally, but try to change the subject as fast as I can. "So… how do you know where you are going? It's all just a tangle of trees to me. Is there a secret trick to it?" I ask, hoping to not be too obvious in my topic change. Patryk, who leads us at the moment, navigates his horse expertly down a slope blanketed with grass as he calls over his shoulder to me.

"A secret? Yes. Though not one we are privy to."

What the hell does that mean? I begin to ask, but Ivrik beats me to it.

"Are you trying to be a riddle master? Just answer her!" He says, sounding bored, shaking his head and giving a hearty eye roll, and I swear I catch Ladir do the same as she trots beside us.

"Fine." Patryk snaps back with a huff before answering me. "It's the horses. They are the descendants of the ones long ago who used to live in the forest. They have some mythical ancestry to the Creatures of the Forest that used to live in this land." He shrugs, leaning forward to pat the kind-eyed roan he was riding. "You just have to tell them where you want to go and somehow, they always know the way. Nearest anyone can figure, it's due to some magic still left in their blood, even though it has been watered down by the centuries." I look down at the large, beautiful beast I ride with different eyes.

"Used to live in this land?" I inquire. "Where did they go?" Out of the corner of my eye I see Türë, who had begun a separate conversation with Ivrik suddenly whip his head towards us. His eyes are full of obvious concern at the tone in my voice and my body language; the tension now spreading from my clenched hands to the rest of my composure.

"It—well, it was a very dark time." Patryk pulls on the reins, slowing down until his horse walks alongside my own, allowing us to talk more comfortably. "Much has been lost to time, and honestly Noran is the history buff of us all, but I will do my best to explain." He rifles around his saddlebags, distracted for a moment, before pulling out a pair of bright ruby apples. He takes a crunchy bite out of one and hands me the other. I take it gratefully, my heart warming at his unexpected gesture. I bite into the perfectly sweet and crisp apple and I have to stifle a moan. I begin to wonder if all food in this kingdom is magically-made delicious.

"Let's see," Patryk taps his fingers across his cheek, his brow furrowing in concentration. "The Massacre at Dothsmerna was about eight hundred star-cycles—"

"Eight hundred twenty four." Türë's sharp voice interjects.

Patryk glances nervously over his shoulder before continuing. "Okay, eight hundred and twenty four star-cycles ago, but really the conflicts truly started even before that. The Creatures of the Forest were mostly good—from what I know—but there are a few where it is just in their nature to be predators. It is like holding a wolf pack responsible for taking out a flock of sheep." He shrugs and sighs deeply. I feel my stomach twist with apprehension. This was one story I knew would not have a happy ending. After all, it had apparently led to a massacre. "The population spread as your kingdom grew and flourished, which lead to tension as we began to push into their territories. The tension grew as attacks began to happen. I guess what the people who would move into these new areas didn't realize is that they were occupying the hunting ground for creatures, like Kelpies and Wendigo. That is until their livestock, pets, and eventually loved ones began to go missing." He heaves another heavy sigh, looking down at the apple core in his hand before chucking it into the trees that still surround us. I watch it vanish and realize the forest is not as dense as it had been the day before and this morning. *The trees are much smaller too, so we must be closer to the forest's edge. I wonder what the world will look like outside of the trees.* My pulse quickens from both anxiety and excitement before Patryk's voice draws me back to his story.

"Unfortunately this was before we had the system in place we do now. You were alone, trying to rule the entire country single handed. It had worked until then, but it was inevitable with the speed Tesindren was growing that it would not continue to go smoothly. Because of that, by the time word had reached you about what was happening, the people had decided to take matters into their own hands." My fists tighten of their own accord onto the saddle horn in front of me, and I suddenly am not so sure that I want him to continue.

Do not be a coward. This is your history and your people. You need to know.

"What happened?" I ask again, this time in a strained whisper.

I force a hard swallow, trying and failing to calm my racing pulse, and wait for Patryk to answer.

"Well..." He clears his throat and shifts, uncomfortable in the stiff leather saddle as he too realizes Türë's attention is still sharply focused on us. "I guess by the time you were able to rush there, the villagers had begun to round them up, the Creatures of the Forest, and—slaughter them." He begins slowly, but by the end, he rushes to get the words out. Like they wouldn't sting or land as harshly if he spit them out fast enough. "It was before my time but—" Patryk's eyes dart forward to Türë and Ivrik, who had been drawn in to our conversation.

"That was far before any of us were in your court or alive, but it is said when you returned, you were covered in blood, and completely distraught. You then locked yourself in your room for fourteen days." Türë finishes, his dark eyes filled with pain and sorrow, mirroring the emotions that rush through me. "Even when you emerged, sullen and grey, nobody could get you to say what happened. Only once word came by messengers did anyone else know about the massacre that had taken place. And that was the last we ever heard from of any of the Creatures of the Forest."

We all fall silent, lost in our own thoughts and mental images conjured by this piece of history. Even though I cannot place why, something doesn't seem right in that story. I strain my focus into the vast darkness of my mind that once had held all my memory, to no avail.

"There was *some* good that came from the atrocity." Türë murmurs after a few minutes.

"Really?" My eyes meet his, and silently beg him for that silver lining that I desperately need right now. He nods, understanding without words.

To my surprise, it is Ivrik who answers, his usually bored pout transforming into a vibrant smile. "The atrocity brought to light the genuine need of swifter communication with the capital, as well as the idea of giving more power to local rulers in each individual territory. It was that decision that led you to bestow the greatest gift you could to those you could trust the most; a slice of your kingdom to call their own, to love and care for. Those who you chose became the very first Underkings."

I blink hard, but it is too late; a sudden betraying tear slips out and I grip the reins, the leather releasing a faint squeak at the pressure. Silence fills the space for a while. I am not sure for how long, but soon the horses come to a stop. The world around me still tilts and sways as I process this. I hear the others dismount around me and go about their business; Ivrik disappears into the vibrant green foliage to relieve his bladder, and Patryk pulls out a smaller wrapped package from his saddlebag and chooses a large boulder nearby to serve as our apparent lunch table. I watch as the wrappings are removed to reveal a chunk of bread and a wedge of cheese. Türë, as he had the day before, watches me carefully. He seems to make a decision and approaches me, holding a steady palm out to help me down from my sizable grey mare. But I don't take it. I remain stubbornly in the saddle, still enveloped in the wild tangle of thoughts. Making me jump, Türë suddenly snarls and clenches the outstretched hand shut, anger tightening his face. My wide eyes flick up from the hand to his own dark, piercing eyes and for the first time see true irritation in them.

I gape, startled at this shift from his usually calm demeanor, but am unable to speak. I am again struck with the realization of how little I know these men, despite my instincts and the letter telling me to trust them.

"We will be back. Don't go anywhere." He snaps to Ivrik, who returns from his jaunt nearby. Ivrik looks at me, eyes narrowing, and to my surprise I see his hand drift to his own dagger slung across his hips. I realize, if I refused to go with Türë, Ivrik would intercede for me. Even against his own long time friend. I feel a gush of emotion for him, but shake my head subtly. Lowering his hand from the weapon, Ivrik crosses his arms across his chest. Clearly accepting my choice, but not entirely happy about it. Patryk remains frozen in place with a piece of bread held midway to his mouth, evidently unsure of what to do. Even Ladir tilts her head, confusion filling her dark eyes.

Türë bounds smoothly onto his horse again and, with a few unfamiliar words, he gives his stallion a gentle yet firm tap to the side. Our two horses take off, mine following his eagerly. Riding at a gallop that I am not used to, I bump and bounce all over the saddle and wince at the thought of the bruises and stiffness that will surely be there in the morning.

We ride like this for about five minutes, until he deems us far enough away from the other two. By the time he at last reins in the horses and dismounts again, I still have absolutely no idea what could have set him off. Even more importantly, I have no idea what we were doing alone again in the middle of nowhere with only the trees and brush, and no sign of a trail back anywhere.

"What in Jera's name was that all about?!" I snap at him. He holds out his hand again to help me, but I smack it away and manage to maneuver my way down. It isn't pretty, but I make it to the ground after a few awkward wiggles. My temper rising with each second.

"I'm trying, Evara. I really am. For you, for the others, but *fuck,* you are making it hard!" I am thrown at how upset he is. For the first time he has shifted from the calm, chaperone figure he had been up to this point. I wasn't sure what to say, so I let him just get his feelings out. He had obviously been bottling them inside for at least a day and a half. Maybe even longer. Türë storms ahead for about ten paces, before spinning in a huff, and pacing back to me. Then again, and again. "This was *your* decision, Jera damn it, and I am trying to help where I can. I don't know what..." he fades off into more muttering that I can't understand. But I do realize suddenly is that it is not even me he is talking to. Continuing to pace, his disjointed dialogue doesn't stop as I realize it is a completely different language. He switches back to words I understand. "But how am I supposed to know what to expect? Then we get there and you truly don't even recognize any of us. I knew what you had said, but—" more muttering in words I don't know breaks through the peace of the clearing. Loud enough it scares a tree-full of birds out of their nests nearby. I realize I may have driven this man to madness. He passes near me on his now trampled grass path, but I step in his way, blocking him. Türë freezes a breath away from colliding with me. This time when our eyes meet, his eyes are full of desperation.

"Türë," I interrupt, my tone far too timid and careful. *That won't do. You are a Queen.* My inner voice scolds and I try again. "Türë," I say, this time rolling back my shoulders and standing tall. "I apologize for making you feel as if you are alone in this and having to take care of me. I am certain that is not what I wanted for you." His chest heaves and, as close as we are, I feel it press slightly into my own, but neither of us step away. In fact I swear he gets even minutely closer. My heart thunders in my chest and I take a deep breath of my own, trying to disregard how close my nose is to his, or how our fingers are a feathers-breath apart. And especially of how handsome he looks all disheveled from his outraged stampeding. My fingers twitch with the urge to run them through his tousled hair, even as I want to throttle him.

"I just thought that this was what you *wanted* and, I guess, I figured that would make it easier." He whispers, so near inaudible that only with my Sidhe hearing can I make out the words. "But then seeing you so scared, so unsure—so unlike you... I just couldn't handle it. Why did you do it?"

My breath hitches at this and I try to rack my brain for anything that I could say to reassure him. I remember the words from my letter. *My power.* That was the reason why I had put myself, Türe, *everyone,* through this. My fingers twitch and feel them briefly brush against his. It's like an electric spark jumps at the caress. Everything slows down as time seems to stop and my awareness grows, and I realize there actually is a spark. One that blows us apart with its energy.

The bolt jumps out of my skin and, with its force, throws Türe and I in opposite directions. I don't see where he lands before my back and head slam into a nearby thick trunk and the world fades into the grey haze of unconsciousness before I can even scream in horror at what I had done.

nine

My gaze spins before shifting into a thick gray mist. It begins to ebb away and, from its depths, only a few feet from where I watch in the shadow of a large throne carved from stone, is a man who stands tall, his back towards me. An intimidating black iron-tipped crown encircles his head and my breath catches. He grins at whatever is spread out on the table before him, and my interest grows with every second that he mutters to himself. Too quietly for me to make out what he was saying, but enough to glean that he was excited about something. After a slight hitch of hesitation, I risk a step forward for a closer look. Before I can glean what he is examining, the fast click of footsteps approach and the door to the cavernous room is thrown open with an echoing boom.

"Your Majesty." The soldier greets the now silent man and falls to his knee in respect. His chest heaves in his anticipation of the news he carries with him. From the unrestrained glee on the King's face, I know it has been long awaited—whatever it is. "The throne sits vulnerable." The soldier says at last.

"Then our time to strike has come." The King responds with a victorious laugh, returning his attention back to the table. "Ready the men. The gods have blessed us with this opportunity and we will not waste it." I shudder as a chill and ominous feeling snakes its way up my spine at his words. Who is this man? A King of somewhere. I can't help but be frustrated at the black canvas that was my memory and take care to remember every detail of his features so that, when I saw him again, I would be sure to be extra cautious. Because I knew in my soul that I would see this man again.

The soldier recognizes this as his dismissal and, with a click of his muddy boots turns, and pulls the doors closed again, leaving the man alone. His attention is returned firmly on what I see now is a scroll of aged parchment. As I try to look closer again, I feel a slight tug pulling me back to the shadows, but I dare a last hopeful glimpse and at last see a familiar sight: a map of the kingdom.

My kingdom.

Again, I wake with no idea of how I ended up lying on the forest floor. This time a sharp sting on my forehead throbs. I press my eyes shut against the onslaught of colors and light while my brain tries to catch up, but that only leads to more confusion. *There was a man? No. That was a dream… I think. But it was so real…* I feel the press of something cold and wet suddenly nuzzling my cheek and I push it away, startled at the unexpected sensation. A grumble of impatience responds and my eyes snap open. *Ladir!* It is my turn to grumble at the pain that burns across my back and the bruise I know is already blooming there. I push up to sitting and am greeted by a sopping rain-wet wolf. Before I can complain, though, I remember with a start what had happened.

"Türë!" I shout, looking around for him in a panic. *The lightning. I threw him!* My breaths come in deep heaves as I push to shaky legs and look around for his prone figure. My eyes catch on a figure and I step towards it, sure it is Türë, before it moves and vanishes into the forest again. Not Türë. Some other forest creature I had no doubt disturbed. I curse and spin, trying to find him. Out of the brown and green of leaves, old and new, that make up the forest floor, I can barely make out the tip of a leather boot. I gasp at the fear that overwhelms my pain at the sight of him unconscious and sprawled on the ground. I race to his side, followed closely by Ladir. "Türë," I say again, only this time barely above a whisper as my hands flutter helplessly over his body. "Wake up, please. I am so sorry." I choke back a sob when he doesn't move. "What do I do?" I plead, though there was no one else to answer. I grasp his hand and squeeze, as if that would somehow push breath into him. *Breath.* I could smack myself at my stupidity. My shoulders droop in relief when I notice for the first time the rise and fall of his chest. *He still lives*! I send up a silent thanks to Jera and shuffle myself around to brace his head on my lap. Rather than leaving it where he lies on the damp forest floor, blanketed with twigs and leaves.

"Türë! Evara! Where the hell are you?" Ladir's ears pick up the shouts first, her ears twitching towards the noise, but breaths later I catch them too.

"Here! We are here." I try to make myself loud enough, but my voice is quickly lost among the branches that tangle around us. I chew my lip nervously, racking my throbbing brain, trying to decide what to do. If I left Türë here to go to find the others, I could not be sure that I could even find him again. But I also knew the others hearing was not nearly as good as ours, Patryk and

Ivrik being human and not Sidhe. I remember Ladir's intelligence and how she had seemed to understand me somehow. "Ladir, can you go get them?" I look deep into her eyes and know instinctively that she understands. Yet she doesn't move, other than a twitch of her ears. I am about to ask her again, my heart twisting with uncertainty as their voices begin to grow more distant. "Ladir—" I start again, but she cuts me off.

Throwing her head back and taking a deep gulp of air, the leaves seem to quiver with the reverberation as she begins to howl. Like a tolling bell, the howl rings even after she stops, echoing around us. Lowering her head, she looks pleased with herself and her apparent success, as the direction of the voices again change, growing quickly closer.

Whether the noises finally stirred him, or simply the passage of time took effect, Türë's eyelids begin to flutter. The clench of nerves I didn't realize had been a tight ball finally begins to uncoil. *Maybe he will be alright.*

He grimaces before his eyes even open, and I wince along with him, sympathetic with my own soreness. The other two finally break through the brush as Ladir leads them the last bit of the way with a final piercing howl. Their looks of annoyance shifts immediately when they see the two of us on the ground. Patryk pales at the sight and they both dart towards us.

"What happened?" Ivrik snaps, though obviously more concerned than he wants to let on. They both fall to their knees beside me and I catch the should of their panicked hearts racing.

"I lost control and..." I confess, trying to keep the tears from spilling out. "I—I zapped him," I stammer trying to explain through my tight throat. "and the force blew us both backwards into the trees. I just regained consciousness myself and found him like this. I have no clue how long I was out." I run my fingers down his cheek and through his hair, too worried to think about its inappropriateness. "He started to move a second ago, but still hasn't woken up fully yet." I look up when they don't answer and catch a look between the two. I immediately pull my hands back and blush from the embarrassment that rushes through me. "What?" I bite, daring them to say anything about it.

"What do you mean you *zapped* him?" Patryk asks gently, returning his attention to me, and pulls a vial of deep golden liquid from a pack strung across his back. "As in, you conjured lightning or more like a push of fire?"

I think on it a moment, trying to remember through the buzz that fills my head. I realize now, looking back, it was kin to the small zap I had stung Patryk with the night before, the *singe* I had brushed off as part of my emotional fire. "It was a small spark of lightning, but it just exploded when—" I cut myself off when I remember now the events leading up to the spark and look down at Türë, still unmoving in my lap. "When we were talking." I finish, not looking up. I hear a scoff from Ivrik but choose to ignore it, my mind swirling on what Türë had asked. *Why did you do it?* Any answer I could provide him I knew wouldn't be enough. That much was clear.

"That is… interesting." Patryk extends the vial to me and I take it. "Give this to him. It will help with the pain."

I do as he says, trusting that he knows what to do far more than me right now. Türë groans, but makes no further sounds as the golden liquid disappears through his lips.

"Why is that interesting?" I ask, passing him back the now empty vial.

"Well because you told us that lightning took you star-cycles to discover and manipulate. It certainly wasn't one of the first gifts to return." Ivrik says dryly, eying me closely with suspicion, clearly also remembering the night before.

"But that isn't necessarily a bad thing." Patryk interjects, with a sharp look towards Ivrik. "It just could mean that this time things are just different from last. You also told us that you couldn't remember what order they all came back the first time."

I mull this over, trying to let the steady chirping of birds quiet my still pounding heartbeat and matching thoughts.

"Am I safe to even be around right now?" I mutter to myself, though desperate for one of them to reassure me.

"I hate to break it to you," a rough voice answers me. "You have never been safe to be around." My eyes drop to the source of the voice—Türe—teasing me in spite of the fact he had just been knocked unconscious. It takes all of my self-control not to throw my arms over him and sob. Even so, I heave a choking sigh of relief.

"I am so sor—" I start to gush, but he cuts me off with a glare.

"Enough of that. I pushed you farther than you were ready, and in turn you kicked my ass." He grunts in a bit of pain as Patryk prods at his ribs. Ivrik chuckles under his breath, but Patryk only responds with a tight-lipped smile that doesn't reach his eyes. *He must be more concerned about the lightning than he let on.* I feel my gut twist a bit, but then see Türe grinning up at me and the feeling lessens.

"Are you really okay?" I ask him, needing to know for sure before I will truly let any amount of relief sink in.

"I am perfectly fine. In fact, I—" He stops short, looking around. "Am I in your lap?" He inquires with a raised eyebrow. I feel the heat rise in my cheeks and stand abruptly. He grunts as he hits the ground with a soft thud.

"Next time I will just let you lay in the mud." I say, indignant at the bemused grin still on his face.

"Hey," He says, voice changing as he grabs my hand before I can pull away. "Thank you for not leaving me in the mud." A strange feeling washes over me as our eyes meet, his thumb tracing an arch across the back of my hand. Suddenly, I find it hard to swallow as warmth shoots up my core. I nod in response, unable to think of any reply. Thankfully, Ladir pushes her way in between us and starts jumping excitedly all over Türë, breaking the moment and our grip. I take the opportunity to retreat back a few steps to where Ivrik watches, silent and stone-faced.

"Are *you* okay?" He turns his attention full on me, surprising me with his rare, genuine concern.

"Shaken, and confused, but okay." I reply, honestly. He seems to understand that and nods towards the others. Patryk trying to help Türë back to his feet, and Ladir's fuzzy bulk doing everything she can to prevent him from getting out of her reach until she was satisfied that everything was alright.

"Türë is stronger than us. He will be okay. As for Patryk and me, we knew the risk coming out here today." I stiffen, trying to make out if that was a slight or just pure honesty. He seems to sense his misstep and shifts his weight from foot-to-foot nervously. "That was supposed to be reassuring..." He huffs a laugh at himself. "I am not so good at this. What I *meant* was that no matter what, we are here to help, and that is because we all care deeply about you. So the little chance that you might send us sky high with a magical flare up is not anything we are too worried about. It is worth it—to be here for you."

I blink rapidly in surprise at his admission, feeling my eyes burn with unexpected tears. "Thank you, Ivrik. I needed to hear that more than you know." He grins, feet shuffling with embarrassment, before walking over and helping Patryk ease Türë to his feet. I feel relief at seeing Türë standing tall again. To even greater relief, I do not detect even a bump, bruise or even a wince of pain now. *I think I am actually more banged up than he is.*

"I am fine, really." I hear him say, "I can't believe that you wasted a vial on that." He chides Patryk with a laugh, though I get the soft undertone of worry in the statement. We start to walk back to where all of the horses stand waiting for us.

"Well when we got here, you were unconscious and she said she zapped you and," Patryk glances over his shoulder to find me staring and winces in apology, "we weren't sure how bad it was."

"What was in that vial?" I ask, now that they know I have been listening in on their conversation anyway.

"It is a simple healing concoction; actually an old Sidhe cure that you taught the healers. It is no miracle cure, but it will help with most ailments. Kind of like a jump start to the healing process. This is one of the last few made by your own talented hands. Thankfully it was one of the things you had written down before it was lost forever." To my surprise, I detect the faintest bit of irritation in the words. I wring my hands as I try to fathom why this would upset him so. I realize then how much power I truly possess. Should I choose to go through this Awakening and decide to not tell anyone anything or write things down, like the letter, and the vial of healing potion, it would have been vital information lost forever. With a pang I realize how little say these men probably had on any of the decisions I had made, despite the fact they were as close as family to me. I feel my voice crack slightly as the words spill out of me.

"I apologize for whatever pain and anger I have caused—with all of my decisions that have affected you. All of you." I stare at the forest floor, unable to meet their eyes. The crunch of leaves and boots stop abruptly. I bump into Ivrik's chest before I realize the others have turned and stopped to look at me.

"You do not need to apologize for anything." Ivrik says, looking down at me with the softest expression I had seen on him as he grips my shoulders to steady me. "What you did was hard, for all of us, but we still understand your reasons. And even if we didn't —" I fight the urge to avoid his bright, sky blue eyes, but force myself to not look away.

"It is not our place to question. It was *your* choice, about *your* life. And we are here to serve, assist, and protect you." Türë cuts in, and I pull my gaze from Ivrik to face him, and Patryk who stands just a step behind.

"But that—" I start, but Patryk cuts me off now.

"We are your friends, your chosen family. You may irritate us every once in a while with some of your choices," he teases. "But in the end, we still love you and will have your back." I look back to Ivrik as I feel his gentle grip on my wrist tighten slightly at these words. He smiles for the briefest breath and then pulls his hand and eyes away from me, returning his attention onto the path ahead.

"Let's get back to the horses and see if we can make it home before dark tonight, shall we?" Ivrik calls over his shoulder as he continues his march through the emerald maze of trees. "Patryk gets cranky if he has to sleep in a cot too many nights in a row."

ten

It is only shortly past mid-day when we at last leave the canopy of the forest and join the traffic that travels the *River Road*. I had wept lightly as I gave Ladir a big hug, and received a sloppy wet kiss in return, before she bounded back into the trees, vanishing from sight. Thankfully, the only teasing had come from Ivrik, and it had been an obvious attempt to cheer me up. Aptly named, it follows the Keena River along its entirety from the harbor at the northern-most port town of Grezon, all the way through the kingdom to the southern stronghold of Charobi. Patryk had, in great detail, taken the opportunity of the last hours of travel to delve into even more information about my kingdom, a lot of which centered around the rushing river to our right that had fingers spread into each corner of the land. Helpful as he was trying to be, by the time we come into the very distant view of Yvonya Castle, just an indistinct shape in the distance, my head swirls with all the new information. My mind tries to fill the black void with it all. But before long, the seemingly unending list of cities, towns, strongholds and rivers, as well as the major lakes, ports, forests, cliffs and plains, quickly became an overwhelming jumble. The disappointment Patryk clearly felt, but tried his best to hide, made me feel worse. After I failed to remember the difference between Eludar and Saroch's location and which territory they belonged to—it dawned on me that he was hoping something would jog my memory. As if the right word or phrase would unlock the vault that Jera had locked my memories in. My inability to reach the expectations he still held onto makes him grow more quiet each time I failed. I couldn't bring myself to crush that thinking with the truth. How could I explain it to him, after all? How could I explain the complete surety with which I knew my memories weren't locked in some vault somewhere? That even with the right password or spell, they still would not be released.

They were gone. Like dirt washed away in a stream, my memories were washed away and would never be returned. Not fully, anyway. Maybe a fleck of dirt or piece of sand might rise to the surface now and then, bringing with it a glint of my past. But never would it be—would I be—exactly what I was before. That fact I knew in my soul, like a whispered answer from Jera herself.

In a way, it was both a freedom and a curse. I could start anew in my life. I had the opportunity to discover all of my likes and dislikes again and find new ones. Yet I did feel sorrow for those who had some idea of the person they expected me to be, like Patryk. But lingering on those hopes, when there was nothing I could do, would be a waste of the time given to me.

I touch the pocket of my dress where the letter to myself still sits, and try not to think about how hard of a decision it was for her to leave these people behind, knowing they would mourn her loss—even as I walked beside them. For her—for me— I would appreciate it all.

We crest a large hill in silence and I can't help but feel my breath catch at the sight. For the first time I can truly appreciate the size of my kingdom, as well as its beauty. Spread out below I see rolling hills, fields beginning to bloom with crops, and the winding turquoise of the Keena River as it fades far into the distance. And straight ahead, standing immense against the horizon, a bustling city at its feet, Yvonya Castle. Still far off, another few hours ride, the stone towers and surrounding walls are big enough to make out. The maps and the stories about it that the others had been telling me all day did not do it justice.

We continue along the road and I feel my head begin to throb from the overload on my senses. Despite adjusting a bit to my exaggerated eyesight and hearing, it begins to grow overwhelming when the forest hues and soft woodland sounds are replaced with colored fabrics of the curtains billowing in the windows, and flowered gardens filled with buzzing wildlife. Coupled with the rushing roar of the close by river mingling with the rattling of wagon wheels pulled past us, it all becomes stifling. I edge up to Türe who looks somehow still comfortable in the leather saddle with his face towards the sun, humming a lively tune to himself. Only the subtle upturn of his mouth gives any hint that he knows I am watching him.

"How do you get used to the—" I search for the appropriate word to use. "*Extraordinariness* of it all?" He looks around, as if he doesn't understand at first what I mean, then he laughs under his breath.

"It is hard to describe the sensation, isn't it?" He says, realization filling his eyes as he turns his full attention on me. I exhale in relief, somehow comforted that, at least in this, I wasn't alone in experiencing the sensation.

"So you have felt all of this too before?" I eagerly ask, shifting uncomfortably in my saddle.

He nods, "Every Sidhe has. It is part of our magic, our heightened abilities. Even those who are not born with extra gifts has, at the very least, increased sight, smell, hearing, and strength." I feel my eyebrows raise. I wasn't sure why, but this surprised me. He had mentioned the better than mortal sight and hearing, and up until this moment, I had figured it was simply biological rather than magical. Despite the questions that well up at this realization, I let Türë finish answering my first question. "Because of the influence of magic, however, when we are very young, or sick, or even maybe injured in battle, " He flexes his right shoulder absentmindedly at a memory. "Those abilities wane and can even vanish for a time until your strength returns."

"So basically, when you need it the most, it is gone?" I stammer, incredulous at the irony. This makes him laugh with a grimace.

"Unfortunately, yes. But to answer your earlier question, your body *will* adapt and adjust to what all feels overwhelming now. In the meantime, I can show you some exercises we used to teach the young ones to help them when their senses start to bombard them at the beginning." I push down the sense of pride that rises up and nearly has me rejecting the offer. *I am not a child and do not need to be taught like one.* That feeling is quickly shunted aside when a packed caravan of musicians passes us going in the opposite direction. The screeching cacophony that reverberates in my ears has me quickly agreeing to his helpful offer. I wince but bite out the words, ignoring the pride that scoffs at the fact that a few subpar musicians had me so disoriented. "Yes, please." By the time the various noises of drunken singing and laughter, mixed with the screeching of an off tune lute, have passed blissfully into the distance, I am panting and holding my head from the overload that had my mind and stomach swirling. I don't try to conceal it. One glance at Türë, who watches me baldly, and I know there is no point in even attempting to brush off the pain. He nods, thankfully brushing over it with nonchalance. I try not to blush at the fact that his supposedly infamous queen is weak enough that she needs training given to children. I clamp down on these thoughts, reminding myself that this was the whole reason my past-self had broken her pattern and let these people in. To help me. The least I can do, as a thank you, is to accept that help.

"One thing that is the easiest and quickest to teach you, when it starts to grow overpowering—whether it be sight, hearing, even one of your magical gifts—cut away everything but one thing." I stare at him, wholly confused. He sees this and laughs openly, though not at me, scratching at the scruff that darkens his jawline as he thinks. "I explained that horribly, didn't I?" Not waiting for my confirmation, he tries again. "Here. If you are walking through a garden and suddenly all the flowers are too bright, hone your focus on one flower, then one petal. Trim your focus down to smaller and smaller details until it no longer feels so overwhelming." I think over this before responding with a question.

"So like with those musicians—" I begin, glancing up to see him grinning widely, then with an encouraging nod, he beckons me to continue. "I should have thought of the wagon, then the man with the lute, then the lute, and then..." I trail off trying to remember what could have been smaller than that.

"Good. You have the general idea. And it doesn't have to be so straightforward either. From there you could focus on the man's lips, then breath, and so on. It is only really a distraction tactic, like pinching your arm if you stub a toe to pull your mind away from the pain."

"Okay, and if that doesn't work?" I ask, adjusting myself in the saddle again and fighting the urge to wince at my tender backside.

"Well, you're fucked." He responds bluntly.

My attention snaps up in shock. "What?" I stammer, fear

rushing cold through my body, until I see the glint of mischief in his dark eyes. "That is a cruel joke." I snap. I pull my horse to a stop and glower at Türë, "When I ask for your help on something, it doesn't bode well for our relationship if you try to tease me in those times. If I am asking, it is because I genuinely need your help." Shame colors his face at my scolding and he opens his mouth to respond. I talk over him. "Do you fully understand how hard of a situation this is? For me to wake up and have people tell me what my life is, what I need to know... how to live and who to be? I'm trying, Türë. But telling me I'm *fucked?* Well, that is not exactly reassuring." I stare up at the azure sky and blink back the angry tears that well up.

The heavy tread of two other horses approach and pull to a stop as they join our now silent stand off. I don't look at the other two, sure I would see the concern there, and feel immediately apologetic. I take a deep breath before returning my gaze to meet Türë's. Sure enough, apology is easily read there, but it still doesn't lessen my surge of despondence.

"Please keep riding. I need a moment to myself. I will follow the road. Wait for me at any turns."

eleven

I ride alone for close to an hour before I pass through a valley and gasp at what lays before me. As far as I can see spreads a field of wildflowers. Despite the beautiful view, I snap my eyes shut. The intelligent mare jolts to a halt as she feels my body lock up stiffly, and understands that something is wrong with me. Already the color was overwhelming, though not as much as the scent. I switch to only breathing through my mouth, thinking that might help. It doesn't. So strong is the scent that I can *taste* the aroma. My head begins to swirl and I feel sick with the sensation of it all. Until I remember what Türë had begun to teach me, and I swallow my pride as I resolve to do as he instructed. Trying my best to not linger on the 'you're fucked' comment should I be fully overwhelmed. I decide to not even consider that as a possibility. Instead, with extreme slowness, I pry open one eye and do my best to ignore the pounding that immediately begins to thrum in my head, as my mind tries and fails to process it all. I have to snap it shut again after only a second.

"If you are walking through a garden and suddenly all the flowers are too bright, hone your focus on to one flower, then one petal. Trim your focus down to smaller and smaller details until it no longer feels so overwhelming." With his words echoing in my head, I slide from the saddle into the soft grass and force myself to walk ten steps into the flowers that stand waist high. I realize now that had been his way to prepare me for this very field. I take another breath, trying to soothe my panicked, racing heart. Annoyance floods me at the fact he did not just simply *tell me.*

Okay, one flower. I instruct my brain, and again pry open one eye. I pick a larger flower, ornate and deep violet, so dark and prismatic it shines with hues of navy, lilac, and ruby. In spite of the pain surging again at such a sight, I can't help but appreciate its dynamic beauty. *A petal.* I train my focus on the inner spiral, and find even more colors radiating there. I never could imagine so much brilliance could come from a single flower, let alone a sliver of it. *Smaller details.* I tell myself as my breath hitches again. *Smaller than a petal? Let's see.* I swallow hard and narrow my focus again. *Was that—?* My attention catches on some movement. *A small flying creature!* Stepping forward, I look closer and find a tiny green woman flitting around the interior of the flower. I laugh aloud, astonished, startling the thumb-sized woman who spins around at the sound and stares back at me in terror, then awe, before blushing and bowing deeply at me. I lower my head in return and smile widely at the unexpected surprise.

Then I notice the pain is gone. The panic too. I take stock of myself and realize that, even though the colors and world around me were just as bright and stimulating, I could handle them a little better now. Even more gloriously, I could *appreciate* them. Distraction indeed. Everywhere I look I now see a whole miniature world, in nearly each of the flowers I can see held a little home. Yes, there was its tiny door, and a window made of twigs! The green woman I had seen initially must have called to her friends somehow because suddenly there were hundreds, all flitting and fluttering just barely above the field. Not high enough that they would be unable to flee if something should happen, but enough so that they are able to see me. I edge closer, trying not to scare them as they watch me warily. I don't get any uncomfortable or uneasy feelings around them and figure I am safe enough to approach. The growing crowd that now watches me, their tiny iridescent wings holding them aloft, told me that they knew exactly who I was.

"Hello!" I say with an awkward wave, and like a bubble popping, within a blink of an eye they all had vanished. Only the first little woman remains, crossing her arms and stomping her foot with irritation. With the sound of a chirping bird, she calls out to the rest who begin to appear one by one again. Their heads peak up from the flowers and respond with lovely whistles and chirps of their own. "I am sorry! I only wanted to meet you." I try to start again, this time with a softer tone and a matching smile. The grins that are returned seem to brighten the field more than the sunlight and the clear, sapphire sky above.

"They don't speak our language, though they always did try to communicate with you." A familiar voice says from behind me. I heave a heavy sigh and turn to face Türe. "I see you were able to regain your control." Türe says after a pause, saving me from trying to figure out what to say.

"Yes. I—" I shuffle my feet, my head lowered feeling shame now at my reaction earlier. "I am sorry I reacted so poorly. I just don't..." I struggle to think of the words to say to explain how much I was relying on him. I look up to find him shaking his head in emphatic disagreement.

"I shouldn't have made that joke. It was in bad taste and

absolute wrong timing." He looks up, still shaking his head. "I guess I just fell back into old habits and didn't think before speaking. I should have known you would not find that funny."

"I just don't know how to be *her.* I don't know how to be the girl you all know and love." I confess with a broken voice. "You all have this history and expectation of me and… I just don't know how to be the *normal* you all expect."

He closes the distance between us so suddenly I inhale sharply as his rough hand cups my cheek. "Be yourself, Evara. Whoever you feel that is. And please stop apologizing for it. We understand how difficult this is for you, and truly just want to help. I feel I must redeem myself for making it harder."

We don't speak for a while, though every second that passes I grow increasingly aware of his closeness and how warm his hand on my cheek is. I can't help but feel a surge of disappointment when he steps away again. As the wind rustles through the flowers, the flickers of a different field—a younger one appears in my minds eye. I shake it away, and find Türë watching me with a curious expression on his face.

"This place feels… like a memory." I trail off, not wanting to spread false hope where none should be. "Don't tell the others I said that, please. It was a foolish thing to say. I know I don't remember anything." Türë smiles in response, eyes filled with a glint of sadness and understanding. "I thought you said that the Creatures of the Forest were all gone?" I ask, looking down upon the field that nearly shimmers with the constant movement of the small little beings.

"There are a few tiny creatures who manage to live in plain sight. Nobody looks close enough to them to think they are anything but insects, or small birds." He shrugs. "Only your Underkings and us even know that they exist here, as far as I know. And I have not heard of any other beings like them being reported elsewhere. I can only assume that being so close to your seat in the kingdom kept them safe from attack, so they never fled or were exterminated." The thought makes my heart ache. I notice how low in the sky the sun sits at the same moment Türë remarks on it. "We should continue on if we want to reach Alessandra by nightfall. Luckily, I know a shortcut from here."

I nod in agreement, and take one last deep breath and look around the enchanting field of flowers and its occupants who flit back and forth across the rainbow of petals. Turning back to the still waiting mare, I eye the saddle with trepidation and silently apologize to my backside, growing ever more sore. It had just begun to de-numb from the hours long ride it had already endured. Already back in his saddle, I see Türë watching me.

"What?" I ask dully, wondering what he was staring at. It wouldn't surprise me if I had started to glow or grew a tail at this point.

"Do you need help back up?" He asks, doing his best to not sound patronizing—and failing.

I scowl at him and lock my grip tight around the saddle horn. With a deep inhale and tapping into the muscles I feel suddenly wake up in my arms, I pull with all my strength and swing my leg over like I had done this a million times, making it onto the saddle. I manage to emit a single *ha!* of triumph before I realize my mistake. I had done too much to pull myself up and didn't even think to worry about going over. My momentum wins and I start to fall off the other side until a sudden burst of wind swoops under me. Just enough for me to catch myself and regain my center balance. Breathing heavily, I look around in confusion. *That wind came from nowhere and felt almost... solid.* I spin to face Türë, who is doing his best to examine the empty sky and trying not to laugh at my reaction.

"Was that *you?*"

"Maybe… will you get mad at me again if I say yes?" He asks warily.

I glare at him, but wanting to open the door to lighthearted teasing that I had slammed shut earlier, I huff a laugh.

"Well, I could have let you fall on your face, if that is what you prefer." He scowls back playfully, but I don't let him dodge the question..

"How did you do that?" I ask him, incredulous. "You have magic?" I feel stupid that it didn't occur to me that he, or anyone else, might also possess any gifts.

"A bit." He replies. "Nothing as strong or as impressive as yours, but what I do have comes in handy." Though his voice remains casual and light, his eyes seem to grow darker as he stares into nothing. He shakes his head lightly and a glazed lightness falls into place, masking his true emotions that I had caught the barest glimpse of. Türë changes the subject. "Are you ready to see your castle?"

I make a mental note to revisit the whole *Türë has magic topic* later. But at the reminder of what waits for me, I swallow hard, feeling my heart rate quicken with re-surging nerves. "Where are the others?" I remember them suddenly and feel guilty I had forgotten them completely. Well, I suppose not *completely* again. I fight down a laugh at myself and wonder briefly if I was going mad.

"I sent them on ahead to wait at the gates. I wasn't sure if you would still be angry with me. If you were going to light me up again, I didn't want them to see that. I would never live it down." Chuckling, he nudges his horse forward, leading us towards the spire now standing silhouetted in the sunset that slowly paints the deep indigo sky with strokes of radiant pinks and oranges. Instead of returning to the road, however, he leads his horse into the flower field. I prepare myself for the onslaught of angry little voices, certain that we were about to either knock or trample at least a few of their homes. Instead, a nearly invisible path opens up as we approach. The little people bow and pull the stems back so we can pass safely through their miniature city. I do my best to smile and nod at all that we pass, but there are so many that it is staggering. The sight is so breathtaking I have to remind myself to keep my mouth from falling open more than once.

"What are they?" I whisper to Türë, hoping my voice is quiet enough that they wouldn't overhear and be offended. He slows his stallion back to walk beside my mare. The path adapting for both of us to pass side by side. I can't help but appreciate the beauty of his stallion, Jerboa, against the bright flowers, so deep onyx and shiny that the coat reflects the various hues of the flowers we pass, now beginning to glow as the darkness of night grows.

"They have many names; the fae, field sprites, *florenta,* little people…" He leans in closer, "or if you are Ivrik—pain in the asses." I side-eye him, immediately intrigued, so he explains. "There was an incident before he became king and he was chased for a good half mile by about fifty of them. You will have to ask him about it, and please do. Nothing gets him more embarrassed than having to recall the time nearly all of Alessandra saw him getting chased by a herd of tiny women in nothing but his underthings." Wide-eyed, I laugh quietly and mentally it log away to definitely ask Ivrik about that.

"What did I call them before? Just to be consistent." I return to my original question.

"*Florenta.* That is what they told you they were called when you first arrived on the continent those four thousand star-cycles ago, so you stuck with that ever since."

We ride without speaking the rest of the way through the field, and when we emerge on the other side the only light that illuminates our path is the dim shimmering glow from flowers behind and the city waiting in front of us. Led by the *florenta*, the path had taken us directly to the gates waiting open, only about two hundred paces away and lit with large torches— a beacon to all travelers, Türe explains. We both come to a halt, and this time I am unable to stop my jaw from hanging open in awe. I stay there a few minutes, taking in the impressive, yet welcoming sight of the castle walls of Alessandra.

Of *home*.

twelve

My heart races as I stare up at the spire, neck craned as far back as it can go to try to make out its point that slices into the night sky. It, and the massive gates, had looked large in the distance, but now that I stand at the gaping mouth, I am overwhelmed and nauseous again. The guard tower that stands at the entrance to my castle looks imperious with its grey stone and crossbows bolted into them, large enough to fire an arrow as tall as Ivrik. But beyond that, I can make out flickering firelight from torches hung along the main road and the glowing light that dances inside the windows high above. The speckles of light from the various soaring towers within the walls of the city warm the heavy darkness that presses in. According to Türe, these dark grey, now weather worn, stone walls had been the first part erected on this ancient castle.

"Who all knows about my choice?" I ask, swallowing hard and pulling my focus back to Türe as we continue to approach the city.

"Only those absolutely necessary and who you trusted the

most." He reassures me.

"And who all would that be?" I prod for a more precise answer.

"Your Underkings, of course, myself, and your handmaiden, Ilithyia, and Patryk's wife, Athene." Türë tallies the small number off before turning to face me fully, his brow furrows in obvious concern. Apparently, I was not hiding my nervousness as well as I thought I was. "Are you okay?"

"I—" I try to say yes, to reassure him, but the words can't seem to come out, so I nod as enthusiastically as I can muster.

"Liar."

I gulp and laugh, breathless and high pitched. "Wh—what? Why did you say that?"

"You are on fire again." He responds dully and with so little concern that I think he is joking at first; until his gaze flicks up to the top of my head. Following his gaze, I see that I am indeed on fire again. Only this time, rather than my body, it is the top of my head that is lit up like the head of a torch. It is a testament to my horse's training that she doesn't immediately throw me and take off running. Her nose flares with concern as her tail flicks with annoyance, and I tug her to a sudden stop.

I gasp and pat at it until the warmth of the flame is replaced with the cool night air, smoke billowing around me. I sigh with relief as I run my fingers through my hair and around my gently curved horns, making sure everything is normal as before, rather than the ashy cinders I feared I would find.

"You will find that with most of your powers, they will not affect you or your clothing—unless you absolutely lose control. And should *that* happen, well, you will have bigger issues than burnt hair." He explains, but doesn't elaborate further. I bite down on my irritation. It wasn't that I didn't *understand* that he was trying his best to help with this new situation. But the utter helplessness that I feel at being *told* about myself without further explanation continues to grate on me. Maybe once I am back inside my castle I will feel more settled. Or maybe I am just cranky and tired and need a good night of sleep. The long day and a half on horseback had made my ass numb and my patience short. "Please tell me how you are truly feeling. I cannot make it out." Türë asks softly. I hesitate, but then the tears begin to well up and along with them, the truth begins to spill from me.

"I am so *nervous*. Everything is brand new, and I feel so lost. I feel so helpless, and I hate it. I just don't know how to do anything, even something like not lighting myself on fire. I want to be strong and wonderful like you all seem to remember me as." I confess.

"There will be time for you to understand and learn about everything. For now, lets just take it one step at a time. All you can do is your best, and for the rest of it—well, that is why you have us. We have no expectations for you other than that. You were able to build this kingdom on your own back without any guidance or previous experience, and that is why Jera chose you. Why she continues to choose you. Again and again you have proven that you are the most ideal Queen this kingdom could ever have, because each time you take the opportunity to learn more and grow more. To thrive." I take this in, and try to use it to bolster me, guilt filling me at the frustration I had felt for Türë only a minute ago. "When you are ready, we will take you through Alessandra properly and you will see how beloved you are by all your people. Even if you do light yourself on fire. Which by the way is something you have always done when you get upset." He grins widely at me, and I return it. "The people still adore you. And so do I."

I blush, but the words aren't flirtatious or possess any double meaning. They ring with truth and he doesn't break my gaze for even a breath.

"Thank you, Türe. I value your hope in me, and I pray to Jera I don't fail you."

He cuts in, his voice rough, "You could *never* fail me."

My breath catches, eyes filling with tears that I blink away. My heartbeat thrums in my chest with something I can't quite put a finger on, but it ripples through me so strongly I curl my toes in the leather boots. "Well, let's not keep the others waiting much longer. I still need to apologize for my earlier actions and if yesterday was any indication, Ivrik must be very hungry and cranky by now." I respond, more breathless than I was expecting, and I see Türe's eyes drop down to my mouth at the airy sound, but I can't make out the look that shadows his face before he looks away again.

I click my tongue, mimicking what the others had done to encourage their mounts into action. To my great relief, my horse starts forward again eagerly. As we grow closer to the waiting walls and towers of the city beyond, I begin to hear the noise of its occupants. The mixture of music and voices grows along with the glow from inside the city itself, chasing away the darkness that surrounds Türe and I with the bright, welcoming comfortability that radiates from the city and castle within. A feeling that grows with each step. The first rays of torchlight fall upon my face as we get within a hundred paces of the mountainous stone walls. I had appreciated their strength upon our approach, but now that I was at their base, I can't help but be awestruck at their beauty. What appeared at first to be simple grey, upon closer examination, looks as if billowing smoke had been captured and solidified, and veins of silver, gold, and onyx paint a dancing pattern across its surface. I smile at the brush of warmth, feeling an immense weight lift from my shoulders. Even if I have no memory of this place, my spirit seems to recognize it. For the first time, a calm washes over me, like coming home after a long trip. Or maybe it is the vibrant city beyond that creates the sensation. Either way, I don't feel as close to a frantic trapped rabbit as I had earlier in the day.

"A smile is a good sign." A familiar voice drawls from the shadows cast by the wall that divides the warmth of the city from the now solid darkness from which we emerge. "I see she didn't fry you, Türë. How disappointing." Ivrik leans to the left of the iron gate, his hands shoved deep in his pockets. His foot taps the wall in his impatience as he watches us approach with the smirk I am already beginning to get used to. We pull the horses to a stop just outside the gates and I can't help the flicker of impatience. I am so close to what had been my home, my city. To be this close and to be delayed, even a few moments, suddenly seems too much to bear. Uncrossing his arms with a huff, he digs into a bag resting at his feet, pulling out a thick velvet emerald cloak that spools to the ground like some kind of enchanted liquid. It gleams around the collar and up the arms, all intricately decorated with amethyst and silver filigree that glints in the flickering lights nearby. I am grateful for the stronger light so I can appreciate it even more. I make a mental note to examine it closer, because it is clearly worthy of my awe. And I would guess it cost a small fortune. He approaches and hands the cloak up to me, somehow smirking even more at my unrestrained reaction.

"What is this for?" I ask, but his attention gets stolen away almost immediately as my mare begins to nibble affectionately on his shirt collar. A rare smile transforms his face and he begins to mutter to her, teasingly chiding her for it. I watch the interaction, and can't help my intrigue at this softer side of Ivrik that continues to show itself in unexpected ways. He catches me watching and a shadow crosses his face before he quickly looks away.

"It's to hide who you are as we pass through the city." He responds, running a hand down the side of the horse's neck before meeting my eyes again. "While the people are used to you coming and going as you please, we don't need to risk anyone asking unnecessary questions."

"Or pushing you further and faster than necessary." Türë cuts in, and I jump. He had been so silent in the last minutes I had forgotten he still sat on his similarly silent horse only a few feet away. "When you are ready, you will walk among your people freely again. But until then, we will keep to ourselves." I nod in thanks for their foresight and sling the thick cloak across my shoulders. The dress that had been waiting for me in my tent this morning, along with the thick, broken-in boots, are on the warmer side. This afternoon, in the bright sunlight, the warming rays had me wishing for something lighter. But now with the wind picking up and the sun long dropped below the horizon, the night time chill had begun to bite through the material. I hadn't even realized the cold seeping into my bones until the warmth of the cloak drapes over me. Tugging the hood up to mask as much of my identity as possible, I sigh, wrapping it even tighter around myself with a content *hmm*. Ivrik and Türë both chuckle at me, but I don't care. Filled with warmth and the light ahead bolstering me, beckoning me, I feel ready to take the last steps into my city.

"May I?" Ivrik asks, gesturing at the saddle. I tilt my head, confused. He cracks a half smile at me before explaining. "Patryk took my horse in with him. One of his hooves was starting to ache and I didn't want him to have to wait any longer for you slow Sidhe. May I ride with you?" Ivrik glances only a moment at Türë, before returning his attention to me.

"Oh! Of course." I sputter, so elegantly.

He ties, with expert fingers, the bag at his feet to my mare and, with a much smoother attempt than I managed, pulls himself up behind me. I try not to notice how close we now sit. Close enough that I can feel the defined muscles hidden beneath the layers of clothing. Türë eyes us, his face blank. I blink, thrown at the difference in him. I flick a look over my shoulder at Ivrik, only to see his face is stretched in a wide grin. I roll my eyes and look forward again, following as Türe nudges his stallion ahead without a word.

"So it seems like you get along with my mount. Is she yours?" I inquire, both from genuine curiosity and from desire to distract myself from all the thoughts tumbling around my head.

"Her name is Afina," he responds, reaching around me to tug at the reins as the horse gets distracted by a nearby bale of hay stacked against one of the walls. I try to ignore the slightest brush of his hands as they return to rest gently on my waist. "And yes, she is one of mine. I found her as a foal, hurt and abandoned by her herd on one of my trips north. I decided I couldn't leave her and so I set my tent up right there and stayed with her until she was strong enough to make the trip to my home in Naro. From there, she followed me everywhere and was soon one of my best, and favorite horses." He explains. After a pause, he leans, lowering his voice, and I swear his lips brush against the shell of my ear. "I find animals easier to understand and get along with. You used to always tease me about it and say if you were a bird or dog then maybe I would be nicer to you." Ivrik huffs a laugh and I feel the breath brush my cheek. My stomach twinges and the tingle that buzzes down my spine has nothing to do with the wind that swirls around us. Even so, I pull the cloak tighter again, hoping he won't notice. But as close as we are, of course he does. "Are you cold? I should have brought a thicker cloak, but never would have guessed it would get this chilly tonight. I am further south, so it is already warm throughout the night there." He starts to rub my arms beneath my cloak up and down, more gently than I ever expected from him. The warmth I feel though has nothing to do with the heat generated from the kind motion, but more the blood that rushes to my cheeks. At the look we get from Türe,

Ivrik quickly drops his hands and clears his throat, obviously uncomfortable. I raise my chin in challenge of Türë's stern look, irked by his apparent disapproval of Ivrik's friendliness. "This here is the entry courtyard with the public kitchen-gardens and orchards. To the left there is also the pavilion where on the first night of every full moon you host music and dancing all night—as well as other events from time to time." Ivrik says, loud and obvious enough to make it clear he want's Türë, who sits stiff backed ahead of us, to hear.

Distracted by this, my head whirls immediately with a list of questions. So I ask the one that caught my attention first. "Public kitchen-gardens and orchards?"

To my surprise, it is Türë who answers, calling over his shoulder. "It was one of your first mandates as queen." He explains, his face dances between light and shadow as we pass the massive square filled with all kinds of plants. The torches that line the vast vegetable beds and miniature rivers carved out intricately between them dance in the breeze. Even now, with the moon making its appearance, a group of people still could be seen with their hands dusted with dirt, and smiles upon their faces. One tall, ebony-skinned woman watches us pass and bows her head low in respect and reverence when she realizes who we are. Türë continues. "You were visiting the other villages that were now a part of this kingdom, right at the very beginning. When you saw the beggars, the homeless and starving, and then the locked lush, garden gates of Lord Waven—the man who was in charge of the city at the time—you blew the gates apart and demanded that all who wished to enjoy them could do so. No matter their status or abilities. All were to be allowed to enter and eat their fill. Just as long as those who took, would also assist in the maintaining and care of the garden. From there, you went to every city and did the same to all the others. The cities that didn't have a garden, or at least a well-stocked or large one, you personally oversaw the creation and employed head gardeners to ensure their survival. Since that time, there has not been a single report of starvation, or even theft of food in the entire kingdom." Türë pulls to a stop, dismounting, and at last turning to look at me again. Pride glimmers like an unshed tear in his eyes. I look around us, trying to glean why we stopped beside an undistinguishable section of wall that extends from the garden and out of sight. Not nearly as big as the exterior walls, it is still immense. Ivrik slides off Afina, then holds a hand out to help me down. Stretching my arms up overhead to ease my aching back before taking the offered hand, I feel thankful to the horses for carrying us all that way, but am even more thankful that our journey has come to an end. My tailbone screams in objection as I land on my feet and stand upright, looking around us. Taking advantage of the moment, I truly examine the interior of my city for the first time. As I do the mental math of everything I had been told of the kingdom and the city's history, as sturdy as it all seemed, I still can't fathom how long it has stood. Upon my initial inspection, Alessandra appears to be a series of walled rings layered within the outermost ring. That had been the thick stone wall that surrounds the perimeter of the vast city. If I had to guess, I would estimate that it would take a full day to walk around the top of the outer wall, and probably another to figure out how to safely return to the ground. Standing fifty feet in the air, there were no steps to be seen, nor any other reasonable way to reach the top of the walls or get down again. Unless maybe if you could fly.

"Can I fly?" I ask, staring up at the imposing stone. I hear a barked laugh followed by a rough bout of coughing. I pull my focus from the wall and turn, baffled. Apparently Ivrik had been in the middle of drinking out of his wine skin when I had asked the random question. I watch him, wide-eyed, as he scowls and tries to hopelessly dab at the deep red stain that now blooms bright against his previously white shirt.

Türë continues to laugh, hands braced against his knees as he catches his breath. "No, that was something you never managed to do—much to your annoyance." He catches his breath, then calls to a young boy walking nearby. Flipping him a coin, Türë convinces the boy to take the horses to the palace stable and sends him on his way with the promise of whatever sweets he would like from the kitchens as well.

We watch the boy lead the horses away, leaving us standing on an abandoned street beside one of the inner walls.

"So," I say, looking around uncertainly. "What are we doing now?" Before the words can leave my mouth though, a soft sliding sound comes from my left; from the direction of the wall. If not for my sensitive ears, I am not sure I would have even heard the noise. Spinning towards the sound, I find a grinning Patryk waiting on the other side of a doorway that had previously been invisible, now slid open to reveal a dark tunnel leading into the inner wall.

"Would you like to see your home?" I can't help but grin, then eagerly step into the passage.

thirteen

I stare up at the tall, immaculate ceiling of my bedroom. Well, what they said was a bedroom. It was, in truth, a gigantic cavern of space with a bed in the middle. In different parts of the room there is a reading nook with a luxurious pile of pillows, a large flower-covered balcony with a fire pit large enough to roast a hog on a spit, and a whole couch and chair set up in front of a stone fireplace. An entire family could live here comfortably, and I use it to simply sleep. I toss to my side, willing myself to seize the brief respite of unconsciousness. No matter how hard I squeeze my eyes closed, or tell myself to relax, it continues to evade me. The bell tower across the city chimes three tolls. I groan and toss again with a sigh. It wasn't that the bed was uncomfortable. No, quite the opposite. Like everything else I had seen on my quick, back hallway tour of the castle, it is complete luxury. Everything from the candlesticks, to the doorknobs, to the tiles cut into finger length pieces and positioned into an image above my head. I examine the image displayed above me, a *mosaic,* according to

Türë. It depicts a large grove of lush green trees that, in the flickering candlelight, seem to dance in a non-existent wind. It was beyond magnificent, and I couldn't imagine how long it had taken. Everywhere I looked was a wonder in this place. I could stand on my shoulders three times over and still not be able to touch any of the ceilings.

I roll onto my other side and scold myself for the continuous worries that swirl through me on repeat. The ones that echo through my tired mind and keep me awake. Patryk had led us through the darkened tunnel with only a single torch to give us any sort of clarity on where we were going. My anxiety climbing with each step as I came to grips with the reality I had been trying to push off all day. In the dancing shadows of the secret passage, there was only a stone path pockmarked with muddy puddles to be seen. Not enough to look at to distract me. When we came to an apparent dead end, he pulled a large brass key from the depths of his scarlet cloak, unlocking the door with a hard twist, followed by a clunky grinding sound. Despite the ominous sound of the lock itself, rusted and clearly rarely used from this side, the door itself was silent and sleek. An emergency exit, in the event of attack or disaster, one kept secret and had never been used until tonight, Türë had explained. *Sneaking the queen into her own castle, how incongruous.* I couldn't help but be amused by the situation I had found myself in. Holding my breath as the door swung open to reveal the opulence beyond, I could only gape at what was to be my home.

It had been at the threshold of the secret door that I realized I could no longer put off the denial of who I was. This isn't some trick, or joke. I am the Queen of a rather vast kingdom, and I have no idea how to do anything.

Hours later, I mostly mull over what my role will be for the coming days. How will I keep up the appearance of the people's beloved ancient queen? Would I even be able to pass off as a competent ruler when I was still trying to figure everything out as I went? The biggest blessing was that we at least were at peace, and the kingdom was fruitful. There were no immediate crisis's to handle while I re-learned everything. I flip to my back and huff in anger and frustration. I had spent the last hour trying to ignore it all in the apparently useless hope that I would be able to drift off to sleep. I consider taking another bath. Not to clean myself again, but just to *enjoy* it. That bathtub was more than a beauty. It was a gift. The tub had been big enough to fit myself and a dozen others if I had wished it. Once I had arrived in my room I had been exhausted, but encouraged by a chambermaid to get in the freshly drawn water. Lit by the light of the moon from the window, I had immersed myself into the warmth and soothing scents of the oils added to the water and nearly squealed in delight. For the first time in two days, I felt my muscles finally, truly, relax. After the combination of stress pulling my muscles tight, and the long hours in the saddle, it felt glorious to stretch out and unclench.

I don't honestly know how long I would have stayed there, the water seemed to never cool or grow stagnant, but now that I had begun to relax I knew it was only a matter of time before I would fall into a deep sleep.

Or so I had thought.

I give up, throwing the silky covers off with a soft whoosh. I step into waiting fur-lined slippers and pull on a robe draped over a nearby chair. Due to the late hour and waning Frë temperatures, the air is crisp and I shiver at the chill. I make my way over to the immense fireplace to see if I could at least manage to figure it out without having to wake anyone else. It takes a few minutes of poking around before I find a matchstick that I had seen a young woman light a few candles around the bath with. I strike it against the stone mantle like she had and nearly cheer at my success when a small lick of flame ignites its tip. Remembering how Patryk had started the campfire, I mimic what he had done the night before and hold the flame out towards a wrapped bundle of what appeared to be a long-stemmed, fragrant grass sitting in the hearth among the fresh wood. It ignites and quickly grows bigger, catching a large log in its grip and setting it afire too.

I lean back on my heels, watching my success with pride. Even though it was such a small, mostly insignificant thing, it made me happy to know that I could do *something*. Maybe with the help of the others I *could* learn how to be a queen again. I look around and spot a pillow propped on a nearby couch and pull it down beside me. I decide to curl up there, as close to the warmth as I could get. Watching the mesmerizing flames and thinking on what I would do next. I let the heat radiate through and over me until finally the room doesn't seem so expansive. Until I don't feel so alone.

❋ ❋ ❋ ❋ ❋

I feel something nudge my toe and my eyes fly open before I wince and groan. I roll over, shoving my face back into the darkness of the pillow and out of the rays of morning sunlight that stream in through the glass balcony doors. I hear a rough laugh and hesitantly lift my face out of the pillow again. Squinting against the bright rays, I find Türë staring down at me. *Down?* I look around, confused for a minute as to where I was, before realizing I had fallen asleep on the floor of my bedroom.

"I thought that you were aware you could have chosen any of your couches, chairs, or the bed to sleep on. I guess I should have told you they were an option." He teases, a mischievous look gleams in his eye. "And if yours didn't suit you, mine was always available."

"Ha. Ha." I fake a laugh, even as I swallow hard at the suggestive comment. I shoot a sideways glance at him, frantically combing at my tousled hair with my fingers as I tuck my legs behind me, sitting up. Though I can't see them, I can feel the disheveled curls sticking out in every direction and tangle around my horns in a bramble. My hair is a mess thanks to deciding to climb directly into bed rather than calling for my handmaiden to brush it out after my bath. To be honest, I am a bit hesitant about meeting her. And I had for sure not been up to it after the extremely long day. I give up after a few rakes through the strands, realizing it was hopeless. "I couldn't sleep." I confess, pulling the pillow into my lap and plucking at a loose piece of thread. Türë joins me on the floor, leaning against the olive velvet couch, our thighs brush as he extends his legs out. The embers in the fireplace emit enough heat for the cool morning, but still I feel goosebumps flicker across my skin.

"You don't have to do anything that you aren't comfortable with today." I feel the heavy weight of his gaze on me, but continue looping the thread through my fingers. I take a deep breath and look through the glass door to the balcony, where I can see the bright sunlight and the azure sky.

"No, I need to do something. Putting it off will not help anyone, especially me." I say with more conviction than I feel, but my heart tells me that it is the right step forward.

"Are you sure?" Unconvinced, he narrows his eyes at me, scrutinizing my face for any hesitation. I stick my tongue out and roll to my feet. His eyes widen before flushing, his pupils blowing wide. He stiffens, eyes watching my every move with a predator's focus. My brows rise in surprise, mouth opening to ask him what the problem was. At first. Then I remember the gown that had been left out for me the night before. The one I had been too tired to throw a fuss over. The nightgown I didn't think twice about wearing, because no one was going to see me in it anyway. Except now Türë was definitely seeing. I watch as a look of hunger washes away the blush and his eyes trail openly across my body. I inhale sharply, not from fear, but rather from my body suddenly awash with a heat that has nothing to do with the fire snapping in the hearth. His eyes flick back up to mine at the sound, and he stands smoothly. Stepping forward, he traces the outline of my jaw with a finger, before looping a it through a curl. I bite my lip, heart fluttering in my chest.

"I—" He starts, voice low, but then the sound of voices leak through the open doorway.. He shakes himself at the sound, stare breaking. "Fuck." He steps back, and I feel suddenly as if ice water spills down my head and neck. "Excuse me." Türë growls before suddenly storming off, fast enough that he is gone before I can say a word or take another breath. I take a single step after him, before falling into the nearby armchair, shaking knees giving out. I stare at the door that slams shut behind him as my heart beat races. "Well shit." I mutter to myself.

Ilithyia and Athene are just what I didn't realize I needed. I hear the pair before I see them. Both young and vibrant and clothed in a set of silky flowing gowns that dance with each of their approaching steps. Deep in loud, joyful conversation, the two don't acknowledge me for a moment as the doors to my room swing open and they enter, their laughter filling the room. I turn from where I still sit, trying to dissect my confusing moment with

Türë. I stand, my feet shuffle with excited nerves as I tug at the hem of a blanket I had draped across my shoulders. To both ward off the chill and to try to cover up myself more to prevent another incident like I had with Türë. One with waist-length honey-gold curls catches sight of me and screams. Actually *screams*. Not in fear or pain, but delight.

To my surprise, no guards come barreling into the room in a panic and I realize the noise must be a regular occurrence. The issuer of the scream rushes over to me, skipping and dancing the entire approach. I don't know what to do as she takes my hands and pulls me along with her, twirling me in a circle and still laughing as she goes. The eldest of the two, with russet hair, braided back into an intricate, and familiar, plait, has a bit more grace, walking to join us at a reasonable pace rather than joining the energetic flight of her companion. She takes one of my flyaway curls in her hand and gives it a gentle, playful tug as we, thankfully, stop spinning around.

"It is so good to see you! I know we only just saw you a few days ago, but I know this is the first time that you have seen us, so I am just so excited to meet you—again—oh, it's so wonderfully confusing, don't you know!" My enthusiastic handmaiden bounces on her feet and, in spite of myself and my nerves, I can't help but smiling with her.

"Let her breathe, Ilithyia." The other chides, rolling her eyes at me with a grin. "I am Athene." She says, dragging her friend away from me and over to the couch where they both sit down without encouragement, like this was as much their room as it was mine. *I suppose as my handmaidens and closest friends, they would be as comfortable as I would be—should be.* I stand in silence, suddenly shy and unsure of what to say.

"Now I see why Türë was in such a fuss when we ran into him just now." Ilithyia says coyly, with a pointed look at my close-fitting and revealing gown that peaks out from under the blanket. I can't help the heat that inflames my cheeks.

"I am afraid I made him horribly uncomfortable..." I mutter before pausing, then decide what the hell. "I keep getting mixed signals." I hope the answer I am looking for isn't too obvious and I try to appear nonchalant. Nothing truly aside from a few hidden looks had passed between us—until this morning. The hunger that had seemed to rush through us both in those few breaths could have been a momentary weakness. Aside from that there had been nothing, other than my own distracted thoughts, that would lead me to believe there had been anything other than a close friendship between us before the Awakening. The two girls exchange a look, but are so suddenly quiet and unable to look at me, and I know I have my answer. *They are staying out of it.*

"I heard Patryk and Ivrik came along to get you." Ilithyia says, trying to not be obvious about changing the subject, "Ivrik is wildly handsome, don't you think?" I almost laugh at this. I had enough going on without having to deal with any sort of romantic drama. I did not need to be having *moments* with Ivrik. I did not need to be having *moments* with Türë. What I needed now, more than anything else, was friendship and guidance. Anything to risk that or make things uncomfortable wouldn't be worth it. *Even if he does make my heart race and—* I shove those feelings down deep in the vast emptiness of my mind. I also make a note to be more conscious about my sleepwear requests, since apparently Türë had unquestioned access to my rooms.

"I refuse to answer that!" Athene says with a pretend sniff of importance, shaking her head at me and wearing a grin.

Ilithyia actually titters before turning and tugging me down onto the couch beside her. "Athene is Patryk's wife." She explains with a heavy sigh. "They are wildly, disgustingly, amazingly in love! She came with me today to make sure you were alright after the day with the boys, and to introduce herself. She used to be your other handmaiden before Patryk swept her away to be Lady of the Castle." Ilithyia teases her long-time friend.

"I should let you two ladies get to know each other. I promised Lord Eldgren's new wife that I would meet her for morning tea. I wish I had gotten out of that one, but what else was I supposed to do? Tell her no in front of everyone at the last council dinner?" Athene says, with a pointed eye roll at us, standing and curtsying to me before leaving Ilithyia and I alone.

"So what first?" I break the silence, and try to bring back the jovial mood. Ilithyia gives me a wary look before grinning widely and apologetically at me.

"A bath." She says with a pointed glance at my hair. I remember how glorious the bath had been the evening before, even with my exhaustion.

"I would be entirely okay with that." I huff a laugh and with another squeal she bounces to her feet again, pulling me into the bathing chamber and the musical sound of her voice bounces around the room. Everything else weighing me down seems to lift away as she begins to tell me about the castle.

fourteen

My skin is scrubbed pink and each knot that had tied itself in my sleep is gently pulled free, all while Ilithyia makes the room bright with her barrage of stories, information, and gossip from throughout the castle. It had taken until I was about halfway through the bath before I realized she had not made me feel different or even asked me a thing about my choice. It was a relief after the previous day of feeling like an outsider looking in. Even the stories she told me, I didn't think about how I wasn't familiar with anyone she spoke about or even how I didn't know *her*. Definitely a breath of fresh air after the last two days of feeling scrutinized.

When she at last deemed my nails free of dirt and my hair free of tangles, I was ushered from the bath and into a closet that I had not noticed the night before. It was big enough it could have been a suite of its own. Filled to the brim with various shimmering ball gowns, day gowns, and even battle worn leathers, I gape in awe. In the end, I let Ilithyia choose. I didn't have any idea of what to expect for the day and didn't want to guess at how formal I needed to be dressed. She did not take much encouragement before vanishing among the rainbow of fabrics, somehow even *more* enthusiastic, though I couldn't comprehend how that was even possible. In the end, it was decided a simple floor length day gown would suit. Though it too was fine enough for a queen. The material was soft and stretchy, a deep amethyst with gold embellishments embroidered across the hem and neckline. Beneath, I don a pair of worn in burgundy leather pants, which could be seen thanks to a waist-high slit that divided the skirts of the long-sleeved gown up the middle. I examine myself in the mirror and take in my attire with confusion, comparing it to the outfits I had seen Athene and Ilithyia wearing. Both were dressed in full gowns, complete with corseted bodices. Mine, while holding the appearance of an elegant dress, diverted enough from their gauzy, flowing skirts to be noticeable.

"You always insisted on being prepared for whatever you needed to do." Ilithyia explains, catching my confusion. "The dress keeps you formal enough for meetings, appearances at court, and the like. But the pants allow you to move freely, for your trainings, horseback riding, and fighting—should the need arise. After all, you are as capable as any of our best trained warriors."

I run my fingers down the woven golden belt she had added to the ensemble, struck silent, in awe of both the beauty and practicality of it all. "Thank you for all your help." I say, turning to face the bubbly woman, who drops into a fine curtsy again. "I know we are going to be great friends—" I grimace, my mouth quirking into a half smile in apology. "—you know—*again.*" Sharing a soft laugh, we both jump slightly when a cough interrupts us. Turning towards the noise, I hope to find Türë, but instead find a different man standing in the doorway. I grimace and scold myself for the disappointment I feel and decide to analyze *that* feeling later. Out of the corner of my eye, I see Ilithyia bob a curtsy before leaving the two of us alone.

"Hello," the man cautiously takes a step forward before dropping to a deep bow. I blink, unsure of what to do. He looks up at me and I decide to just nod, hoping there wasn't some protocol I should be following instead. Thankfully he rises again, amusement glittering behind his deep russet eyes. I examine his finery, nothing outlandish, but still notably exquisite enough to guess he was a higher member of my court. I wince and wish Ilithyia had stayed—or at the very least had whispered a name or some clue who this man was.

He must catch this because he quickly introduces himself as Noran. Recognition flickers somewhere in my mind, and I run through the few things I did know so far to see if I could place it.

"Bethos!" I blurt out in excitement, so loudly that he jumps slightly in surprise. But then he smiles slowly and nods.

"Yes, I'm sorry, I should have said that. I am your Underking of Bethos." Running a finger through his thick jet black hair, he chuckles under his breath. "This is weird." He confesses, and I laugh loudly in surprise at his blunt honesty. "The others warned me, but still it is..."

"Weird." I finish for him in agreement. He shakes his head. "I suppose I should begin my day finally. Did they send you to fetch me?" I attempt a a joke and his eyes flash in a silent thank you.

"I actually volunteered." He runs his fingers down his thick beard, flecked with a few strands of silver hair, and his mouth quirks in a smile. I blink in surprise.

"You did?"

He nods and looks around the empty room. Either looking for a way out or someone to helpfully cut in and speak for him, I am not sure. I watch him openly and make sure to keep my face as unfazed as I can.

"We used to be pretty close, before. We bonded over the histories you used to tell me." He explains. "I know that you don't remember any of that, but…" Noran trails off, sadness clouding his already darkened gaze. "Well, I just had to see for myself, I suppose." He confesses with a soft laugh. I smile in return, and though I hesitate after a step, I cross the room and hold my hand out, which he quickly takes and shakes, his shoulders drooping in relief.

"It will be wonderful to get to know you, and again earn your friendship, Noran." He beams, his cheeks flushing at my words. "I hope you will indulge me in the millions of questions I have rolling around up here." I gesture to my head.

"I can't imagine." Voices echo down the hallway to us, interrupting the conversation at the right time. I didn't think I could take the sadness in his eyes any longer. We both turn our attention to the approaching group, and I am grateful to see some faces I know—well, as much as I could know anyone at this point. It is Ivrik who swaggers into the room with Ilithyia and Athene, one on each arm, and Ilithyia giggles uncontrollably at an incredibly inappropriate joke we had only just heard the punchline too. I purse my lips together and try not to laugh. Noran just looks embarrassed for his friend. When the trio spot us staring, their laughter only starts anew and Ivrik smirks, his ego aglow from the attention.

"Well, look who is back to her radiant, royal self!" He now turns that attention on me, circling and eyeing every detail. I try to hold my chin high, tapping into the confidence I'd had when I glimpsed myself that first time in the floor to ceiling length mirror that stood in my enormous dressing room. Ivrik steps close enough so I can hear, whispering in my ear, "Though I bet you looked even better in that nightgown Türe was all flushed and tripping over this morning."

I whirl and my mouth drops open, ready to scold him for teasing me so, until I see his eyes locked on my own, though now dark and seductive. His eyes flick to my mouth and I feel my cheeks flush. *He is just teasing me. Right?* Only the realization that Noran, Ilithyia, and Athene still stand mere feet away stops me from berating him for answers. Instead, I turn my back to him, my skirts swirling from the sudden movement. Though I can tell, the others were dying to know what had been said that agitated me, I ignore his soft chuckle and quickly walk to Noran's side. Taking his arm, I pull him towards the door that leads to the rest of the castle. Between Türë and Ivrik, my morning had been confusing enough. I needed a distraction right now, and Noran and his infamous love of history would suit perfectly.

"Will you give me a proper tour of the castle, Noran?"

He beams with delight, and with a new energy, takes over leading. Already describing to me the various histories of the tapestries, artwork, and crystalline decor displayed on intricate marble columns that we pass. Behind us, Ivrik again takes the arms of the other two ladies and continues with his flirtations, following at a slower pace as we navigate the maze of halls that make up my castle.

Patryk and Ivrik had not been lying when they had teased about Noran's passion for history and extensive knowledge regarding *everything* in the castle and kingdom. My heart had nearly broken when, in response to my question of how Noran had come to know all of this, he had sadly replied that I had been the one to tell him. It had taken four hours to walk only half of the castle, the newest section—which still was almost six hundred star-cycles old. We had made it that far only thanks to Ivrik's impatient prodding and encouragement to continue on, rather than stop every fifteen paces. Each time I fought the urge to shoot him a grateful look, I held off, remembering his earlier teasing.

How much knowledge has been lost because of my choice? If I had just allowed myself a normal lifetime, which would still be longer than most, would that have been better for all?

At lunch, I can't help but stare at my still full plate as the others chatter animatedly. If they notice my melancholy, none comment on it—something I am grateful for. We had returned to my rooms for lunch, after Ivrik's complaining had finally become too much and a doting cook had brought a wide selection up within minutes of the request being sent. Even though there are five of us, the table that makes up the centerpiece of my personal dining room wasn't even a third full. When I had asked if this was where events were held, they all had laughed until they realized my question had been genuine. The rotund yet kindly woman had patted each of our cheeks with her surprisingly powerful hands before disappearing with a cheery whistling tune. I return my attention to the others, doing my best to catch up with their conversation. The door to the dining room suddenly opens and Türë strides in to join us. His gaze immediately lands on mine with a shy, apologetic smile. The others cheer at the sight of him, encouraging him to join us, but he only declines before returning his attention to me.

"May I have a word, Evara?" He asks politely, though with an edge to it. Almost as if he expected me to say no and was preparing himself for it. Ivrik shoots me a sideways look that I can't dissect but doesn't say anything. While the others still talk, I can tell that they are closely monitoring every word, though they all do their best to pretend otherwise. I remember Ivrik's earlier comment about Türë's reaction and suddenly feel wary when I recall the look of desire and hunger that had rushed through me. I clear my throat and nod.

"Of course. I was through anyway." I answer. Türë's eyes flicker with concern as he takes in my still full plate, not a single bite taken out of the sandwich.

We exit the room together, the quiet that had taken over the dining room since Türë's appearance falling away the second the door swings shut behind us. Minutes pass without another word, though not in an uncomfortable way. More of the opposite actually. The sunshine streams freely through the floor to ceiling windows and I can't help but linger over the beauty that I hadn't been able to take in on my previous tour. Now that I didn't have to hear about the histories of every object we pass, or my exhaustion after a day of travel to contend with as I had last night, I am able to see it all and appreciate it. Everywhere I look seems to glimmer. As if every surface is iridescent or even made of diamonds. While it seemed overly colorful, mainly from the rainbows dancing off the gleaming surfaces, upon closer inspection I realize that there is really only a few colors that made up the castle's color palate. An ivory cream, with shades of eggshell painted through it made up the columns, walls, and marbling of the floor. Everything else was either a soft blue, the hue of the clearest freshwater stream, or a rosy pink that matched almost identically the gentle tones of the sunset I had beheld the night before. I manage to keep my mouth closed as we silently pass through the monstrous halls, that somehow despite their size, still managed to feel warm and cozy. We pass a wide variety of people all carrying out their duties. Each of whom stops to curtsy and smile widely at me before continuing on their way.

"What are you thinking?" Türë's soft voice cuts into my thoughts as we stop in front of a large ornately carved set of wooden doors. I take a long breath, contemplating how to respond. No words seem enough to convey what I am thinking.

"It is intimidatingly perfect and beautiful." I say, breathlessly laughing. He barks a laugh in return, loud and ringing in the quietness of this empty hall.

"This always was your favorite part of the castle—the old wing. I suppose with Noran leading, you only got through the newest half." I nod, but with only half my attention on his words. I look around at where he had led me. We stand at a set of doors with an intricate set of stained glass set into them, depicting a scene of lovers embracing in a lush garden. I stare at them as they ring with a familiarity that for some reason makes my heart ache. Following my gaze, Türe reaches forward and gives the doors a gentle shove. They ease open and I take in the scene. Past the doors is a set of arches woven with rose vines that open to the outside. His face transforms with the smile he shares with me as I walk, speechless, to the swirl of vines that stand waist high—what I had initially thought were simply more immaculate carvings that make up the balustrade. Just when I had begun to think that nothing could be more beautiful than all that I had already seen, I am proved wrong. Through the empty space, I take in the unobstructed view.

Alessandra.

Standing at the railing, my grip tightens and I brace myself on the surprisingly sturdy vines and feel my breath catch in my throat. Looking out upon the entire city, I can see the small houses with smoke rising to the sky from their chimneys, busy preparing their various dishes for the evening. The streets lined with small shops where people walk, making conversation and laughing freely, to the gardens where I can hear a lone man singing heartily in a language I can't recognize as he works in the dirt. And the lily-covered ponds where a group of children play in the sunshine.

And past that, past the white and grey marble wall that sparkles from the midday light, surrounding the city and standing as a beacon of the capital and a symbol of steadfast safety to my people. Beyond that lies the expansive field of flowers that I had found myself in yesterday.

For the first time, I am truly thankful for my position and what it had brought these people. My people. This is what I had been protecting. What I had been willing to give up the memories of my friends, my loved ones, for. This was what I had given up my own history to save. To ensure many, *many* more star-cycles of safety and happiness for all of them.

For the first time, looking out on my city, on my kingdom—I understood who she had been and the reason for every choice she had made. I understood the queen she was and who I needed to be—wanted to be.

I understand you.

I want to say it aloud as relief rushes through me at last. This was the puzzle piece I was missing.

The reason for it all.

"Thank you for showing me this, Türë." I manage to whisper as my eyes fill with tears. I turn to find Türë looking at me again, his gaze guarded. Like he wanted to say something but didn't. He blinks and the look vanishes.

"Like I said, I know this was always one of your favorite parts of the castle, I figured that past-you would have kicked my ass if I didn't bring you here." He comes to stand beside me and we both let the comfortable quiet weave around us as we look upon the city.

fifteen

I try to remember the pattern of halls that Türë had led me through to reach the castle's front mezzanine with zero success. After only one passage, I was completely turned around and couldn't find my way back to my room if it was life or death. Instead of letting it demoralize me, I instead decide to see it as an opportunity. I embrace our missed turn as a chance to not only get to know more of my home, but also to try to catch a read on Türë. Something about him makes me both comfortable, but also unnerved. It must have something to do with the one-sided aspect of our relationship now. He seemed to know everything about me, whereas I know next to nothing about him.

We stroll down a large open air hallway lined with life-sized statues and I linger, reading the names on the plaque set into each one. "Who are these people?" I ask, staring up at a middle-aged man with a stern face but dancing eyes. An impressive feat to be done with stone. I notice the empty spot where a plaque had been and frown in disappointment. I would have liked to know his name.

"They are various warriors, or advisors, who did great things for the kingdom. They do something in your service, they end up immortalized in here, the *Hall of Heroes*." Türë explains, looking up at the same statue of the man. His eyes narrow as he stares and I swallow at the anger that simmers behind the look.

"Did you know him?" I risk asking, looking between the two. Türë blinks and looks away.

"No." He says shortly, then begins to walk away. I take quick steps to catch up with him, confused by his mood swings, but my stride falters at a strange noise that echoes into the hallway through the open.

"What is that?" I ask, pausing to try to discern what it was. "It sounds like chanting." Türë doesn't answer, instead he turns to lead our path away from the sounds coming through the large gate across the open-air courtyard. A flicker of defiance rushes through me and I huff, grabbing a handful of my skirts and hurrying to follow the noise. The rhythm of the voices set my heart racing, drawing me towards its source as Jera had drawn me to the tree when I had awoken. My quick steps keep rhythm with the chant as I follow it through one of the large exterior gardens, filled with workers tilling up the dark earth in preparation for planting. I reach the origin of the sound and step onto a large balcony that encircles a gigantic pit. Set deep into the ground, it stands about three times my height. My breath stutters in my lungs as I take in the sight, the source of the chanting. Over a hundred people, men and woman, all stand in a formation in the pit, calling out in a language that I don't understand as a drum keeps beat with their movements.

Though silent, I feel Türë step next to me. I fight a snide remark and smile at the irritated look on his face. "What is this?" I ask him, not bothering to hide the demand now.

"These are your warriors. This is where they train every day." He says simply,   glancing up as the sky darkens with a low hanging cloud. "We should get back inside. It looks like it might rain." Türë tries to grab for my wrist and I yank my arm out of his reach, not taking my eyes off the figures dressed in black below. Even from this distance I can see that many arms and a few of the bared chests are painted with thin lines of varying color. *Not painted. Scarred.*

"Do not grab for me." I bite, and turn to face him fully. "Why did you try to hide this?" I ask, bewildered by his intention. I spot the flash of anger in his own eyes before he inclines his head and steps away. I do notice he doesn't answer me, but I don't care right now. I return my attention below. My eyes track the warriors, all moving in synchronized patterns. I realize, with a start, their uniforms look extraordinarily similar to my attire. Though they all are outfitted in either grey or black, and with none of the fine embellishments that decorate mine. But the style, the cut, the symbols that pattern the fabric?

"I wondered how long it would take you to find this." Ivrik's familiar drawl makes me smile and I turn to find him sauntering up the walkway to join me.

"Who are they and why am I dressed like them?" He grins, before taking a large bite from an apple he pulls from his pocket. I wonder distantly if he and Patryk sprout apples. They always seem to be plucking them from no where.

"Technically," he mumbles through the juicy mouthful. "They are dressed like *you*." I roll my eyes at him. "Alright, you want the truth? The others don't think you are ready." I try not to flinch at that honesty.

"Why would they think that?" I ask, unable to hide the hurt in my voice.

"Well because you have set yourself on fire twice, electrocuted one of us, and hardly slept the last two nights." I open my mouth to argue before snapping it shut again. There wasn't anything really I could argue with.

Fair.

"I still want the truth. Who are they?" I pause before adding. "And by *others,* you mean Türë, don't you?" Ivrik barks a laugh.

"Now, now. I am not here to start a fight." He tilts his head, eyes dancing. "But yes, Türë."

I grit my teeth in frustration. "Just tell me. I can handle it."

He sighs. "Fine. For the record, I voted that you could."

I wait as he leans his forearms on the ledge that looks down upon the group below. To my surprise, a few of them notice me and wave congenially. I return the gesture, then look pointedly at Ivrik, urging him to explain.

"Okay, so I won't probably explain it as in depth as Noran can, but the gist is this; when you liberated Tesindren in the beginning, you had a group of warriors called the Nefriti. You were their leader and trained every single one." He waves a hand down at the group below, now bobbing a weaving around each other with what I now see are blades. "This is what remains of that legacy. They are still known far and wide as the elite of the elite warriors. Only ten are selected each star-cycle to enter training. After completing their training, if they wish, they then can endure the trials to further split into a two factions, the Tomyris and the Magnar, or they can choose to remain Nefriti. In each elite group, only twenty are chosen. Once in, the only way to get out is to die in service or to be discharged by you, the Queen. These warriors devote their entire lives to training and serving you and the kingdom. They do not marry, they do not have children, and they do not quit." I stare at him in shock.

"That is..." I search for the word.

"Intense?" He finishes for me, and I nod in silence. He shrugs.

"Like I said, it is an honor to be chosen as Nefriti, let alone Tomyris and Magnar. I was Nefriti before I started down my current path. I had actually put forth my name to be Magnar. You convinced me instead to be an Underking." I thought my eyes would pop out of my head they widen so far when I catch up to what he said.

"You!?" I look at him with fresh eyes, trying not to offend him completely but unable to picture the stoney look I see on each of the warriors on him.

He only laughs at me, then shrugs again, before returning his gaze to watch the training. "Believe it or not. It was why you put me in charge of the territory to the south, the one bordering our most notable enemy." It makes sense, but I still cannot reconcile the sarcastic, flippant man with a brutal warrior. "Why do you find that so hard to believe?" He asks me, genuine curiosity pulling his attention back to me as he straightens.

"I guess you just don't seem like the type." I confess, blushing slightly as he catches my eyes drifting to his muscled arms. My mind lingers now on how hard his body had seemed behind mine last night on the horse and realize now that apparently he had not completely given up his training. Ivrik smirks, as if he catches my trail of thoughts. I clear my throat and try to get back on track.

"I still don't understand why Türë didn't want me to know this." I scoff, glancing over my shoulder where my supposed friend had disappeared.

"That isn't exactly the part we aren't supposed to tell you." My brow raises and he sighs again. "Like I said before, the most elite of the Nefriti are in two factions. The Tomyris are all women, the Magnar all men, and there are twenty warriors in each. Well, you are one of the twenty Tomyris." I stare at him, not fully understanding. Thankfully he continues without my prompting. "You train with them, you battle with them, you are *one* of them.

It is brilliant, actually." He turns around and sits on the wall edge, facing me. "Not one of your most popular ideas with your council, naturally. But you managed to convince them."

"I am still confused." I admit. "Why would I do that?"

"Well, for one, how better to gain complete allegiance from your warriors? An immortal ruler ordering strangers to die for her will only be so loved. But you, you not only went to great lengths to befriend them, but you keep yourself to the same standards that you expect from them. You bleed with them, you fight with them, and you mourn with them. They do not just fight for their Queen and land when you call for them. They fight for their friend, their *shield-sister.*" He shakes his head, and I swear for the first time I see reverence in his eyes as he looks at me. "Like I said, brilliant."

I think over this, before comprehension sets in. "So let me guess, the reason Türe says he doesn't think I should be told this is because he thinks I am going to want to continue to train and remain a Tomyris."

A smirk tugs at Ivrik's lips as he drags his gaze over my face before locking onto my eyes. "Well... don't you?"

Again, I spend the night tossing and turning in my bed. All the thoughts of the day tumbling together and keeping my mind restless. My consciousness stubbornly ignores the lull of sleep that my body pleads for. I sigh in frustration and roll onto my back. Staring at the ceiling, I pound my fists into the mattress with a quiet scream of irritation. I glance out the window, its gossamer curtains sheer enough that I can see the full moon through them. Deciding I don't want to lie here and stew any longer, I throw off the covers and slip on a nearby cloak. I had made doubly sure that Ilithyia had found a much more comfortable nightgown as she helped me prepare for bed tonight. Though a flare of deviousness had alighted in her eyes at the request, she didn't comment thankfully. She had insisted that this was the most appropriate nightgown I possessed, though it still left me self-conscious enough to chide past me on my night wear choices. A light lilac silk gown with lace decorating the gentle scoop of my neck, it was beautiful. I could not deny it was exquisite, the way it hugs my body, comfortably clinging to every curve and, what I now realize, is muscle from my continual battle training. But it still leaves way too little to any imagination. Not to mention the slit in the skirt that goes all the way up past my knee to mid thigh. I roll my eyes and pull the cloak tighter around me as I tug open the door to my hallway. A quartet of guards snap to attention outside the doors and I nearly jump at the sight of them. *Of course, I have guards. I am the Queen.* One to the far right steps forward with a concerned look.

"Your Majesty, can I help you with anything? Or shall I fetch Ilithyia?" I shake my head as one of the other guards turns toward the suite opposite mine where she slept.

"No, no, please." He stops, immediately turning back to his original position. "I just—wanted to go for a walk, if that is..." I sputter and trail off, embarrassed. But the guard who spoke first only gives a sharp nod. *You don't have to ask permission. You are the Queen, remember?* I flush and straighten up. I see the corner of the guard's mouth quirk up for a second before returning quickly to neutral, his eyes remain focused ahead.

I mull over some more words, but then decide that anything further would only make it all even more awkward. I trusted that these guards were closed-lipped enough to keep this encounter to themselves. I knew I needed to get myself together and act like the Queen everyone in this castle was still under the impression I was. But it is late and I have enough thoughts swirling around my head to make me dizzy. I nod again at them, ignoring another smothered grin from the men. I make it down to the end of the hallway before I hesitate at the adjoining hall that runs in either direction. *Left or right to the private garden.* I strain my brain, trying to remember any of the paths I had taken on my tour with Noran. We had passed it at some point, and I knew it had to be close by. If I had just jumped off my balcony, I would already be there. I chew on my cheek, debating whether to give in and ask the guards to lead me. Hell, I should just get back in bed and give up on this silly idea. *Well, the idea was to go for a walk, so what if it is just through the castle. The gardens were just an idea.* Without letting myself hesitate anymore, or contemplate how I would find my way *back* to my room, I decide to turn left. With my head held high and cloak pulled around me, I set off into the dark, sleeping castle.

sixteen

The good news is I found the garden after only wandering around for an hour. The bad news is that I fear the only way I am going to be able to navigate my way back to my bed is to climb up to my balcony. I stare up at it now as I sit among the fragrant rainbow of thousands of rose bushes, daffodils, and dahlias. I still feel some victory at making it here. I must have retained some of the unending information that had been poured into me today. Or is it yesterday? Glancing up at the moon beginning to descend in the sky, I would have to guess that it is past midnight and well into the next day. Walking around the unlit paths, the moon provides plenty of light to still see all the manicured arrangements and fountains that make up the castle gardens. According to Türë, these were the gardens that I had enlisted the help of the *florenta* in managing. It definitely explained how the blossoms seemed extra plump and vibrant, and why some even seemed to glow in the light of the full moon. I shift on the bench I found. It, to my surprise, is still living and surprisingly comfortable. Made of a vine wrapped and grown in such a way that it forms a platform on which I could sit, the bench was a perfectly hidden sanctuary. I had giggled in trepidation when I first dared to sit on it, expecting it to immediately collapse and spill me into the dirt. But now, it might be the most comfortable seat I had sat upon. I have to wonder briefly at this, wondering if it was grown purposely for me it fits my body so perfectly. I scuff my feet across the path, lost again in the endless thoughts and questions that whirled through my brain at every moment. Knowledge about the kingdom, its cities, ports, and strongholds, the final Underking, Eivan, would be arriving tomorrow. And, especially, my thoughts return to the group of warriors that I had spent decades strengthening and fighting alongside. I groan aloud at that recollection, and run a hand down my face as my anxiety surges so hard that I wonder for a moment if I am going to throw up all over the lovely garden. Thankfully, I regain control of my stomach before I could mar this beautiful place. I trace my toes across the border of the stones at the bench's base, attempting to quiet my thoughts with a feeble reassurance that it would all be okay. My toes catch on something and I narrow my gaze to see what it is. Then I notice my toes weren't randomly tracing anything—they were actually following a carving etched deep into the stone that had been hidden in the dirt. My curiosity peaking, I ease off the bench and onto my knees beside the carving. *Some sort of drawing, or a symbol maybe?* I look closer at it, wondering why it was here of all places. I hadn't noticed it before, nor any other carvings of its sort anywhere else in the garden. *But then again I wasn't looking for it either. Everything is decorated around here. Why wouldn't the path be as well? Probably a marking from this bench's creator.* I shrug and begin to stand when a shadow falls across the ground where I kneel.

"Why are you outside, in the dirt, in the middle of the night?" A male voice drawls, and I gasp, startled a bit—until I see Türë standing a few paces away with his arms crossed. Watching me with an eyebrow raised, an ornery grin crosses his face. I brace myself for the anger he had shown me earlier today. We had not seen or spoken to each other since. However, the Türë I see now is one I had not yet gotten a glimpse of. This Türë is lighter, more teasing, and not as tightly-wound with stress. I feel my shoulders relax, even as I wonder how I will get used to his constant mood changes.

"Why are *you* outside in the middle of the night?" I fire back in turn, dusting off my hands on the cloak as I rise.

"The guards let me know that you had left your rooms and grew concerned when you still hadn't returned after an hour."

"Of course they did." I groan, though not in anger. After all, they were only doing what they could to protect their undeserving Queen. "I'm so sorry they woke you for this." That explains the weapons at least. Though I had begun to suspect that he never was without a weapon, except for maybe in the baths. My cheeks warm at the thought and images that follow that line of thought. Türë cocks his head, obviously curious why I had suddenly blushed and fallen silent. I clear my throat and decide to change the subject. "Just when I thought it couldn't get any more beautiful, somehow the moonlight transforms it and makes it glow." I gesture around us and indeed the blooms all sparkle in the silvery-blue moonlight.

"I know what you mean. It has a different kind of beauty at night. You always used to come here on full moons and sit on that bench and sing old songs long since forgotten. And you don't need to apologize, I was awake anyway." He trails off as the tolling bells of the sleeping city reach us, singing their tune and letting us know it truly was deep into the next day already. Thankfully, the walk in the garden's had accomplished my desired result and a yawn ripples through me.

"How did you know I was here?" I ask him, taking the first steps alone on the path that weaves back to the castle, but he quickly falls into step with me, his pace slow and ambling.

"I have a lot on my mind, and figured you did too. This is where you have always come when your thoughts become overwhelming." He answers after a long pause.

"I didn't realize I could sing." I say in an attempt to change the subject. It hadn't occurred to me that I would have had *time* for any hobbies other than running the vast kingdom. "Was I actually any good, or was there a reason I would come here in the middle of the night to sing?" I joke, and hope that isn't the truth after saying it aloud. I make a point to try the next time I was alone to test out the ability to be sure.

He snorts at that, and I laugh along, relaxing slightly and matching his mood. I yawn deeply again and feel sleep calling me at last. "You are a wonderful singer." Türë says as we reach the gate to the garden, his voice suddenly rough with emotion, though not one I can identify. I turn towards him, startled at the shift, but find him not looking at me but back towards the garden behind us. "Are you ready to go back to your rooms?" He asks, clearing his throat and turning back to face me. I openly stare at him, trying to peel back the mask he seems to wear, hoping to get to the man underneath. I sigh, but nod. Türë seems to have so many layers, but I just can't seem to make it through them. My letter said he was my most trusted, yet he seems to be keeping so many things from me. I want to get to know him... but the question that remained unanswered seemed to be if he just does not want to get to know me anymore? After all, to invest centuries into a friendship to only have it all wiped clean. It had to be exhausting to think of having to start all over again. Unable to give a voice to my worry, I just hope that given time, for both him and me, we could be friends again. I so desperately wanted—needed—that.

Everywhere I went in the castle, I felt so alone. Like I was missing something everywhere I went. And the bed, so large for just me... so lonely. No matter how I try to shake it off, it lingers. The best I can do is hope to know those around me again and to chase away the feeling.

Türe leads me, much more efficiently, back to my room. In my hallway, we find four very pale, worried guards waiting for us. After apologizing profusely for causing them any distress, and their assurances in return that there was no need, they return to their posts at the ends of the hallway, leaving us alone at my door.

"Thank you for coming to find me tonight. I was actually contemplating if I would be able to shimmy up to my window to get back here." He laughs hard at that—too hard. I shoot him a playful glare, but laugh, too. I open my door and turn to say one last goodnight, but the face I find watching me freezes my heart in my chest. *Longing.* But different from the hunger and desire that had colored his face that morning. No, this was dismay. Torment. A loneliness of a different kind than what I had been feeling. My shock must have shown because like a gate slamming down, his eyes shutter and the look is replaced with cool amusement. I blink a few times, wondering if my lack of sleep was beginning to affect my mind at last. "I—" I start, but my breath freezes in my chest as Türe reaches out, pulling my free hand into his own. I can do nothing but watch and try to keep my heart from beating out of my chest as he pulls it to his lips, warm and so soft, pressing them gently into the inside of my wrist. Based on my own senses, I know for a fact that, even if he can't hear my heart racing wildly, he can feel my pulse thrum as his mouth lingers on my tender skin. His eyes darken and the longing seems to fight to emerge again. But then he blinks, and the mask is back.

"Sleep well, my Queen." He says, his voice a cool tone that doesn't match his fiery eyes as he straightens up. Before I can respond, he is gone. Vanishing around the corner and into the dark halls beyond.

"Goodnight." I manage to whisper to the emptiness that now chills me. I slip into my room, and push it closed, a smile tugging at my lips. Leaning my back against the surprisingly warm wood, I try to catch my breath as my thoughts whirl about again.

I gasp as he pulls me into a hidden alcove. "What are you doing?" I whisper, even as his lips descend on my neck and I groan in desperation for more.

"Do you want me to stop?" He asks, hesitating.

"Please, please, do not stop." I lean into his warmth, his touch, like it was the only thing connecting me to this earth. When he had invited me to meet him in the garden, this was not how I pictured tonight going. But I was not going to argue with the results. I inhale when his lips return to their path, trailing from my ear down to my collarbone. The surrounding garden, where we had met for our 'innocent' picnic, grows even more dark. The night cloaking us, as much as the corner we had found. In almost two thousand star-cycles, I had never met someone who had turned my blood as molten as he does. What was I doing? This man was a youth when I was far past a thousand star-cycles old. But Jera help me, he knows what he is doing, as he grinds into me, his body hits all the right places. The delicious friction makes the last of my inhibitions vanish. I moan his name, which he takes correctly as a queue to continue. Goddess forbid he ever stop.

The stone wall scrapes against my back, but I care about nothing other than his lips. He mutters soft curses against my neck, before he pulls my face into his, kissing me deeply on my lips. I taste us both in the kiss and twine my fingers through his golden locks, pulling him closer to me.

I had always pictured giving myself to some stiff royal in my cold bed for the betterment of my kingdom. To give this piece of myself to someone I yearn for in the dark shadow of my garden? That was even better.

"Please." I put everything I want to say, but can't bring myself to in that single word. To my surprise, he pulls away. Concern darkens his irises, the most beautiful emerald green I had ever seen, as they scan my face for hesitation.

"Are you sure?" He asks, more sincere than I have ever seen him.

"I have never been more sure of anything in my entire life." I say, meeting his eyes without wavering so he can see my sincerity.

He kisses me again, filled with longing. We both moan into the kiss, then huff a laugh. If he had any idea how long I had wanted him...

We had trained together for nearly an entire star-cycle and each session, my eyes had lingered too long on him, obviously so. Far too long for a queen to linger on someone who had been a peasant, many of my councilors had lectured me.

I did not give a fuck.

Live over a thousand star-cycles, then tell me what I should do with my body.

This. This is what I wanted to do with it.

He teases me, nipping at my lip. Right now, I would not be sated until I felt him inside me.

"Please." I say again. Looking him dead in the eyes, before I pull him in for another kiss that melts my bones.

This time when he mutters, it's my name.

I revel in its sound on his lips. Eyes meeting, joy fills my heart as he kisses me again, this time slowly, deeply. The kiss is filled with more passion than I had ever experienced in almost two thousand star-cycles. Not that there had been many to turn my gaze or tempt me.

According to my last letter, none had tempted me then either.

But now...

I kiss him back, trying to fill it with the words I was too terrified to voice. My heart races at the implications of what this could mean. Aside from sex—he is only twenty-three.

I am two thousand and twenty-four.

But I love him.

Even though I am not supposed to.

In all the times we had talked and began to know each other more, it had grown.

Until I now can't stay away.

Even if I wanted to. And I don't.

But I am supposed to go through the Awakening in less than a star-cycle.

Needed to.

Fuck.

What do I do?

seventeen

I wake again to another laugh. Groggy and disoriented, I try to catch the threads of my dream that hang in the air. Something about a garden, and a man. My cheeks flame as a piece of it becomes clear and I shake it away. Looking around, I find the source of the laugh. This time it is Ilithyia who wakes me with a wide smile on her face, shaking her head at my appearance. Scolding me playfully for my windblown hair and dirty feet, she tugs me back into the bath. For the first time, I wake up feeling optimistic and lighter. After everything that had happened between us during the day, it had been nice to clear the air. I appreciated what he was attempting to do for me, protecting me from too much at once. But deciding what things I knew about myself and what I *deserved* to know was going way too far.

I brush my hand back and forth in the bubbles that coat the top of the water and an idea comes to me. "Ilithyia?" I sit up, looking for the young woman who bustles with quiet, relaxed efficiency about the bathing chamber. She pauses, looking at me from over a stack of fresh towels.

"Hmm?" She sets the fluffy stack down on a nearby stool before grabbing a brush and coming over to sit on the edge of the tub.

"I saw the Nefriti yesterday." I trail off, unsure of what exactly I want to know. I just have a feeling that if anyone would know something about me, it would be Ilithyia—my handmaiden, who I trusted enough to help conceal my current situation.

"Oh! Did you?" She squeals with excitement, picking up my hair and lathering it with some floral-scented soap. "I hoped you would! It didn't seem right—" Cutting herself off, she pales slightly, biting her lip in sudden anxiety. I narrow my eyes, watching her reaction carefully.

"You knew they were trying to hide that from me?" It appears I know what direction of questioning to go in. "Why? I know what Türë *said*, but it still doesn't make sense. I think I have the right to know who I am, even if I am… different now."

"I agree." She sniffs. "And I tried to argue that for you. But Türë was so certain and made us all promise that we wouldn't say anything. The others caved too, especially when he argued that he didn't want you to be overwhelmed and hurt yourself by accident. He mentioned something happening in the forest where you got thrown into a tree." My anger flares at this and I spin, eyes wide in disbelief that he had brought that up.

"First of all, that was only on the second day and I was still coming to grips with everything. And second, that was because he started yelling at me and lecturing me over how much responsibility I had placed on his shoulders, and how hard it was for *him!*"

Ilithyia gapes at me in surprise. "He did *not!*"

"Yes, he did. So I got upset and accidentally threw his ass into a tree." I huff, folding my arms across my chest as Ilithyia rinses out my hair, her brow furrowed as she listens to me vent. She works silently, long enough that I know she is mulling over something.

"Evara, it is not my place." She begins, before hesitating, obviously conflicted about what she wants to say versus what she should say. I spin in the tub, water sloshing slightly over the edge in my ferocity, and grip her hand tightly in my own.

"Please, Ilithyia, if you are truly my friend, tell me what you are thinking. Because I feel so lost and have no idea of what to actually think, or who to trust. What else could he be hiding from me, in the guise of keeping me safe?"

She opens her mouth to speak when the clack of footsteps approach. Her eyes widen and she quickly leans down to whisper in my ear. "Be careful who you trust. There are some who look to take advantage of the current question of your ability to rule."

It is my turn to gape as she sits back up and begins humming as if nothing had happened. The lightness I had felt upon waking this morning pops like one of the many bubbles that float beside me. I struggle to mask my face with calm indifference as Athene steps into the room.

"Oh my! You are still in the bath? I had better help or you will be late for your first meeting!" She greets us, hands on her hips with faux disappointment. Only when Athene mentions this do I remember the meeting I have with the *others*. I had been excited to meet the remaining Underking, Eivan. Now, I can't help but question everything. My stomach churns and I duck underneath the bubbles into the deep, warm water of my gigantic bathtub. I let the muted sounds of Ilithyia's soft singing, buffered by the water, relax me. I hold my breath as long as I can before re-emerging. Ilithyia stands waiting with a fresh towel and eyes on the nearby clock, as if she too just realized the time.

"Come on. Out of the bath, or you truly will be late! I will help you get ready." Athene impatiently bustles over to the door of the closet before freezing mid step as she realizes what she said.

"Forgive her impatience, my Queen." Ilithyia glares at her friend. "She has been like that since finishing school. It drives her absolutely crazy to be late, and she seems to think that affliction plagues everyone. I thought she would be better after she and Patryk were married and she took on other duties to distract her. But lo-and-behold, she somehow got even more bossy!" Rolling her eyes, Ilithyia helps me out of the tub and wraps me in a thick towel.

An idea hits me and I hesitate, mulling its practicality over. "I will on one condition." I set my gaze on the two women who watch me with apprehension. Chewing my lip, I debate the question I want to ask, and if it was even smart to broach. "You have to tell me what exactly is my relationship and history with Türë."

"No deal." Athene snaps, turning her attention to Ilithyia, staring her down with a true firmness I hadn't seen in her yet. Ilithyia winces, but meets my eye with an apologetic smile. It was obvious from both of their reactions that they would be unwavering in keeping their mouths shut on that one. But why? Was there something between us at some point and it ended? Does it have to do with Ilithyia's warning to be cautious? The two women silently shuffle me over to the closet and into the waiting gown. Similar to yesterday in its general tailoring, this one is an emerald green and turquoise gown that flairs out into more of a flowing, regal fit. Definitely more formal than the one I had worn yesterday, though still with a pair of comfortable cracked and worn in leather pants beneath it. Another reminder of the warrior queen that I must continue to give the impression I was. The final touch, a floral golden band that Ilithyia rests carefully on my head, once they had dried and curled the hair into an elegant style. Sitting right above my brow, it pulls the golden hues out in my eyes and I stare at myself in the mirror. Even dressed like a queen, I still find this hard to believe.

The two still don't speak, and I begin to wonder if there was some unspoken line I had crossed with my question. But then a bit of anger surges in my gut. First Türë. Now them. *How dare they shut me out like this? I can't ask a* question! *One about my own life without fear of them shutting me out?* I turn to face the two, who stiffen immediately at the look on my face.

"Evara?" Athene says, cautiously shooting a glance at Ilithyia beside her. They both take a step back, and I blink in surprise. I catch a glimpse of myself in the mirror and I see why they are suddenly retreating from my anger. From me. The water that had been warm and bubbling in the bath, was now hovering head high and swirling behind me like a whirlpool. And my eyes, Jera help me, my eyes were alit with orange fire, flickering like my own anger. As quickly as it had flared though, it receded. The water falls with an echoing splash and lapping of waves. I watch myself in the mirror as the flames in my eyes cool to mere embers.

"What is going on?" A wary voice asks from the bedroom doorway, and we all three spin in surprise to find Türë watching wide-eyed, one hand still on the doorknob. The two women sputter a bit, fear clouding their minds. I try not to dwell on the fact that the reason for their fear was me.

"I lost control again." I admit with a croak, attempting to hold in the desire to weep. My emotions, my self-control, all of it were like a rising wave crashing upon me again and again, and behind me I hear the water mimicking the feeling. The water sloshes along my feet and Ilithyia and Athene scurry backwards, pressing against the far wall. My heart sinks further, and I do my best to steady the breaths that now come in huffs as the tears begin to pour from my eyes. I hear Türë bark something that I don't catch. I feel, more than see or hear, them rush out of the room. I vaguely wonder if they are going to lock me in the room alone until I can pull myself together again. If that is what it takes for me to not hurt them, I can't help but agree. Exhaustion, mental rather than physical, sweeps over me, and I fall to my knees as a bolt of fire pulses from me. The sizzle of steam sweeps through the room as the two elements combat each other. Apparently Türe had been right to keep me in the dark about so many things, I can't help but think.

Still kneeling, I stare blankly at the stone floor, now covered in water as it mingles with petals of flame. I watch a pair of boots emerge from the fog of steam. I blink slowly at them, not even attempting to think. I look up to see Türe braving the chaos to kneel beside me. His mouth moves, so I know he is speaking to me, but I can't hear anything past the roaring in my ears. His face is calm as he reaches out, ever so gently gripping my chin and pulling it up until I meet his eyes.

"Breathe." His mouth says, and I obey. I inhale deeply and notice how much he smells like the garden from last night. Like fresh soil, the forest, and the wind before a storm. I inhale again, letting it distract and soothe me, and I feel my heartbeat begin to even out. Around the two of us, the circle of flames gutter like a torch in the wind and finally they succumb to the water that still swirls, though slower, around us. Türe releases my chin, but I still don't look away as he moves his cool fingers to my cheek, then forehead, then tucks a piece of hair back beneath the band of my crown. The sensation is relaxing and this time the exhaustion that rushes over me is physical. I collapse completely to the floor and into darkness.

* * * * *

It feels like only a mere blink before I regain consciousness, thank Jera. I struggle to pry my eyes open as the warmth of arms wrap around me, lifting me off the bathing chamber floor with reassuring whispers, though in a language I don't understand. Türë carries me easily back into the bedroom. From what I can tell, he lays me down on my already favorite couch, cozy and warm, thanks to its position in front of the fireplace. My head spins with vertigo and I realize for the first time how cold I was as the wash of heat envelopes me. The arms vanish and, against my pride, a whimper slips out. Only a breath later, the weight of a blanket drapes over me and someone lifts my head enough for them to slide a warm pillow underneath it. I hear Ilithyia's concerned voice mingle with Türë's muttered reassurance. My whimper changes to a blissful sigh, and I let sleep overtake me completely.

❋ ❋ ❋ ❋ ❋

I wake disoriented, sore, and starving. I stretch my legs out, only for them to hit the arm of the couch that I lay on. Blurry memories of what had happened in the bathing chamber begin to emerge and I crack my eyelids open with a groan. Feeling the toasty pillow move beneath my head, I twist to try to squash it into a more comfortable position.

A dry chuckle greets me and I realize suddenly that what I thought was a pillow was actually Türë's lap. I pray to Jera that I hadn't been drooling, or worse, snoring. But then as I push to sitting, ready to begin profusely apologizing, he hands me a glass of icy water. Realizing how thirsty I am, I gulp it down, reveling in the chill. A wonderful balm on my dry and rough throat. My muscles quake from even that gentle of movement, and I feel like a herd of horses has run me over.

"Did I really flood the bath, then set it on fire, then flood it again?" I manage to ask, my voice rasps as if I had been screaming. I hope the fuzzy memories were all just a crazy dream. But the worry that sends a shadow across his face gives me my answer.

"Do you remember what made you so upset?" Türe hesitates before asking, "Did Ilithyia or Athene say something?"

I think carefully back, hesitant to reveal too much of what I had asked. I grow even more hesitant when the memory of Ilithyia's warning resurfaces. "No. It was more something they *wouldn't* tell me." I sigh, deciding I should just be honest. Though the voice in the back of my mind cautions me on the limit. "I got so upset at the fact that they wouldn't tell me things. That *everyone* is not telling me things." I shoot him an apologetic grimace, but continue any way when I see he doesn't look mad or offended. "I know you are all trying to protect me, but do you have any idea how hard it is to have everybody else know more about *you* than you do yourself? And then to have them determine what *I* need to know." Now that I started unfurling the anger that had been coiling like a snake in my thoughts, I find it hard to stop. I stare into the fire, trying to stop the tears that brim my eyes again. "And then I have this magic constantly stirring like a never ending *itch* underneath my skin. How do I control it? Did I ever say anything about how to help?" I heave a deep breath before turning to face Türe again with a hoarse whisper. "The way they looked at me, they were so *scared*, and I couldn't even reassure them that I wouldn't hurt them—because I *didn't know*." I feel my lip tremble and my face falls into my hands as the tears begin to fall in earnest. A tender hand presses onto my back in a careful caress, letting me know that he was there and understood.

"It is my fault." He admits, his own tone strained with pain. I look up at him, my brows furrowed in confusion. "You and I talked about it all before you left for the Awakening, and I suggested that we just take it slowly and fill you in as needed so we wouldn't overwhelm you. You actually disagreed with me then too." He chuckles softly. "But I convinced you that it would be better in the beginning for you. I should have listened then. I will let the others know that any questions need to be answered, and not make those decisions on your behalf. If you ask, you will be told. And don't worry. I made Ilithyia and Athene promise to tell no one what happened. Not even Patryk. Alright?" I nod, relief causing my shoulders to droop a bit. "As far as the powers, well, abiding by the openness you desire..." Türe pulls his hand back, and I immediately miss the warmth and steadiness it provided. I watch him as he struggles over the words. "In the past, after you went through the Awakening, you said it took decades and extensive training before any of your powers began to resurface. Even then, you said it took nearly another century before they were substantial enough to do what you just did." I mull over this revelation.

"A century." That is all I am able to get out, my words seemingly lost in the rapid fire of my thoughts. Until my mind tugs on the word he had actually used to preface it. "Wait. *Another* century." I manage to stand on my wobbly knees, and begin to pace in front of the couch were he still sits. Türe's eyes follow me carefully and I know that at the slightest inclination that I would either collapse or set the room on fire again, he would be at my side in an instant. Whether it is to catch me, or help me regain my control. Whichever happened. "You mean to tell me that all these powers should not have started to reveal themselves to me for at least a hundred star-cycles?" I need to hear the confirmation, to be sure that I understand.

Nothing, you understand nothing of this.

I almost growl aloud at the inner voice that seems to be egging me into the flames, water, and lightning. He watches me carefully. Eyes wide as he tries to determine if I have snapped already, or am about to. Whatever conclusion he comes to ends with a nod. I feel a stone settle in my gut.

"One hundred and sixty five star-cycles last time, according to your extensive notes you had kept, if I remember correctly." He admits with a shrug. "The time before that it was apparently even longer then. Though only slightly. One hundred and ninety something, I think." I chew my lip and turn to face the fire. I try to puzzle out the various possibilities of what this could mean. Even behind my eyelids, the glow of the dancing fire is bright, stoked on unintentionally by my racing thoughts.

"Okay, well maybe after each Awakening the powers reappear more quickly? Just part of the whole process..." I turn back to face Türë, my hands gripped tightly around each other and only when I feel the sting of my nails cutting into my sensitive palms do I release the pressure. He thinks on this, giving no clues to what he theorized about it all.

"Possibly." He responds.

I growl again in frustration at the evasive answer and his brows raise in surprise. I fight my immediate reaction, which is to apologize for it. My anger wins out in the end instead and I stride towards the door that leads to the hallway beyond. Before I can make it ten steps however, Türë intercepts me halfway. Not to stop me, or even to respond with his own frustration.

"I'm sorry." He forces out. "I am trying. I just don't—" He runs his fingers through his hair and I notice then how drawn his face is. How shadows now hang beneath his piercing eyes. I realize that I am not the only one this is having a heavy effect on. And from his reaction, it is obvious I am not the only one who is completely lost and scared. I reach out and take his hand into mine from where it hangs clenched at his side. I feel his muscles tense from the action, but he doesn't fight me as I pull it closer. One by one, I pull each finger free of the ball they had been pulled into, until his hand lays loose, cradled atop my own palm. I trace the lines that make up the hand that dwarfs my own, somehow soft and warm, yet still firm and cool against the fire that now purrs beneath my skin. I feel his eyes on me, but I don't take my own off of the tapestry of scars, grooves, and calluses that weave across his skin. *Jera help me, this is just his hand.* It was clear from the long-healed wounds that he was a warrior— one who is deadly and ancient. I realize how lucky I am to have someone who had decided I was worth spending time with for the last few hundred star-cycles. I look up to meet his gaze. A fire of a different sort alights in his eyes, each one a pool of melted chocolate that sends a shiver from my toes up to where our fingers still touch. Against my will, I swallow hard and pretend not to notice as his eyes flick down to my lips that fall open as I try to catch my breath. *I want him.* My mind registers this as my body seems to beg for him. His touch, his kiss, his gaze on every inch of my body. Türë's eyes return to mine and he too seems to be suddenly breathless. The longing to close the distance and melt into each other is near irresistible. *Damn the consequences.* I take a step closer until his still outstretched hand tucks against my ribs. Against my chest that heaves with my rapid breaths. All it would take would be for him to lean down and to claim my lips that his gaze keeps returning to.

The door suddenly opens and, before I can blink, Türë is gone. I whirl around as my mind tries to catch up with what had just happened. Instead of Türë standing in front of me, it is Ivrik. The reminder that the Underkings were waiting to meet snaps through me. He stops in front of me, his eyes narrowing to examine the look on my face. I am sure it was a comical sight; cheeks bright red, chest heaving in gulps of air, and still blinking like a mad woman. I turn slowly to find Türë lounging on the couch in front of the fire, as if nothing had happened.

"Let's *go!*" Ivrik snaps impatiently, wrapping an arm through my own and tugging me until I begin to walk. I turn back to look again at Türë, who follows without another word. I truly begin to wonder if I had dreamt it all, but then I see the flush on his cheeks, twin to my own. I watch as he gently unclenches and examines the palm I had held in my own so carefully mere breaths before. *It* wasn't *a dream.* I reassure myself, but then I silently groan when I think about the complications I might have just caused as Türë glances up to find me watching, before looking away again, just as quickly.

What am I doing?

eighteen

That night I, yet again, find myself wandering into the gardens as the moon reaches its peak, staring up at the star-pricked sky. And again, Türë finds me. Sitting with my back pressed against the bench made of vines, I pull my knees to my chest, attempting to ward against the chill that manages to cut through even my cloak. I hear his footsteps first. And I know at least enough about him now to know that it is only because he wants me to. I don't look towards him this time. My eyes stay locked on the navy blanket that stretches above the world. He doesn't say anything, obviously gleaning that tonight's mood was different. It wasn't anxiety keeping me awake tonight—it was fear, confusion, and the overwhelming desire to *scream*. My introduction to the other Underking, Eivan, had gone well—good even. Unfortunately, it had been marred by the lingering itch of what Türë had at last confessed to me. Confirming something I had begun to fear, even on my first night in the forest.

This time it is different. Something has changed.

"I—" My voice cracks and I cough to clear the emotion that had peppered holes in my voice. "I need to know how to control myself. Do you know how I learned before? You mentioned that I had kept extensive notes prior to my first Awakening for myself. Would those be of any help?" What are the chances that they even still exist after two thousand star-cycles? Unless I had taken attempts to preserve them, they were no doubt dust in the wind after that much time. The guarded look and silence that follows answers my questions enough. I pull my knees in tighter as an especially powerful burst of wind buffers against us and tugs at my cloak.

"I don't know how you learned last time, other than the notes. And no, you unfortunately burned everything after you decided you had re-learned what you needed to." He refuses to meet my eye at this revelation, though thanks to my Sidhe ears, I hear his heartbeat increase suddenly. I gape at him, not wanting to understand what he had just told me. The muscle that tightens and flutters in his jaw, coupled with the sudden anger that burns in his dark eyes, tells me of his own fury at that decision. Silence overtakes us and whole minutes pass before he speaks. "The *plan* was that when you were ready we would begin your training to, hopefully, ease you into your strength and abilities. But now..." Türe trails off, tracing the etching I had noticed yesterday. *Maybe he knows what that means.* I can't help but think, then realize that in the scope of all the questions I had for him, *that* definitely was not on the top of the list.

"What is different now? What changed? Other than the speed of its return, of course."

"Your strength, out of the gate, is more than I can help with. If I push you too far, or you lose control, there will be nothing I can do to stop you. It is not like last time. When I still had my full magic it was different." He continues to trace the stone until he at last seems to realize I have gone rigid. Once he glances towards me, brow furrowed, he sees the look on my face. And realizes what he just said.

"*Had* power?" I rasp. "But the other day in the field, you caught me when I nearly fell off the horse."

Türë only sighs, apparently frustrated at his slip and the direction this conversation had taken. "I used to be much stronger, almost as strong as you. Now I can only do small magic. And even that drains me." He does his best to conceal the true pain he feels at the loss, but I can see it in the lines of tension in his shoulders and the way he clenches his jaw even tighter. In the way he too looks up at the night sky.

"How did—" I begin to ask, then hesitate, wondering if it was too personal of a question to ask.

He chuckles, the sound low and rumbling, returning his attention to the garden around us. "It's a long, complicated story, and one I am not in the right mood to re-live." In other words, he was not going to tell me. Not any time soon. I suppress the annoyance of him already going back on his promise to answer any of my questions. The promise he had made mere hours ago.

Technically he promised to tell me my *story. Not his own.* I try to rationalize and not snap at him in my re-surging frustration.

"Okay. Well, I still think you are the best option I have. Whether you believe you are strong enough to stop me or not." He snorts a sarcastic laugh, but I ignore it. I reach out and grip his hand tightly in mine, spinning to face him, fully sitting on my knees and ignoring the sharp stones that dig into my kneecap. The touch between us now differs completely from what had been between us this afternoon. Not warm and electric, but cold and desperate. "Somehow, every time, you have been able to pull me out of it. You have been able to help me control it. And unless you know of any other Sidhe that knows my secret and would be willing to help me… then you are my only hope." Türë's hooded eyes convey nothing of his thoughts. No glimmer of a window into his emotions. At last, he releases a sigh before nodding, albeit extremely unenthusiastically.

"Very well. We will start your training in the morning." Narrowing his eyes to a glare, he adds, "but if you think I am going to take it easy on you because you are my Queen, understand now that is not how I train. What I ask of you in training, I expect you to comply." I swallow hard as sudden nerves surge in the pit of my stomach. I realize then I am still grasping his hand and release it with a nod.

"I also plan to rejoin the Nefriti in their training. Beginning tomorrow." I say, choosing my words carefully. Making sure that he understands this is not a request for him to agree to.

His eyes dart to mine in surprise, and he opens his mouth to respond.

"Türë," I start, deciding that if we were going to take this opportunity to clear the air, I should try to figure out what to say regarding what had happened between us this afternoon. The sound of footsteps approaching has us both turning towards the unexpected company, however. Türë quickly launches to his feet when the door to the garden pushes open to reveal Ivrik. Reaching a hand out to me, Türë pulls me to standing and I dust off my cloak as we walk, meeting Ivrik halfway down the garden path beside a large bubbling fountain. In the moonlight, he looks exceptionally pale, the silver tones in his hair almost shimmering in its luminescence. I begin to wonder if everyone in this castle has trouble sleeping as he gives me a wan smile.

"May I have a private word?" Ivrik asks Türë, his eyes wide with something unspoken. If Türë is worried or baffled, he doesn't show it. Instead, he turns to me.

"Do you know the way back to your rooms, or shall I call for someone?"

"I know the way now." I answer, my chin held high, not trying to hide my pride at that fact. I had made sure to memorize each turn he had led me through the night before. "Goodnight Ivrik, Türë." I drop a curtsy and give them each a smile before passing and heading for the door. They purposely wait until I am out of ear shot before speaking. I reach the door and turn back, hand resting on the door knob, my smile dipping into a frown. I wonder what it was they didn't want me to hear. Whatever their conversation was about, Ivrik looked…shaken. And Türë, well he was the stone-faced Sidhe he became whenever he didn't like what he was hearing. I shake the thoughts away, and slip through the garden door back into the palace. Whatever it was, they didn't want me involved. Besides I had enough to think on for one day. And now, starting in the morning I had my first day of training.

By the time I make it into my bedroom and discard my cloak, slipping in between the warm covers of my bed, I actually feel excited about tomorrow. *Finally I might better myself rather than continue feeling out of control. Tomorrow will be a fresh start, and one in the right direction.* I turn my face to the balcony windows, looking out at the stars still hanging bright in the sky. I picture the image of the warriors, dancing around each other as they duck and weave from the training blades. At last, I fall into a deep sleep.

As much as I initially insisted that this cabin was ridiculous, I have grown to love it. Our neighbors, miles away, have no idea that we were, in fact, the King and Queen of their kingdom. And we enjoyed immensely vanishing from society.

It had been his idea. A small, one bedroom cabin in the middle of the plains outside of Anopthe. Our own place to disappear to.

To be just us.

I had laughed when he first brought the idea up. Now?

I am elbow deep in bread dough, flour scattered everywhere, when he enters the cabin. I turn, then freeze, raking my eyes over him, head to toe, without shame. He hums a familiar tune to himself, arms full of the wood he had spent the afternoon chopping. Blessedly shirtless and dripping with sweat, his sculpted body almost begs me to lick every single one of his muscles. He pauses in the doorway, feeling the weight of my attention. He, in turn, takes every inch of me in before dropping the freshly chopped wood into a pile, not caring as it cascades in front of the door, blocking the entry, and advancing towards me. His eyes grow increasingly ravenous with each step.

I instinctively gulp and take a step backwards, my legs pressing against the wooden table behind me. This doesn't affect his feline-smooth approach. If anything, it encourages it. Bracing an arm on either side of my waist, our faces, our bodies, end up mere inches apart. Close enough to join into one, his breath sends tendrils of my hair dancing as he moves in even closer. His warm lips brush against my earlobe as he whispers. "You, my love, are covered in flour."

"Am I?" I ask breathlessly. His attention focused on kissing the tender skin beneath my earlobe, he doesn't notice as I softly scoop up a handful of flour. Not until I reach up and release it above his head. The powder coats us both, head to chest, and he gapes in shock before throwing his head back and roaring a laugh. I shriek in surprise as his arms suddenly wrap tight around my middle and he lifts me off my feet into a tight hug. "As if I thought I would get enough of this in the garden that night. Of you." His damp, sweat-soaked hair from chopping wood falls coldly onto my neck and a shiver vibrates through me. His words register, and I pull back, far

enough that our eyes can meet, my own arms rest on his shoulders. A playful light joins the longing that dances behind his unrelenting gaze. I smile back, still breathless and at a loss for words. "I love you, more than words could ever possibly say." He sets me down and pushes the few loose strands of hair back from my face, before his hand, warm from the fire-heated kitchen, cups my cheek. "My Evara." I lean into the touch. "I should apologize for pushing this morning... I know your reasons are valid. I just still wonder at how I am lucky enough to be the one for you, and those insecurities came through at the wrong time and in the wrong argument." He strokes my flour dusted cheek, leaning his forehead in to touch against mine. "I lost you once. It is hard to forget how long you looked at me like I was a complete stranger." He confesses.

"I know. I am sorry that I had to put you through that. But you know that it was the only way to keep my power from overtaking me. My letter said it was growing uncontrollable, remember?" I don't mention to him that already I feel it rising. Worry chases me everyday with what it could mean. The implication that the reprieve and time my past-self had bought with the Awakening was growing less and less keeps me on edge. Was the Darkness just going to keep calling to me until I gave in and became the very thing I held at bay?

I always tell him everything.

Except for this.

I don't even want to speak aloud the doubt and fears that plague me almost daily. And the terror that had rushed through me at the question that he had posed this morning had shaken me to my core. We had never discussed children, but now we were married it shouldn't have surprised me the topic had at last arisen. I shake my head and the words away. "Everything else aside though, there is no one else in this world or the next for me, my King. Trust me. I have been around two thousand star-cycles and spent all of it looking for you." He quirks a smile, though I see doubt flicker there, before leaning in tentatively, as if waiting for my rejection. My heart aches at his uncertainty. There just weren't words in existence to convey my love for him. I can only tilt my face further up, encouraging him. He devours me with a deep, gentle kiss that sets my knees trembling. I knew him well enough to know he still wonders at me choosing him. I kiss him even deeper, trying to pour my unending love for him into the touch. The Goddess herself had declared us soul-bonded at our wedding. No matter how many lives we lived, and were parted, we would always come back to each other.

A clap of thunder startles us both, setting off a round of laughter as we cling to each other in surprise.

"I love you." I murmur again, wrapping my arms around him in a tender hug as we watch the rain outside pour down.

"Forever." He says.

nineteen

This morning I had woken before dawn from a wild dream. My mind races from a mixture of arousal and curiosity. Mainly it lingers on one thing. Who was that man? Most of the dream was foggy, but the parts I did remember—*damn*. I shove the dream to the back of my mind and. In an effort to distract myself, I had decided to bathe and dress before Ilithyia came to help me. I mentally review through the breakdown of information that Ivrik had yammered away last night, giving me a crash course on the Nefriti and what to expect.

The Council of Elders has five members, two Magnar, two Tomyris, and me. I struggle to remember their names. Elder's Dakar, Makal, Ygrette, and Varine. They are the upholders of tradition and are the final authority. To become Elder, you have to win a battle challenge to take the place of a previous Elder—one to the death. All Nefriti, once you had passed the final trials to become one, were given the honorific of Viktu. *Tomyris and Magnar were given* Eliviktu.

Ivrik had then delved into describing the various ceremonies and explained the scarring, *Ynrya* lines, he called them, that marred, especially the Tomyris and Magnar's bodies. As hard as I try to recall it all now, the information turns into a jumbled mess instead. I forgo this for now and focus on remembering the things that I would have to utilize most today: the titles and hierarchy levels among the Nefriti.

Turning my attention to the day ahead floods me with nervous excitement. Bleary-eyed, Ilithyia had walked me down to where I was supposed to meet the rest of the Nefriti, and then departed with a yawn and a half-hearted *good luck*.

Elder Dakar did not bow upon my arrival. Though I didn't expect it of people, he had been the first to not at least volunteer to do so. If that had not clued me into his stern, unyielding character, the fact he had immediately begun yelling at me to get into line, with hardly another look, certainly should have. Starting off with what he called a 'light run' the group of warriors take off at a brisk pace that has me grunting in pain within minutes.

But they are expecting their queen. Their fearless, strong, relentless queen. So I do not let myself stop. Even when it feels like I am inhaling shards of glass. To my disappointment, I end up at the back of the group, with a warrior named Arne, who introduces himself between my gulps of air, as a new recruit that had been a part of the ten that just started last week. Even though the newest were in great shape already, it was clear they were not yet to the caliber of the Tomyris and Magnar, who lead us all with ease. I had tried not to stare at the painted scars that stripe their arms and chests. The *Ynyra* lines were beautiful, in a morbid way, and made the difference clear in the Eliviktu versus the Viktu. I spot maybe one or two marks on the Nefriti I am surrounded by, which is nothing compared to the dozens marking those that lead the sprint.

We end up running around the entire city at a brisk pace, and as we approach the pit that I had spotted them training in two days before, I feel my stomach sink. My worry is only confirmed as people start lining up in organized rows. Spread about ten paces apart from the next, I watch as people start stretching, jumping, and swinging body parts around.

That run had just been the warm up.

Not even ten minutes in I already dream of slicing a dagger through the heart of the giant drum that beats in time to our movements. Sweat pours down my face, back, arms, hell even my quaking legs now. I gasp for breath and take advantage of the break in exercises. Arne, who had chosen the spot next to me, shoots me a look that says he shares my misery as I spout off a stream of curses. I drop my hands to rest on my knees, not even three breaths, before Elder Dakar shouts over the drum at me. I raise my head up to meet his icy glare with my own. *What the hell is his problem?* But I continue along with the others, even as my mind drifts to thoughts of my warm bed and the lull of sleep.

"I know they said he was a hard ass, but I thought he might at least be a little nicer to you." A woman named Helene who is set up on the other side of Arne grumbles as we do a series of squats that have my knees wailing in despair.

"I know, right?" I can't help but agree with her. It wasn't like I wanted special treatment, but at least some respect of my station.

"Wait, has he not always acted this way to you?" Arne asks at the next pause in the set of movements as we all move to the ground.

Shit. I lay on my back, preparing to hike my hips up for the next set of exercises. My mind races to come up with something to say that wouldn't be obvious that this was my first time to this training. It was a very different, much stronger, much more bad ass Queen who they were thinking of. *Definitely not me.* "He has." I say, hoping it was the truth. "It just gets me every time, you know?" I thank Jera they can't see my face. No doubt it was a dead giveaway that I had no idea what I was saying. At this point, it is taking all of my focus to not pass out from exhaustion and pain. Thankfully they must buy it, because no one speaks again for a long time, we all are too focused on moving our muscles in the complicated instructions barked out at us from the podium.

I nearly cry in relief when the Elder calls out final set, and by the time that is done, I am uncertain if I can even hold out through another second of standing—let alone walking out of here. I fight to keep my eyes open until I spy a familiar white blond haired man climbing the stairs to where the Elder glares down at all of us. Ivrik has a conversation with him, his back to all one hundred and sixty-eight of us that wait, sweating and shaking, for next instructions.

"What do you think they are talking about?" Arne asks Helene, then both of their attentions shift to me. I almost ask them why I would know, but thankfully bite down on that before it can slip out. Instead I stay quiet, taking advantage of the moment to catch my breath, not taking my eyes from the two men who remain locked in quiet conversation.

Finally, they seem to come to a resolution as Ivrik turns, leaving the podium and walking down the center aisle of the warriors. He pauses at the start of the row where I stand, Helene and Arne staring at him in awe before lowering into a bow and muttering *Viktu Ivrik*. Ivrik only smirks at their attention before turning his to me.

"Your Majesty, there is a matter I need to discuss with you. The Elder has dismissed you. Please follow me to the throne room." I feel my jaw drop, then close it with a loud snap. I start to take a step towards him, before I remember that here I am equal to the rest and pause to dip into a respectful bow towards the Elder. He simply waves his hand in dismissal, though I swear I see a pleased tug of his lips, before returning his attention to the rest and resuming giving instructions. Without another moment's hesitation, I stride on shaking legs to Ivrik, praying to Jera my body will hold out another few minutes.

"What is the matter?" I ask the second we are out of earshot of anyone else. I flash to the image of him and Türe in the garden last night, and a wave of fear washes over me. Apparently, I had been right to worry.

He laughs quietly before leaning in to whisper to me, even as we stride at a quick pace from the training pit and into an empty hallway. "Nothing is the matter. I had been watching and thought you would keel over and die if you had to stay there another second, let alone for the rest of weapons' training."

I blanch. "There was *more?*" I groan, then feel gratitude wash over me for Ivrik. "Jera help me. Thank you for the rescue." He just laughs and slows his rushed walk down to a casual stroll.

"It was the least I could do. I honestly was a bit surprised you made it even through the run. Then to keep going... I was beginning to worry your heart would give out after four thousand star-cycles, simply because you were too stubborn to refuse to do a set of crunches!" His voice is light and teasing, so I am not offended.

"It's harder than I thought." I confess, my voice soft enough that he glances over at me in concern. "I know everyone has this idea of who I should be and what I should be capable of. Even if they don't realize it. I try to keep up, and to be as close as I can to that person. But those warriors," I gesture back the way we come where the drum still beats. "They have an expectation that I am one of them. And rightfully so, because I have been for the last however many centuries!" I huff a sigh of frustration, letting my hand fall back to my side. "How am I supposed to keep up with *that?*" I roll my eyes and playfully glare at Ivrik, who watches me with a soft smile. "Without my heart giving out after four thousand star-cycles." He tilts his head, and thinks before responding, all trace of teasing gone from his face.

"Do you want my actual answer?" I blink in surprise before nodding. "It has been my opinion all along that you tell them."

"Tell them?" I can't keep the surprise out of my voice.

"Yes." He responds with a single shrug. "They are your brothers and sisters in arms, some of your most loyal followers and citizens. *Every single person* in that arena would gladly, enthusiastically, give their life for yours without a single hesitation or regret." He points emphatically back towards the training pit. "That level of loyalty, in my opinion, should earn at least a little trust." I stare at him.

He was right.

There was no way you could argue with that. It had not really made a lot of sense to me from the get go, this plan to not tell anyone about the fact my memories were gone. Okay, I could understand not telling the greater populace. That would put the safety of the kingdom at risk if our enemies found out Tesindren's primary protector had been wiped clean. But I had, obviously, decided to tell my Underkings and the most trusted others, such as Ilithyia and Athene, to help me learn and adjust to my new mind and abilities. Why would that logic suddenly be inapplicable to the warriors whom I had bled and lost with?

"You are right." I say, not bothering to hide my surprised tone. He blinks a few times in astonishment, as if he had been prepared for an argument. "You are right." I repeat, reaching out and squeezing his hands in silent thanks. "I will arrange a meeting to inform Elder Dakar tomorrow and will get his advice on how to proceed with telling the others in a confidential way." His grin is so wide and unrestrained it lights up his pale face. He tugs me into a hug and places a gentle kiss on the top of my head. I blush, and that only makes his smile grow wider.

"You will not regret it." He states firmly. "Isolating yourself from those closest to you only makes you vulnerable." Ivrik makes the comment in passing, but I can't fight the chill that races up my spine at the words that ring so similar to the ones Ilithyia had whispered to me.

Ivrik had raced off immediately after ensuring I made it back to my suite to set up a meeting with Elder Dakar. I smile to myself at the memory of his face lighting up as I peel off my sweat slick clothing. Each movement warns me of the pain that is to come. My muscles wail in protest of each movement. Stepping into a freshly laundered pair of loose silk pants and knitted top, I sigh in relief before sinking into the velvet couch. I lounge back and stare up at the illustration on the ceiling, mulling over how exactly I am going to explain to the wildly intimidating Elder the truth when I remember Türë. I groan and flop an arm across my eyes. He is going to be seriously angry when he hears what I am about to do. Though Ivrik hadn't said outright or even hinted at whose idea it had been to keep everyone not deemed necessary in the dark about my *situation,* I knew that it had been Türë's idea none the less.

Then another realization hits me. I had promised Türë that today I would begin my magic training, too. I groan, then wince as even just making the sound tightens my abs and sets them on fire. Yeah, I was definitely going to be in serious pain.

❋ ❋ ❋ ❋ ❋

Hours later, I limp into my bedroom again. This time I am covered in soot and I think that, despite the bucket of water Türë had dumped over my head, I am still smoking slightly. Ilithyia lounges on a chair filled with pillows, waiting for me, and looks up in surprise when she takes in my worn figure. Launching to her feet, she darts into the bathing chamber and I hear the water begin to splash into the tub. She reappears and begins to wordlessly help me remove my singed jacket, easing the sleeves free.

"I don't think I will be able to move tomorrow." I moan as she leads me slowly into the bathing chamber where the steaming tub is filling.

"You will." Ilithyia tinkles a laugh before moving to tug the last of my clothing free from my near immovable limbs and helping me into the water. She grabs for a large glass jar filled with sparkling crystals and dumps a few handfuls into the water with me. I eye her warily. "It is a salt mixture that you perfected a long time ago to help ease your muscle pain after battles or really intense training days." I lean my head back, luxuriating in the soothing warmth and scent that envelops me. Ilithyia begins to wipe at my face, at the smudges of black soot that coated my skin in a thin blanket. Relaxing into the touch, I almost fall asleep right there, but Ilithyia interrupts me. "So, how did it all go?"

I fill her in on the nightmare that had been this morning's training with the Nefriti, then my decision to tell the warriors the truth about their queen, and finally the magical training that I had endured with Türë.

"It all started with breathing, like he showed me in the woods. But then he started shooting fire arrows at me and insisting I divert them! Basically, he kept doing crazy things to irritate me to the point of anger, and I essentially exploded into a living fireball. After that, he had me focus on the sensation and try to repeat it. Nearly ten times he had me do that, but then I got too exhausted and my clothing caught on fire. He had to dunk me in a nearby horse's trough a few times to get me put out fully. Even then, he had to empty the water bucket over my head to get the last few flames." I splash my face a few times with the fragrant bath water and try to rid myself of the embarrassment. "I knew it would be difficult, but…" I confess, trailing off.

"But not to that level right away?" Ilithyia finishes for me, her voice sympathetic. Her tender touch washes away the remnants of the day as she rinses my hair one last time before wringing it out. "I think you should be proud." She states matter-of-factly. "I don't know anyone else who has ever gone through what you have, in the last few days alone, mind you. Let alone continue to strive to do better each day when you have every excuse in the world. You could decide to not train with the Nefriti any longer, or to let your Underkings continue to rule without you overseeing. You could make every attempt to stifle your power and hide out in your rooms. Nobody would blame you in the slightest. But you don't. And that is why I am proud to have you as my Queen, why I believe you will master it all, even if it takes a little time. And why I *know* Jera chose well." She stands and walks away without another word. I hear the door to the bathing chamber shut and the slight creak of the chair in the next room as she returns to it, giving me a breath of privacy to relax and allowing me simply to have a moment to myself.

Tears fill my eyes as her words repeat in my heart, and I don't stop them from falling down my already steam damp cheeks. I didn't know how badly I needed to hear someone tell me those things. Until now.

twenty

"Again." Elder Dakar's firm tone echoes across the training yard and I shoot a glare that would have anyone else stumbling a few steps. But with his back towards me, the only ones who see it are Arne and Helene, who both stifle a giggle. They too pant heavily, but ready themselves to restart the obstacle course we had only just survived. I brace my hands on my knees, sweat pouring from everywhere. *Jera damn him.* I gulp in the air, but manage to pull myself to standing and back to the start of the course. It had been five moon-cycles as of today since I had Awoken. Five moon-cycles of becoming Queen—though not the one everyone had been used to. No, I had decided to just figure out who I wanted to be as I went along, learning about my kingdom, its people, and getting my ass kicked in training every day. Surprisingly, the physical training had been the easy part. Well, *easier* part. The Nefriti had taken my reveal well, and even Elder Dakar, though reasonably stunned, seemed to respect my honesty. None had gone easy on me, but I would say they were more understanding when I had run at the back of the group or failed during weapons training. Though I was improving rapidly. A fact I was proud of every day, even as I collapsed into bed. My muscles had managed to retain some of their memory there, at least.

But my magic, already having now spread to all the natural elements, still was the hardest lessons. When I wasn't dripping either my sweat or blood onto the sand and stones that made up the training pits, I was in the nearby forest, lake, or field, trying and failing to hone the power that roars inside me like the wild creature it was.

Türë had not been bluffing when he warned me of its difficulty. It was intriguing watching him become more Sidhe than human during those lessons, delving into things unknown entirely to humans. I had been surprised when he showed up one day stating he had to give a demonstration to the guards. Not the Nefriti. They had different trainings. Ones that Türë was not allowed to participate in, since he was not one of the Nefriti. I had asked, only once, why he wasn't one. Only the wide-eyed, too late warning look from Patryk stopped me from asking about it again. But I had expressed curiosity about the guard's training regimen, so Türë had arranged for me to look in. Turns out that whether guard, soldier, or Nefriti warrior—every member of my military were well-trained, honed, deadly weapons. Which made it even more impressive when Türë stepped into the ring, moving with lethal grace. Unapologetically, he had decimated the newest group of royal guards, ten strong and deadly looking men and women. All of whom had been unconscious and drooling within minutes of entering the ring with him. I had watched openmouthed at the demonstration and finally began to understand why I had chosen him to be at my side as my General all those centuries ago. When they had awoken, however, he did not mock. He took time to explain to each what their fatal flaw had been and then set about instructing them how to fix it. Because it *was* a fatal flaw. Should the worst happen, these guards were the protectors of his home, of his friends, of his Queen. Any fault in their training could be fatal for someone indeed. His words had struck something deep in me as well. A fact that I could not run from, and had to remedy as fast as I could.

All of me was a fatal flaw.

My body, my unbound magic, my inability to protect myself— all could cost me and mine their lives. This realization had set a fire in my soul, and from that point my training had become my sole focus.

Arne, Helene, and I watch a trio of Magnar set off in front of us, taking their turns on the obstacle course as we catch our breath in the burning summer sun. All of my personal guards stand off to the side in the shade, watching with barely hidden smiles on their faces. They had initially watched my training with the Nefriti with awe, though now they had seen me getting knocked on my ass regularly, the reverence had worn off. One catches me looking and flashes a grin. I learned his name was Isos. He had been the one who had first spoken to me the night I had decided to wonder aimlessly until I found the garden. After I had expanded the knowledge of my secret to the Nefriti, it became obvious that a few more people would have to be let in on my secret, mainly to aid me in unavoidable times—my chosen guards had been some of the lucky few. I make an obscene gesture at him and he laughs aloud, shifting his sword belt a bit so he can sit more comfortably. I grind my teeth as Elder Dakar barks a reprimand at my distraction.

I wouldn't say *he* had treated me differently since I had revealed my secret to him. But the others, well, their feelings of understanding had obviously shifted. It was hard to not feel a chill now when I would walk in each morning and the whispers would stop. Thankfully Arne and Helene had continued to welcome me without any judgement, as they had from the beginning.

The bell dings, signaling our mark and together we dodge, weave, jump, and crawl through the intricate loop of athletic torture. I spit blood and curses as a spinning post with multiple wooden arms circles around and smacks me hard on my cheek and chest. I sprawl on the ground, coughing and trying to right my swirling head. My jaw rings from the impact, but I still manage to hear Elder Dakar yelling at me to get up and keep going. I spit again to clear my mouth and push to my feet. A pulse radiates from me before I can stop it and, between blinks, the wooden post vanishes in a puff of smoke and ash as my fire incinerates it. Helene, already another obstacle ahead of me, snorts a laugh but doesn't stop. She had long ago stopped fearing my magic and simply called it my *tantrums* now. I glance at Arne with a grimace, and see Türe standing in the outer ring of the training pit. Great. I could now expect a lecture for losing control like that. At the moment, however, he gives no sign besides a twitch in his jaw and the barest shake of his head. I also don't fail to notice a group of Tomyris turn away from watching me with a scoff and disappointed head shake. I step through the still smoking remnants and chase after Helene and Arne, trying to make up the time I had lost, even as my stomach sinks. My cheek throbs with every heartbeat, but I still manage to catch up to them and together we cross the finish line. Our chests heaving, and lungs burning, we sprawl out on the ground—no care for our manners or the dust now certainly coating our bodies. Isos and the others all whoop and cheer for us, and I can't help but grin back at them now. I show them a smile that shows all my blood-stained teeth, courtesy of the inside of my cheek that had torn open from the impact of the post. Satisfaction rolls through me, until a shadow blocks the beating sun and I turn to find Türe staring down at me. My companions quickly pop up to standing, but I have no desire to move ever again.

"Go grab some water and cool off in the shade." Türë says quietly to them with a surprisingly proud smile on his summer-tanned face. Even though he was not a Nefriti, the legend of General Türë still held some awe for the newest initiates. Arne and Helene gape a moment in reverence before they scurry off. When he turns his attention back to me, I brace for a lashing about the post and the fire I had unleashed.

"You controlled it." Is all he says, and my eyebrows flick up in surprise.

"What?"

"You controlled your fire."

"No, I *lost* control of the fire." I stammer, but he shakes his head in disagreement. He reaches out to help me up and I groan, already feeling my legs beginning to cramp.

"You *lost* control of your temper, but your fire you kept isolated to the post that had offended you so." He explains, with a teasing nudge to my shoulder. I turn to look at the still smoldering post. *Had I actually controlled it like he said?*

"What does that mean?" I ask eventually. The responding grin that spreads wickedly across his sun baked face has me groaning aloud again.

"That means we are going to have to amp up your magic training."

✱ ✱ ✱ ✱ ✱

"You have to keep your feet *planted*, Evara." Türë growls as I fall into the sand for the third time. He hadn't been bluffing about increasing my magic training. My muscles quake as I lift the dulled blade up again, re-stabilizing my feet and bracing myself for the impact it is about to take again.

Normally, I did the physical training first with the Nefriti. Surviving the obstacle course, running, strength trainings, and the like. Then I would proceed to drilling with swords, learning new forms, and practice dueling with each other. After I had told them of the Awakening and revealed the truth of my non-existent abilities, I was now always placed with Türë for weapons training, and began to join the soldiers of Tesindren and guards of Alessandra, rather than the Nefriti. I tried to pretend it worked better with my daily schedule, rather than admit that it was mainly to avoid the unwelcoming stares. *I will get better, then rejoin them.*

Türë seemed to enjoy it greatly, teaching me various blades. Gleefully whooping my ass daily, he held back only enough so I would not zap him, or light him ablaze. But it was both disorienting and amazing to watch when he morphed from my friend and advisor, into the feared and beloved warrior that personally trained every guard and ranking officer in my military, aside from the Nefriti. Only when those guards were deemed worthy by Türë were they then sent to the various strongholds across my kingdom, selected for the palace, or chosen to become one of the rare and honored Nefriti. Even the newest arrivals were brilliant and lethal, and I could see why my kingdom had survived and thrived for so many centuries, unthreatened.

The first days after revealing the truth about me to the small group of the trainees I had joined had been a bit strained. All were cordial and overly cautious at first. So I made it a point of often joining them on their end of day commiseration at the nearby tavern, to show them I was one of them, not their superior. At least not during training. From there, we had become a group, even meeting up at the local pub on the evenings preceding our one day off each week to moan and complain about our various blisters and bruises.

Finally, the week prior, I had been granted approval by Türë to step into the dueling ring against one of the training Captains. I had actually successfully landed a blow—before he sent me careening into the stone wall outside the ring.

I missed that camaraderie now. Instead Türë and I stand alone in an empty field outside of the castle, trying to figure out how to meld the two practices into one.

"When you take your step to block, try to summon the wind to brace you." Türë says again, and I clench my teeth, growing more annoyed each time he repeats it.

"You know, no matter how many times you say that, it doesn't change the fact that *nothing* is happening."

He rolls his eyes, but lifts his own blunted weapon. I take a deep breath and try for the tenth time to do as he instructs. I call to the wind, the element we were working on today, and my favorite. It was more willing to mold to my instructions and, when it did disobey, it was much less destructive than the rest. Only a few days ago I had accidentally channeled a lightning bolt into an innocent farmer's cottage a mile away. He had been quickly and handsomely compensated for the destruction, and for his silence. I step into the move, bringing my sword forward and angled to stop Türë's steel. A sudden gust of wind ripples from behind me and I grin in victory as it tugs at my braid, pulling half of the strands loose, before wrapping around my forearm like a snake and up the extent of my blade. Together, my own muscles and the support of the wind, take the blow dealt.   Quick as the lightning that suddenly crashes down from above and joins the tangle of wind now freely circling us, I push the blade downward and twist. The look of surprise that ripples across Türë's face has me laughing aloud. First surprised pleasure at the wind and lightening, then bewilderment at the sword suddenly mid air and torn free from his tight grasp. It lands with a dull thud in the shortly cropped grass nearby and we both stare at it for a few moments before a roaring laugh comes from Türë. He crosses the short distance and wraps his arms around me, spinning me around in a circle before setting me back down, his own grin wide and proud.

"How did I—?" I ask, staring at the again quiet sky, the windless field and the sword that remains in my hand.

"A channel. That is what we have been missing. Having the sword in your hand and an object to channel your power around was the key. I got the idea this morning when you took out that pole. When your fire hit, it looked like a fist. Exactly like how you punch in your combat trainings." He shrugs, as if the idea had not been genius and probably life changing. But the joy still radiating from him says otherwise. Moving to retrieve the weapon, I have an idea and chew my lip in concentration as Türë walks the few feet to pick it up. I ground my feet and picture vines sprouting from them into the soft, warm dirt. I imagine my fingers spreading through the field until I feel the metal resting atop. I picture a hand reaching out from the vines and giving the sword a tug backwards to me. Just as Türë bends to grab it, the weapon is gone. I watch his face, doing my best not to laugh and spoil the joke. Annoyance and confusion wipe his smile away as he tries to figure out what just happened. He glances up at me and his face goes slack as he takes me in. Smirking with a sword in each hand.

His eyes widen, lips parting slightly in words he can't seem to get out. "How did you—?" He starts, and I laugh so hard and long that my core muscles begin to quake and I start to wonder if I will die from laughing. When I finally catch my breath, tears streaming from my eyes, Türë approaches and wipes them away.

"I am so proud of you." He whispers, and I swear I see silver lining his own eyes for a moment before he inhales sharply and turns towards the horses grazing in the distance. "We are done for today. Go take a bath, you smell truly awful." He calls back over his shoulder to me. I roll my eyes before cautioning a whiff of myself. I gag a bit. *Jera help me, he wasn't wrong.*

twenty-one

My day begins horribly. After being up all night, plagued with terrifying nightmares and bloody scenes that have me waking in pools of icy sweat, I finally decide to give up, throwing off the covers and digging around in my immense closet until I found what I was looking for. While it wasn't unusual for me to wander the castle and garden at night in my nightdress, I knew that I was going to be up for good, whether I liked it or not, so I might as well dress for the day. Pulling on my now favorite dark red leather pants and an emerald green dress atop them. I run a finger through my loose hair before shrugging and deciding to wait for Ilithyia's help with that. The idea of braiding seemed too complicated to do by myself. The bell tower chimes its tune and signals four in the morning. I heave a sigh as I slip out of my room and into the hall. Isos grins at me.

"Another late night jaunt?" He asks, casual yet I still see him shooting looks towards the open end of the hall, checking with all the other guards who stand ready at their posts, making sure to double check that it is safe for me. As always, his priority of his queen's protection surpasses the friendship that had begun to grow. Once he feels reassured that an assassin won't suddenly jump out at me, he relaxes—slightly.

"Yes, I think I am going to take a walk through the garden." I shrug, trying to keep hidden how much the nightmares had actually shaken me. *They seemed so real. And the man in them, he was so familiar somehow.* I feel a tingle of something slide up my back and I glance over my shoulder towards my door. I stare there for a minute, frowning at the sensation and wondering if I am losing my mind.

"Your Majesty?" Isos watches me, concern darkening his gaze. He follows my line of sight to the door and takes a step forward, voice rising loud enough that the other guards step closer too. "Is everything alright?"

I nod my head and attempt to laugh it off, but the feeling grows. Almost a breeze on my neck, but not in a loving caress, more of a warning—a hissing—in my ear. My head snaps toward it, and immediately Isos and two other guards are between me and my door. Rapiers raised, the other guards now summon their companions from where they stand throughout the wing of the castle. Two of the guards approach the door as Isos pushes me further away from it, towards the circle of guards that have joined us to guard my back. I curse myself and my lack of a weapon. But I had always been safe in my own castle. Or I thought I had been. *This is just a mistake. It is nothing!* I want to say, but that ominous feeling remains and grows with each step the two guards take as they reach the door and push it open. We all peer into the darkness. I take a deep breath and try to pin my focus, not hard since every one of my senses thrums on high alert. It takes a few blinks, my mind straining with the effort, but finally the candles in my room flares with light. Every single guard around me jumps at the sudden brightness. The two men inside spin to find the origin of the sudden light in the room.

"That was me!" I stammer, shooting an apologetic smile at them. There are a few nervous chuckles, but the tension remains thick. The feeling begins to fade and the embarrassment for causing such a commotion starts to flood me. "I think I was just imagining it." I whisper to Isos, shame flushing my cheeks. Until one of the guards inside shouts, making each of us tense and the group tightens their protective circle.

"Go get General Türë. Now!" One of the guards down the hall takes off at a sprint and my blood rushes cold. Barely a minute passes before Türë comes sprinting around the corner. He rushes to me first, the encircling guards pass to let him through without hesitation.

"Are you hurt? Are you okay?" The panic in his eyes is so fierce I find it hard to speak, but I manage to tell him I am fine. He examines me closely, head to toe. Not romantic in anyway, just pure fear and desire to resolve that trembling that only comes from assuming the worst and needing undeniable proof to reassure himself. He puffs a breath of barest relief, and then cuts a path back through the guards and into the bedroom. I shudder a bit, the look of fury that had shuttered over his eyes was unlike anything I had seen before, and I wonder what was in my room that had scared *him* so badly.

All of us wait, nervous and on edge. A few more guards go in to see if they need help, but don't return. Finally, Türë calls out the all clear and we collectively sigh in relief. Still unwilling to let me out of his sight however, Isos is my shadow as I go to Türë, who remains in the room with the other six guards.

"—didn't see anything at first, and thought there was nothing. Until Her Majesty lit the candles and we could see this." One guard was saying as I join them where they stand around my bed looking closely at something. I don't understand at first, but then I follow Türë's unmoving glare and my heart leaps into my throat. I fight the urge to be sick. Against the headboard, was pinned my cloak. No—not *pinned*. Two gleaming ornate daggers hold up the cloak, one positioned in the throat and one in the heart. I see it dripping a dark liquid and my head spins. *Blood. But whose blood??* I hear my breaths coming in gulps and I fold into myself, trying to control the magic that surges in my panic to protect me. Türë is immediately at my side, his hands surprisingly gentle as they grip each of my arms, trying to shake me from my shock. *I was* just *laying here. That could have been my body.* A shudder rolls through me and I turn my focus to Türë who is shouting something at the guards, despite not taking his eyes off of mine.

"Whose blood?" I manage to whisper out, my voice hoarse from my dry throat, and the taste of smoke coats my tongue.

"Shit." That is all he responds before giving more orders to those who scatter around me. Despite the situation, the guards who had remained in the room all flee, and I know he told them to get the hell out before I incinerated them all in my panic.

I had been doing so well. My control has been close to perfect— well I at least hadn't shocked, or burned, or doused anyone in a while. I snort a laugh, and Türë tilts his head in surprise at the sound. *He looks like Ladir.* I can't help but think, and that makes me give another sharp laugh. He takes a step back and looks around the room. I look too, and realize two things. First it was now dark in my room again, all the candles had been extinguished. Only light from the hall torches illuminate the room in its eerie distant flickering glow. And second, I see what had been causing him concern. Everywhere there had been candles, now only black scorch marks remain. *But I had regained control of myself.* I flick my eyes back to where I had been laying not an hour ago.

"Whose blood is it?" I ask again, this time my voice a lethal calm.

"An animal." My brows furrow in confusion. "A deer, I would guess."

"It's not—" I can't find the words to say, to let myself fully hope that someone's life wasn't taken in this threat to me. Türe steps closer, his hand halting in midair. Like he wants to reach out, to touch and comfort me, but thought better of it.

"It was definitely an animal." He reassures. "But this definitely is a danger. How they got in, what they wanted… if they came for just a message, or if they had actually come for you." *The message was received alright.* Another shudder rushes through me. I wrap my arms around myself, chilled to my bones, in spite of the warm summer air that rushes in from my balcony. I turn towards it, my mind in a fog.

"That's how." I point towards the door, swung open to the outside. "I had shut that before bed."

More quickly than my brain processes, Türe crosses the room and is through the door and onto the balcony. I hold my breath until he prowls back into the room, his eyes darker than normal and almost snarling. Before I can ask what he found, Patryk and Ilithyia rush in to the room. Patryk pales slightly at the sight of the blood-stained bed, but then relief as he sees Türe and me, unharmed. Ilithyia just stares, open-mouthed, in horror at the gory wall display.

He whistles slowly, shaking his head in disbelief. "Took over two thousand star-cycles, but someone at last dared to infiltrate the castle." He tries to force a smile, but only manages to grimace.

"Did anything happen on your end?" I ask, hoping that the threat was not to the castle entirely. As the Underking of this territory, he had his own section of the castle to call his own, as well as his own guards and staff. Thankfully, he reassures me that the only thing anyone had seen was in my room.

"The guards are now rousing those asleep in the Guardhouse, as well as the Nefriti, and are on high alert checking every inch of the castle and grounds. If they are still here," he shoots a pointed look at the cloak. "They will be found."

I chew my lip, knowing what we are all thinking. *They are already gone. Whoever it was, their message was delivered.*

Because there was no doubt in my mind it was just a message. The mysterious intruder had waited until I was out of the room before slipping in.

If they had wanted me dead, I would already be.

❋ ❋ ❋ ❋ ❋

What was left of the night was certainly not spent sleeping by anyone in the castle, and I certainly wasn't going to be left alone any time soon. Instead, I was quickly ushered into a secret room hidden off of the throne room. Sealed with a blood lock, only Patryk's, Türë's or my blood could open and access the room, so it was deemed the safest place of any to wait while the entirety of the staff determined that the castle was safe. I sit in silence in a large ornately carved chair and stare into the monstrous fireplace until my eyes burn. Restless, I am not sure I can take the quiet or the idea of sitting here any longer.

"What if—" I start again, but a sharp look from Türë, who lurks in the corner beside the door, cuts me off.

"We have already had this discussion. Let it go." I glare back until he sighs in annoyance. I turn my attention to the centerpiece of the surprisingly large room. A giant detailed map of all of Tesindren. I had seen the smaller ones on parchment, but nothing to this scale. I run my fingers down the Keena River all the way from the harbor at Grezon, down to where it passes through Lake Naro, and down to Charobi where the map ends—the southern border of Tesindren.

I had argued with Türë to let me go along when Noran, Eivan, and Ivrik had left for their territories about a month after I had Awakened. But it was determined that it would be too much too soon. With my magic being too unstable, they argued it was best for me to wait to travel through my kingdom and meet my people. Though now with the obvious threat that had been left for me tonight, I wondered if the castle was even the place for me to be any more. There had to be something kept from me. I couldn't believe that this *message* would suddenly come with no precursors or warning signs. I turn slowly toward Türë, remembering the night that Ivrik had come to him in the garden, pale and nervous. That had been before I understood or was aware of Türë's position in my court. It clicks now that Ivrik had come looking for the General that night, not his friend, or the friend of the Queen.

Türë stiffens as my gaze locks on him again.

"What is happening in Paith?" I ask. He only blinks in response, but the flicker of uncertainty in his eyes gives away his true surprise at the unexpected intensity of my question.

"I am not sure what you mean."

I narrow my eyes and he actually flinches. I know now that my question is on the right path. "What is happening in Paith?" I repeat, standing slowly and not pulling my eyes from his face. I force the words out through gritted teeth. The room grows brighter as the fire surges slightly in the hearth. He steps forward, hands upraised, trying to placate me.

"I was going to tell you." He starts, but then falls silent. Apparently words suddenly become difficult for him. I was interested to see how he would try to explain in a way that wouldn't light up the room. But as angry as I was becoming, more by the minute, I feel my control remain. Yes, the fire in the mantle burns hotter and brighter, but remains where it is. I let the silence hang heavy in the air, an eyebrow raised as I wait for him to explain. When he sees that I will accept nothing but the truth he sighs, his hands dropping in surrender. "It was that night about two quarters ago when Ivrik came to find me and we were in the garden." I roll my eyes but give a sharp nod.

"Yes, I figured that much out."

"He had received word that Mirinth, the country that borders us to the south, had begun moving." I let the words sink in, my mind whirling with all that implied.

"What do you mean *moving*?" I manage to ask, my tone flat with annoyance.

"They had reports of great numbers of people setting up camps and assembling in large groups south of the stronghold at Charobi."

Silence rings through the room.

"And you didn't think this was *important* for me to know about?"

"We talked and decided that you had enough going on. Even before, we would have handled it without needing to get you involved. They hadn't moved in on us, or even seemed like they were declaring anything by it. For all we knew they were building a town of their own there."

I turn to face the map, my jaw tight from fighting back the words I want to shout at him.

"And *now*?" I ask through my gritted teeth, unable to look at him. Even across the room, I hear him swallow hard and brace myself for the bad news that will change everything.

"We learned a few days ago that one of King Tanth's best captains just arrived at the encampment and our spies report military training and weapons being made."

I heave a deep sigh and stare at the model of Charobi on the map. "Have we sent any supporting forces down?"

"Yes, a legion from both Merga and Anopthe. They will be in Charobi in three days."

I nod, thankful that at least *some* action had been taken. The last few moon-cycles I had been not just training my body back into its own weapon, but every other free minute I had was spent learning about the kingdom and its various historical battles and events. Each week Noran helpfully selected and sent a book to me to read, following it up with long list of questions for me to answer and send back to him. Five moon-cycles I had spent studying my kingdom and had learned more than I had ever thought possible. Including the threat posed by the country to the south. Many decades before, King Tanth had set his eyes on my kingdom and it seemed like now he was done waiting to take it. How he had discovered that the strength—my strength—that had kept him at bay was no more, I had no idea. I jolt up straight, a revelation striking me like a bolt of my lightning.

"That's why they were here tonight." I whisper, spinning towards Türë, who I realize too late is now only a step behind me. I collide into him, but he manages to grab me and keep us both upright. We are both wide-eyed as I explain to him my sudden realization. "They were here to test and see for themselves if my power was truly gone. If the kingdom is truly vulnerable." I feel nauseous, and the room spins. I clutch at Türë's shirt, not caring about the black singe marks that burn holes in his shirt from my grasp. "They were here to see for themselves how easy it will be to conquer us."

twenty-two

By the time every last nook is checked and the intruder confirmed to be nowhere in the castle, I am a boiling pot of rage. I storm from the room, leaving Türë behind. Making my temper even worse, he has the audacity to look *bothered* by my anger. I don't know where I am going, or what I am looking for to soothe the jumbled thoughts that rush through my mind like the rapids of the Keena River. I just need time to think. From the fast-paced footsteps that follow me as I cross the throne room and out to the hallway beyond, I realize that my time of being left alone in this castle is done. At least for the foreseeable future. I hesitate at the intersection of two hallways, and a wave of sorrow sweeps through me. *I have nowhere to go, and no one I can truly trust. Türë has been deceiving me—if not intentionally, then by omission. Patryk, Ivrik, Noran, and Eivan too. And I sure as hell am not going back to my room again.* I find myself not too dreadfully upset by that decision, at least. That room had always seemed too large, too empty. Too lonely. No, I would tell them that I needed a different place to stay. I did mourn losing that bathtub though.

"Your Majesty?" A gentle voice interrupts my silent conversation with myself. I turn, startled slightly, to find one of the guards, a shorter, curly red-haired woman. Extremely young looking, she had to have enlisted for training the second she had come of age. And then risen rapidly through the ranks to become one of my personal guards already.

"Yes?" Aware suddenly of how insane I probably looked. *Maybe I am actually going insane.*

"Do you need pointed in the right direction?" She asks this with a knowing smile, though not in a haughty or insolent way. Looking closer, I remember seeing her now, on the few nights the group of guards in-training and I would go out to the local tavern. Always smiling and shy, she was pulled into our group by Isos. He always seemed to find constant reasons to have her close by, never further than arm's reach.

"Um… yes and no," I confess, smiling back at her. The once hesitant grin blossoms into a full smile. "I am not quite sure *where* to go." I look in the direction that would lead me to the garden, and back to my room. I return my attention to her. "How long have you been a guard here?" She blushes, but straightens in obvious pride.

"Six star-cycles, Your Majesty."

"Six star-cycles…" I repeat, thinking a moment. "And I bet in that time you have at least found or heard of a cozy place where, let's say, a queen can go and hide out when she needs a moment of quiet privacy."

She glances over her shoulder at the rest of the guards who stand with her, all watching to see how she would answer. I purse my lips to keep from laughing as she stammers a bit, trying to figure out how to reply.

"The rest of you can leave us. I am sure there are better places for you to be than waiting for me to make a decision." I wave them off, and they blanch, but refuse to take a single step. I heave an annoyed sigh, but try to reign it in. After all, they were just trying to do their job. It wasn't their fault I was in a shit mood today. Lighting my right palm with a tendril of blue and gold flame, and letting the electricity rise in my left palm, sparking and crackling in its own miniature storm; I meet each of their eyes. "I am the Queen, and this is my command. I am fully capable, at the very least, of protecting myself until the rest of you can come running. There seems to be a dozen of you around every corner of the castle today." They still don't take a step, but I see uncertainty flicker in their eyes. I douse the flames and point at the female guard. "Here, I will take her with me. Everywhere I go. I swear it. *Now* will you please go?" My head throbs, exhaustion suddenly sweeping through me, along with the desire to curl up in some dark corner and sob. Though disgruntled, I see their willpower give and one by one they leave, disappearing around different corners until it is just me and the copper haired girl. "Oh, thank Jera." I look up to see her staring at me, disapproval plain on her face. I blink in surprise. "Do you have something to say?" I ask, not unkindly, genuinely curious what she was thinking.

"They are just trying to help you, Your Majesty." She says, gently. Not angry or even upset. *Interesting.* "A lot of them owe you their lives, you see. They would be horribly distraught and ashamed if anything happened to you at all—let alone on their watch." I turn in the direction they all had vanished, and a twinge of regret and guilt pulses through me.

"What do you mean they owe me their lives?" From the way she had asked if I needed directions and her close association with Isos, I knew she was one of the chosen few royal guards that had been told my secret. A group of maids turn down the hallway where we stand, and we both fall silent until they pass, leaving us alone again.

"Walk with me?" She asks, pointing with her chin and sending her curly locks bouncing. I nod, perplexed at her casualness, and she leads the way down the hallway opposite the one I had become familiar with. "It was twenty two star-cycles ago, you were in Saroch," she begins, her voice hushed. I try to remember where Saroch was but struggle to place it. "It's a harbor port in South Eri, just west of the Cliffs." She turns down another hallway, I glance back over my shoulder to try an orient myself, but I was already throughly turned around. "Word was received while you were there that a ship had been spotted off the coast and it was engulfed in flames. You didn't hesitate apparently as you jumped aboard a nearby boat and single handedly sailed it out to the ship in time to rescue all on board. Once there—" Her voice cracks slightly and her steps falter. I reach out and softly grasp her arm pulling her to stop and face me. "Once there," she starts again, staring up at me, her eyes shining with tears. "It was discovered the ship was not one of Tesindren's, but Mirinth's. Though it was a merchant's ship, the cargo wasn't cloth or spices." Both her face and tone shift to one of disgust and my stomach churns with awful suspicion. "After you doused the flames and boarded to see what you could help with, you heard them—the cries of the two hundred slaves that had been packed in and concealed below." I swallow the bile that rises in my throat, and I fight the urge to interrupt her, to spare me from hearing anything more. But I have to know what happened to those people, and how they related to those guards I just dismissed so disrespectfully. "You pulled them each out, and had them board the boat back to Saroch, and then once all the innocents were free, you set the boat ablaze again." My jaw drops, the implication of her chosen words. *The innocents. Not the Captain. Not the crew.* But to my further surprise, it is not disgust or horror that shines in the eyes that look at me, but adoration and pride. "You then released every person on that ship. No—not just released." She corrected herself, pointing back down the hallway we had just walked down. "You found and gave them each respectable, paying jobs, wherever they wanted to go, and the children were given everything they needed and an education to rival the Underkings. But nearly all of us chose the option to come here and train to become a guard in your household—to protect the Queen who chose to fight for us. And when King Tanth demanded you return what was *his* and pay for the damage to the ship and crew, you told him he would have to cross your borders and declare war."

I suddenly find it hard to breathe, and I stare into the dark green eyes that look back at me without shame as the line of tears paint her cheeks. "Us?" I force out, the lump in my throat burning with each inhale as my own tears begin to fall. Each one burns like boiling water, and I wonder if there will be blisters later, showing the evidence of my sorrow. I swallow the lump in my throat and bow my head to her. "There are no words I can—" She reaches out and takes my hands and I relish the comforting contact.

"I just thought you should know. That is why many of us are slightly overprotective of you. We all care for you, Your Majesty. It might be unfair to put such expectations on you when you are going through so much, but just know that none of us are here to make life harder on you. We are here to help you, even though sometimes we don't know how to do that, any more than you do."

"Thank you." I squeeze her hand and take a deep breath. "I did need to hear that. My Underkings and General can be overbearing with their protectiveness." I shake my head. "I took it out on you all. I am so very sorry." She smiles and begins leading me down the hallway again.

"What is your name?" I ask, after a few minutes of following her in silence, digesting everything she had told me. She stops in front of a door in the middle of the dimly lit hallway, and I notice for the first time that the polished marble has shifted into faded, yet still beautiful, soft carpet.

"Rhodie." She answers before grabbing a bronze doorknob and pushing the door open to reveal a room. "And this is that secret place where no one will bother you." Her grin now borders on devious as she leads me in, and my caution quickly shifts to delight as I look around.

I am struck speechless at what the room holds. It must have been an old private office, or even a personal library. Floor to ceiling stained glass windows decorate the far wall of the room, and the colorful streams of light fill the space, large but not overly cavernous. Unlike my rooms upstairs had been, this space was cozy. Every single wall was filled with ancient thick volumes wrapped in leather and dust. I realize distantly that Rhodie is speaking to me, and I turn slowly to find her carefully lighting the numerous candles that fill every inch of spare space.

"—they used to be used. I don't know why they moved you so far away from the General, but—" She cuts herself off at the look on my face, paling everywhere except her cheeks that deepen into a ruddy shade of red. "Apologies, I shouldn't have said anything."

"No, what did you just say? Those rooms upstairs—they weren't mine *before*, were they?" The words come out almost breathless and she nods slowly. "I knew something felt off about them." I look around the room and feel more at home than I have ever since leaving the forest. "What were you saying about the General? His rooms are down here too?" I ask, wondering why this simple secret was being kept from me. Or if it wasn't truly a secret at all. *I am becoming dangerously paranoid.* I can't help a twinge of sadness at the realization.

"Just around the corner from here, actually." Rhodie admits, and I turn away from her, examining the room again as I try to mull over this newest revelation. At the doubt that now fills every thought.

"Hmm…" I spy a shut door across the room and stride over to it, hoping to make everything easy by finding a bed already there. *Then I can just inform everyone I am sleeping down here, and there will be no further discussion or moving anything.* But when I try the gilded handle, it doesn't budge. Locked.

"Damn." I mutter, and turn to find Rhodie standing by the windows, a scared look on her face. Then I see why. Taking up nearly all the study doorway stands a glowering Sidhe. I groan and turn to face him fully. I roll my shoulders, preparing for whatever lecture I am sure is coming.

"What are you doing?" Türë asks, his calm words scarier than all the times he yelled at me in the training pits.

But then I remember that I am supposed to be the one upset with him, and I straighten my spine, readying myself for the shouting match. Embracing it. "Rhodie, please give us a moment. Thank you for accompanying me on my wandering." I don't look away from Türë's piercing eyes, but I do hope that my phrasing is such that she gets the point—*put the blame on me.* I certainly didn't want her to get in trouble on my account. She gives me one last hesitant and thankful grin before slipping past Türë, like one would edge around a deadly viper.

Once again alone, Türë sighs and rubs a hand across his eyes. "Do you have *any* self-preservation at all?" His exasperation differs so entirely from the angry onslaught I was expecting, all the retorts I had prepared vanish from my mind. "We just had an intruder break into your bedroom, which is in a *tower* surrounded by multiple walls, and protected by dozens of highly trained guards. They then stake a bloody cape—*your* cape—to the wall above where you were just sleeping. And not *hours* later I have a troupe of guards come find me, frantically telling me that you ordered them away and now couldn't be found." The last word ends in a growl, but I see the true concern in his eyes. Guilt starts to trickle in again past the hard wall of anger I had built up around my mind.

"I know I shouldn't have ordered them away, trust me, Rhodie already scolded me for that." The corner of my mouth twitches up slightly at the impressed look that flashes on his face as his head tilts in the direction the guard had just gone. "I just needed a moment and I was angry and—" I take a deep breath to calm my racing heart and to slow the words that have started to pour out. All of my feeble excuses seem flimsy and selfish, now that he had laid out the danger so eloquently. "I am sorry, Türë. And I will make sure to apologize to those guards as well."

Silence fills the room and I sink into a nearby chair, staring at the carpeted floor, thick with dust. The soft pad of his steps approaching is the only noise, and for the first time since the forest, we are truly alone. He too sits on a pillowed chair beside mine, sending up a puff of dust that catches in the softened rays of sunlight that filter into the room.

"I apologize for my part, too. If I had been open with you about the threat Mirinth posed, maybe—" I silence him with the cautious touch of my hand atop his knee. He freezes, and I pull it back quickly, chiding myself for breaching the boundary we had both built up. We had never spoken of the day when we had nearly kissed so long ago. *Stupid.*

"You did everything you thought you needed to. I cannot begrudge you for that. I just wish you all trusted me more to be queen." It has been five moon-cycles, yet everyone seems to be content with me remaining as the Queen in nothing more than image. "I want you, Patryk, Noran, Ivrik, and Eivan to begin to trust me again, to *believe* in me again. Because if I don't have that, well, I might as well leave the castle and the kingdom to you five." The words, finally spoken, were what had kept me up all those nights. The thoughts I had never even allowed myself to think fully until now. "I am the Queen," I add softly, angling my head around until I manage to get Türë to look up and meet my gaze. "I need to start *being* the Queen again."

He nods and responds with a crooked smile, oddly endearing, and the first of its kind I had seen on his face. "Of course, Evara. And I am sorry if we ever made you feel less than that." He casts his gaze around the room, growing brighter with each minute as the sun moves further in the sky. "How did you find this?"

"I was looking for a new room to sleep and just happened upon it." I bluff, not wanting to get Rhodie in any trouble for leading me here if she wasn't supposed to. "There is no way I will sleep in *that* room again." I add, shaking my head. He only chuckles with a dark gleam in his eye. "Even this couch will be more comfortable than that room and that bed will ever be for me. Especially now."

"I can't *imagine* why?"

I lean back in the chair, suddenly feeling the sleepless night and the heavy weight of exhaustion that only can come from worry hit me. Together, we sit in the comfortable warmth of the sunshine and the quietness that surrounds this area of the castle. I think over the revelation that I used to be down here with Türë, and wonder why I had decided to be relocated upstairs to a brand new suite, either by him or me. But I decide against going down that road for today. Instead, I think over something that had been in my nightmare. I had been weaponless and calling out for one, though I couldn't remember what name I had been saying.

"Did I ever have my own named blade?" I ask him, and if the random question surprises him, he doesn't show it. A few days before, he had gone into detail in our lessons about various historic and powerful named blades, but had never mentioned one in connection with me.

"Yes, you carried it with you everywhere you went." He looks mournful as he explains, his brows knit together. "You called it *ahtorainë*." The word peals through me like the ringing of a bell, and I nearly gasp out as a flash of an image appears in my mind. Then, as quickly as it appeared, it vanishes again, leaving only a splitting headache and bewilderment in its wake. Thankfully, Türë is too lost in his own memory to notice.

"What does that mean?" I ask breathlessly as I try to blink away the pain that already begins to subside, rubbing my temple.

"Peacemaker." He smiles at me and then reaches to his hip, where a few of his own weapons are slung around his waist. "Unfortunately, you took the sword with you when you left, and it was not with you when we found you." Now his failure to mention it makes sense, and a wave of grief over its loss washes over me. But I look at what he unhooks from his belt and hands to me. "But you did thankfully leave your dagger in my possession. I have been keeping it safe until you were ready to wear it again." He extends the gilded sheath to me and I am unable to withhold my gasp at its beauty. The dagger he had loaned to me on my first day in the forest upon Awakening had been beautiful—but it now seems dull and ordinary in comparison to this work of art. I am surprised I hadn't noticed it before he calls attention to it now. *If this is the sheath, what is the dagger's appearance?*

I pull the blade free of its perfectly fitting cradle of leather and gold and bite my lip to stop my jaw from dropping to my chest. Dark onyx metal with gold engravings down the blade end with a carved…vine?—no, a tail. *A drakon.* I see it now, carved so intricately that the entire handle makes up the body, complete with emerald eyes and glittering ruby that captures its flicking tongue perfectly. The gold too, I now realize, adds to the artwork that this blade is. Not just simple gold engravings, but the shimmering flame that pours from the drakon's gaping and lethal maw. It takes me minutes to inspect every delicate detail, and I am left speechless. When I at last find the words, they don't seem to suffice. "It is… *beautiful.*" Türë nods in agreement, an appreciative smile on his own face, despite the numerous times I would guess he had already seen it himself. "I am surprised you were willing to give it back to me." I tease with a wink, and to my delight, he barks a loud laugh.

"I wouldn't dare keep it." He responds, eyes glittering like the drakon I hold in my hand. "The metal is actually made of a drakon scale." My eyes widen in disbelief.

"There are drakons here??"

His eyes dim, growing sad again and I know the answer before he can say it. "Not for a few millennia. They were all hunted to extinction before you took control." He clarifies, catching a glimpse of dread on my face. "That scale," he nods at the dagger, "came from the last drakon before he died back during First Tesria. His name has been long since forgotten." My mouth goes dry at the realization again of how old I truly was. Even much older than the male who sits across from me.

"And is this blade named?" I manage to ask, both in genuine curiosity and the desire to change the topic. His mouth twitches up into a sly grin before answering.

"*Nehtarûmarth.*"

"Which means…?" I prompt.

"Bane of Evil Fate."

"Huh… A little different than *peacemaker* then." I slide the dagger back into the sheath, and look for approval at Türë as I move to attach it to the simple brown leather belt already looped around my waist.

"It is yours. I wouldn't dream of taking it back." Then he reconsiders. "Well, maybe *dream* about it, but I won't." I laugh at his teasing, thankful that the ease had returned since our confrontation this morning. As the weight of the weapon settles on my own hips, I look up at him and set my shoulders.

"Okay, Queen duties. What is first?" I ask enthusiastically. He snorts in response and pushes gracefully to standing.

"Council meetings, then training, and then the Solstice celebration."

I groan, picturing the long day I now had ahead of me. *Maybe this was a bad idea.*

twenty-three

I am exhausted, but for the first time, I feel certain of my position. I had spent the morning listening to the various lords who attend to commerce, construction, and other things of the like throughout the kingdom give their reports, I was proud of how much I *could actually* assist and give voice too. I make a mental note to include an extra thanks and even a gift with my next letter back to Noran in return for all of his study suggestions and help since I had Awakened. I did notice, however, that nothing about King Tanth, Mirinith, or the intruder the night before was mentioned. Or even alluded to. *Maybe I am not the only one that they were keeping the truth from.* I am lost in my own thoughts when Türë's voice stops me from leaving the room.

"Where do you think you are going?" He asks, and my brows raise in silent question. "Just because you survived a council meeting, quite well might I add, do you really think you are now spared from training?" I try not to ruffle at the pride that shines from his face, then the rest of what he says hits me and I groan.

"Oh, come on… I *barely* slept." I try to argue, but his head is already shaking in disagreement, the General returning.

"If we were in battle, do you think that a sleepless night will stop a fight the next day? Or that it will stop someone from taking off your pretty little head?" I stick my tongue out in response, but can see that arguing is pointless. His reasoning is a sound one that I couldn't even find a rebuttal against.

I follow him from the throne room where the meeting had taken place, and try to hide my surprise as he leads me out to the garden I had spent so many nights in. The heat of the summer had reached its peak, but this morning had surprised us all with a chilly wind that seemed to whisper that summer's end was approaching.

"I thought we were training?" I look around at the peaceful surroundings and wonder what he is up to. I stand in the middle of the path and look over my shoulder at the sound of steps that enter the garden behind me. Smiling, I realize who it was.

Thankfully, they had pulled in more guards from surrounding areas and adjusted the sleep rotations of the guards in-training to ensure that more were present and fully aware on the castle premises. This meant that my trailing of guards had dwindled down to only Isos and Rhodie—both of whom I specifically requested. I also got the feeling that Türë knew I would only continue to dismiss them if a whole detail was assigned to me. The two smile back at me, and then position themselves in front of the double doors, the only way in and out of the garden. Other than climbing the twenty-foot stone walls that surround it. Fighting the urge to sigh in annoyance, I remind myself that they are only so protective because they care. I suddenly wonder distantly if Isos was one of Rhodie's companions on the slaving boat that day too, but then a soft splash has my attention quickly flicking back to Türë, who shakes free his hand that he had dunked into the garden fountain. I eye him warily.

"Splash me." He instructs, gesturing at the bubbling fountain he stands beside.

"Pardon?" I stare at him in surprise.

"Splash me." He repeats, and I try my best not to gawk at the order. Though I do catch a chuckle from Isos. I take a step forward, and extend my hand out, trying to find the connection I had managed in the field with the wind and earth.

"Breathe." I hear him say, a gentle reminder that makes me realize I was holding my breath. Minutes pass and my frustration builds at my ineffective attempt to get even a drop to move. I grit my teeth and drop my hand, my eyes wide with exasperation. I look to Türë, hoping he has some further instruction or suggestion even to help me. He studies me openly before motioning with his chin to approach. I reach his side and try to hide my swallow as he takes my hand into his own, scarred and callused grip. "Close your eyes." I narrow them at him instead, and he glares back at me until I obey. "Take a deep, slow breath." He prompts before I feel him submerge them both into the wide basin, and as the cold water wraps around my skin and his, a shudder ripples through me. Habitually, I wiggle my fingers, feeling the weightless current that flows through the fountain. I also realize how close and warm the body pressed against mine is. His chest lining up with my back so perfectly that if I leaned any closer I could nuzzle his neck. My heart thrums at the thought. *Why did I think that?* Pulling my hand from his grasp and the water, I snap my eyes open, and find his own looking down at my face. So close I feel his breath mixing with my own. He flushes and steps back immediately, clearing his throat and glancing at Isos and Rhodie, who thankfully appear to have their attention conveniently focused anywhere else but on us.

"Now, try again." Türë shoots a grin at me, daring me to do it.

"Splash me." He says again. I close my eyes, and this time instead of extending my hand out, I wiggle my fingers slowly like I had done while in the water. I picture Türë's face, how he looked at me in the bedroom all those moon-cycles ago, this morning when he had finally told me about the threat of Mirinth, and then when we smiled at me as we sat in the sunlight and he showed me the dagger.

"Evara." His breathless voice pulls me from the images and I look to see what had changed his tone so drastically. Circling around him in a swirl, a tendril of water dances around him. Glinting in the sun, rainbows pirouette across the flower beds and walls as more and more water from the fountain joins in, encircling him completely. Türë watches it, transparently stunned at the display, before turning to face me. His eyes open wide and sparkle with delight. I feel every drop of the tendril that unfurls and cascades around him and, against my better judgment, I give it a little encouragement until it obeys. Twirling upwards it tenderly reaches out, an extension of my own finger I hold aloft and, without breaking Türë's gaze, I gently caress his cheek, down his sharp jawline, and across his bottom lip. I bite my own unconsciously as I do so, and can feel every bit of his skin and stubble that the water tendril brushes against.

He doesn't move, but I see his breath hitch. For once, he doesn't pull away from the touch, or even take his eyes from mine. I smile widely, and with a bit of fiendish glee, another thought from me pools the water into a ball above his head, so quickly that, with his distraction, he doesn't see it coming. I release the tendril and it drops, dousing him from head to boot. He sputters and spits water, still staring at me. I hear Isos and Rhodie gasp aloud. I tilt my head, crossing my arms across my chest as I give him a slow, sly, wicked smile.

"You told me to splash you."

His laugh echos loudly off the stone walls for many minutes, until Rhodie, Isos, and I have all joined in, clutching at our stomachs.

Türë sketches a bow to me, his soaking hair hanging limply and sticking to his face. I still feel the touch of his skin on my fingers, and absentmindedly, I rub my thumb across them. I try to pretend I don't feel the heat of Türë's eyes on me. He straightens from the bow and indeed his eyes are on my fingertips that still tingle. A muscle in his cheek twitches, like he can still feel the phantom touch too.

"Well done, Evara. I would say you have a knack for water." His voice comes out husky, and I try to convince myself it is from the chilly water. I smile back at him and don't sense the attack in time. A set of invisible hands suddenly buffer against the back of my knees and I lose my balance, falling backwards with a gasp. It is not stones I fall against, but the full basin that swirls at the bottom of the fountain behind me. I sit up, sputtering and sopping in my too thin lacy gown, and hear Türë roaring with laughter again. I realize now that the invisible hands that had been the culprit of my involuntary swim were the same ones that had caught me before I could fall off of the horse next to the field of *florenta*. Türë's magic. I grin wickedly at him and reach for my power again, giving the surrounding water a yank that sends it shooting at Türë in retaliation. He manages to duck out of the way of the first liquid spear I launch at him, but not the second. Nor the third or the fourth. With a frustrated bellow, he races at me and throws himself onto me. Together we fall back into the pool, soaked to the bone, but still laughing hysterically. I hear the click of a door and realize that Isos and Rhodie have gone, leaving Türë and I breathing heavily as I realize that somehow I ended up basically on his lap. My shoulder leans against his strong, chiseled chest, clearly evident through the soaked shirt that sticks to every band of muscle and crevice of his torso. I fight the urge to let my gaze linger, but I shiver slightly. Unsure if it is because of the cool water that we sit immersed in, or the closeness we share now.

"I think we should probably go get dry." He murmurs, though doesn't loosen the arms that encircle my waist, holding me in place atop him. Water trickles down both of our faces.

"Probably." I agree, breathless, as my mind races through all the reasons why this is inappropriate. It was not worth the risk of losing a centuries long friendship. He was one of the leaders of my kingdom's military. I was still trying to figure out who I am. He had been lying to me for nearly an entire quarter. Really the list could go on and on. But still neither of us moved, aside from both of our chests rising and falling rapidly. I get the feeling that he too is trying his hardest to keep his eyes from drifting over my own form, as wholly obvious as his own, in the soaked gown that now sticks to every curve of muscle.

His restraint breaks first, throat bobbing the only warning sign as his eyes, now predatory, rake openly over me. I lean into him, unable to hide the action given the fact I was still sitting atop him. Thanks to the shift, I can feel the length of him that now presses hard against me. I fight the shudder that ripples through me, but fail. Catching the movement, the hunger evident in his eyes flares and I could swear he stifles a moan as I brush against him again. I tell myself it is accidental.

He slams his eyes shut, taking in a deep breath before gently rising from the fountain, though he still holds me in his arms. I wonder if it is for my benefit, legs quaking now with true cold. Or if he just couldn't bring himself to pull away any more than I could. I lean in to the warmth of his breath that ghosts against my cheek, and against my better judgement, I rest my head against his chest. We clear the ledge of the fountain pool too fast. He sets me down, making sure my legs are stable before stepping away. I realize how tired I have become from the rush of emotions that had just swept through me with the force of the water I had been flinging around. I had noticed before that with each time my control over each element increased, so did my exhaustion from it. But that was something to consider at another time. Right now, Türë stares at me, a flicker in his eyes letting me know that he was fighting the urge to do *something*. Whether it be to say something, to sweep me back into his arms, or to scold me for my actions and putting him in such a position. After all, he had never truly hinted or suggested that these feelings I was struggling with were truly warring inside of him as well. *Other than what I felt harden beneath me.* I can't help but think. I swallow a sigh. He is a man, I can't help but rationalize. Sometimes those reactions didn't require actual feelings.

I take a step back, this thought thudding through me like a stone dropped into a well. Whatever he had been debating seems to resolve itself in his mind as he too retreats back before turning and scooping up the fresh towels Rhodie had brought in at some point while we were distracted. I take the towel he hands to me with a shy, grateful grin and again the flicker of something gutters in his eyes.

"Evara!" Ilithyia's voice cuts across the silence of the garden and we both jump at the sudden sound. "What are you doing?? You may be all magical and immortal, but let's not test that by catching your death of cold." She turns her reproachful gaze to Türë, who actually looks shamed. "This dress is lace and *velvet*. Do you know what that means? It means it is ruined thanks to your actions." She loops an arm around my shoulders. I am truly shivering in earnest, now that I was far enough into the shade and away from the General's warmth. Ilithyia's arm tightens and starts to pull me towards the doors now full of Isos, Rhodie, and Athene, all who watch the ordeal with barely concealed laughter. "A fountain. Really?" She mutters under her breath and I glance over my shoulder to see Türë's lips pursed against his own grin. Our eyes meet and I smile back. Something in my heart flickers and a weird sense of wrongness simmers in the back of my mind. I shove it away.

"Would you do something for me?" I ask suddenly, my mind racing back to the present. "I need to go down to the city. *L'aiguille* is preparing a new gown for me. Would you and Athene go pick it up and make sure it is ready for the event tonight?" I thank Jera that I had remembered the dressmaker who was the artisan for all of my formal and everyday gowns. While she was notoriously hard to get along with, she indulged me each time I went in for a fitting. Partially because I was her queen, but I got the feeling that was a secondary reason. In truth, it was because I showered her with appreciation and praise each time I was in her studio. I prayed that she indeed had the gown I requested a week ago ready in time for this excuse. I had actually been planning on a different gown for tonight, one I already had in my closet upstairs. But this was a convenient excuse to get my handmaiden occupied enough so I could have a conversation with Türë. *Just a conversation.* I order myself. There were some things we needed to clear up, and that was not going to be a discussion I was having in front of anyone else. Especially if I found out that the feelings were actually only one sided.

Ilithyia and Athene both were thankfully my size and height, so in a circumstance where I was occupied and a fitting was needed, well, they could conveniently fill in for me. I pull the towel tighter around my shoulders. I force myself to meet Ilithyia's piercing gaze, but at last she concedes, taking a step towards where Athene waits with her hand outstretched for her.

"Will you be alright in your bedroom alone though?" Her eyes darken in concern for me. "After the events of this morning..." She trails off, her eyes drifting to Türë.

"Türë will make sure I am safe." I interject before they can decide whether I am capable of being alone or not. I try not to feel a pang of irritation, and to keep the snip of annoyance out of my voice. I feel the touch of a rough, battle worn hand take my elbow —not in protectiveness or control, but reassurance. In spite of myself, I luxuriate in the feeling of that simple, warm contact, and bite down on my lip as my heartbeat accelerates again. From a sideways glance and smirk he shoots at me, I know immediately he can hear it.

Damned Sidhe hearing.

twenty-four

Wrapped in a towel and shivering, I follow Türë as he accompanies me through the castle and back to the cozy study that Rhodie had shown me earlier. Neither of us speak, but I assume that a change of clothes will be brought to me here. I still felt no desire to return to the room where a stranger had snuck in. Snuck in and gotten away. There was still the matter of where I would sleep, I suppose. The study only had an ancient dust covered desk, a once fluffy chair, and threadbare couch. Until it could be arranged for a bed to be brought down, and when I figured out where to squeeze it in, the couch would suffice. I still wonder at what could be in that locked room, but decide to add that to the bottom of my list of things to figure out. It probably was no more than a dusty, forgotten coat or broom closet that wouldn't even be worth the hassle of tracking down a key. Türë suddenly slams to a halt in the middle of an empty hall and I am so distracted I run right into his back.

"Sorry," I start, peering around his tall frame to see why he stopped. We weren't at the door I remembered from earlier, though the hallway looked almost identical in its lack of traffic and use. He pushes the door open, and I am overwhelmed by his scent. Not coming from him, lingering as he steps into the dark room and vanishes among the shadows. No, the scent was coming from the room itself. *His room.* I realize with a bit of surprise. Almost half of a star-cycle of spending every day with the man and I had not once thought of where the General spent his time when not with me or training the guards. Knowing what I did about his practicality, I always just assumed he maybe slept in the barracks, or some plain, dingy tower. Not that I had even thought about it much at all. It too featured on the ever-growing list of things that I did not have time to contemplate. But now the flicker of an army of candles being lit chases away the shadows enough to give me a glimpse into yet another side of Türë.

Where my study had been ancient and dusty in its coziness and my absence since the Awakening, his was meticulously tidy. Somehow it felt *right* for him though. It was still comfortable, yet in the completely opposite way of what I was imagining. Every surface seemed to be either exquisitely carved wood, fur, or leather. The floors were a dark polished wood that was so deeply stained it appeared black at first glimpse. Softening the floor was a fur rug that sent a ripple of terror through me to consider the size of the beast it must have come from. But then, on either side of the fireplace were obviously specially chosen, well-loved, and leather-worn books. I do my best not to openly gape as I step in. And I definitely do my best to not look too closely at the bed that is tucked against the wall in the far corner of the room. A tickle of satisfaction rushes through me, against my better judgement, to see that it was only big enough to fit one person comfortably. And, not that I was looking, but no signs pointed to a secret lover that called for a bed large enough for two. While he busies himself with lighting the candles, I take the opportunity to walk through the room, running my fingers across the gilded books as I pass them.

I was reading the title of a particularly massive tome, *The Ancient Beasts That Lurk In The Shadows*, when a throat clears, interrupting my thoughts.

"So." Türë gestures with his eyes around his room, a hint of uncertainty as he seems to drink in my reaction. "This is my room, I thought you would be more comfortable changing here than back upstairs."

I tilt my head in confusion. "What about the study I found earlier?"

"I figured a warm bath would chase the chill away. If you get sick I have no doubt I will never hear the end of it from Ilithyia." He laughs a bit with the shake of his head. I catch the slip of his tongue, and my mind begins to whirl. My brow furrows as I try to detect any hidden meanings. I would like to assume that inviting me to his bedroom, then to into his bathtub, would have *some* alterior motive. But I detect nothing. I nod instead of prying that proverbial door open. Dealing with it after a bath seemed like the better option rather than freezing to death. The castle constantly remained cooler than outside, even now during the high heat of summer. From some hidden magic or if it just was the way the castle had been made, I wasn't sure.

With the upcoming party looming only hours away, I can already hear the lecture from Ilithyia if I wasn't clean and dry by the time she returned to prepare me for the night. I cast my gaze towards the door standing open, a soft rush of water lets me know that the water was already running and filling up a bath that might equal, if not rival, the one I had grown used to in my old rooms upstairs.

"Thank you, Türë." I say, passing into the bathing chamber

before I can do or say anything further to embarrass myself today. I push the door shut with a click, and lean against it, inhaling the surrounding scent with a sigh. There were things I still needed to clear up with him. Whether he realized how I was feeling, if he felt anything in return, or if I had crossed all boundaries and put him in a terrible position. We needed to be open with each other after the few electric moments we had together.

But first I needed a warm bath and a clear head.

I fight the grin when my eyes at last adjust to the dimness and see that my assumption had been right. His tub, set into the massive bathing chamber floor, did rival mine upstairs. This tub was so large I could do laps across its width if I wanted.

As the steam washes over my face and I detect my favorite scents of lavender and lilac, I knew I was going to enjoy every moment of the soak.

✾ ✾ ✾ ✾ ✾

I let myself float in the water, doing my best to shut out the numerous thoughts and unanswered questions that whisper through my mind, threatening to distract me. I sigh and raise my hand above the water, letting the drops fall slowly back into the enormous tub. Each sound echoes in the surrounding dimness. Other than the soothing glow of the candles lit in and placed methodically into carved out alcoves in the stone wall, there is no other source of light. I hear a soft knock and turn my attention to the door.

"Come in." I say, assuming that my time of hiding out is up and Ilithyia is here to help me dress for the night. Instead, it is Türe who steps in, after what was clearly a moment of inner conflict with himself. I nearly swallow some of the bath water in surprise. *Shit.* His gaze thankfully remains locked on the ceiling as he shuffles in. I quickly take stock of what can be seen beneath the still lingering bubbles and douse a few of the dancing candles that flicker around the room, plunging the tub into darkness.

"Quit staring at the ceiling before you fall in!" I nearly shout before I can delve too much into the logic of my words. He tenses, and I know that his mind whirs over the possibility of a trap. Bit by bit, I see him lower his line of sight ever so cautiously, but as much as I can tell, they don't drop past the wall on the far side of the room. My eyes had already adjusted to the dark, so I can see what he carries, and my heart pangs with appreciation for him.

"I brought you some tea." He shrugs halfheartedly, as if the gesture didn't mean the world to me.

"Thank you." I murmur, but from the way his shoulders relax, I know he could hear the depth of my gratitude for his thoughtfulness.

"Of course." Even in the dark, I see the corner of his mouth twitch upwards and feel my own smile widen.

I knew he still wasn't telling me everything, even after our conversation earlier. But right now, I found it hard to hold it against him. After all, he was only doing his best to navigate this unfamiliar territory of dealing with keeping my secret, getting me back to the woman he used to know, and helping organize the Underking's, continuing to ensure the kingdom's safety.

"Will you sit and talk with me?" I ask, careful to make it clear that this was a request and not an order from his Queen. He doesn't answer right away, and I know he is mulling over the implications of the invitation. Silence passes and my embarrassment begins to grow. I open my mouth to tell him never mind, but then I see his dark figure move. The plink of china on the tub's edge is followed by the scraping of someone sitting a few feet away. I release my held breath and feel some tension recede. While the bath was not the *most* respectable, or even practical place to have a deep conversation like the one I was about to start, it did provide a few advantages. For one, should he decide to flee I could not very well chase after him. Not without scandalizing myself and the entire castle. The second was the dark. I knew of my unfortunate ability to give away all of my thoughts with my blushing. Third, should he reject me completely, well, at least I could drown myself quite easily and spare myself having to live through the aftermath. The fourth reason was the most optimistic. Should it go better than I was hoping for—well, I would already be undressed. That thought sends a pulse of heat through me that has nothing to do with the steamy water.

A light splash, and faint outline of the silhouette across the room tells me that he has submerged his feet on the far end and I take another deep breath and try to figure out how to even broach this subject.

"About today—"

"Listen, Türe —"

We both start speaking simultaneously, then fall silent. A rough chuckle reverberates off the walls, and I grin into the darkness.

"Please, what were you going to say?" Türe starts again when it becomes clear I was waiting for him now. I summon all of my courage and nearly choke on the words I have been debating for many moon-cycles. My first few words come out as a jumble of unintelligible sounds, so I inhale deeply and try again.

"Look, I think there is something I need to tell you." Even across the pool, I hear his heart thrum louder, as if he could tell what I was about to reveal to him. I pause, giving him time to run out, if that is what he chose to do. When he doesn't, I continue. "I have been... struggling with some feelings." I strain my eyes in the dark, wishing I could see his face at the same moment I feel grateful he could not see mine. Only silence answers me, so I proceed, forcing the words through clenched teeth. "I don't want you to feel uncomfortable because of them, or for me to put our friendship at risk. But when—" I swallow hard, mustering up my courage. "—when I walk into a room, you are always the first person I look for. Even after you have been a huge pain in my ass. And you make me laugh, even when the weight of the kingdom and who I should be presses down on me so hard I can't breathe. And I don't know if you feel the same, or anything for me at all—" I break off, still staring at the soundless dark. Not even his silhouette moves to give me a clue into what he is thinking. Minutes pass. "Will you *say* something?" I whisper, embarrassment surging through me as tears brim my eyes and threaten to fall. "Or just go. I will have my answer and swear I will never bring it up again." Silence presses in. Then the shadow moves and a wave of nausea crashes into me as he stands and walks away without a word.

The wooden door shuts with a cavernous echo and I lean my flushed head against the cool edge of the tub. *You fucking idiot.* I try to steady myself with deep breaths, but the bath now feels icy as I force the tears down past the tightness in my throat. "Now you know for sure." I say aloud and listen to the words vibrate around me. I wave my hand and the candles reignite. Across the pool where Türë had sat was a platter filled with a pot of tea and a set of dry towels. No longer warm or comforted in the bath, I pull myself out. Drying off while sipping at the tea, I delay as long as I can, while trying to muster enough courage to emerge from the room. Hopefully, Türë would not be there, and I could flee to my chambers. At least until the party tonight. I groan, but grab a nearby wine-colored robe and tug it on. I notice with a heart-wrenching pain that it is a woman's. Intricately embroidered in gold and silver wolves and smelling of jasmine and yarrow. I curse under my breath. *Of* course *there is a woman. Have you seen him? Why would you assume there isn't one you imbecile of infinite proportions?* I look around for something else to wear out. *Anything* else. But find nothing. I make a mental note to never do anything this foolish again. I reach the door and stop with my hand resting on the handle, bracing myself for the reality of whatever awkwardness would be on the other side of that door. It will not come from me. I had meant what I told him—I would not hold this against him. Nor would I let my pride ruin the past few centuries of friendship. Especially not now when I needed him for, well, everything. I shake my head and lean my forehead against the cool wooden door before cursing under my breath again. I tug the door open and, holding my head as high as I can, I leave the sanctuary of the bathing chamber.

twenty-five

Tiptoeing out of the bathing chamber, I peek around the corner and nearly laugh in relief upon finding the bedroom empty. I look for a change of clothes first because, Jera bless me, if Türë caught me in his lover's clothing after *that*... I shove the thought away before it could manifest into reality. I chew on my lip, debating if it was worth it to escape in just my robe—pardon, *not* mine—and attempt to find my old study. But there I would have no clothing either and would have to wait and hope someone would find me. Or I could wait here in the damned robe, and just pray that Ilithyia, Athene or Rhodie would return soon and save me then. I am still debating the merits of each when I hear the creak of a wooden floorboard behind me. I spin towards the noise and freeze. Türë had apparently not left the room and instead had been hiding in the shadows like a ghost. His eyes land on the robe and darken with something I had never seen before. I swallow hard.

"There was nothing else to wear." I stammer my feeble

explanation. "I will buy her a new robe, whatever she wants to pick out." He tilts his head, content to watch me babble. I tug my fingers through my still slightly dripping hair nervously, before turning towards the door. *Screw it. Just get me out of this damn room.*

"I will see you later." I manage to mutter at him, rushing for the reprieve of the hallway.

"Wait." Türe says, not a shout—but in his commanding tone of the General I had come to recognize from training. I freeze, my body obeying the order before my mind could even register it. When I turn to face him again, he hasn't moved a step, but something about him has shifted. "You got to say your piece, so now it is my turn." I stiffen in surprise.

"You had your chance, and you left—remember?" I can't help but snap at him, my blood starting to heat with anger. "I know your answer, okay? Sorry for even bringing it up. I thought that you—" I sigh in frustration and shake my head at him. "I don't know what I thought, but I guess it was wrong. So, like I said, just forget it and I will never mention it again. Trust me. Never."

I spin on my heels and stride for the door.

"Did you think I was going to say what I wanted to when I couldn't even see your face?" He growls. My heart stops and I freeze, my hand hovering above the doorknob. I feel my pulse accelerate, leaping into my throat as I slowly turn back to face him. He still stands across the room, arms crossed firmly across his chest. But it is his eyes that make me pause. That has me curling my toes, blessedly hidden beneath the robe.

"What is it you had to say then?" I ask, carefully, surprising myself with how hard it is to force the words out. I try and fail to keep my voice steady, but every inch of my body quivers with nervousness.

He inhales deeply, and I swear I can feel the air pulling me in towards him. "Every time you walk past me, I have to physically restrain myself from touching you. Any time you speak, it becomes my new favorite sound. And when I enter any room, you are the first person I look for too. But then I die inside if you are smiling at anyone else. Rhodie, Isos, Athene, Ilithyia, Patryk... Ivrik... Anyone. I wouldn't feel like that because you were happy. But because in that moment, I wanted to be there and to be a part of that joy. For so long I have restrained myself because it would be inappropriate for me to approach you as I wanted to. For a multitude of obvious reasons, that I am sure you have recognized. But most prevalently, because you had so much going on. How unfair would it be for me to put my feelings upon you too?" He starts to pace slowly towards me, his face shifting from pained into hope with each step he gets closer. I am fully aware that my mouth has lain open in a silent gape the entire time he speaks, but I can't find the time for a spare thought to close it again. My mind is too busy trying to remember each word he says.

"Why did you think it would be unfair?" I manage to ask, breathless, as he stops close enough that I can feel his warmth through the thin robe.

"How could I ask you to choose me? Over the centuries you have had innumerable options. How unfair for me to try to snatch you up before you had the chance to see the world and all of those options with fresh eyes. Hell, even Ivrik..." He trails off at the confusion that snaps across my face.

"What about Ivrik??" I ask, completely bewildered. Türë looks regretful at bringing it up. He still answers me, though he retreats a step while doing so.

"Back when you two first met, about twenty star-cycles ago, he tried his hand at winning your heart. You let him down easy, then told him he could still be Underking only so long as his feelings wouldn't get in the way of his duty, and wouldn't compromise your friendship." He shakes his head with a snort. "On the trip returning here after the Awakening, the entire time he was testing the waters to see if this was his second chance." Something akin to satisfaction darkens his amber eyes and he lets loose a rough chuckle. "That day he walked in on us in the bedroom, he realized, I think, he had no chance yet again. He left the next day, if you recall." I roll my eyes at such a blatant display of male territorial glee, but I step closer. Closing the slight gap that he had put between us at the mention of other men, I see his pupils dilate. In spite of my earlier resolution to never do anything stupid or courageous again, I reach out and trail my fingers down the side of his arm. In the time I had been in the bath, he had changed out of his own soaked clothes and was already dressed for the Solstice celebration that was happening that night. The shirt was a crisp white, pulled tight across his chest thanks to his toned muscles that strain against the seams. I had seen him in the training pits only once this summer with his shirt off. The heat of the day too much for even him to remain in his usual black and gold doublet as he sparred with one of the other guards. When I had one day gained the courage to ask him why he opted to stay covered, he only looked at me curiously, an eyebrow raised in an unspoken taunt. "If you and the other women are expected to remain fully clothed in the heat, why should I not be tormented the same? But if you want to see me shirtless more often, you just have to merely request, my Queen." I smile at the memory and flick my eyes up to him. From the humored glint in his eyes, I would guess that he is remembering the same conversation.

I pull my hand away from his arm, not to stop touching him, but to instead move my fingers to the delicate bone buttons that clasp it shut. I look up at him as his breathing catches beneath my touch. Eyes wide, his mouth quirks up at the corner and he raises his hands to wrap around my own. Not to stop me, but to undo the first clasp, his consent—his plea—to continue. I don't unlock my eyes from his as I undo each button, slowly driving the both of us mad. I pull the panels of cloth apart and nearly melt as I at last lower my gaze to take in the tanned and toned planes of his chest. Flecked with faint white scars, that I feel confident in assuming were older than most inhabitants of the castle. I trace my fingers across each one of them until I come to one that is much larger and in a much more worrisome spot. A silvery palm sized splash of skin on the right between his heart and stomach is all the remains of what appears to be an axe or spear wound. And from my training on battle injuries, one that I know should have been fatal by all accounts. I trace the outline around the faded wound, looking up at him, my concern obvious in my eyes, wide as I inspect the lingering scar.

"That was how we became friends." He whispers, breath ticking my cheek.

"I *stabbed* you?" I tug my hand back, horror filling me.

"No! You saved me. When we first met, you *despised* me." He chuckles and traces a rough thumb against my cheek. "I admit you intrigued me, but when I presented my attempt at your hand, you laughed and called me a child." He smirks, but I gape at him.

"Well, that was rude of me." I mumble.

"That opinion of me lasted until a battle where I took an axe to my side, nearly dying on the Great Plains of Merga." His hand drops from my face, eyes becoming unfocused, and I can't imagine what he is picturing from the memory. My heart pangs in sympathy, and I reach up to cup his face. The touch seems to pull him from the past and his eyes refocus on mine, glinting in the candlelight. "Then an angel stormed past me and fate made her look down at the poor soldier, one of the thousands left for dead on the field." I swallow against the bile that rises at the thought. "You cursed impressively at my wound, then dropped to your knees, not even caring that you were ankle deep in muck and gore." He again reaches up to caress my face. This time running a thumb along my bottom lip. I lean in to the touch, my eyes falling closed against the spine-tingling sensation. "You chewed my ass out for getting hurt in the first place. Then some more for just laying there and waiting for death like a pathetic fool." I blink in surprise and fury at my past-self and the hateful words I had said to him as he lay dying.

"Don't be mad. I saw the truth in your eyes, the true panic you were trying to shove down. And despite the General of that time, General Kahlin, telling you to leave me and to not waste your energy on healing one of the thousands who were already basically dead—you used the last of your power to save me. Then, right there, you promptly discharged Kahlin from his duty and told him if he had so little care for your warriors, then he was no longer who you wanted in charge of the military." He laughed softly before adding, "Then you promoted me to General on the spot and healed me yourself. I only found out later, the reason you were on that field in the first place was to find me. You had learned I was one of those not returned and insisted on joining in the search for my body. You claimed it was because I was the only other Sidhe left, but I think even then I knew that maybe you felt more for me than you had admitted."

"So you and I, our relationship was never more than friendship before?" My hands drop of their own accord again to his chest, trailing my fingers across the corded muscle beneath.

"Our relationship was..." He contemplates, pulling the silk hem of the robe I wear through his calloused fingers. "—complicated. We were always closer than friends, but our friendship was undeniably always what came first. I am not sure if that makes any sense or not... but that's the only way I can think of explaining it." I think over his words and decide that yes, in its own tangled way it did seem to encompass even what was between us now.

"Then this robe—?" I trail off, unsure if I will get the answer I am hoping for, but force myself to finish the question anyway. "It isn't some other woman's?"

He hesitates. "It was. But one that was not nearly as important as you, and is no longer in my life." His fingers find their way into my still damp and tangled hair. "There is no one else. Nor will there ever be anyone else for me, but you." With that breathless confession, his mouth descends upon mine.

The world fractures around me at the kiss. Warmth and longing seep from every inch of contact our bodies make. I press up against him, my mouth opening to him with a whimper of elation. His fingers tangle more into my wet hair as his other hand wraps around my waist, pulling me even closer until I feel like the two of us could meld together into one soul. I shiver at his touch.

His lips set me on fire, yet the burning is unfamiliar. There is attraction, yes. But it is not the feeling I have been longing for since I had first woken in the forest with no idea of who I was. The one I continue to blindly grope for in the dark. For a lost piece of my soul that beckons constantly. Always present, like the breath in my lungs.

I pull away, stifling a sob that threatens to shatter the look of utter happiness that shines from Türë's face for the first time. Brushing the tendrils of hair free from my face, he murmurs, "I have been aching for that in a way you can't even fathom." His eyes flick to the door, and a glint of irritation glints in his eyes now. I struggle trying to find something to say. To explain the disappointment in my heart, in some way that wouldn't forever crumble our friendship. He gives me one more deep kiss, and I beg myself to this time find the spark I was looking for.

"Our tryst is unfortunately over for now." He nearly growls as the door flys open, but his hands don't remove themselves from my waist where they grip. His own desire not allowing him to let go just yet. Ilithyia scowls at the two of us, before her eyes widen at the sight. Myself clothed only in a thin robe, and Türë's shirt gaping open with barely a breath of space between us. Athene is right behind her, eyes going wide as well, before bursting into a fit of giggles that has me smiling sheepishly. Suddenly shy now that we have an audience, Türë thankfully drops his hands from my waist, taking a step back, and quickly buttoning his shirt back up.

"So you sent us to the dressmakers to frolic with this one did you?" Athene manages to ask between gulps of laughter, looking between Ilithyia's scowl and my blush.

I straighten, trying to redeem some of my decorum. "I did need a bath and a dress for tonight. Was the gown ready?" My unspoken dare for Ilithyia to push that line of questioning clear in my eyes. I would not let her try to shame me for kissing Türë. *Because Jera help me, I need her advice.* She nods sharply before turning her attention to Türë.

"General, if you would allow us the use of your chambers. We need to prepare the Queen for the celebration tonight." She demands. I wonder what she sees in my eyes and if I am failing to conceal the desperation for a moment alone. Türë nods at her before turning and bowing deeply to me, a silent promise of *more* to come later glinting in his eyes. I swallow hard as he gently takes my hand, planting a tender kiss to the inside of my wrist. The gesture makes my heart dance wildly, even as my gut screams at me that it is wrong, and he grins for a beat at the noise before turning on a heel and vanishing through the door.

"A *bath,* eh?" Athene asks, coyly. "That is not what I call it." Ilithyia rolls her eyes, but we both break into laughter that I know echos down the hall, because Türë's own laugh rings happily in my ears before the door clicks shut.

twenty-six

I swish back and forth, reveling in the masterpiece *L'aiguille* the dressmaker had crafted for me. A mixture of alternating layers of cream, gold, and pine green that catches and shimmers in the lights of the crystal chandeliers that hang above our heads in the massive ballroom. Tonight is my first night of seeing the hall in its full splendor, and it is a joy to behold. Glimmering with candles, crystals, diamonds, and flowers of every color, fill every table, banister, and column I pass. I had left the decorations to Athene, and I made a mental note to commend her on such a magnificent job. It was summer incarnate. Now that night had at last overtaken the long day, the dancing had begun with such fervor that my smile had not fallen once in the hours that passed. More people than I had expected had come, though according to informative whispers from Patryk, this was not unusual. All of my subjects were invited to attend each of the Solstice balls thrown by the castle every star-cycle and all who could attend did. It was a night of pure elation and a celebration to the Goddess Jera, he tells me. The happiness and unity that were created by the celebration, not just here but also in the towns across the kingdom, fueled the Goddess's strength. Another thing that kept us all safe. When I pause for a minute to look around at the crowd, all twirling and bobbing across the dance floor, I can see how that would be possible. It was even fueling *me*. My soul feels like leaping and dancing with the pulse of the music. The double doors that surround the entire wing of the ballroom had been thrown open, turning the indoor room into more of an outdoor pavilion. The warm summer air dances through the crowd, like it too is joining in the frivolity. I inhale a garland of amethyst chrysanthemums that had been intricately braided and wrapped around a column.

"You look *glorious*."

I immediately smile at the voice. His hand rests against my mid-back in a possessive motion. Nearly shivering at the touch, I can't help but think of how I had imagined such a caress when I requested the dressmaker to lower the back further. I never let myself hope it could actually come true, and now... *Why can't I shake this feeling of wrongness?* Ensuring my smile is in place before turning to face him and notice that the vest he had donned after I had seen him last is a green, gold, and cream that matches my own perfectly. I take in his handsome form and the rest of the crowd seems to fade into the distance. The song that was playing ends and the dancers applaud with appreciation before the ensemble takes a quick breath, then jumps right into yet another song.

"As do you, General Türë." He returns my smile and takes my hand, pressing a kiss. I curse the gloves that Athene had insisted would complete the outfit, wishing that I had disregarded the warmth of the day and worn them. They put an unwanted barrier between my skin and the caress of his lips. "Clever Athene thought

I would like something more fashionable than just a plain white shirt. Though she failed to mention how similar it was to a gown Your Royal Highness would be wearing." He shoots a look to Athene, standing across the ballroom, who has her arm looped through Patryk's. I look around for Ilithyia, finding her watching the pair of us closely. She flashes a playful smirk at me before returning her attention to Isos, who seems to be enraptured and hanging on every word she says. My attention perks at that, my eyebrows raise and I hide a smile behind my champagne flute.

"That flirtation has lasted star-cycles." Türë says, following my gaze. I decide not to get involved, while also thinking of finding more excuses for the two to work closely on a few things. Türë seems to know what I am thinking, but he just shakes his head, a humored grin slanting his smile and revealing a dimple on his right cheek I had never seen before. I fight the urge to poke it, then he steps closer, his hand finding the curve of my back again. His thumb finds a rhythm with the music, the band now slowing into a gentle waltz.

"Would you dance with me?" His lips brush against my ear as he whispers and I nod, swallowing hard. I know I should tell him how I am feeling. The sooner the better. But maybe, in the beauty of the night and party, I can overcome the hesitation in my heart. He takes my hand in his, leading me out to the floor. The others make way for us, dropping into deep curtsies and bows. One elderly woman even drops to a knee, planting grateful kisses onto the hand not grasped in Türë's. I try not to tug my hand away in surprise, and thankfully, a nearby guard intercedes on my behalf without making a scene. "You saved her crops, animals, and her entire family and house last star-cycle from a flood." Türë whispers into my ear as he pulls me close, our clasped arms outstretched, the others rest on his shoulder and my waist. With the start of the next song, we are off, joining the wave of swirling skirts and closely pressed bodies. He leads me through each beat, and somewhere deep inside me, I know I have done this before. Like with wielding a sword—the forms come to me before I can think on them. A flash of an image flickers in my mind, but I am in a navy and silver gown. However in Türë's place, also wearing a matching vest, is another man who leads me through this same song. I blink and gasp a bit, but the image is gone in the next breath. Türë frowns in concern, his Sidhe senses missing none of it. I smile weakly at him. Neither of us miss even a step, despite the shock that flows through me.

"Nothing." I mutter, trying to reassure him, even as my heart betrays me. Its pulsing beat races, a harsh contrast to the slow rhythm of the music. *Did I just have an actual memory? It is impossible, right?* I knew I have had dreams, incredibly realistic dreams, and at the beginning flashes. But this feels different. *They are all supposed to be gone—permanently gone.* Türë eyes narrow. He obviously doesn't believe me and begins to press more, but then he freezes, his head whipping towards a sound only he and I can hear.

My name. Being shouted again and again. Not from inside the room, but from the hallway approaching. Running footsteps accompany the call, growing louder with each step closer they get. All joy seems to seep from me. My blood feels like ice in my veins. I know that, either from Jera herself or just my intuition, something was horribly wrong. My heart races, screaming at me that everything is about to change.

Türë starts to tug me through the crowd with him toward the noise, not running or even appearing hurried enough to cause a panic. We reach the open doors that lead to the source of the still yelling voice. We meet the pair of guards already there who had begun searching the crowd for us. Their faces both pale as they pull the door shut behind us, the strains of music and laughter muted with the thud of them closing. We meet the shouting man in the next hall down, and I couldn't help but take a moment to marvel at the range our ears had. Even above the cacophony of the party that was raging around us— I could still hear my name shouted from halls away. We spot the source and rush to meet him. The man is gasping for air, but relief hits him as he sees the two of us now running at him, and he finally stops shouting my name.

"What's wrong?" Türë growls at the man, fully the General now, placing himself between the stranger and myself. I can clearly see his own fear at what this man is about to say.

"Your Majesty," the man gasps out in between gulps of air and a quick bow. From his attire, at first glance, I would have guessed a guard, but then I notice that only the coloring remained the same, emerald and navy. It was not nearly as fine as the castle guards uniform.

"What is your assigned post, Messenger?" Türë snaps and I realize the reason for the difference. *A messenger?* I shudder to think what would send the messenger careening through the castle in such a fright, yelling for the Queen.

"Naro, General." The man snaps upright into a salute and I notice his hands shaking violently. "I rode through the night to carry grievous news from his Highness, King Ivrik of Paith." I feel Türë's fingers tighten almost imperceptibly around my own. *Bad, bad, bad...* the voice chimes in my head as I remember what he had told me just this morning about Mirinth being on the move.

"Has something happened to Charobi?" I manage to ask, though I feel a wash of desire to plug my ears and instead just pull Türë back into the party. To put off the inevitable words that I knew were about to strike us both with cruel blows.

"No, Majesty..." A rush of air puffs from both Türë and I as we exhale in relief. Then the messenger grimaces in apology before continuing. "Dulen." We both freeze and the man's throat bobs in a hard swallow. "Dulen has fallen to Mirinth."

twenty-seven

I had vomited all over the poor man the second the words had sunk in. I cover my mouth, stammering apologies. Türë springs into action, calling over a number of the nearby guards, instructing one to spread the word to others, but to keep it from the guests. The other guards present form a circle around me, as if they were worried King Tanth would just waltz down the hall and stick a dagger through my heart. Though after the uninvited visitor this morning, it wouldn't be an impossibility. *Jera help me. Was that just this morning?* Despite my earlier insistence on stepping up in my queen role, I was perfectly content to let Türë take charge on this one. War had not come to our door for hundreds of star-cycles. Nearly a millennium, according to the history books Noran had instructed me to read. A kind faced guard gives me a tight smile before taking a cautionary sip of the water brought to me by a nearby servant. He pauses a few breaths before nodding and passing me the cup then. I stare bewildered, trying to make sense of it. Then the truth registers. He was testing it to make sure it wasn't poisoned. That hits me with an invisible blow.

"Don't do that!" I hiss at him and he jolts in surprise. "Don't any of you do that." I glare around at each of the guards who watch me, speechless, obviously confused at my order. "Don't you dare check my food and water like that. What if it *had* been poisoned?!" The guard who had tested the drink returns my gaze, solemn yet resolved.

"It would be an honor to die in your stead and service, Your Majesty." He murmurs, bowing his head in respect. He looks pointedly at his brothers and sisters in arms who all nod, pale with worry, but entirely serious. "We all would." Even the messenger who still stands a few feet away, covered in my vomit and waiting for further questioning, nods in agreement. I take a shaky breath and straighten, fighting tears with each word that he says. Now I have to be the person who is deserving of all the lives lost in Dulen and that will be lost in the war that was most definitely on our doorstep.

"Thank you for your willingness, and can only tell you what an honor it is to have you in my guard. I pray it will not come to that, but I can tell you Jera walks with us all in these moments and those soon to come." My words seem to bolster them, as well as me. "Please tell the General I will be in the gallery. Summon each of the captains, as well as Elder Dakar. Tell them to meet us there in one hour." I instruct a different messenger who nods and strides off to where Türë is in deep discussion with Patryk. I didn't know when he had joined us, but I could guess they were trying to piece together a plan on wrapping up the still riotous celebration that now feels like another world to me. I look at it longingly, before my gaze catches on Türë staring back at me. The sorrow I feel fills his eyes in return. A silent apology and guilt radiates from him. I share a sad smile and hope he can tell that there is nothing for him to feel guilt for. Then I tear my attention away, spinning on my heel and leading my parade of guards down the hallway to the gallery where we will plan our next steps. I hear the messenger passing along what I had instructed and knew he would not be long behind me. The popping of fireworks sound from behind me, then cheers. I do my best not to wince at each sound of merriment. The realization that, while we had been laughing and partying, my people lay dying, hits me hard. Striking a deep wound into my already aching heart. But I am for glad it. This may be the last night for a time that many of them would go to bed with joyful memories, and happiness thrumming through their veins.

Tomorrow word of Dulen's fall would spread.

The world would all change.

"Why would we pull a legion from Charobi to retake Dulen when Mirinth will just turn around and take the then vulnerable Charobi?" Captain Ivia snaps at Captain Borke, slamming her hand against the table around which we all stand, rattling all the glasses rested atop.

"Because the encampment near Charobi was a *distraction.*" Borke sneers at the small woman, her stature a clever deception that hides her true strength and ability. I had seen her in training defeating men three times her size with ease. All while smiling gleefully. "It's clear now that the movement they have been seeing across the border was to distract us from the secret movement against Dulen!" I tune out the argument—the same one that had been circling for the last three hours. During that time, the

Captains who had not been on duty and were therefore enjoying the party, and numerous flute-fulls of champagne, had since had enough water and time to more coherently participate in the discussion of our counter. My head throbs and I turn to look at the map of my kingdom spread in front of us, thinking over everything that the messenger had passed on about the attack.

Ivrik is alive in Naro, waiting for further instructions. A regiment now stands guard at the Glin Ford to stop anything or anyone from traveling up river. Erit is locked down by now, waiting for further instructions as well. Charobi remains untouched, but Dulen had been taken. Not from the Field of Pilar that stands between it and Mirinth borders. No. They used longboats that had been run up the coast. Thousands of soldiers had poured in from the ocean gate on the west side of the stronghold. Dulen hadn't stood a chance. Until now, we didn't even know that Mirinth had an armada, let alone enough longboats to hold the number of soldiers that had taken Dulen in an *hour*. I massage the bridge of my nose with my forefinger and thumb. My focus returns to the conversation that has now turned into a full on argument. Realization strikes me that any solutions that we might have been able to make had long since lost any thread of possibility. It all was quickly devolving, thanks to the late hour, lack of sleep, and excess of worry. I glance at Elder Dakar, who sits silent and stern faced as ever. What surprises me is that he is looking at me back. He only inclines his head, as if giving me the support to take control of this situation.

"Enough." I say, looking around at them all. They either ignore me or don't hear me. "Enough!" I raise my voice to a yell and release my grip on the tether of my power. The candles surrounding us surge, their flames reaching nearly a foot in length to accompany the order. Silence falls across the room at that. Out of the corner of my eye, I see Türë purse his lips against a smile, but he too looks to me for an answer. I flick my eyes to Elder Dakar again, who watches me just as closely. All these people and more are relying on you, his steel-grey eyes seem to say. I tuck that thought away into the pocket of my mind. The stress of it all pools in my gut, making my nausea rise.

"Call in the messengers." I order a man near the door. He immediately disappears. Not even ten breaths pass before ten others, all dressed in the same uniform of emerald and navy, hurry into the room. They each stand at attention, waiting for their instructions. A pad of paper sits in front of one of the Captain's who waits, quill raised at the ready, for the missive. The only other one besides Captains Ivia and Borke to be on duty, and therefore completely sober. The rest still sit, almost dazed. Though it could be alcohol or shock induced. I push to my feet, staring blankly at the image of my kingdom, as I feel the weight of all the eyes on me. "For King Ivrik of Paith." I begin. The Captain begins to scrawl the words with surprisingly elegant handwriting. If he hadn't been a Captain, I would have commissioned him to be the court calligrapher. "Prepare Naro for siege. Pull all resources and people you can within the city walls. A legion from Anopthe will be sent to you to bolster and support. Another legion will be sent from Dolunt to support Erit. Three legions from Alessandra will go to support Charobi, Saroch, and Zanda. The armada we have will be patrolling the waters between Eludar and Zanda." I take a deep breath, praying my voice doesn't break. "Dulen is lost for now. Attempts will be made to reclaim when further information is gathered." I pause before adding, "we are coming to help." I can't stop it. My voice breaks with emotion on the final sentence and I feel more than see Türë step forward. He does hold himself back from reaching out to me though. "Stay safe and wait for further orders." No one speaks as the Captain finishes transcribing the orders and passes me the parchment for my signature and royal seal. I press the stamp in the hot wax and look to the others for one last sign of disagreement or concern. Looking to Türë for final approval, he nods his support, and I pass it to one of the waiting messengers. He takes off immediately and I send a prayer to Jera that I had done everything right. If Türë was surprised by my knowledge of strategy or our military setup through the kingdom, he doesn't let on. Though he *was* one of only two people in the room who knew the truth. That their Queen leading them into war was not the person they all thought she was. Only Türë and Elder Dakar know the full extent of our weaknesses. But there is a glint of pride in Türë's eyes. I feel the wave of reassurance when I realize that he would *never* let me send orders in this situation that would not benefit us all. Not when it came to war and our people's safety. Even without his approval, I knew it was a good strategic move. If Mirinth had a secret armada, we needed to bolster each of the harbor cities. But we could not afford to lose Charobi. It was the main military stronghold between Mirinth and Naro. Should Charobi fall too, they would have control of nearly all of a territory, not to mention unobstructed access to a major river that would take them almost anywhere in the land. I sway slightly, exhaustion hitting me from the stress filled, unending day. *Almost done.* I tell myself. "Send missives to Dolunt, Anopthe, and Merga telling them of my instructions, as well as sending a copy of the letter I sent to Ivrik. Include a summary of what has happened at Dulen to each of the other Underkings. They need to be prepared for an attack to come from land, sea, or river." I had instructed Patryk to skip this meeting and to instead begin preparations should Charobi fall. If that were to happen, all of us here in Alessandra also would be vulnerable. We needed to prepare for the worst, which included a precautionary lockdown in preparation for a siege, and eventually a final stand. As the capital, we needed to be prepared to hold, feed, and protect an inordinate amount of people for an uncertain amount of time. Patryk had gone to investigate how long we could stand under what was currently in our stores.

"And who, might I ask, do you have to fill in the gaps of all the legions you are planning to send out, Your Majesty?" Captain Ivia asks, worry furrowing her brow. I look to Elder Dakar as I answer.

"Elder, I believe this is your opportunity to run some preparedness drill for siege attacks." He grins back at me, for the first time, and a wave of relief rushes through me.

"We would be honored." He says in his usual snapping tone, not matching the glint of excitement that flashes in his eyes. "The Nefriti are here to protect. We look forward to the day you call us back into battle, my Queen. It has been too many star-cycles since we have seen our enemies blood and entrails."

Graphic, but I will take it. I heave a sigh, before turning my attention to meet the eyes of each of the Captains who watch me with complete trust. "My Captains." I turn to Türë. "My General." he returns my attention with a bow. "My Elder." I let my eyes run down the table as they all stand together. Sadness, yet firm resolve pull tight each of their paled faces. "King Tanth and Mirinth think they will try their hand at stealing our kingdom, our home, from us." I make a show of sneering at the thought. "Well, he will find we are not so easily taken." I turn from the table and stride to the door, not letting a single step betray the weight that presses down on top of me. I radiate my fury into the room, trying to convey all the confidence that I can muster. My skirts swish around me, a notable clash of how the evening began to its ending. I slow at the door held open for me and pause at the threshold before calling over my shoulder. "Raise the army, my friends. It is time for war." And I stride from the room.

twenty-eight

I don't know where to go after I leave the meeting. There was no way I was going to go back to the party, the sounds of which could still be heard, in spite of the extremely late hour. I was in no mood to be cheery or put on a show. Instead, I flee to Türë's quarters. It was the only place I vaguely remembered the way to, besides my old rooms. And it was deep enough in the less than frequently traveled part of the castle that I would be less likely bothered by wandering party guests. Picking up the numerous layers of my gown that now feels frivolous, I take off at a sprint. I needed the exhausted euphoria that comes with exercising or running hard after sitting and thinking so hard for so long. After a bit of a startled pause, I hear the thundering of my guards who huff along on my trail, doing all they can to keep up with me. I can't help but be impressed as they do manage to keep my pace. I may have had a ball gown slowing me down, but they had their full armor and weapons. Türë's training was not for nothing as our parade storms down the hallway. Luckily, with everyone either celebrating or in bed, there is no one to fly into a panic aside from the on-duty guards we pass. But with a reassuring nod from one of my entourage, they relax—or more accurately, they see that at that moment they do not have to fight a deadly pursuer on my behalf, and return to their position along the wall.

I reach Türë's door and nearly throw myself into it. *Locked. Jera help me. Of course it would be locked.* I mutter curses under my heaving breath and turn toward the group standing behind me in the dark. All of whom are bent over their knees, gasping for air. I wince, but fight back my apology. I can't deny it is good practice to have us all ready to run through the castle. Even armored or gowned. I try to shove away the dark thought, a reminder of what cloud of impending doom threatens my kingdom.

I look for Rhodie or Isos in the group, but spot neither before I remember they were both attending the Solstice celebration. "Do any of you happen to know where my previous study is? I know it is somewhere around here. I just can't remember exactly." One of the young women catches her breath first and points to her left.

"That way, Your—" She starts to answer, but Türë's voice interrupts her.

"I can take you, if you still wish. Or I can let you in." I nearly sag in relief. It wasn't the room I had truly wanted. It was the person who would eventually return to it. I can only nod and point at his door in response. I didn't trust myself to speak more than I had to in front of the guards right now—in front of anyone, really. "You all are dismissed. Report to your Captain for further orders." Türë says, not taking his eyes from mine as he waves his hand a bit in the air and a click comes from the door behind me. The guards bow to both of us before turning and disappearing down the hallway.

Only when we stand in the candle lit hall alone do I realize how presumptive I had been in coming here. After this long of a day, I have no doubt Türë was as ready as I to climb into bed and let unconsciousness overtake me. And after my doubts, it would be cruel to tease him with the idea that it could go further. But tonight, I just couldn't stand the thought of being alone.

"I'm sorry." I blurt out. "I didn't know where to go. I am sure you are ready to be by yourself for a while and get some sleep. You can take me to the study. I doubt I will truly sleep anyway, so maybe all the books will be a good distraction." I realize I am rambling as he quirks a smile at me.

"I doubt I will sleep tonight too. You *never* have to apologize for coming to me. No matter the hour or if you just want to sit in my room." He peers openly at me. "Either way, I will be with you in either place. Especially since I just sent away your guards." I purse my lips before answering with a huff.

"Your fireplace did look divine earlier." I admit, managing as much of a smile as I can in my current mood. With that, the door behind me swings open and the crackling of a fire sounds from inside. I spin towards him as he chuckles, his eyes flicker with the reflection of the light now seeping from inside. "How did you do that? I thought you just had the solid wind." I ask, stepping into the warmth oozing from the room.

"It wasn't me, actually." He admits with a shrug. As he clears the doorway, the door swings shut and locks with a click.

"Then how…" I gesture to the fireplace.

"When you first built the palace," he begins, stepping around me to cross the room. "—and I mean *first* built it. After the war that freed Tesindren—you lifted each stone, each plank, each piece of it, into place yourself. In doing so, you somehow imbued it with a bit of your magic. So now you don't even have to really think about doing anything for it to react to you." He fills up the copper kettle with fresh water before striding to the fire and placing the pot on the hook to bring it to a boil. "I bet you were thinking about how you wanted to sit in front of the fire when it lit. Am I correct?"

I inhale slowly before nodding in awe. "Does the rest of the castle have the same ability? Why haven't I noticed it before?" A multitude of questions distract me from my melancholy that fills my bones with icy tension. I kneel down on the large fur rug laid out in front of the warm fire, spreading my skirts in a fan around me in a way so they aren't in danger of catching on fire.

"No. When the rest of the castle was built much later it wasn't built with magic. All that remains of the living magic in is your study and my quarters down here."

"Why did I not try to preserve it in some way?" I feel mournful over the loss of it, despite just learning about the magic for the first time.

"Well because you are the only one it worked for, and your abilities were such that you didn't really need the magic in the stones. Not with your powers able to do it what you needed anyway. But that also answers the question of why you haven't noticed it before. It wasn't in the part of the castle you spent much of your time in, until now." The kettle begins to whistle and he pulls the pot free of the fire, filling a tea pot resting nearby for us. I watch the steam rise, mirroring the fog that clouds my mind. "Are you alright?" Türë asks me gently, throwing a pillow to the ground and grabbing a set of ornately painted teacups before joining me in front of the fireplace. I blink hard, trying to clear my mind and lean my back against a nearby chair. I pull my attention from the dancing tendrils of steam to his face.

"No." I say, honestly. He nods, understanding the words I am not able to voice. A minute passes without either of us speaking. Not an uncomfortable silence, but one where you can feel the tension of both of our days slowly releasing itself through the tangle of thoughts that swirls in a chaotic storm.

"I am proud of you." Türë finally says and I turn a questioning gaze to him as he pours a cup of tea for me. "For your reaction to the news, and your decisive orders afterwards." I snort unattractively into the cup as I take a sip of the soothing rose and lavender tea. It is perfectly honeyed and I luxuriate in it as my body fills with warmth.

"You mean how I vomited all over the poor messenger without warning?" I grimace at that memory. A fact that, until now I hadn't had a chance to dwell upon. But I still straighten a bit with satisfaction at his complement. He too laughs and winces at the memory.

"Well yes that was unfortunate—but I was talking about how you didn't set the castle on fire or send a hurricane thundering through the hallway." Setting down his cup, he reaches out, taking my free hand into his own. "You have come so far in such a short span of time. Please don't forget that."

I sigh and put down my own cup, suddenly overcome with nausea again. "But is it enough?" I whisper, even though we are the only two around. Fear courses through me and I realize my hands have started shaking. Türë pulls me closer until our knees are brushing against each other and my hand braces against his chest. Our eyes meet and only the reminder that I had been sick very recently keeps me from leaning in to brush my lips against his. I had hoped tonight would give me the spark I had not felt earlier. Was this, familiar warmth, kindness, and comfort, what I need instead?

"Evara, you are always more than enough. When are you going to see that? No one is expecting more from you than yourself. I wish you could see that. You have spent centuries—millennia, actually—protecting and fighting for all of us. Until you are ready, let us return that honor. Just keep doing what you have been. Training, learning, and adapting to your full queenly duties." He bats me softly on the tip of my nose before giving me a soft smile. "You are already doing admirably. Just feel comfortable leaning on the rest of us until you are ready, okay?" I nod, feeling my eyes begin to brim with tears, threatening to fall. A soft knock on the door has both our attention snapping towards it. Why would someone come to his door at this hour? Everything from another city under attack to King Tanth rapping at the door himself rushes through my mind. "Don't worry. It is probably Ilithyia." He stops to reassure me with a pat to my knee before standing. However, I don't fail to notice the dagger he slips free from its sheath. I hold my breath until the door eases open to indeed reveal my handmaiden. I do my best to mute the rush of air that puffs out in relief, but Türë's ears still catch it and smirks playfully at me over his shoulder before returning his dagger to its hidden sheath. Ilithyia's pale face glimmers with concern as she enters, a bundle wrapped in her arms. She is still dressed in her peach and silver-colored gown from the party, eyes red from her own tears.

"Please, come in." Türë says, stepping back to let her into his room. She shuffles past him with a shy, wan smile before dropping to her knees beside me and throwing her arms around my neck.

"Are you okay? I never thought this would happen." She chokes out through her own sorrow. The sudden desire to cry into her shoulder is overwhelming. Ilithyia has never felt like a subject or person relying on me. Simply—and most importantly—she felt like just a friend. I could break into pieces around her and she would not judge. She would only help build me back up. I knew I had Türë and Rhodie and Isos, and Arne and Helene. Really, a castle full of people who would do anything if I asked it of them. But to all, I still felt like their superior. Someone they looked to or expected something from—even if they did not realize or mean for it. I curl my arms around her and sniffle a bit as a few tears trickle out. She was my safe space.

"Would you like some tea, Ilithyia?" Türë asks kindly through our soft sniffles.

"No, no, no," she answers, pulling away and wiping at her eyes. "I just figured you didn't want to sleep in your gown, so I brought you a few things. I already have it arranged to find you more suitable rooms tomorrow."

"Thank you." I say, hoping she can tell all of the unspoken things I feel in my heart for her thoughtfulness. I squeeze her hand and she passes over the bundle that I now see is a robe, nightdress, my favorite pair of leather pants, and a few dresses to tide me over for the next few days.

"My pleasure." She squeezes back. "Just let me know if you need help getting ready tomorrow. I tried to grab your easiest gown so you should be able to lace yourself up. I know how you like to do things on your own." She gives me a watery smile. "Is there anything else you need?" She looks between Türë and me, her dark brows raised, examining the room. "Where are you planning on sleeping tonight?"

"She will sleep here." Türë says before I can respond. Ilithyia turns to me, arms crossed and waiting for a confirmation that I was comfortable with that. I fight a grin as I nod in agreement. Türë may be the General and she would follow his command any other time. But when it came to her friend, her Queen, I had no doubt she would fight with everything she has against him if she caught the slightest hint that I needed her to. She relaxes her stance at my agreement, but still sends a pointed glare at Türë.

"Let her *sleep*." The emphasis makes her point clear to the both of us, and I blush into my teacup. Türë manages to mask a laugh with a cough, but bows his head in obedience. While I knew we had started down a path of such things, I tried my best to keep those thoughts from entering my uncertain mind. Up until a few hours ago, I had only the barest of hope that he returned some of my feelings. *Jera help me what a long day.* Now apparently Ilithyia was expecting, though without a hint of judgment, for us to tumble into bed and ravage each other through the night. My exhaustion betrays me as a yawn slips through of its own accord at the mention of sleep. My eyes drift toward the bed hidden in the corner of the room. Despite the urge to sleep, my imagination suddenly betrays me and sends heat spearing through my body. I recall the urge to touch him, to feel him closer and closer this morning in the fountain before we were interrupted. My gaze flicks to Türe who watches me with eyebrows raised in teasing surprise. His eyes darken, and the rise and fall of his chest gives away his own excited thoughts on the matter. He had seen where my mind and gaze had been drawn. His eyes flicker with mischievous intent in the firelight and he doesn't pull them away as Ilithyia groans in irritation at the two of us.

"Jera help me..." she mutters, rolling her eyes before striding to the door. But she hovers at the doorway, turning her back to Türe so only I can see the roguish grin and wink she bats at me. "See you in the morning." She sings lightly before slipping into the hallway and pulling the door shut behind her with a click. I shake my head, truly smiling for the first time in hours as I refill my tea cup. Silence yawns between us, now with Ilithyia's mention of *other* activities hanging between us.

"I think..."

"I don't know..." We both speak again and laugh loudly.

"Please go on." Türe says. Almost word for word the same start to the conversation we had so many hours ago. I shake my head in disagreement.

"Not a chance. I went first last time." I smirk at him with an encouraging wave of my hand for him to continue. He chuckles, but obliges.

"I just want to say that, no matter what is running through your mind right now, I want to reassure you that I have no expectations. Looking into the foreseeable future we are going to have long stressful days and nights ahead. That doesn't mean I will not dream of someday ravishing you, correctly and diligently." My cheeks flush as my body fills with delicious heat that has nothing to do with the fire. *This. This spark was what I was looking for.* "But I have no expectations. Even if you decide to share my bed tonight and many nights going forward, I will follow your lead." He concludes firmly. A tightness that I had not been aware of until now loosens in my chest at his reassurance. Not breaking his gaze, I set the cup aside and slowly stand. His eyes trace me with each movement.

"And what if I request you to ravage me, General Türë." I reach him and run my fingers across the plane of his chest, a sultry smile on my lips. No longer in my heeled shoes, the top of my head comes even with his nose. I look up at him, wide-eyed and feigning innocence. He swallows hard, his throat bobbing with emotion.

My mind suddenly flashes, and I see the warm steam of a bath, dancing and spiraling in candle light as it prickles my bare skin with sweat. The sound of mingled breaths and moaning echos off of the stone walls of the dim room. I inhale sharply and freeze. That didn't seem like a fantasy, but a memory. *A memory?* I blink rapidly to clear the throb of pain that reverberates through my skull. My vision clears and I know whatever I had been building to in those moments is gone. Concern has now washed across Türë's face and I realize, as if at a distance, that he is calling my name. "I think I am a bit tired." I manage to force out through sharp breaths, trying to re-orient myself. My knees buckle slightly, but Türë is there holding me up against him as I talk more to myself than him. "Stupid memories." I mutter under my breath, causing Türë to harden, stilling beneath me like a living statue.

"What?" He breathes back, but I pitch forward with a hiss as my head throbs again. With a frustrated growl, he sweeps me off of my feet and strides across the room to where his bed stands in flickering shadow cast by the dancing candles. Laying me gently among his clean, crisp sheets, I nuzzle down into them. My body sinks into the mattress that must be either made of clouds or magic. The room spins as I try to sit up, despite his admonitions in protest.

"I am not sleeping in this horrid corset. You might as well press a pillow across my face and smother me for all the air I would be able to take in." Türe stares at me, bewildered, but motions with his finger for me to spin around. With the numerous layers the gown possesses it is a miracle I can fit on the small, cozy bed at all. With jumbled curses and irritated huffs, he manages to loosen my corset stays enough for me to shimmy free of the gown. I inhale deeply in relief and sling on the nightdress Ilithyia had brought me. I laugh a bit, in spite of the still slowly spinning room when I see Türe politely waiting with his back towards me. With the scenes that now played on a loop in my mind, I had forgotten that it might cause him discomfort to see me undressed so fully. "Sorry." I wince, climbing into the bed.

"You have nothing to apologize for. I just didn't want to tempt myself further tonight. Especially since you are clearly not in peak condition to—how did you phrase it?—have me *ravage* you." He tries to pass it off as a tease, but I can see the truth of his own struggling self-control as he fights the urge to not look too long at my low cut, revealing nightgown. I frown down at myself as I realize this is the same one I had instructed Ilithyia to toss out after Türe had discovered me on the floor that first night I had come to the castle. The one his eyes had silently begged to devour me in.

I grin into the pillow as I fall back, pulling the warm sheets over me and my body relaxes into the warmth and scent that permeates the sheets. Türë's scent. "You can ravage me later then." I hear a snort of laughter then feel the sheets shift beside me as Türë sits next to me on the edge of the bed. I can feel his eyes on me, and I find enough energy to pry my own open to peer up at him. That doesn't last long however as I feel the soft pressure of his fingers brush my cheeks, then drift up to my forehead, continuing up into my hair. I nearly purr as his fingers begin to pull the pins, jewels, and strands of my hair free from it's decorative entrapment. Once that is accomplished and every strand of my hair now is freed, falling gently down across my barely covered shoulders, I lean into his touch as he continues to run his fingers through my hair. Türë whispers something to me, but I am too far gone to make it out, or to ask him to repeat whatever it was. With that, I drift into long awaited, restless sleep.

twenty-nine

"Evara Caturthirian, come to me." The words clang through me, making me toss and turn in a tangle of warm sheets. A cold sweat prickles on my forehead. The grey image of a sapling shifts and grows into the image of an ancient oak, one as tall as the castle towers. Each of its branches whirl in a sudden gust of wind, shifting each of its leaves. They too change in the lapse of time that swirls in my vision, growing from simple green buds, to a rainbow of green hues, to the yellow and orange of fall. The scene flickers and I toss as the voice speaks again. It is a familiar woman's voice, as gentle on my soul as my mother's had been. Kind, yet demanding, she calls to me again. "Come to me, Evara." Then the image flickers before vanishing into the black abyss of a starless sky.

✱ ✱ ✱ ✱ ✱

I wake with a jolt and gasp in an unfamiliar bed, blinking and trying to rub the fog of sleep from my eyes as I look around again in confusion. I start to sit up when a soft huff of a snore stops me. Startled, I find the source of the noise closer than I expected. Laying—sitting—beside me in the too small bed, Türë sleeps with his back pressed against the headboard. Still fully clothed, his limp hand rests against the pillow I had been asleep on. My heart aches as the realization hits me. He had fallen asleep playing with a strand of my hair. I take the rare opportunity to look at him, unhindered or without worry of someone seeing. He inhales deeply, but doesn't wake. I fight the urge to prop up his head from the horridly uncomfortable angle it had dropped into, knowing the second I did, he would wake. His shoulder length raven hair, pulled back with its usual leather strap, but slightly disheveled as a few strands had come loose in the night. His usually close-trimmed shadow of a beard, now a day-old and rough, makes me realize he must shave each morning. A simple enough realization, but one that gives me true insight into the normally polished male I still barely knew. A soft smile pulls at my lips and my fingertips hover only a breath away when his eyes snap open. They immediately meet mine—as if he tracked where I was, even in sleep. His attention catches on my fingers, still frozen, extended to brush the tangled hair that curls against his cheek. His brows flick up, silent question in his eyes. I start to pull my hand back in when he leans into my hand. It is surprisingly soft in comparison to the sharp bone structure beneath.

"Good morning." He says at last, his eyes brighter than I had ever seen them before.

"Good morning to you." I breathe the words, as if worried that too much noise would break the calmness that fills the room. Normally, the balcony in my previous quarters did little to filter the sounds of the waking city below. But here, encased by stone and positioned on the south side of the castle, it was utterly silent. The rays of early sunlight filter in through the colored panes in the window, throwing rainbows across the bed and floor. I move my fingers up from Türë's face to hold them in a particularly bright stream and immediately feel its tingling warmth. I contemplate that feeling for a moment before biting my lip in concentration. I can still feel Türë beside me, though he has gone impossibly still, watching me. I split the beam into two, then three, then turn my focus to the rest of the room and split all the other rays as well. I laugh aloud, sitting up fully and marveling at the kaleidoscopic jumble of light I had just made. I pull a few of the sunbeams into my palm and let them weave through my fingers like a serpent. "It is beautiful!"

I turn to see Türë stammering, pale, and awestruck. "How did you—?" He asks, and then stops at my frown.

"What—this wasn't something I could do before?" I suddenly realize why he looks so shaken and suddenly the beams stop dancing, snapping back to the individual, natural streams of light they originally were. With a creak of the bed, he stands stretching his neck with a wince.

"No, it wasn't." He takes a settling breath before clearly forcing what he tries to pass off as an unconcerned smile. "But that is good that you are able to control your power to such an extent already. I wonder what else you can manifest." Forcing one more wide, obviously fake, grin, he turns and enters the bathing chamber, leaving me suddenly feeling numb and worried. I sink back into the tangle of sheets, curling my knees to my chest. I tug the sheets up around me as a worried chill brushes my skin.

I don't have to possess some extra sense to glean that he had just openly lied to me.

It *wasn't* good.

And it is my turn to lie to myself as I swear that I don't want to know why.

* * * * *

Türe had left in a rush after a messenger had delivered a list of questions that the Captain of the castle guards sent about their new post positions and rotations. I swiftly change and ready myself for the day ahead when a knock at the door, accompanied by Ilithyia's friendly voice, interrupts my gloomy thoughts. I throw open the door, not bothering to mask my foul mood, when the serious look on her face stops me in my tracks.

"Change of plans." She greets me by holding out another stack of clothing. The material is solid black, like my leather pants, but this fabric is *different*. Bordering on other-worldly, it shimmers with an iridescence, though the black is so dark it seems to absorb the light that now pours in through the window. I had thrown it open for some fresh air, ignoring the humid morning, but a chill creeps slowly up my body. I run my fingers across it before eying Ilithyia with confusion. "I dug out one of your old suits." She says, as if I should understand. I hold the outfit up by the shoulder panels. It is light and flexible, yet I knew instinctively that no blade or arrow could pierce it. "One of your *very* old suits." She adds, nodding lightly to encourage me to put it on.

"Why?" I manage to ask, shrugging out of the dress I had donned for the day. I leave on the pants I already wear and pull the new outfit on. It glides against my skin, fitting like a glove. It still had skirts like a dress, but rather than layers of fabric, the leather is slit all the way up to my mid thigh on each side of my hips and between my legs. Cut very specifically, the modification allows my movement to be unrestrained, yet still manages to cover every inch of my torso and legs with its specialized material. My other training uniforms allowed for movement and were elegant enough for everyday use. But this was a dress for battle. Almost too beautiful for the endless death it had probably helped me cause. The bodice of the gown was simple and strapless to free my arms, but the material was thickest around my midsection. Providing better protection and padding for my vital organs. I notice then, it possesses no seams that I can see. I tug up the hood and see that it too is seamlessly attached to the rest of the piece. Whatever beast this leather had come from had to have been monstrous to get this entire outfit cut from without having to sew bolts of it together. My mind can't even fathom how one would get such a hide capable of providing a dress with a single cut. Running my fingers down my body, from my covered head to my waist, I realize that other than my arms and the dip of the low cut of my neckline, I am protected head to toe in this. Battledress indeed. My Nefriti armor would cover anything that was not shielded by the outfit.

"What is this?" I ask, awed. If I wore this at night, I would transform into a shadow. Impervious and undetectable—I would be the Queen of Death.

"It is Drakonskein." She says, amazed, just as I was. "This is the first time I have even seen it, though you told me about it before. When the last drakon fell a millennium ago, you had a few things made from its body." I cannot hide the horror I feel at those words and immediately try to rip it off of my skin. "At his request." Ilithyia adds quickly, snapping out to grip my hands before I can try to.

"What?" I manage to stammer out.

"The last drakon was *ancient* when he died and it is said you protected him to the last second. So when he did pass, his final wish was to protect you in turn. To honor his noble request, the hide was turned into suits and other protective items, while his bones and teeth were fused in weapons. One such weapon was your sword *ahtorainë*. It was made of one of those bones, and your dagger was crafted from a tooth." I swallow hard, fighting the aching sadness and multitude of questions about the old drakon. *I truly had a drakon for an ally?* So many stories had been now lost with my memories. I mourn them before a glimmer of a thought strikes me. *Some memories are resurfacing... maybe they are not truly gone.* But I have other things to worry about at the present. Ones that created a need for me to wear a battle dress of drakonskein within the walls of my castle.

"Why?" I ask again. "Why should I wear this now?"

"The people have heard now. They have certain..." She mulls over the words. "Expectations. Your next movements are going to show this kingdom what to expect from you. Tesindren has not had a war for nearly seven hundred star-cycles. There is nobody around anymore to tell the tales of how fearsome you were—are —" she corrects herself quickly, but the sting of the slip still lands. She takes my hands gently again, giving them an apologetic squeeze. "People need to see that the warrior they know their Queen to be still exists. Because if the people lose faith—" Ilithyia's voice cuts off, but I finish for her.

"—then everything will be lost." I nod and attach the emerald sheath with *nehtarúmarth* to the belt of the suit. I roll my shoulders before lifting my chin and heading for the training pits.

I enter the training pit where the rest of the Nefriti wait for

Elder Dakar. Spotting my friends, Arne and Helene, stretching together and aim for them. I try to let all the sharp looks my way from the rest bounce off, but silence falls. Word had spread quickly about the fall of Dulen this morning, and now everyone watches me. Their unease fills the already cloying air. The kingdom holds its breath, each and all waiting to see how swift and deadly the retribution of their Queen would fall upon Mirinth. Only those who knew the truth, including the Nefriti who surround me, felt the concern even deeper. After all, I was the famed warrior queen of old... who they knew was greatly weakened and vulnerable. The fear of my wrath and destruction is what had kept the rest of the world at bay. Now? Well, we just had to wait and see if my legacy and the warriors who serve me are enough to inspire my kingdom. Especially after it is clear that now King Tanth is well aware of the chink in our armor. I swallow nervously, but don't let my chin drop or steps falter.

The news of Dulen had indeed fallen upon the city, stifling the normally convivial tone that fills the air from the morning market. Before now, I had enjoyed the distant voices and music that filled the halls each morning, pouring through the windows propped open to allow the morning breeze to cool the castle before the heat of the day descended upon us. Today it is silent. No voices, no laughter, and no music. I swallow against the ball of tears that lodges in my throat and straighten my shoulders.

Today I had slept in due to hosting the solstice party the night prior, so I had arrived just in time for weapons training. I had no doubt Türë would be far too busy for the foreseeable future to take the time to instruct me himself anymore.

Without waiting for approval or prompting, I stomp into the pit, where two Nefriti warriors already clash in a duel of swords. The two men stop mid-blow, glancing at me in surprise, before dropping into a bow then exiting the circle of sand and sawdust.

Indeed, this outfit made me a fearsome sight to behold, yet the look on my face I think was the true reason for them fleeing. My silent walk through the castle, coupled with the cascading torrent of my thoughts, had certainly swelled into a foul mood. I was ready, and needing, to pick a fight. The way the others suddenly avert their gaze tells me what I already knew. None of them were going to fight me today. Nor did I want them to. Because it wouldn't be a real fight. They would play their part, I knew. Even after the encouragement to treat me as a fellow warrior in the training pits. But not today. They would be too afraid to hurt me, now that they knew I was not on their level. They would pretend at first, but then after a few strikes they would suddenly let their grip slip, or trip on an invisible stone. Today was different. They would let their queen win, rather than risk embarrassing her or hurting her. Not with a war on the horizon. They had no reason to believe that I could hold my own after my private trainings with the General. I look to Arne and Helene, both who look away. Even my friends did not want to risk it. *How am I supposed to show them, inspire them, if they do not even trust me to hold a weapon?* I want to scream aloud in rage.

I grit my teeth, my jaw tense, desperate to pour my anger out with blade or staff. I hear the singing whine of a blade being drawn and spin to find Türë along with a large grim looking man standing next to him, a gleaming two handed sword drawn. *Perfect.* Türë nods to me, his empty hand flexing in anticipation. A silent conversation and understanding sweeps back and forth between us. This man, whomever he was, was willing and ready to fight me. Though he wouldn't aim to kill, he was still going to hurt me if I allowed him to. This would not be training. This man was to be a demonstration.

In my periphery, I see a crowd beginning to gather. Not just the Nefriti were present today. I recognize a few Lords and Ladies from the party last night who were just waking and beginning to meander through the castle, gossiping enthusiastically about the ball and the attack on Dulen. Even down in the pit I make out the excited whispers that provide my answer as to my opponent.

"—a gladiator. Best in Tesindren they say!"

"—undefeated, if the rumors are true."

"—ruthless, and loves to inflict pain." "

"Does the Queen truly believe she can beat him?"

I glance again at Türë, nervousness surging, as the man enters the circle with me, swinging his sword around as if it weighed as much as a butter knife. A cruel smile on his lips tugs at the map of scars that paint his otherwise handsome face. I swallow hard and my hands start to shake. Türë reaches my side and hands me his own sword. I take it without hesitation. I was going to need something better than the dull, chipped blades that we usually used in the pit during training.

"Try not to use any magic. You haven't yet mastered turning it into a weapon and it will only distract and drain you from his physical attacks." Türë mutters to me. I nod, doing my best to quiet the ringing in my ears. The adrenaline in my body spikes for the upcoming duel at the same time the pressure of this moment crashes upon me. I realize then however, I am not shaking from fear, but anticipation. Not yet had I been able to unleash my full strength. Aside from Türë, and sometimes Isos, I had rarely had a true partner to battle. Even they used it more as a training and endurance opportunity, rather than the simulation of an attack that it was meant to be. And though they would never admit it, I knew they too held back from delivering real blows. I slip on my leather bracers and realize that the ones I had been using all along were of the same material as the suit I wore today. I recall Ilithyia's mention of other items and wonder what else was made from the treasured drakonskein. I swing Türë's sword around a few times, quickly trying to familiarize myself with its weight and balance. I start to pace in the dust, my feet testing for any irregularity in the ground of the pit that could create a twisted ankle or a loss of balance and traction. Finding none, I roll my shoulders and narrow my focus before nodding to the man. A grin tugs at my lips and I don't miss Türë's sharp, nervous intake of breath before his voice rings across the pit to us, and the now large crowd that has gathered.

"Begin."

thirty

Despite bracing for it, the first clash shoots a shockwave through my bones that makes my shoulder throb. I mutter a curse under my breath and spin away, rolling my shoulder through the pain and re-collect myself. I have to adjust my stance away from how I have always approached sparring. This man would not pull his blows. In fact, from the glint of excitement in his nearly solid black eyes, he enjoyed the thought of putting the queen on her ass. The gladiator advances, and I take the moment to glance behind me to locate the boundary line. *Two paces. Too close.* Taking a step forward as he approaches, swinging the sword towards my left side, I dodge in a swirl of my skirts. I feel the air as the blade passes within a hairsbreadth, but it doesn't land. Having switched places, he is now the one mere steps away from the border's edge. I struggle to tune out the cheers that sound from the spectators. I have not won. Not even close to it yet. The gladiator Türe had found to fight me was a brute, slow, but incredibly strong. Plus, he had the advantage with his bulk to simply lumber about. He did not have to worry about wearing out as fast as his opponents, who had to exert way more energy ducking and dodging around him and his blows. Because taking just one of his hits would be brutal. There was also the fact he was used to a true fight.

By the time the man has turned back around to face me, I have planted my feet and hold my sword up, ready for the coming blows. *Faster.* I tell myself. *I just have to be faster and smarter.* Türë had said not to use my magic, and I knew he was right—it took too much of my mental focus and energy to do anything really worth the effort. Using magic for victory in this battle felt like it would mar the victory. Because I would win. I had to win. The weight of all the eyes on me sits upon my shoulders as the man strides forward again with a snarl, already swinging his blade down. I take a guess where he will strike and guess wrong. A long deep gash is opened down my right arm from shoulder to elbow, the skin parting like I had seen happen to a pig carcass in the market. It catches on my drakonskein bracers, but it still inflicts major damage. I bite down a scream against the pain, spearing the feeling into my mind and soul. Through the ringing in my ears I hear a collective gasp from the ever-growing crowd. I risk a glance up at them. The many pale faces watch me enraptured, all masks of shock, and my attention catches on Türë. He steps forward and I see his intent to end this. I stare him down, giving a single shake of my head. No. I need to do this. I return my attention to my opponent and the fight ahead of me.

I rotate my injured arm, letting the sensation fuel me. This is the burning pain my people felt as they died in Dulen. This is what will be felt across the kingdom should I fail them. I hear the man laughing loudly as thick, deep red drops of my blood fall into the dust at my feet. I remember, now a distant haze thanks to the pain that mars my concentration, Türë's mention of how I healed him on the battlefield the day he had almost died centuries earlier. My power has other uses in battle, and I would show them off. Narrowing a glare at my gleeful opponent, the anger that has been compressing in my gut since yesterday churns into a lake of fire that surges upwards. Not into my flames.

I redirect it.

It itches horribly, but it is a much better alternative than the pain that it replaces. The wound stitches itself up with brand new, baby pink skin, and it is my turn to laugh now at the look on the gladiator's face. Dry and rough, I barely recognize my own laugh. Face shifting from shock to disgust, the man snarls in fury. I manage another sideways glance at Türë, who watches closely from the side. I see a shocking look of absolute joy wash across his features before he returns it to his previous stone-faced mask. I have no doubts he will scold me for not following his instructions, but in order to win, I have to be able to swing my sword. I give a few test waves of the blade through the air again. I feel the new skin tug uncomfortably, but breathe a sigh of relief to learn it is manageable.

It is I who advances now. The magic I had used barely scraped a thimble full from the writhing, seemingly bottomless pool that contains my power. *Good to know for the future.* I strike, my anger coiling like a snake in my skin. I knock his blade out wide and he is too slow to recover in time for my next slash. Down the length of his immense body, from left rib to mid thigh, I part the skin. His blood joins mine on the pit floor. His doesn't heal though. He hisses a particularly vulgar curse at me, but now my blood is singing so loudly with my fury that I barely register it. I bring the sword down twice more. One to his arm and twin to the gash he had given me, the second movement to block his returning blow. Even though I prepare for the force, my wrist snaps and my blade goes flying with the hit. I cannot stop the scream of pain this time, but I see the victory in my opponent's eyes breaths before he sees the truth. He had landed what he imagined was the winning blow, only to realize the deception it had been. I had pulled my dagger, *netarúmarth,* free. Its razored edge now rests against his throat.

He had landed the blow, but lost the battle.

We breathe, gasping ragged and hot puffs into each other's faces before I lower my dagger and step away. He manages a surprising bow, respect washing his features for the first time into a man, rather than the prowling beast he had entered the ring as.

"Well met, Your Majesty." He huffs, pain paling his cheeks more with each step he takes on his injured side. Turning, he limps out of the ring, among cheers of the spectators rejoicing over their queen's victory.

I had truly beat him, a fact everyone present knew without a doubt. The man was not one to fake a loss, not with an unblemished record and nothing to lose. The reason Türë had brought him in the first place. I manage a grin, breathing through the waves of pain that radiates from my wrist I hold tucked in close to my chest. I raise my unhurt hand in the air, waving at the crowd calling my name. Türë watches me, his face still the mask of unreadable calm, though his eyes scream the opposite. I knew it had killed a part of him to watch me be hurt in such a way. First with the gash to my arm, and then my wrist. But he also understood it was a necessary evil, for many reasons. The least of them being that I needed a true opponent who was not afraid of hurting me. If—No. When—I ended up on a battlefield, whoever I encountered there was not going to pull punches simply because I am the Queen. That fact would actually ensure I was a prized target. If I continued to solely train against those who refused to truly fight against me, I would be dead within breaths of a real fight. I send a tendril of thought down into my power again, wondering if I could accomplish my feat a second time. I nearly utter a most unqueenly squeal of both excitement and relief as my wrist snaps back into place. I test it with a gentle rotation. I would have to be careful in the next few days to make sure I didn't weaken the bone or break it again. I could instinctively tell it needed to still do the bulk of its own healing. But my hand was usable again, thank Jera.

I look over to the side of the pit where the man carefully and slowly sits wrapping the gash I had torn open on his body. Türë watches me closely, but I go to the man, stopping by his side with a bow. I hear the crowd fall quiet at the movement, and the man too gapes at me. One of the first things I had been instructed by Türë was to bow to no one below my station. But I didn't give a damn. This man deserved my respect.

"Thank you for fighting with me. It was a rare opportunity to find an opponent willing to not hold back on my account."

"Aye, I bet." He manages a smirk, followed by a wince as his leg no doubt throbs beneath the bandages he pulls tight. "You fight well. I know they said as much, but you are—" He thinks over the appropriate words before saying what he was thinking anyway with a shrug. "—fragile."

I laugh, and the man looks somehow even more surprised. "Will you allow me to heal you?" I ask, not wanting to offend. I wasn't sure on protocol of such a thing, and indeed the man stills his wrapping looking up at me with a narrowed, wary gaze.

"Why?"

"Because I don't want that to get infected, and I am hoping if I am nice enough to you, you will continue to come here and spar with me."

He doesn't answer, contemplating my offer with suspicion of some hidden catch. But he drops his chin into a sharp nod. I drop to my knee, holding my hand out above the two large wounds I had inflicted.

It is harder. *Much* harder to heal him. I pour sweat by the time the last of the gashes inch their way closed. I gasp in a hard breath, and sway slightly where I kneel. The man eyes me and, surprisingly, concern fills his face.

"I heard someone say you are a gladiator?" I manage to say.

"I am."

"I didn't know we had gladiator fights in Alessandra." I comment as Ilithyia joins us, holding two canteens of fresh water for him and I.

"You wouldn't."

I snort, taking a few deep gulps of the cold water. "You are talkative, aren't you?" The man's jaw tightens briefly, fighting against the urge to grin. "At least tell me your name." I press.

"Ionel Vacos." He says finally. His eyes flick to Ilithyia then quickly away when she smiles widely at him.

"So will you oblige me?" I ask, knowing that he wasn't going to continue speaking with me much longer.

"With what?"

I huff in slight irritation at the glacial pace of the conversation. "Will you come back and help spar and train me?"

This time he turns his full attention on me, examining me head to toe. Not in the way Türë does, or even Ivrik. This was simply a test whether I was worth his time.

"I will." Ionel says at long last.

"Once a week, meet me here at sunrise and we will compensate you for your time. Agreed?"

He nods sharply, then shoves to standing, testing out the leg and side I had healed. Ionel does his best not to look impressed, and succeeds. Only a grunt signals his satisfaction before he lumbers out of the training pits. Ilithyia and I exchange a look, uncertainty fills her eyes.

"I think you two will be best friends!" She says sarcastically, looping her arm through mine with a laugh as we watch him lumber away.

thirty-one

Though much more reserved than usual, the sounds of the city begin to return by the time the sun reaches its peak that afternoon. Türë and I stroll through the now familiar stone streets, my guards trailing leisurely behind. We had determined that my continued presence in the city would be a reassurance and a show of power, though a silent one, to tell my people, and my enemies, that I was not afraid. To the casual eye, the entire entourage appeared unconcerned, but I knew that each of the guard's knuckles were white from keeping their grip tight and ready on their weapons. Their eyes open wide, alert for any sign of trouble. We had received no further word from Ivrik or from anyone in Dulen whether there were any survivors. The worry grows more awful by each hour that we hear nothing.

"I had a thought." I say, lowering my voice as I smile at a nearby shopkeeper who stares at us before dropping into a low bow.

"Oh?" Türë keeps a light slow pace beside me, his wrists

clasped behind his back. His beard had been trimmed back to its clean cut, but I still remember its texture beneath my fingers. I shake the thoughts away, reminding myself where we were. I hadn't had time to confess my hesitations, and after the past twenty-four hours of chaos, I didn't need to add another thing onto Türë's shoulders. Though to be honest with myself, it was mainly selfish reasons that kept my mouth shut. It felt wonderful to have someone look at me and take care of me the way Türë does. I didn't want that feeling to go away yet. Even if it did make me horrible.

I smile and take a vibrant orange zinnia from a little girl who runs up, dropping a quick wobbly curtsy. Her tight curls bounce as she blushes and runs away again with a smile. "I think I need to take the time I have been spending on magic and instead focus on weapons and combat." To my surprise, Türë stops suddenly and grabs my arm to stop me as well.

My brows furrow. It isn't just disapproval, but anger that flashes across his face. "Why would you think that?" He growls at me, his voice lowered, aware of the people that could be listening. "Look at what you were able to do in the fight today! You *healed* yourself. Think how *vital* that can be in days to come. Your power is growing, whether you like it or not. You must learn to harness it. Why do you run from it instead?"

"Because you and I both know that time is running short for me to keep the pace of what we are doing now. Yes, I have come a long way from sending tidal waves across the bathing chamber and lighting you up with electricity, but you know more than anyone that my charade as the warrior queen is about up. If I were to step out on the battlefield as of this moment, can you honestly tell me I would live? Or would I just be a distraction to all those around me, causing more harm than good?" His mouth opens to argue, but I can see that he has nothing to fight back with. I speak only the truth. I had come a long way in the few quarters of training, but that time was now up, and I was nowhere near ready. "If war has come, then I will lean on what I can hone and what will serve me and the kingdom best. That is fighting with a sword and dagger. I will use what of my magic that I can now, but won't waste the time now to increase it." Türë's jaw tightens, eyes flashing in anger. *Why is he so against this?* I ask him as much, and he casts a look around without answering. The unspoken message is clear. He would not speak of it here. *Fine.* I tug my arm free from his grip and spin away, continuing towards the shop I was looking for. Türë's eyes follow my path before he sighs heavily, acting like I was leading him into a beauty salon rather than a smithy. Though I don't understand his resigned attitude, he trails along, ignoring my questioning look.

This morning at the training pits, I had asked the Nefriti who lingered after their training for their recommendation, and all had answered the same. The best blacksmith and armorer in the territory was Yessin Arboff. To my surprise, the man standing at the shop's work table does not fit the image that I was expecting. With his reputation, I had been picturing an older, stout, coal-covered man. Instead, I find a man who looks about mid thirties, with pale gold hair, and an athletic build. I manage to conceal my surprise, ignoring Türë, who stomps in, scowling after me. The guards all remain outside, but Türë alone still cuts an imposing figure, towering over me, his arms crossed with a sour look on his face. I glare at him. The foul mood now seems to be less because of our conversation as his annoyance that seems to grow sharper as he looks around the shop. That idea is quickly confirmed as Yessin looks from me to Türë, face shifting into a cocky smirk at the glowering man behind me.

"General Türë." he simpers, sarcasm coating each word before he snaps. "Get out." He turns to me, a genuine grin shifting his face to handsome. "Your Majesty, of course, can stay as long as she pleases." He bows deeply, not taking his golden eyes from me now, shifting from irritation to enchanting as they rake over every inch of my body. I shift uncomfortably under the probing, open stare.

I guess there is a history here I wasn't expecting.

"Do I know him?" I mutter, soft enough for only Türë to hear. To my surprise, he doesn't answer me, his attention focused on the blacksmith.

"The old you did. But not now, I suppose. The next cycle has begun, right?" I blink rapidly in shock at the casual revelation that this blacksmith knew my secret.

"If you truly think I am going to leave the two of you alone again, you must be even more of an idiot than I already knew." I shoot a look at Türë, silently demanding an explanation, but they both ignore me. Yessin flashes a cocky smile at Türë before suddenly spinning around and disappearing through a door that leads further into his shop. I raise my brows in silent prompting as Türë finally deigns to acknowledge me again. He answers, though without looking away from the doorway the blacksmith had vanished through. "Last time you two were left alone, it led to Alessandra being set ablaze." He shakes his head in disapproval. "It is a damn shame he is the best blacksmith in Tesindren." He follows after the man without waiting for me, and I sigh in frustration at the continued half answers that I always seemed to get. Just when I think I am getting used to this whole forgotten past thing... something always pops up and throws me into another whirlwind of questions. My mind lingers on the possibility that my memories had, for whatever reason, began to resurface, before I shove those thoughts away. It was more than likely a fluke and not one to waste my time on. With one last glance towards the front door, where the guards all were stationed and waiting outside, I follow Türë and Yessin.

My jaw drops as I step through the unassuming door. I look over my shoulder again, this time to make sure that the shop was, in fact, still there. Hoping I won't be swept away somewhere, never to be seen again, I take a hesitant step into the space and feel it surround me with a tingling warmth. *Magic.*

I feel so foolish as I gaze at the wonder of the hidden oasis. For some reason, I had fallen into the assumption that Türë and I were the only magic wielders left—in this land, at least. After the tale of the Massacre of Dothsmerna, and other than the hidden *florenta,* there were no further tales or occurrences that I have come across of remaining Creatures of the Forest. I had come to the assumption they had fled or died. Yet, as I step further into the grotto that pulses with magic, I see proof how ignorant that conclusion had been. In the center of the room grows an enormous tree covered in a moss that is so green it seems to shimmer, as if a glowing ball of starlight lives within its trunk. The room is filled with a symphony of birdsong that seems to dance with the air and light itself. As large as the city gardens, I am astounded at all the wondrous things that had been concealed under the guise of an ordinary shop front. At the end of the winding stone path, lit with fairy lights and the radiant glow leaking from the tree, a row of clear blue waterfalls cascade down from above into a deep pool that leaks into a river that rushes by me. The bubbling trickle joins the melody of the magical grotto. Only a hedge appears to stand between this hidden garden and the shop, and where the waterfalls originated, I couldn't tell. But there were so many other things to discover that I am continually distracted as I make my way down the path, following the sound of Türë's familiar voice. I catch enough from the tail end of their conversation to know that he was telling him about the loss of my ancient sword. For the first time, the man looks shaken. Even distraught, as his face pales and the light in his eyes dims slightly.

Mopping at his sweaty brow, his cool demeanor cracks.

"—at least I can rest easy knowing it protected many and completed its purpose. Enough to fill many average blade's lifespans. As heartbreaking as it is to hear about the loss of such an amazing blade, I am glad it is to me you returned for a replacement."

I jolt to a stop as the Yessin's words land. "You? You made *ahtorainë?*"

"No, but my father did."

"But—how? You can't be more than thirty! I thought it was made thousands of star-cycles ago." I look to Türë for an explanation, before I realize again how naïve I am. I, a four thousand star-cycle old woman who appears mid-twenties, stands in a magical oasis hidden under the guise of a normal blacksmith's shop, next to a man who was also over a thousand star-cycles old. I blush in embarrassment. Türë had made it seem that way. In fact, I thought he told me that we were the last two Sidhe in Tesindren. Yet here stood the son of the man who had made the legendary blade over two thousand star-cycles ago. *So what is he?* Though my intrigue is great, I can't force myself to ask such a blunt question. How do you phrase *what are you* without sounding insulting?

"Eganël is not a Sidhe." Türë says, eyes softening at my clear rush of emotions and confusion.

"Bless Jera for that!" The blacksmith snorts, flashing a wink at me. Türë shoots a look of irritation his way, which he ignores completely.

"I thought your name was Yessin Arboff?" I ask dully, feeling completely lost.

"He is an elf. Similar to us Sidhe, he possesses certain gifts and qualities that grant him a longer life. But he likes to keep his true identity hidden. For obvious reasons, as one of the Creatures of the Forest, he doesn't like to put an unnecessary target on his back. His true name is Eganël Dervishi."

"My life won't be as long as Türë's and certainly nowhere close to yours—but long enough to know I have to keep my heritage a secret. Even under your rules and protection. Even in Alessandra." Eganël's voice shifts into a melancholy that has me wanting to reach out and console him.

"Creatures of the Forest, of which Elves are one of the many that were grouped under that distinction, were hunted to extinction centuries ago. Well—near extinction—a very rare few are still alive, though hidden." Türë's voice drops, low and respectful for the first time since talking to Eganël as he explains. The words don't seem to register fully as I struggle to absorb all of this information.

"But—" Eganël says, clapping his hands together and rubbing them as if he were trying to start a fire. Or maybe brush off the ashes of the past. Türë and I both jump at the sudden noise. "You didn't come here for sad tales of a history long past. You are here for a new blade, I presume?" I nod, but file away the topic to pry answers from Türë about later. Or maybe I can ask Noran about it. I wasn't sure how honest Türë would be regarding Eganël, if I had to base their relationship off their greeting. "Now, as an elf, I am blessed with a special talent of creating deadly masterpieces. Come, come, come!" He enthusiastically waves me over to a massive work table. Its top is scattered with a wide array of designs and drawings, as well as a selection of different blade styles for me to peruse. As he works, it is made clear how truly gifted and passionate about his work he is. A spark of joy and anticipation glitters in his eyes again, chasing away the ghosts of his past, and he begins his process.

✿ ✿ ✿ ✿ ✿

Returning to the castle three hours later, I can't help but marvel at all the details Eganël had taken in that time. All to factor into the final result. A weapon worthy of legend. "I see now why I held on to *ahtorainë* all of those star-cycles. I was not expecting it to take *that* long." A twinge of guilt ripples through me as I realize the unending list of things I could have, *should* have, been doing with that time instead. My pace quickens.

"I'm surprised you aren't peppering me with your questions yet." Türë's voice cuts through my sudden tension. I can't help but laugh, in spite of the stress that was beginning to rise.

"Maybe I'm still trying to sort out which ones I want to ask first." He huffs a soft chuckle but still waits for the first of many questions that inevitably were coming. As if they had been waiting patiently to be remembered. "I think the first—and most obvious —did we truly set a town on fire?" Türë's eyes glaze over, and I know he is picturing it.

"You did." He shakes his head, trying to force a smile for my benefit. "Eganël had made a claim that a pair of fire bracers that he had invented could beat your magic for fire strength and distance."

"Fire bracers?"

"Like these." He stops and takes my wrist to hold up the drakonskein bracers that still wrap my forearms. "But the ones Eganël made could, on command, blast a stream of fire—like a drakon—or like you when you direct it from your palms."

"H—how would that even be possible? To enable anyone the power to control a sliver of magic, even if the power was limited, it would still be uncontrolled power over fire." He nods, agreeing with my disapproval.

"Hence the challenge issued. You set out to prove why Eganël should not create such a thing."

"But I am assuming something went wrong."

"Very wrong. You gave a demonstration of your fire, your control, and the distance you could send it out. It displayed what centuries of training and the blessing of Jera could accomplish. But then came Eganël's turn..." Türë runs his fingers through his hair, dark eyes flickering with the reflection of the torches that line the streets of Alessandra. He begins walking again, though his steps are heavy and a weight seems to press on his shoulders. As if the memory sits leaden in his mind. "He pushed the magic he had forged into the bracers too far to try to surpass you. It did as commanded and sent a wall of fire in every direction for five hundred paces." My steps falter and horror surges through me as I picture the scene. My hand flys to my mouth, covering my silent gasp of revulsion. "We still don't know if there was a gap in the stonewall or if Eganël's magic bracer had somehow overpowered and slipped through the surrounding barriers—but the fire got into the stores of black explosive powder. It ignited." I can't breathe I'm so appalled at this piece of history I am hearing for the first time. Unfortunately, Türë continues. "The blast could be heard as far as the Port of Eludar, hundreds of miles away on the far side of Tesindren, it was so loud." Neither of us speaks for several minutes as I try to gather my mind back into pieces, scattered as far as the debris from the explosion had no doubt been.

"What happened? How many—?" I swallow down the words I desperately, simultaneously, want to and don't want to know. But Türë knows my question.

"Two perished."

"Two?!" I repeat, hoarse from fighting the tears that threaten to choke me. I frown, disbelief clearing the haze of dismay. "How is that possible?"

"You realized about three breaths before the shockwave of the explosion hit and threw out your abilities, somehow, around every person and animal you could sense. When the fire-wave receded, there was nothing standing for half a league—except for those you threw the barrier around. They did not even have a fleck of ash or soot on them, let alone a scratch or burns. The most severe effect felt by the survivors closest to the explosion was akin to a mild sunburn."

"That's—that's *impossible.*" I breathe, unable to comprehend the scope of my previous control.

"Well, I wouldn't suggest doing it ever again if you can avoid it. You paid dearly for it." He laughs halfheartedly, trying to lift the mood. "You took a look around—as if you had to reassure yourself that everyone was safe—then promptly collapsed. I wasn't with you then, but it was said they couldn't wake you for half a moon-cycle."

"Who were the two I did not save?" I manage to ask.

"Two of the guards who were stationed at the powder stores." He explains, as gently as he can. "They were too close to the explosion and there wasn't time for your protection to reach them." I can't think of what to even say now, so we just continue our walk in silence. The castle looms ahead of us, and for the first time I don't wish to return.

"What happened to all the other Creatures of the Forest? Why is Eganël all that is left that we know of? You said they were hunted to extinction. That had to be before my rule, right? Patryk said that I established the Underkings to prevent anything like the Dothsmerna massacre from happening again. Why wouldn't others like Eganël re-emerge?" We pass through the first round of castle gates and I nod in greeting at each guard and warrior we pass. Now manning the walls with increasing numbers and attentiveness since the news had come the evening before. The Nefriti had been paired with the castle guard for night watches, to show unity in my kingdom's protectors as well as getting them used to mingling. I had been shocked to learn the two groups rarely, if ever, associated with each other. Türe still doesn't answer, and I glance at him, concerned. My stomach drops at the pained look that tightens his already sharp features. "Explain. Now." I demand, gripping his arm tight enough that he winces. I realize a second too late the reaction is not from my nails digging into his forearm, but from the bright white sparks of lightning that dance across my skin. But I ignore them and pull him to a stop, spinning Türe to face me, even as he looks away.

"Fine. But let's go in here." With a resigned sigh, he motions with his head to a nearby dark arch. Through it I see a small flower garden, tucked away in an alcove. I let him pull against my grip, leading me inside for some privacy. Just off the main road that leads to the castle, I am surprised to find it empty and I ignite the surrounding unlit braziers with a focused thought. My icy mood is a sharp contrast to the delicious heat I feel at the brush of my fire. I push away the feeling, not wanting anything to distract me as I strive to find a reasonable explanation for why I would allow an *extermination* to happen. We reach the farthest point in the small, unoccupied garden. Türe finally stops, apparently deeming it safe enough to talk as he turns to face me.

"It was nine hundred and fifty star-cycles ago when all of this began. I had just come to Tesindren, along with an unprecedented number of others like me. Us. Word had spread that a kind and powerful Queen had extended sanctuary to all. So all manner of beings, now grouped under one title—Creatures of the Forest— began to flee other kingdom's where persecution and segregation had begun to take hold." He takes a breath and starts to pace back and forth on the small dirt path woven among the flowers bushes.

I notice a nearby boulder, large enough that it could function as a bench for ten people, and plop down on its edge. Mental and physical exhaustion overwhelm me as I try to keep focused on the story.

"That all sounds positive. What went wrong?"

"It was going to create a utopia, and it was that way for a while. Sickness was rare, starvation non-existent. Peace filled the kingdom. But magic is power, and power can lead to fear if abused—even if there are only a few who do take advantage of it. The fear grew and began to meld with jealousy. It began to rot in the hearts of the people. This led to neighbors turning on each other, casting out any of those who were deemed *different*. It didn't matter then if their magic was being used to help the crops, or heal the sick. They were different and therefore untrustworthy. What was once a haven quickly turned into just another place to tread lightly or remain hidden. Mind you, it took over a hundred star-cycles for things to begin to sour. But once they did, they were never the same. It seemed to be almost over night."

"Why didn't I do anything?" I say through clenched teeth, thankful to be sitting as my head begins to swirl with anger.

"That is exactly what we all tried to figure out. Where was this Queen? The one we had heard such amazing things about?" His tone is filled with sour rage and I feel sick at his words, but don't interrupt. He had been one of these people I had let be hated and shunned I realize. Then he smiles softly at me and his pacing stops. "Turns out, she was going city to city across the entire kingdom herself. Ensuring that every citizen saw her and knew that she stood by us. Hell, that she was *one* of us. If we were going to act against those perceived as different, well then they would have to act against her." His eyes glimmer with respect and adoration as he gazes at me openly. I blush and return his piercing gaze with a careful smile. It had been a long day and I realize, with the wild thumping of my heart, that I needed to see that look, especially after all of the feelings I had confessed to him the night before, and my second thoughts since.

Then his face falls and another memory sweeps him into the past. His eyes dim as it hits him, a shadow descending across us both like the front of a storm. I shiver against the chill that washes across my skin as Türë's limited wind whips around us both, sharp against the warm summer night air. "Then we were all beckoned. We were told there was to be a celebration in our honor." His voice cracks slightly and he turns away, hiding his face from me. I sit, rigid atop the rock, waiting for the horrible story that I know has yet to come, to be over.

But I have to know. I don't want to run from my history, even the worst parts of it. I owed it to myself, to my people—past, present, and future— to learn from it.

"Instead," Türë continues, "the music came to a screeching halt in the town square, replaced by loud, wooden thuds. Then a man standing above us on a turret told us that the Queen had been playing with her magic and set her own city ablaze. He told us she now lay dying, and it did not look favorable that she would last the night. I remember the shock that rippled through the crowd. But we still didn't understand, didn't realize, until it was too late that everyone that stood around us was *different*. Not until we realized the thudding had been the doors being shut and barred. Not until we realized we were locked in. Only when the first arrow struck and a young female healer elf dropped did the confusion clear and the screaming begin." His hands tighten into fists at his side, knuckles white as bone as his tendons flex beneath the skin. When he looks over his shoulder at me, I see the tears painted silver by the moonlight streaming freely down his face. Tears drip down my own cheeks as I imagine the horrific scene. As clear as if a picture was sitting in front of me.

"That is why you are so angry with Eganël. You blame him for this."

"If he had not allowed his ego to play with magic, you never would have overextended yourself, and would not have fallen into unconsciousness." He bites, crossing his arms tight across his chest.

"But you survived...? How?" I force myself to ask, to reassure myself that even though he stood before me, he somehow lived another seven hundred and twelve star-cycles.

"I was shot in the arm and the side, somehow only two of the hundreds of arrows finding me, and lost enough blood that I lost consciousness. My Sidhe body was able to heal, but slowly. Too slowly. The townspeople who had signed our death warrant then dragged us out of the town and to a nearby field. Apparently, we were to be burned the next day, to hide what they had done. I, thankfully, regained enough strength in time before that horrific end and fled into the forest.

"Why didn't anyone use their magic to fight back?? Why didn't you?"

"It happened too fast." He spins fully around to face me, anger flickering in his dark eyes. Night had truly fallen around us, and the glint of tear tracks catch in the torchlight. Even with the town just on the other side of the wall, in the darkness and quiet of every one tucking in for the night, it feels like we are the only two in the city. The topic creates a heavy distance between us, however. The past that will haunt Türë rises up like a wall. Him on one side, forever trapped by the grief of that day, and me, mind empty of those same memories that I gave up in payment for immortality and magic, on the other. Payment to keep the very thing that so many had lost their lives *because of*. I am deep into my spiraling when I realize Türë is still talking. "They coated the arrows with poison. Not one that killed, but one that nullified any trace of magical power once you were hit." My hands shake in rage. The desire to avenge my people, my friend, overtakes me, even though I know this happened over centuries before and all who had participated were long dead. I still want to rain down hell upon those who had done this.

"Where did this happen?" I ask, trying to mask the shaking in my voice.

"Dothsmerna." He spits, as if the name itself was acid in his mouth. My brows furrow as I gasp.

"You were there?" I stammer, racking my brain. "Patryk didn't say—"

"Patryk doesn't know." Türë hisses softly. I try to picture the map of the kingdom in my mind.

"I don't remember seeing a town called Dothsmerna. I thought it was a field somewhere, or... I don't know. Not that *that* matters." I mutter, more to myself. I feel like vomiting.

"That is because it no longer exists." A cruel, satisfied grin cracks across his face, not reaching his eyes that shimmer with hate. "You woke up to news of the massacre, the Massacre of Dothsmerna as it's called now. And when you arrived, you wiped it off of the map. The retribution for action against your people that you promised would come, did. It descended swift and terrible in its vengeful beauty. I didn't know you then, nor you I, but I sat in the forest as I healed, slow as a mortal thanks to the poison, and watched you avenge us."

"What—what did I *do* to them?" I swallow hard, my mouth completely dry.

"You strode into town and told the children to leave. Then you called all the adults into the square. You walked through them, row by row, watching them closely. The ones who plead and shook you separated from those who dropped to their knees and rejoiced that you had lived. The latter you ordered out of the city after the children. You then gave all those who remained, the guilty and evil, a last chance to admit their wrongs and beg for forgiveness for all that they had done to us." He sneers. "None did. Not a single one. They all had their *reasons*." Shaking with disgust, he wrings his hands. A path below his feet had already begun to form from his fevered pacing. "That was when you announced that a fire death was too good for their sort. It was too swift and merciful. For them, you gave the ultimate punishment. You called up the ground. The earth itself swallowed Dothsmerna and its remaining inhabitants up whole. Left to die a slow, suffocating, starving death. Away from any light and open sky. A fitting punishment for killing so many innocents with no remorse."

I taste bile and barely turn in time to spill the contents of my stomach into a nearby bush. Türë's warm hands pull the hair back from my face, rubbing my back in an attempt at comfort. *Comforting me... after what he had gone through. After what I had done.* When the nausea passes, I stand again, wiping my mouth with the handkerchief Türë holds out to me.

"That is *horrible*." I rasp. "How could I do such a thing?"

"How could *you?*" Surprise flares across his face, eyes wide in disbelief. "How could *they?* I don't think you grasp the level of the atrocity, Evara." I wince at his volume, and he tries to soften his voice as he realizes he had yelled, without meaning to, at his Queen. "There were children—even a day old newborn—that were included, without consideration, in the carnage. The humans you punished were matured adults who knew what they were doing and the evil they conspired together to carry out. Even *then*, you gave them a chance to repent. They chose to remain. Their hatred of us was so great that, for their own lives, they were unwilling to waver in their fear. Their prejudice." I gape at him. The loathing and disgust that sharpens each of his features into a deadly mask was so unfamiliar to me. I had never seen such hate and rage before, and definitely not from Türë.

"I understand your anger, but that doesn't excuse the hell I rained down upon those people. All that did was prove they were *right* to fear magic and its wielders."

The look of incredulousness that wipes away any part of Türë I thought I knew from his face has me taking a step back as his lip curls into a snarl of rage.

At me.

I take another step back, my quarters of training have me falling back into a protective stance out of habit. I had no idea what to expect from the man before me.

He sees this and suddenly utter sorrow replaces all the anger. Flattening the features back into ones I knew and trusted. But it was clear something had shifted between us. I could see from his eyes, now doing everything to avoid mine, that respect had been lost. For both of us.

"This is what is coming, Evara." He says, voice flat and emotionless, turning his heavy gaze on me again. "You say you want to be Queen. This is it. Hard choices. Lives lost. Your own morals getting damaged to protect and stand for what is *right*." My breath seems frozen in my chest as I try to find the words to argue, to prove that he was wrong. "We are at war now. You are going to send people to die and will kill others yourself. You need to evaluate yourself, right now, if that is something you will be able to do." My own anger surges and I step forward, jabbing my finger into his chest. A bit of smoke curls up from where my touch singes his shirt.

"How *dare* you. You over step, General." I snap at him, and it is his turn to step back and I swear the smallest bit of fear flickers on his stony face.

"Excuse me, Your Majesty. I need some—time." He forces out, his voice going chilly, using the same manner he reserved for courtiers whom he didn't care for. I watch, my heart beat warring with itself as it seems to stumble in my chest. Türe drops a sharp deep bow and vanishes through the archway and back towards the city we had come from. I start to wonder if I knew anyone at all.

Including myself.

thirty-two

I do my best to smile at every person I pass in the halls. Praying I exude a confidence I don't come close to feeling. I meander down random hallways after realizing that, apart from my old rooms, I had nowhere to sleep now. Though I am sure Türe would not begrudge me sleeping again in his bed, even with his foul disposition at the moment, I didn't think it would feel right. Not to mention I didn't particularly *want* to. I regret dismissing my guards now outside of the blacksmith's shop. But it wasn't like I was expecting Türe to abandon me in the streets. With a sigh, I rub my eyes, which water from exhaustion, emotions, and stress. I decide to try to find my study again, remembering the couch and deeming it acceptable for the night. I was fooling myself if I thought I was going to sleep well tonight, anyway. Aiming for the hallways around Türe's quarters, I remember what Rhodie had said about them being near the study.

Entering the older part of the castle, I trail my fingers along the walls, exhaling loudly. What Türe had said about the magic I had accidentally, and conveniently, infused into them lingers in my mind. After a second of consideration, I reach into the wood and stone with my mind. If I am the only one who can use the magic, well, then maybe it *was* still here, just hiding. Nothing flares against my mental touch, hinting to even the barest glint of power. I sigh and continue on my path through the maze of hallways toward what I hope is Türë's quarters. In the dimly lit passage, every door seems to be the same. I do eventually pass Türë's door, recognizable only by the stag engraved in the wood. I stick my tongue out at it as I pass. Knowing it is locked, I don't bother even trying the handle.

I continue down the hall. What had started as me trying to find a room had somehow become almost a game. Each hallway I travel and each door I open reveals something new. And right now, the simple distraction was a gift from Jera herself.

These days, it was rare for me to find myself not surrounded by guards. Not that I was pushing it much anymore. Everyone was too on edge right now. Still, no word had come from any of the Underkings or territories with further information or actions. With a sigh, I rub my eyes and lean against the wall before sliding down it to sit on the floor. I had done my best at trying not to think about what had happened with Türë. *Was I wrong saying what I did? The way he looked at me...* I rest my head back against the stone and with half of a thought, now well versed in the practice, douse the flicking flames in the braziers that light the windowless halls.

"What the *hell?*"

A male voice from around the corner curses colorfully under his breath to himself. My eyes snap wide open, looking down the now black-as-moonless-night hall. I purse my lips against a laugh as I hear the man, who had been unexpectedly plunged into impenetrable darkness, fumble around for the walls, continuing the endless stream of curses while doing so.

I cast my fire back out to the still warm embers that smolder in their golden bowls. Every torch I had smothered not a minute ago reignites, illuminating the hallway again.

"Jera help me! That is bright as—" he yells, and I wince, realizing too late I should have warned him. In his blind stumbling, he had turned into the hall where I now sit. But whatever the sudden light was as bright as, I would never know because Patryk blinks his eyes rapidly, still watering from the painful sudden changes and shouts loudly in terror. I launch to my feet and stumble over to him, wondering if I had accidentally caused more damage than I thought. "How long have you been sitting there?" He yells, placing his hand on his chest, trying to soothe the rapidly thumping heart that I can hear dancing wildly from fear. Unable to help myself, I burst out laughing.

"I'm so sorry! I didn't mean to scare you. Or blind you!" Patryk takes a few deep, steadying breaths before speaking.

"Sorry to interrupt if you were trying to hide. I just heard that Türe was storming through the city in a fury and you hadn't been seen for a while. I wanted to make sure you were okay and guessed this part of the castle would lure you back." I don't know quite what to say. Part of me is annoyed at how quickly word spreads in this castle, but I am also touched by his concern for me. "Are you okay?" he asks. I tug on a loose strand of my hair that had come loose from its braid. I mull over how to respond. Since returning to the castle following the Awakening, I hadn't sought him out, or any of my Underkings really, since my training with the Nefriti and Türe had begun. Not only had I been neglecting my friendships, but I had been hiding from them. I force my eyes up to meet his bright sapphire ones that watch me openly. From what I already gathered of his character, I knew that whatever I told him—-confessed, confided, vented—it would go no further.

Nor would he hold it against me. I grab for his arm, tugging him down beside me, and tell him everything. The development of Türë's and my attempt at a deeper relationship, my resulting doubts about doing so, what had happened in the courtyard tonight, my fear for my growing powers, my discontent in the castle—and in my role as Queen in general—and finally of the memories that seem to have resurfaced. To his credit, he listens to all of it without any sign of judgment. Only kindness and an understanding that seems to see more than just the words I say.

"I don't see how I am worthy of this—of any of you." I confess, no longer bothering to hold back the tears that slide now fully down my cheeks. "Maybe the person I was before was worth it, but more and more, I am realizing I am not *her*. No matter how hard I try. And I think others are starting to realize that too. Türë certainly is." I stare down at my fingernails, torn and jagged thanks to anxious fidgeting during my lengthy confession to Patryk. "Making things even harder is the fact that I know there are things still being kept from me." Patryk grimaces, confirming without having to say a word. But I can't find the energy or desire to be angry with him. He gently grabs a hand resting in my lap.

"Would you like to know the truth? All of it." He murmurs, soft enough that I have to lean in to hear him. Even with my advanced hearing. I sit back, wide-eyed and try to comprehend what exactly he is offering. "I can help you learn everything you want to know." Patryk's eyes have darkened, knowing what he might risk with his offer. There was a reason Türë and the others were set on keeping me in the dark on a few things, or all things. But he was willing to take that risk, as well as possibly harming his friendships and forgoing the trust of the others. For me, his friend, he would give me those answers I needed. All I had to do is say yes.

"Let me think on it." I say, squeezing the hand in mine. "Thank you Patryk. I am sorry I have not been who you expected me to be. I'm truly so sorry about that. "

"Don't ever say that!" He says loudly, outraged. I jump at the outburst. "You don't have to be anyone but yourself. What you need to do is to find out who that is. Not was, but *is*. You have a chance to start over. To be whoever you want to be. But that is what you need to figure out. Not Türe, not Athene, or Ilithyia, or any of the rest of us. *You*." I blink at him, surprised at the sudden passion. But this was what I needed to hear. And I had needed Patryk to open my eyes to that fact. I have been looking to everyone else to tell me who I am supposed to be, rather than listening to myself.

The minutes pass in silence as we both sit in the empty hall, simply thinking and relaxing in these few, rare moments alone.

"What were you doing down here when I found you?" Patryk asks, suddenly, as if the realization had just come to him.

"Exploring, I guess." I say, looking down the hall in the direction I had come from as I worked my way from room to room.

"I'm surprised you weren't already sound asleep. From all the gossip I have been hearing, you kicked some serious ass today. A Gladiator too, if what they say was true." He nudges my shoulder with his own, a smile furrows a small dimple into his cheek. I fight the urge to poke it with my pinky finger. I snort, humored at the gracious over-exaggeration of the fight.

"As tired as I am, I don't know where to sleep, honestly. Nothing feels right, right now." I admit. He nods, understanding after all I had laid upon him.

"I heard Rhodie showed you your old study. Why don't you just use your old room across the hall?"

I stare at him blankly. "That would be convenient." I muse, barking a sharp laugh. "No one until just now said a word about a room across the hall... I was just planning on crashing on the study's couch—if I could ever find it again that is."

Patryk laughs at me, before rolling to his feet, then turning to help me onto mine. "I can help with that." He tilts his head, looking at me with such affection, I want to sweep him into a hug. "Has anyone told you about the magic that still lingers in this part of the castle?"

I start and narrow my eyes. "I was told that aside from my study and Türe's room, it no longer exists anywhere else. And even then, I was the only one who could control it." He steps closer, a teasing grin on his face as he whispers loudly.

"Well, you were told wrong." My intrigue is peaked, so I watch him closely as he begins to knock on the wall, his volume returning to normal as he shoots me a conspiratorial look of glee. "It was a secret that you only shared with me, as far as I know." Patryk turns to face the wall, speaking directly to it. "Queen's study, please."

I watch, fascinated and baffled, as we wait for whatever it is he is trying to show me. He winks playfully at me, apparently seeing a response to his request that I do not. Seeing my continued confusion, he points to the nearest brazier. I understand suddenly and I gasp at the little ball of light that bobs out, flickering and hovering, about shoulder height. I take a hesitant step forward, hand outstretched to touch the apple-sized fireball. It floats backwards, almost mimicking my step. I watch it in wonder, taking another step towards it. Again, the ball of light floats ahead another pace.

"Were you hiding from me before?" I ask kindly, and the tight seems to bob a playful yes. I giggle as it spins happily. Patryk's eyes glitter in amusement as he watches me play with the little spark of magic.

"It will lead you where ever you want to go—in this part of the castle, at least." He explains proudly.

"Do you know why they changed my rooms upon returning from the Awakening?" I find the courage to ask suddenly. Curiosity overtaking me as I wonder why they would go to the lengths to separate me from this part of the castle.

"I do." His tone has become guarded, and I sigh, understanding his reservation.

"Does it relate to the secrets that are being kept from me?"

He only nods once, before looking ashamed. "Like I said—I will tell you. But you need to understand that you requested certain things be done after your memories had been taken."

"I know. I understand. It's frustrating, but I understand." A yawn forces its way through and he chuckles at me before slipping his elbow around my own and leading me after the dancing ball of light.

"Come on. Nothing good is ever decided by a sleep-deprived mind." Together we follow our silent guide and I feel relief begin to seep into my heart with each step that leads me forward to a warm bed and a good night of sleep. I look at Patryk, affection warming my heart. Steady and comforting, I lean into his touch, letting the reassurance of his friendship chase away the chill from all my worries.

thirty-three

I sigh in relief as I wake up to the soft pink rays of morning light and the muffled quiet that I had only experienced in this part of the castle. Stretching my arms up, I moan at the mixture of pleasure and pain from the motion. Patryk's memory had been accurate, thank Jera for that. By the time we reached the hallway that led to my study, each step was heavy and my body was begging for a comfortable bed. I had been braced for an empty room with maybe a few blankets or even a spare soldier's cot. And as tired as I was, I would not have complained about either of them. Instead, we found an enormous fourposter bed, complete with a fluffy feather down mattress. Squealing with delight, I had nearly launched myself into it, forgoing any attempt to pretend that I possessed self-control. Even more of a blessing, the servants had continued to maintain the room, so I was able to snuggle into freshly washed, dust free sheets. A luxury I had not expected when Patryk had told me of this room. He had departed quickly afterwards, claiming he was satisfied that I would not be sleeping in a strange corner or wandering through the hallways all night.

I curl deeper into the blankets, feeling better rested than any other time I could remember. Any glimmer of a thought that threatens to surface, I shove away, deciding to let myself luxuriate in the peace and quiet as long as I can. A dream in itself.

Yet, that proves to only be mere minutes. A tentative knock comes from the door. I sigh deeply into the pillow I pull over my head, but when the soft knock on the door comes again, I finally sit up and bid them to enter.

To my surprise, it is Patryk's face that peaks around the door. Though upon reflection, I realize that unless he had told anyone else, nobody *but* him knew where I was right now. I wince a little at the realization and pray that I had not caused anyone distress or panic.

"Good morning, Evara." He gives me cautious smile as he finds me still in bed. "May I come in?" He hesitates, "or should I meet you in the study?" He blushes and I realize that I am dressed only in my underthings. I had no nightclothes in the room yet, and I had not been in the mood, nor had the energy to track down something for the night. As comfortable as the drakonskein suit was, it was filthy and not suitable for a good night's sleep.

"Umm... the study is best." I say, pulling the sheets further up as casually as I can. Though I was positive there was nothing more between us than friendship, I did not want to have Athene on my case. He chuckles enough though to let me know my efforts were in vain. Though I wasn't showing anything I shouldn't, he still had guessed from my bare shoulders and obvious discomfort, the predicament I found myself in. I roll my eyes at him.

"Here. I brought you these." He reaches in through the door to place a folded dress inside the room. I throw him a grateful smile and he shuts the door, leaving me again to myself. Curiosity gets the better of me and I am out of bed and dressed within a minute.

He hadn't seemed impatient or worried—which made me feel slightly less anxious. Only slightly. I did wonder at what he wanted to tell me. This had been the first morning he had sought me out, so there had to be a reason. Whether good or bad—I didn't dare guess which.

I make my way across the hall to where the door sits open. The gentle crackle of the fireplace greets me as I stride into the cozy room, then notice the snapping is accompanied by another sound. I struggle to identify it when Patryk answers it for me.

"Quite a thunderstorm, isn't it?" He asks, just as the grumble of thunder shakes the castle. Raindrops plink against the glass panes, explaining the sound that dances with the fire. Looking up from a book he had perched in his lap, reading while waiting from me, he looks just as comforted by this room as I was. I wonder how often we had passed hours here together...before I had been so changed. "Stop that." Patryk chides, somehow seeing the direction my thoughts had gone. The rhythmic *tink* of the rain against the window creates such a merry tune, I stride to one of the windows and push it out. Not enough for the rain to come pouring in as it falls in sheets from the sky, but to better hear the rumbles from above and to feel the fresh electric storm air fill the room. When I at last sit behind the massive oaken desk, I run my fingers across the intricate lines that make this particular grain a true mastery of nature. I return my focus to Patryk, who snaps his book shut with a thud.

"Alright. What news do you have for me?" I ask, sitting tall. I had only seen my throne once, and not felt like even half of the Queen worthy of such a seat. But this desk? Somehow it feels like the right step forward in accepting my place again as Tesindren's true ruler.

Shifting to serious, Patryk sets the book aside, a frown creasing his forehead. "I did the figuring and, under our current population, Alessandra can sustain on its current supplies for four star-cycles."

"Okay. That's good, right?" I hesitate when he doesn't seem thrilled with those numbers. "Why do I sense a *but..?*"

He gives an unenthusiastic half smile that doesn't reach the rest of his face. "*But* if we extend our invitation of protection to the rest of the kingdom, should the worst happen, that time dwindles down to only three quarters. Maximum a star-cycle if we enforce strict rations." I chew my lip as I think over this information. "*But*," Patryk says again, with another shallow grin. "The good news is that if we have a profitable harvest, like we are expecting, *and* if each town and village agrees to give their surplus supplies for us to maintain and store—in exchange for a place to seek sanctuary—that timeline jumps back to the four star-cycle estimate."

"Well, *that's* good... right?" I repeat, frowning at the still lackluster feeling that he radiates.

"My concerns for that option are two-fold. Should we take the surplus stock from the rest of the territory, we are simultaneously drawing them thin *and* keeping all of our eggs in one proverbial basket. So many things could go wrong. What if the storage rooms flood, or a fire breaks out? Or even worse, Alessandra falls and we all have to flee? If all our reserves are here, we will have nothing to fall back on without high percentages of starvation and death."

I stand and begin to pace behind the desk, trying to think through all the options and dangers presented. "And the second concern?"

"I don't honestly know *where* we would put all who would come. While Yvonya is the biggest of your castles, it is also the most populated, due to it being a part of Alessandra. And while its design is beautiful—it is not meant for lengthy sieges. It was why you positioned strongholds along the borders. They were to take the attacks. Not Yvonya Castle, and not Alessandra. The castle, and even considering the city, there is extremely limited space when you are talking about taking in hundreds of thousands of people."

"How many could we fit? Comfortably." I begin to walk circles around the desk as I think.

"Comfortably?" He says. "Around eight hundred. But the maximum before we have to start filling the streets," Patryk checks his notes, tugging a notebook from his jacket and flipping through a few pages before he finds the number he is looking for. "Two thousand. And that is using every room and spare space in the castle, guardhouses, and grounds."

I rub my temples and prop up against the front of the desk. "And we want to avoid the streets as much as possible because of the risk of illness and disease." He nods slowly, and I catch the flash of surprise at my accurate deduction. "Noran has been giving me homework, and one book was an epic poem of the siege of a city that fell due to being overcome with sickness." I explain with a half-hearted smile.

"Ahh!" He nods, but still eyes me with a pleased look. "I admit I am impressed! I didn't realize you have been studying."

I feel myself tighten, bracing against the perceived insult, until I realize that it was a genuine compliment. I nod with a shy smile. "I don't *want* to be a useless queen." Lowering my head, I stare at the stone floor edge I trace my toes along.

"Is that what you think you are?" His voice is pained and I don't let myself look at him even as he leans forward in the chair. Obviously wanting to get close to me, but not wanting to pass through an unwelcome barrier I had erected. "I don't know who made you feel that way, but I hope you know that *none* of us think that about you." Türë's face flashes in my mind, but I shrug, as if it was just something to brush off. Never had I voiced to anyone how unworthy I felt. Not worthy enough for the people who supported me, guarded me, *depended* on me.

"No one has *said* it exactly. But it's hard to think it is anything other than that when everyone keeps things from me." I turn my gaze now fully to Patryk. His eyes harden, seeing through my attempt at nonchalance.

"Is this your decision, then? You want me to tell you everything? Because like I told you last night, it was you who left specific instructions to what you were told and when. I am just doing my best to honor those wishes, as is everyone else." He doesn't yell, but his tone shows his frustration.

With a long exhale, my shoulders drop. "I know. I know. I'm sorry. I am just on edge right now." Patryk sits back, understanding suddenly flashes across his face. I chew my lip against the question that threatens to burst forth.

"Do you—have you—" I struggle to find a way to voice the words that won't betray my desperation. His lips quirk at the corners, and I see him resisting a knowing grin, sitting back in his chair.

"I might have also inquired as to any word of Türe and where he is..." He scratches against the rough stubble that bloomed on his chin overnight.

"And?" I prompt after he doesn't continue. A full grin widens unrestrained now. I grit my teeth in irritation at his obvious teasing.

"He was spotted riding through the castle gates just as I was on my way to find you this morning. He should be arriving at his room any minute now, actually. Assuming that is where he chooses to go first." His brows slide upwards at the insinuation.

"You didn't hear the discussion we had. I doubt he will be coming to find me any time soon." I admit. "And even if he did— I'm not sure I have anything kind to say to him anyway." I cross my arms against my chest, hoping that he won't catch the lie. There were so many things I needed to say to Türë.

"Well then. I will take my leave." I spin, startled, towards the door to the study where a soaking Türë stands, hair limp and face pale in the low light of the rainy day.

thirty-four

My heart stutters in relief at the sight of Türë, even as my happiness at seeing him wars with the anger still lingering from the night before. Our eyes meet, and I see the regret of his actions in their depths. He turns to go.

"Wait." I actually shout at him, before swallowing hard and turning to Patryk to ask him to give us a moment. But my friend is already moving across the room to the door, pausing only to pat Türë's sopping shoulder.

"I will go see if there has been any more word from my brothers." He says, before sliding past Türë's muscular form that takes up a majority of the doorway. There are so many questions and pain in the air right now, it feels silly to take up the precious minutes and energy with this much needed conversation. But things had to be put right with Türë. Now. Before, they could become even more convoluted.

"Please come in and get warm." I say softly, gesturing to the empty couch, filled with warmth from the fire. Suddenly alone with him again, the words I had wanted to say to him all morning escape me. His eyes narrow, examining me closely before pacing silently towards the fire. His shoulders relax slightly in its comforting warmth. I try to focus my thoughts, though they are wrought with distraction.

"Where did you go?" I ask finally. I knew of the numerous brothels in the surrounding villages and realize, with sharp relief, that I didn't particularly care if he had visited one in an attempt at some petty revenge or distraction. That alone was revealing enough to give me the answer to the question within my heart that had been circling like a bird of prey the last few days. After all, we had never truly defined what we were to each other, and after the way he had looked at me last night, I wondered if he now saw me in a different light than he ever had before. As I had seen him, a familiar stranger.

"Did you find somewhere to sleep last night?" He turns the question on me, rather than answering. I shove down my annoyance.

"Did *you?*" I reply, crossing my arms over my chest as my gaze narrows on the back of his head. He chuckles lightly, though the look he shoots me over his shoulder is anything but friendly, his hands outstretched in front of the fire as he tries to get the iciness out of their pruned tips. He turns back to the fire as I clench my fists against the rage that begins to build.

"I did, Your Majesty."

I almost snarl at the honorary term. Because I know he only uses it now as a patronizing quip.

"Good." I snap, forcing my body to relax as I turn away from him and move to take my seat behind my desk. "I am glad you are well rested." He stiffens, then turns to face me fully. There is no attempt to hide his shock at my reaction. It is painted obviously on his face, making it clear he was attempting to goad me. Moves within controlling moves was what Türë was known for on the battlefield and war room. It appears to be a skill in every day life now, I observe sadly. Resolve fills me and I press my flat palms against the desk. "I think we need to clear the air, Türë. What I confessed to you before the Solstice ball was a mistake. One that has not only compromised our working relationship, but also has put our friendship at risk. For the good of the kingdom, and for us, I think we need to reevaluate where we stand.

Türë balks as he takes in my words before he moves quicker than I ever thought he could. Before I can blink, or gasp, he is at my side. Cupping my cheek with his fire-warmed hands he presses his forehead to mine, even as I go rigid. "I'm sorry I left you, and I am even more sorry for what I said to you." He pushes the loose strands of hair back from my face, either not noticing my discomfort, or ignoring it completely. "Will you forgive me, Evara?" I lean into the touch.

"Of course I forgive you. You had me worried sick when Patryk said you were seen leaving Alessandra. But—" I shake my head and, as gently as I can, push him away.

"Please don't do this. I messed up, but you and I, we are meant to be together."

"Türë—" I begin, trying to stand even as he grabs at me.

"I can do better. I just don't know how to navigate this. To you, I am a stranger, but for me, you are the woman I have always loved." He nearly begs and I feel my breath catch. My mind stutters as I try to figure out how to respond. I can only give the truth to him as gently as I can.

"There is no spark, Türë. And you deserve someone who feels that spark. We both do."

"I don't—" He flinches as my confession lands. "Let me try again. I can show you a spark! There is something between us. I know there is!" He lunges forward for me again, something in his eyes growing dark, desperate. I push against his advance, my heart pounds in agitation.

Suddenly someone pounds on the door, surprising us both enough that Türë wavers. I am still frozen in shock as I stare at Türë. Only the words shouted at me break my stupor.

"Evara! It's Ivrik!" Patryk shouts through the door.

Türë spouts a creative string of curses as he finally pulls away from me, furious at the interruption, but my stomach churns.

"We are coming." I say weakly, before I elbow my way past Türë. I needed to figure out what the hell just happened, and what the hell *almost* happened. But right now, my priority was Ivrik.

Türë was a problem I would have to deal with later.

A major problem.

✱ ✱ ✱ ✱ ✱

My skirts billow around me as I sprint through the castle. Türë and Patryk follow close behind me, though I do notice that I quickly leave them behind. I would have to send a note of thanks to Elder Dakar for his punishing regimen that had chiseled my body into one that could outpace the General. Other than the short, stammered explanation that Ivrik had arrived unexpectedly at the gate, we had no further information of what to expect. Patryk had run to get us immediately upon receiving word that his brother, in everything but blood, was now in the care of the castle guard. I knew that it had taken everything for him to run to us, rather than to Ivrik.

Each of the Underkings had their own set of rooms in the castle, a place for themselves to call their home away from home when visiting the capital. An occurrence that happened frequently since the furthest of the Underking's palaces was Noran's in Dolunt. Even then, he was only a three-day ride away. Two, if the horses were pushed to an uncomfortable pace. There was rarely a holiday or celebration that passed without at least one, if not all, of the Underkings present. The only exception to this was the Solstice ball, since each territory played host to their own. Türë had explained to me that our relationships were fascinating to him, a bond that is rare and entwined. We were as close as family —or at least we had been before I had again completed the Awakening, wedging a gap between me and them. Even if there was only one in my mind.

We skid to a stop outside of the double doors that lead to Ivrik's suite. I had never been inside, only had it pointed out to me on one of my frequent trips through the castle. I hesitate and the men behind me give questioning, impatient looks. My mind begins to swirl with all the possibilities that lie beyond the door. Other than the messenger who brought the news of Dulen on the eve of the Solstice, I had not yet seen the proof of the war with my own eyes. Not yet seen the consequences of my choice to remove myself as Tesindren's strongest protector, even only temporarily. Would Ivrik be hurt? Would he blame me for the death that had come to his door? Would hate stare back at me for my choice that led to this vulnerability in my kingdom? I inhale slowly, trying to push away all of these fears to focus on the crucial fact. He was alive. And well enough to make it here. If he hated me, I would take it, and do everything I could to prove to him—to everyone— that I was worthy of his respect again. I would do everything to prove it to myself. I shove open the door and, despite the tension of the moment, am overcome with the urge to roll my eyes at its opulence.

The entire room was decorated in black velvet with silver filigree. Though it was dark, the few windows covered with thick satin curtains that made the room feel more like a cave, it was a surprisingly cozy cave. My eyes land first on the man lounging across the settee, a full glass of brandy in his hand. Isos stands with an arm braced against the mantle, chuckling lightly at whatever conversation we interrupt. Patryk rushes to his friend's side, clapping him on the back before pulling up a nearby chair and sinking into it. It is easy to see his relief at Ivrik's relatively normal appearance. Türë slips by me, but a gentle caress of his fingers trails briefly across my lower back, as I stand watching from the doorway. I flinch away from the touch, and try to not let my revulsion show.

Ivrik acknowledges Türë with a nod before his attention lands on me. Whatever he sees there, softens the tired look on his bruised face. "I'm still alive!" He announces, words slightly slurred, raising his glass in a one man's cheers before taking a large swig of the amber liquid.

"Thank Jera for that." I mutter, feeling some of the weight lift from my shoulders. A weight I had not been fully aware of until it was gone. I join the group as Isos gives us all a deep bow, before spinning on his heel and leaving us to talk. I give him a grateful smile as he pulls the door shut. *When all this is over, I need to fund an extended vacation for him. I don't recall him taking a single day off in this memory.* I return my attention to the three chatting men. We all will need an extended vacation after this. *If we survive.* The dark thought clangs through me, even as I shove it away. "So you are okay?" I ask, sinking on to the foot of the settee with Ivrik. I scan him head to toe, looking for any trace of blood or pain, but find none other than the large rainbow bruise marring the side of his face. He however winces, and drains the still half-full glass in a single swallow. He hisses a bit from the liquid burn, but I know the shine that fills his eyes is not from the drink. Not as his gaze seem to drift far away, seeing things that nobody should. "You are not hurt?" I rephrase, my voice as gentle as I can make it without shifting into sounding overly motherly.

"No, I'm not hurt." He laughs bitterly, setting down the empty glass with a heavy thud on a side table. "Only thanks to a healer who unknowingly spent her last moments healing what wounds I did have before an arrow ripped through her throat." None of us speak. What was there to even say? Ivrik had gotten out. When so many others did not, he had. Pain fractures in his eyes and he tries to cough them away. I had no words of comfort for him, nor any experiences to tell him that it would fade. That the horror and guilt would eventually be replaced with better times, happier thoughts. I remember what he had told me the first day I had seen the Nefriti. He had trained as a warrior. What had it cost him when he could not protect his people? I knew the cost it had taken on my own soul. And I had not seen it with my own eyes.

"You did everything you could do, Ivrik." I say, when it becomes clear that Türë and Patryk were as lost as I was. No, Ivrik may no longer be hurt physically, but mentally, it was clear he was on the verge of shattering.

"Did I?" He snaps, running a hand over his face, leaning in towards me. "I could have died with my people. *Should* have died with them. Instead I ran. Like a coward. So I could make sure someone would know that we were under attack." He laughs joyless and rough, the alcohol already glazing his stare as he looks into the fire. "You know nothing of war. Are you sure you want to be Queen?" I flinch from the words, as sharp and stinging as if he had truly slapped me.

"Ivrik." Patryk growls, his warning clear. As understanding as he may be for Ivrik's anger and despair, picking a fight with anyone, especially me, would not be tolerated.

"You are right." I whisper, staring at my tightly clasped hands, knuckles white and stark against the deep ruby hue of my gown.

The weight of all three sets of eyes lock on me and feel their worry like a second skin. "I am not yet the Queen you need me to be. But I am *trying*." My voice cracks and I fight the urge to fall to my knees. To plead for his forgiveness for how badly I failed him. "I am very sorry for the anger you have in your heart right now. All I ask is that you do not give up on me." Ivrik blinks a few times, startled at my bluntness and apology. It was clear he had wanted a fight. He wanted to rage and hurt others how he hurt now. But I could not give that to him. I wouldn't hurt him any more than he already had been, all because of me.

In the silence of the room, I know a flood of questions need to be asked. Patryk and Türë's minds compile an ever-growing list, now that we knew that Ivrik was, for the physical part, okay. The same questions echo in my mind and heart. *What happened? How many soldiers attacked? How many of our people are lost?* But with a pointed look at both of them, warning them to keep it to themselves, I snatch up Ivrik's empty glass and move to the table against the wall where the decanter of the expensive liquor rests. I reach for the other glasses in the set, hung decoratively from an intricate holder that was shaped like a tree. As I stare at it, another flash of a memory spears into my mind. I blink it away, biting my lip against the jolt of pain, remembering that the three men sit watching me mere feet away. The dreams I have been forgetting upon awakening each morning suddenly return with sharp focus. I start at the surge of dreams, now revealed to be memory, then slam my eyes shut, sending a prayer to Jera that they wouldn't vanish again before I had time to think on them. Later. Right now, I needed to be present.

I attempt to juggle the four full glasses, but Türë jumps to his feet, taking two before I can drop them. I shoot him a grateful smile and his fingers linger on mine before the warm air of the fire replaces his cool touch. I try not to shudder. Returning to the settee, I pass Ivrik his refilled glass and raise my own to the three men in front of me.

"To those lost, to those who live, and to our enemies—whose breaths are numbered." A morbid joy crosses each of their faces. Their anger at King Tanth as potent and raging as my own. We each drain our glasses, letting the burn roll through us. Reigniting the fire in each of our souls.

Türe opens his mouth, brow furrowed, and obviously ready to pull any and all information that he can from Ivrik. Ivrik detects this too and for the first time, our eyes meet and I see a silent pleading from him. I see in them how close he truly is to breaking. How much the attack has shattered his heart.

"I forbid any questioning tonight." I cut in before Türe can speak a word. Surprise mingling with irritation dances across his features, but I don't back down. He doesn't push it, in spite of the clear desire to. I stare back, my silent words as clear as if I had spoken them aloud. *That is an order from your Queen.* He nods in agreement, just once, and far from enthusiastic to obey. For the first time I realize I could care less if he did agree or didn't. I shift my attention back to Ivrik and he gives me a grateful smile, even though it doesn't reach his eyes. We all fall into a comfortable silence.

"Evara finally got to meet Yessin." Patryk says with a snicker, breaking the quiet. Ivrik snorts loudly.

"Oh god, how is that bastard?" He asks, effectively dissolving the tension in the room, to my great relief.

"Asinine, as usual." Türe replies grimly, exchanging a look with me that makes it clear they, in fact *do not* know Yessin's true identity. He stalks over to the table to refill his glass, then with a second thought, grabs the half full decanter and another, bringing them over to set on the floor beside us. Patryk snatches one up, topping off all of our glasses. I had not been the only one to down the entire thing in one gulp.

The rest of the day and into the night, we stay hidden in Ivrik's rooms, sharing stories and laughing until our sides ache. The worries and responsibilities, the nightmares, that seemed to take up constant space in our minds retreat. I am not sure when we silently accepted it, but each of us seem to adhere to the unspoken agreement to take the night off, letting our companionship drive it all away. If only temporarily.

The bell tower signals midnight as Patryk tips the third bottle up, and drains the last drops directly into his mouth. The second bottle had been finished by myself about three hours before. We had somehow all migrated to the floor, each of us laying on our backs or sides as we made a circle so we could still see each other as we talk. Even as exhaustion and liquor pushes us into a heavy sleep, we fight against it. As if we all sense that our time together like this was coming to a quick end. If not forever, than for a very long time. So together, we keep up the conversation. Poking and shaking each other as we each began to drift off in turn. Trying with every ounce of our will to make the night last as long as we can.

thirty-five

The next morning I wake to a stiff neck, pounding head, and a chorus of groans. "What the?" I moan, blinking at the bright beam of sunlight that shines across our group. The three empty liquor bottles clink as a heeled boot toes them in anger. I squint up at the form of Athene who stands in the center of our pile, hands on her hips and a furious look on her face.

"What the hell is this?" She taps her toes rapidly and I look around at the others splayed out and blinking at the intrusion of our quiet sleep. After everything had grown fuzzy and sleep had finally overtaken us one by one, we had all curled up into a tangle of bodies. My head on Ivrik's stomach, Türë's head on my lap, Patryk's on my shoulder. For the first time, I didn't feel like the outsider looking in at a family unit. I was part of them. And now we would all have to survive our hangover and its consequences together. "We have been looking for all of you for *hours* and here we find you in a drunken stupor!" She shoots an especially venomous look at her husband, who only rolls onto his stomach, pulling a pillow over his head. Ivrik snickers, then winces at the pressure in his brain.

"Sorry, Athene." I mutter, shifting from underneath Türë, who just tugs a pillow off the settee and shoves it into the crook of his neck, curling into a ball against the bright light of morning. *Or was it mid afternoon?*

"Isos did know where we were. You could have asked him." Patryk adds, voice muffled through the pillow.

"Well, your friend seemed to *conveniently* forget where you all were until I threatened to send out the royal guard to search the nearby fields!" Türë barks a laugh that sends us all hissing in pain at the sudden loud noise.

"Good to know Isos isn't a tattletale." Ivrik says, bringing his arm up to cover his face.

"What time is it?" I ask, the unending list of things that I have to do today rushes in and I attempt to stand up. My head swirls and I press a clammy hand to my head, cursing myself for drinking so much.

"It is just past noon." She sighs.

"Good moooooorning!" Ilithyia's voice sings to us as she sweeps into the room and we all push, cursing, to our feet. "Looks like you all had quite a night!" Her eyes thankfully sparkle, a pleasant contrast to Athene's glowering. She carries a tray full of coffee, scones, eggs, and toast. Enough for all of us to fill our empty stomachs. I realize now, we had neglected to eat both lunch and dinner last night. We had been full on memories, laughter, and liquor.

We scarf the food down now. Ilithyia saves us by ushering Athene and her glare away for some emergency that *requires her expertise alone.* Flashing us a wink before pulling the doors shut behind her, we all return grateful grins.

"We owe her big time." Patryk says through a full mouth.

"Don't worry. I am sure she will remind you of that frequently." Ivrik adds, taking a large gulp of the black, still steaming hot coffee.

When we had eaten our fill, our groans now turning to satisfied sighs, a nap begins to already lure each of us, when a knock comes from the door. It is our hero, Isos, who pokes his head in. A hesitant grin on his friendly face.

"Sorry I caved guys." He says as we beckon him in with soft cheers of his name.

"I think you held out longer than any of us would have against Athene's questioning." Patryk says, leaning back in his chair with a hand on his stomach. "My wife is not one who takes *no* very well." Isos laughs, joining us at our insistence, at the makeshift table we had made on the floor.

"Your gladiator friend is waiting in the training pit. Would you like me to send him away?"

"Shit!" I stammer, shoving the last of my breakfast into my mouth and chugging my glass of fresh water. I stand and try to ignore the throbbing in my head at the motion. "Please ask him to wait just a bit longer! I just need to change." I shout as I run from the room and towards my old suite where all of my clothes still remain. Thankfully, it is much closer than the new rooms I had chosen. Ivrik's suite is in the newest part of the castle, so my newly selected rooms in the original castle towers were triple the distance away. I reach the closet and scan for any more of the drakonskein suits. Instead, I find a purple leather suit, completed with a gorgeously intricate golden chain mail corset and armor plates that cover the shoulders and stomach. Another deadly and wearable work of art. I slip it on, thankful that this suit had clasps up the front, similar to the buttons on a man's shirt. My fingers fly over them and I tug on one of my usual pairs of training pants that sit folded in a pile on a shelf. Something tumbles to the floor, a book or journal of some kind, but I shove it back into place before yanking on the pants with a breathy curse, praying to not lose my hearty breakfast. *Far from a graceful royal.* I snort a laugh at myself that has my head pounding, before running again from the room and towards the training pits.

thirty-six

I make it to the training pit, huffing and trying to wrangle my hair into a rough braid. I find the gladiator, Ionel, throwing knives into a dummy with expert aim.

"You are late." He says, his voice thick with an accent I didn't catch in the few words he had spoken to me before. He leans in and sniffs loudly, bemusement crossing his face. "And you reek of booze." He almost sounds impressed by this.

I laugh, and roll my shoulders, doing some quick stretches to try to warm myself up before he can change his mind about training with me.

"A friend came into town and we had a bit of a *night*." Ionel nods and throws the remaining knife into the dummy. Another perfect hit. It lands so close that it sets the other three knifes quivering where they stick, forming a perfect circle around the bullseye. A nearby guard brings me a training sword and I test its balance, giving it a few swings before nodding at Ionel. "Ready."

He only stares at me.

"What?" I flick my eyes to one of my personal guards who stands nearby. Thankfully, he looks just as confused as I am.

"That is not right." Annoyance makes his accent thicker.

"What isn't right?" I lower the sword, my arm already begins to grow tired from holding it stretched aloft in front of me.

"No sword." It is my turn to stare silently at him now. "No sword." Ionel repeats.

I hesitate, but hand the dull blade back to the guard who watches, on edge and growing more wary by the second. I knew that gladiators were not seen as the *best* of my citizens. Seen as objects of entertainment and little value, even prostitutes were often seen as more honorable than they were. But, in my brief experience with him, Ionel seemed to be like any other friendly guard or citizen I had met. Even when sparring, he didn't hold back, but he had taken care to aim for less painful and deadly places on my body. And even the fact he had agreed to additional training with me seemed like an extra hinderance that he didn't necessarily need to bother with. We had given him compensation for his time, but according to Türë, he was successful enough with his fights that he didn't really need the money.

I hold my empty palms out to him, waiting for further instruction. Tucking his arms behind his back, I am suddenly struck by how similar of a posture and air he had to Türë when he stepped into the role of General.

"Have you learned to fight?" He asks, tone clipped and serious.

"Fight? Like with fists?" Ionel nods. "No—I just went straight to the blade." He frowns deeply, obviously displeased.

"What happens if you have no blade?" He doesn't wait for me to answer. "If your weapon snaps in battle, you are dead. If you only train with a weapon, you are dead. You must learn to use your body as its own weapon before you can wield another." I open my mouth to argue, but snap it shut again when I can't find a flaw in his logic.

"Okay." I agree and awkwardly position myself in what I think is a fighting stance. Raising my fists in front of me, I spread my feet wide. "Like this?" To his credit, Ionel doesn't laugh, though his mouth purses against what looks like the start of one.

"No, like this." He demonstrates the appropriate stance before approaching me, then hesitating when the guard nearby steps closer. Obviously nervous to have him too close to his Queen. I glare at the man, a silent admonishment, before nodding my consent to Ionel to continue forward. He positions me. His grip surprisingly gentle as he grabs my wrists and ankles as he shifts me around. "Okay now relax." I let my arms fall and my legs step together. "Now fall back into fighting stance." I do so. He corrects me again, though this time he doesn't have to move me as much. "Relax." I do so. "And again." I step into place and this time, he doesn't have to adjust me at all. He grins, and I return it. "Okay, now we fight." Ionel steps into position himself before slowly swinging his arm up towards my face showing me the motion, instructing me how to block. We repeat this motion before he orders me to switch and I move to strike against him while he blocks. With each pass we get faster and my arms and core begin to burn with the motions. We fall into a rhythm that reminds me of my obstacle training with the Nefriti, and I begin to grin with painful delight.

The castle bells sing twice across the city as he leads me through a variety of forms, until sweat pours down both of our brows and he stops us for the day.

"How was that two hours?" I gulp down the icy water a guard brings me. My cheeks are ruddy with heat and exertion, but also with joy. I felt strong. And even though I knew I was going to be sore as hell tomorrow, I luxuriate in it. I could tell this worked a completely different series of muscles than when I trained with a blade. Plus each of the movements were so unlike those Türë had taught me. He had mainly focused on defensive, whereas Ionel strongly encouraged offensive. A smile transforms his face too. The first one I had seen on his face that wasn't filled with bloodlust.

"You have much stamina for a Queen." He says with a light chuckle, scratching at the dark thatch of hair that covers his jaw line. Then he pales slightly, realizing the offense that could be taken from that comment.

"Don't worry, I take that as a complement." I nudge him gently in the arm with a teasing wink.

"I don't think your friend agrees." I frown and turn to see who he means. Türë stands on the platform overlooking the pit. Arms crossed and brow deeply furrowed, it was hard to mistake that for anything other than displeasure. I sigh, but give him my best winning smile and a wave in return.

"Oh, he just looks like that most of the time." I lie. "How long has he been there?" I lower my voice so just Ionel can hear me.

"About twenty minutes." He says, then to my surprise he playfully cocks his hip out and mimics my wave and smile at Türë. Almost snarling in aggravation, Türë gets the point and turns his attention to the others training in the pit. "So may I ask why you wanted to train with *me*? You have all of these people here who are skilled to help you." We walk over to a nearby wall, clearing the pit for the others who were waiting for their chance at one of the sparring sessions happening in the five other sparring circles around us. Sighing at the relief the shade provided by the overhanging trees, I lean against the wall, contemplating on how to best answer his question.

"It was a few different reasons really. First of all, to everyone here I am their precious Queen. They are too afraid to truly fight against me, and there is no way for me to progress if I am not really tested. Not until it is too late and my opponent is willing to kill me." He nods, as if he had reasoned that out for himself.

"And the other reasons?" Ionel prompts when I don't immediately continue. I shake myself from staring across the sand to where Türe has turned his eyes back to us.

"You fight differently. Everyone here has had the same trainer, the same instruction, and the same methods. I have to know *more* than that, to be who they expect me to be." My voice grows softer, the truth of each word falling heavy on my shoulders.

"You wanted someone who didn't know who you were before." Ionel says, his voice deep and kind, revealing a side I had not expected from such a supposedly ruthless man. Then his words catch up to me and I stiffen. My eyes flick again to Türe, who catches the movement and immediately begins to come over.

"What do you mean before?" I say, my words dull as I push off of the wall to face him entirely.

He snorts, but only leans back onto his elbows, unconcerned. He stands tall enough that they brace comfortably atop the edge of the wall. "Some of your household have big mouths and only think I am some dumb brute. It didn't occur to them to watch their gossip around the *gladiator.*" Türe reaches us, only catching the last part of our conversation.

"Everything alright over here?" He asks, and I can see the restraint he maintains against the urge to put himself between Ionel and me.

"Ionel here figured out my secret." I say, figuring there was no point trying to pretend anything different. Türe's brows flick upwards, both impressed and surprised.

"Well I didn't realize it was a secret." He mutters under his breath, but a pleased smile flickers around his mouth.

"It is *need to know,* more than a secret." I say, before Türe can begin lecturing him. "But yes. I did go away and come back differently than I was before. I need your help to get back to my old strength and ability. But I also need your reassurance that you will keep this quiet." Ionel looks closely at me, watching me so openly, and for so long, I shift uncomfortably. At last he nods, shrugging slightly.

"I have no one to tell anyway. It is just me." He confesses with an air that this sad truth did not bother him. But just like he had seen through me, I saw through him.

"How would you feel about moving into the castle?" Türë shoots me a look of confusion at my offer, but I send him back a silent *not now*. "It makes more sense than having you cross the city every day for only two hours. And if you would be willing, maybe help my General create some new training exercises." I thought Türë's head would explode, it turns so red so quickly. *Male egos.* I shoot him a look that stops his argument before he can start it. I had meant what I said. Türë had done an exceptional job over the last centuries training all of our forces personally, but what I had already learned from Ionel in just a few hours was important. And with both of them working together it could give us the edge we might need to survive against Mirinth's armies.

"I would have to…check." Ionel bows his head in what looks like shame. "My owner might not like me being so far away. Or so busy." Fury ripples through me.

"What do you mean, *owner?*" I don't realize I have ignited until both Türë and Ionel take a step back in fear. Ionel looks so uncomfortable, it makes my anger even more potent. "Slaves are illegal in Tesindren." I look between the two men for some sort of explanation as I douse my flames with a calming breath.

"No, no, it is not slavery. Not exactly." I tap my toes, impatient for the explanation of what it *exactly* is. "My father was a gambler and racked up an unprecedented debt. After he died, those sums passed on to my mother. She could not pay them, and so I agreed to fight for the debtor and work until the money is paid in full." I grit my teeth, but don't have to look at Türë for confirmation to know that there was nothing we could do. *Slavery* was illegal. But working off your debts in an agreement, well, there was nothing I could do to intercede there.

"What do you lose should you decide not to fulfill your end of the bargain?"

"The debt would return to my mother, and the man my father owed would take her home and land. She would have nowhere to go and would have to move onto the streets or into the forest. She is too elderly to travel all the way here, or she would stay with me." Ionel explains.

I sigh heavily, trying to find the words to say, or a solution to help this man who found himself in such an unfair situation. "And what is the sum you owe?" I ask.

"Evara." Türë hisses at me. He knows I intend to pay it. So does Ionel.

"Thank you, Your Majesty. Truly. But I will not say. It is both my shame and my duty to pay for my father's sins and protect my mother. No one else's." I may not like it, but I can only respect it.

"Well, if you change your mind, please let me know." I say, giving him a smile despite the urge I feel to order him to tell me. It was more for my conscience rather than for his freedom. Though I had done much to rid my kingdom of slavery, there were strains of it—like Ionel's situation—that couldn't be stamped out. No matter how hard I tried.

Nodding gratefully, he pushes off the wall and walks slowly across the hot sand, each step puffing up dust. "I will see you again next week." He calls over his shoulder to me, before disappearing through the arch and out of view.

"What if he had told you the sum?" Türë asks, his voice low and bothered.

"I would have paid it." I say, turning around to face him without hesitation.

"You do know we are in a war now, don't you?" His question bites. My lip curls into a snarl at how patronizing the question had sounded, as well as his implication behind it.

"Careful, Türë." I say quietly. He seems to regret his words immediately after however, his arms stretch out to me, eyes softening in apology. Despite what he seemed to think, I had not forgotten his attempts to *make me feel a spark* the day before in my study. My urgency to resolve the issues between us seem to only have grown. I heave a heavy sigh, my shoulders drooping with the weight of everything that continues to pile up.

"I didn't mean it like that." He runs a hand through his hair, dancing in the wind. "I am just beat after last night. Let's go work on your magic a bit and then grab some food. We have to meet up with Ivrik today to discuss what happened during the siege."

I pause, frowning at him, as he begins to turn away.

"What?" He asks, confused, when I don't follow him.

"I told you I am not going to be training my magic. Not until the war is over." Türë shakes his head in transparent annoyance at me.

"I didn't realize you were being serious. Evara, you can't just shut out that side of yourself."

"You said my magic didn't manifest for *star-cycles* normally! So let's just pretend that it never did. I have too many other things that I can hone and control right now. And my magic is not one of them yet. Outside of paltry tricks, it will take too much time to learn enough to make a real difference."

"Why are you so stubborn?" Türë asks, though more to himself than me. Our conversation has grown loud enough that I realize the people around us have begun to turn and listen.

"Leave us please." I say, now purposely raising my voice to ensure everyone in the training pits can hear my instruction. Thankfully, everyone jumps to obey. One of the main perks to being the Queen. Filing out in less than a minute, Türë and I stand alone before I can soothe my rising temper. "I have to make the best choice for me. I had hoped, you of all people, would respect that." My hands tighten to fists at my side, even as I feel the magic writhing deep inside me beginning to crawl towards the surface. I shove it down, the ashy taste of a campfire filling my mouth. I swallow the smoke down and pray none of it curls from my ears and nose.

"I have respected a hell of a lot from you, Evara. It is *you* who doesn't seem to respect anyone else's opinions."

I take a step back, stunned at this retort, as rage flares within me. "What the hell does that mean?"

"Nothing." Türë retreats a step, cursing himself. "Shit. Never mind. I should go." He starts to stomp away, but I quickly catch up to him, blocking his path. Pressing an outstretched hand into his chest to keep him from continuing forward, I hold him from pushing past me as he tries.

"No. You clearly have something on your mind. So what is it?" My mind yells at me to stop. To let him walk away before we both say things we regret. But I don't listen. He can't just keep running away from all of our tough conversations. Not after he had done so the night before last too. If he had things on his mind, they were only going to grow malignant and rotten if they continued to fester unspoken between us. The time to clear the air was now. And he wasn't the only one angry now.

"You just *had* to do this." He snaps, glaring down at me. "You had to decide after hundreds of star-cycles together that you were going to start over. To erase me from your life. Sure, you asked if I was okay with it… but what was I going to say? No? You wouldn't have listened anyway. And you would have just gone on your own and I would never have seen you again. Not to mention leaving the kingdom open and vulnerable. And now you are different. I just don't know how to deal with these feelings. The you I used to love is *gone*. And she is never coming back. I don't see a Queen before me. Not one who can defend her people. That is who I have been trying to keep away from the kingdom, so you don't ruin us all. You are not the Queen, and I don't believe you ever will be again. You can keep trying, and it doesn't matter if you learn to hone your magic or not, it is clear to all you will fail." His chest heaves rapidly, head tilted back as if he was shouting at the sky itself. At Jera who watches us all.

I suddenly feel so tired and cold, as if I just was plunged into a pool of ice. My feet stumble slightly beneath me as my knees go weak.

I feel my cold heart shatter.

My rage, my fear, my dismay, all rushes through me in an icy wave.

Everything I thought he had felt, it wasn't for *me*. It was the woman I used to be. And it was clear enough that he was so angry with that decision that he despised me for it. Not that I blamed him. I had thought similar enough things myself.

But to hear him say it. Out loud. To know Türë, who I thought all this time was on my side, was my friend, was someone who I had *trusted*. All along, he was now only looking to take my place. My mind whiles with all of this controlling behavior, his irritation when I leaned on others, and his derision when I would push to learn more and take on more. Now it was my turn to flee. My emotions rise to a level that borders on suffocating.

"I am so very sorry for your loss." I manage to force out, my throat choking on the sarcastic words. My misery smothers my magic so effectively it doesn't even wriggle as I lose my tight grip of control I try so hard to keep on my emotions, my thoughts, and my power. *No wonder it seemed wrong between us.* Deep down I must have known, even without my memories, that Türë had been playing me.

"No—Evara!" Türë seems to jolt awake at my voice. His usually sun-tanned face drops to the color of curdled cream when he realizes what he has said. But I am gone, dipping around his hand that stretches out to catch me. I don't stop running, even when I hear him yelling for me. I tune out his voice as I run for the stables. I make it there and listen carefully for any sound of footsteps following me. Even as I mutter quick instructions to the stable boy, I keep an ear out for any sound of approach. The little golden-haired boy, brings me the mare I had taken to riding whenever we left the city. The same one I had ridden through the forest and into Alessandra the second day of my memory. I pass the stable boy a shiny coin in thanks, managing a smile at his exhilaration, even with the flood of emotions roaring through me.

"Hello, Afina." I whisper into the sure-footed mare's ear and her bright wide eyes take me in with such intelligence I almost expect her to say hello back. "Let's get out of here." I say, pulling myself up into her saddle, my muscles screaming with fatigue from my rounds with Ionel. I settle into the leather and, with a steadying breath, grab the reigns and tap her sides.

From the stable, through the castle gates and into the city beyond, Afina gleefully thunders through the streets. And finally, we pass through the city walls itself and I realize, for the first time, I am free.

thirty-seven

I make it to the trees before the tears begin to pour, chipping away at the numbness that fills my body. I thought Türë had understood what I had been feeling these last few moon-cycles. The internal struggle that ate away at my soul almost constantly. The fight within me to accept who I was versus who I am now. I thought he understood *me*. Looking back now, of course, I see the signs of his manipulation. But I had poured my heart out to him. Jera help me... It was just a power move for him.

I pull Afina to a stop and dismount before leading her into the tight twine of trunks. We had entered the Forest of Memory, where there was no path, at least not one aside from the small furrows made by the animals that live here. It had been a desperation to hide, mixed with a lure to be among the trees again, that had led me back to the Forest. It was a different part of the ancient forest than where I had woken up and was much closer to Alessandra. Though it had still taken me hours to reach this part. As I weave my way through the white trunks, I freeze occasionally, thinking I hear some noise. My mind wars with itself between hoping and not hoping that Türë had managed to follow me. In this part of the forest, the ground is shadowy beneath the thick leafy canopy, blocking out almost entirely the bright sunlight I know was still shining when I entered not an hour ago. Afina and I sink deeper into the Forest, wandering about without any sense of direction. A few times, the rational part of me tells myself to turn around now before I get lost. But then I realize I don't particularly care. Maybe Tesindren was better off without me. I wonder if I should just leave the others to sort it out and vanish into the wilds. Though my heart rebels at this idea, my mind can't find a reason to go back.

I only decide to stop when my legs begin to quiver from the unenjoyable combination of heavy training boots and the hills that steadily grow taller. Thankfully, the leather and metal dress I had chosen for today was light enough, even with the armor plates, that it wasn't encumbering or stifling. Especially not in the cool shadows. I drop Afina's reigns and try to find a somewhat comfortable patch of dirt and leaves to sit on while Afina grazes on the few bits of grass that managed to grow nearby.

I shuck my boots off and pull my knees to my chest. I, at last, let myself feel the full force of the hurt Türë had inflicted. Even though I had lost any romantic feelings for him, it pained me more than I would ever admit, knowing it was the old me that *he* preferred. The darkest insecurity I fought with myself about each day had been the truth. At least for Türë. *So who else feels the same?*

I don't know how long I cry. But it is loudly enough that I don't hear the soft crunch of leaves until they are right beside my bare feet. I gasp in alarm, roughly swiping a hand across my tear-fogged eyes. I have nowhere to retreat with my back to a tree. I blink rapidly trying to clear my vision. Hours must have passed, because lightning bugs now flicker in the air and the forest is truly night-dark. A single lantern hovers above me, its brilliance enough to hide the person who holds it aloft. I squint against the sudden bright light, and it shifts to reveal who had followed me. I breathe a sigh of relief when I realize it is not Türë.

"Hey, hey— it's just me." Ivrik says gently, squatting down beside me. His eyes glint in the small flame and for a moment I wonder if his eyes might be as puffy as mine. I don't answer, only relax a bit, shuffling over. A silent invitation for him to sit next to me. He does, our shoulders brushing as we both brace against the tree to our backs.

"How did you find me?" I rasp eventually, sniffling and playing with a bead that embellishes the hem of my dress, now dirty and wrinkled from the day's events.

"I was preparing to leave Alessandra myself when I saw you and Afina come storming through the city alone. You looked upset, so I put off leaving, hoping you would come back. I called on the others to see if they knew what happened. Türë decided to brush off your actions as normal, and I knew something was awry. I pushed, but he wouldn't tell any of us where you went or what happened until I told him I had *seen* you. And even then his answer was vague." My irritation surges. *What a coward. Unable to reveal to his brothers what he had said to me.* "So I said if he didn't have the balls to go after you and fix what he had fucked up, then I would find you and bring you back myself."

I stare at him, "You did?" He shrugs, feigning nonchalance, but the smirk that appears fits him better.

"From there it was easy! Ladir was waiting for me at the forest's edge. She led me right to you, then vanished."

I glance around, wishing the wolf had at least stopped to see hello to me before she disappeared again. "Well, thank you for coming after me, but I'm not sure if I am going to go back..."

"That is your choice." Ivrik shrugs again. "If you don't, can I stay out here with you?" He fails to pass this off as a joke as his voice breaks. I look closer and see that his eyes are indeed swollen. The remaining evidence of his own tears that the forest had allowed him the privacy to shed.

"I'm sorry, Ivrik."

He blinks a few times before turning his attention from the leaf he twirls in his hand back to me. "For what?"

"For what you had to endure. For not being the woman you all needed when it counted." Now it is my voice that breaks.

Ivrik sighs, his gaze settling on the leaf again. "When I was a child, I grew up in Mirinth." My brows flick up. It had not occurred to me that any of my Underkings were not Tesindren-born, or even how they came to *be* my Underkings. *Another mistake of mine.* I add it to my ever-growing tally. "Ilithyia is Mirinthian-born too, actually." He adds and I absorb this information slowly, shocked. Ivrik doesn't seem to see my reaction, he is lost in the past. "My father was a Lord of Mirinth and had a beautiful, loving wife, three children, and a magnificent castle. You would think he would have been happy." He scoffs, hand dropping to his lap, as if he had suddenly grown so tired that even keeping it held aloft was too much to bear. "The man was cruel and ungrateful. Always, he desired more. More possessions, more money, more things to be proud of. With my big mouth and attitude, I'm sure you can understand how little he cared for me. So I was pushed aside. Not that I really minded. I had hated always having to be at that horrible man's side to learn my *duties*. I was eight! I didn't need to know about taxes and the prisoners who were set to be executed that week. Eventually, my father grew tired of even having me around and he decided to send me to a boys' school in the northern part of the kingdom. I had been at the school a week when I heard that there had been a revolt due to one of my father's cruel new policies. My mother and two younger brothers had been killed. My father survived. He had been out *visiting* his mistress. When he realized that he suddenly only had one heir—one he had just sent away—he called me back home." I silently absorb each word, picturing the small impertinent child that Ivrik had been, and my heart aches. "That night I ran. We all had heard of the kingdom to the north. The one were wild things lived and a kind and powerful queen ruled." I look up to meet his eyes, now turned on me and they shimmer with tears at the memory. "I somehow made it to the Charobi fortress. Even though I begged and pleaded, the soldiers refused to let me in, or let me pass. I was a Mirinthian—and a lordling at that. They rightfully feared a trap."

"But you were a *child*. And one who needed help!" I feel so sick picturing the scene, though I knew the soldiers were only doing what they thought they had to in order to protect Tesindren.

"It was a trick of fate, or maybe Jera herself tugging at the threads of fate, but the Queen I had heard so many wondrous things about came to my aid herself. You had arrived at Charobi that day on one of your travels through the kingdom and been up on the ramparts when you heard the soldiers turn me away." Ivrik chuckles. "With a thunderclap that shook the walls, you appeared at my side and looked me up and down. I had never seen anyone so magnificent. In those breaths, you took in my dirty face and ripped clothing and seemed to see my entire story." His tone drops low and he sets aside the leaf to grip my hand tightly in his. "You asked me if I would like to be a Tesandrien, one of your people. If I would be willing to leave my family and friends, and titles behind. To be free. You said life would be hard, making my own way, but because I had the courage to leave all I knew behind, to wander through the wilderness to find this kingdom on naught but rumors—well then, I had the spirit of one of your people." I stay silent, no words even coming close to express what I was feeling. "I agreed immediately, and you just nodded and took my hand. Then ordered for the soldiers to open the gates for the Queen and her new ward. For the first time, I entered the fortress and everyone smiled and welcomed me to their kingdom. I felt I was home. And even though I was supposedly surrounded by the 'enemy of my people', I felt more safe than I ever had." Time passes before either of us speaks again.

"So you grew up in Alessandra with me then?" I manage to ask.

"No, actually. You brought me into the care of the Underking before me, Canthos. He raised me as his own. He and his wife had always longed for a child, but never had been able to conceive. Then once I turned seventeen, you had me go to live and learn in the other territories. Eivan had just been named Underking of Eri. Eventually, I came to Alessandra and was selected to join the Nefriti. I trained alongside you and we became reacquainted. About a star-cycle later, Noran also arrived at the castle, but for his training to become an Underking, and we became close friends. It was sixteen star-cycles after you had saved me, to the date, that King Canthos announced his abdication and you named me his heir." Ivrik suddenly snorts a loud laugh, a mixture of pleasure and mirth. "You took it upon yourself to invite foreign dignitaries from the other kingdoms on the continent for my ceremony. It was a great surprise to the miserable ass who arrived to find his own lost son had now risen to be one of the honored Underkings of Tesindren." He laughs again, though I see a solitary tear trickle down a cheek. "I nearly wet myself at the look on the old bastard's face. And when he thought he was revealing some *upmost prized* secret by unveiling my heritage, my true father, Canthos, denied him and socked him right in the face." He brushes away the tear, no shame on his face, only affection. "That was the best day of my entire life..." He says softly, closing his eyes as he leans his head against the rough bark. From the rare gentle smile that softens his face, I know he is picturing it all again.

"I'm so grateful you told me your story, Ivrik." I hesitate before continuing. "And I hope it doesn't ruin the moment, but I'm sorry when you courted me, things didn't work out in your favor. But I'm glad I can still consider you a friend." Ivrik sighs, loudly.

"Türë fucking told you *that*?" He sighs again, opening his eyes and sitting upright. "He is a rat bastard. I was twenty!! And you are eternally beautiful and young. What young rascal doesn't want that kind of woman in his bed?" I blush. "You have nothing to apologize for, Evara. In my heart, we are always bonded. You saved my life, how could we not be? But I know we are only destined for the relationship we have now. And I wouldn't trade it for *anything*." He lifts my hand, still gripped tightly in his, pressing it gently to his lips.

"Do you mean me now? Or the me I was? The one who saved you?" I say, shoulder dropping as Türë's words settle hard on me again, reminding me of the emotional cost of hoping that I was enough—only to find I wasn't.

"What the hell are you talking about?" Ivrik stammers, incredulous at my mumbled question. "There is no difference. You are *you*." He narrows his gaze, and irritation flames behind his eyes. "Did someone tell you differently?"

I debate whether I should tell him, if it would shatter the illusion that he had maintained up to this point regarding me. But I needed to tell someone, to push the words onto somebody else, in the hope that it would get them out of my mind. It is through short, choked words that I explain what Türë had said to me and why I had ended up in the forest. Resolved to live the rest of my life alone and among the forgotten.

He tries his best to hide it, but his fingers shake in fury at Türë's revelation to me. "He is a fool." Ivrik says. "I have always thought so, but he just proved it. I cannot believe he actually said that to you."

"I can." I admit, my voice small and weak even to my own ears. "I have worried about everyone thinking it, and thinking it about myself. He only confirmed that it was true." We don't speak for a while and the sounds of the nighttime creatures begin to echo in the darkness.

"Do you know why the Goddess Jera requires you to go through the Awakening every millennium?" He asks finally. I tilt my head, surprised by the question for a moment.

I scrunch my forehead, trying to remember what Türë had first told me about it. "To keep balance right? If I was immortal with no consequences then I would be an equivalent to a goddess myself. Right?" He thinks on my reply for a moment.

"Yes, and no." He leans forward and begins to trace a finger in the dirt. "Canthos told me it was for *you*. For balance within yourself. A thousand star-cycles is a lot to handle. Uncountable deaths of friends and loved ones, the exhaustion from the pressures of ruling a kingdom, of suffering your power's control, and having to play the all knowing immortal. He said it was a *blessing,* not a curse, bestowed on you by Jera. A reprieve from it all. A clean slate. You get to begin again with new thoughts, new ideas, and a chance to learn and fall in love with everything and everyone all over again. Think of how it would be otherwise. Four thousand star-cycles of never experiencing anything new... That would be horrible. And your power, without the Awakening, who knows how overwhelming it would be. Always growing larger, more wild." I try to absorb this new way of viewing what I had, until now, did view as a curse. Or at the very least, a payment to continue my life. "The *now-you,* as you phrased it, is the result of the weight of all that burden removed. None of us, even Türë, knew the *you* after your last Awakening. So who is he to say who you were after that one? Maybe this *is* the true you, before the weight of the world and your experiences chipped away at you." Silence fills the air.

"You have certainly given me a lot to think on." I say with a thick laugh. He nudges my arm playfully.

"Don't let *him* get you down. Besides, I am sure he has been stewing on what he said and it is eating him alive by now. Just don't let him down too easy." Ivrik says with a slight edge.

"Is there more to you two than just your...um... romantic rivalry?"

He laughs lightly. "I love Türë like I love any of my Underking brothers..." He starts, but suddenly grows hesitant to continue.

"But?" I prompt.

"He argued with you to turn me away that first day at Charobi." He confesses dully, pulling himself to his feet and dusting his hands on his pants. Doing anything to avoid my stunned, wide eyes. "I guess even all these star-cycles later, it's hard to forget that he was willing to do that to a cold, starving, helpless child."

thirty-eight

I pull Afina to a stop at the entrance to the castle. Staring up at its dark walls and the windows that prick with light and dancing shadows of movement, I feel a sense of calm wash over me. Despite the deep conversation we had in the forest, the ride back to the castle was nearly silent. Only a few words were shared here and there, like *look out for that hole* or *careful with this low branch*. So much had been revealed and my mind still whirls trying to decide what to make of it. Reflecting on all that I had gone through since the Awakening, I had revisited everything. My training, my relationships, and, of course, all the memories tied to Türë. Thank Jera things had not progressed further with him. It would have made what I had to do tonight even harder and more awkward. I try to view everything in new light Ivrik had shed. *A blessing, not a curse or payment.*

Ivrik pulls his mare to a stop alongside me. His eyes are filled with concern as he observes me. I don't have to be a mind reader to know that he is worried I will bolt again—and this time for good.

"Ivrik, I need a favor."

He blinks in surprise before answering without hesitation. "Anything."

I chuckle at that. "That's a risky promise." I tease, growing lighter as my plan takes form.

"Even if I didn't agree, you could always order it anyway, so I figured I would skip those steps." He smirks back at me. I shoot him an exasperated look and shake my head before casting a quick look around for eavesdroppers. He catches my thoughts and nudges his horse closer to Afina. Our legs brush and I lean in closer, quickly whispering to him my plan and what I needed him to do.

For the first time, I sit atop my gleaming marble and diamond throne without shaking. Without feeling like a fraud. I can see Ivrik watching me closely out of the corner of my eye, wearing a combination of wariness and pride. I don't blame him for it. The uncertainty. Still outfitted in my armored dress of deep mulberry and onyx stitching, coupled with the glittering gold crown flecked with jewels the shades of the darkest night sky, well, I'm sure it was an imposing sight. Not even taking into account the irritation that radiates from me, giving off a heat that has Ivrik glancing sideways at me in concern. A bead of sweat rolls down the back of his neck and I take a deep breath to try to pull it back before I can scorch him. Even though he had helped me curate the mask I now wore, Ivrik still seems wary of the commanding Queen who had reemerged, if only for the next few minutes. I tap my fingers on the arm of the surprisingly comfortable throne, not having to fake my restlessness. In spite of the semi-late hour, I had called for both Patryk and Türë to come to the throne room.

Immediately.

Ilithyia too had been summoned, but she takes on her role of silent handmaiden, standing beside Ivrik. Ready to assist with anything her queen asks. I couldn't tell if Ivrik had warned her about what was going to happen or not. At last, the heavy doors swing open to reveal a wide eyed Patryk and a pissed off Türë who each take in my demeanor and wisely keep silent. If Patryk had any inclination that my rage was not aimed at him, I couldn't tell. I feel momentarily sorry for the sudden pale green pallor that sweeps over him, but the annoyance that flicks onto Türë's face wipes away everything else. Patryk drops into a low bow, and I don't miss the band of muscle that dances in Türë's cheek, his jaw locking against the words that he bites down on. The bow he barely lowers into is caught not just by me but by the sharp intake of breath by the other three, I know the slight was not just something I misinterpreted. Nodding with the barest of reassuring smiles to Patryk, I motion for him to join Ivrik and Ilithyia off to my side. Türë tracks the movement before his dark eyes snap back to me. He stands up straighter and clasps his arms behind his back. The picture of the ruthless and deceptively obedient General.

"Are you making our private business a public issue now, Your Majesty?" He manages to bite out. Though his tone sounds light and unbothered, his eyes flash in warning.

"Not at all, dear General. I simply wanted to let you know what I decided to do regarding Mirinth's actions."

His eyebrows raise slowly, suspicious about the phrasing. "Oh?"

I snap my fingers, so quickly and loudly that the others all jump. A scribe who had been sitting in the shadows nearby squeaks a bit in alarm, but rushes over to my side. I refuse to back down from Türë's bitter stare as I read my message aloud for the scribe to transcribe. "Her Royal Majesty, High Queen Evara, ruler of Tesindren and the Isle of Sobek declares war against the kingdom of Mirinth and its ruler King Tanth. In exchange for King Tanth's head and crown, she promises land and wealth beyond imagining for its bearer. This will be deemed payment and satisfactory retribution for the attack and subsequent deaths at Dulen this past week. Any and all Mirinthian's be warned. Should you stand against Tesindren, you will die. Rise up against your hateful king who has held slaves and slaughtered innocents in the name of his wealth and failing power. Join us and you will be free." Türë has paled now and I can see him looking for any sign of the woman he had woken to just yesterday. But I was gone. Swept away the second he had uttered what he truly thought of me and revealed the game he had begun to play to take my crown. He thought he had lost me before. But now I was truly lost to him. I continue. "To King Tanth. You have brought death to yourself and your citizens. We were content to be friendly neighbors to the north, but you now will know only vengeful enemies. I, Queen Evara, vow to make you pay in blood and tears for the pain and loss you have brought to my people. You thought you would find a sleeping snake, but you have stepped unknowingly into a drakon's nest. Count your hours. They are numbered." I break my burning gaze from Türë's to look at the quivering scribe. "Sign my usual titles and disperse it to every populous in the kingdom. As well as have my contacts to the south spread these where it is sure to be read and known to the King." The scribe nods and quickly scuttles off to do as I command.

"What are you *doing?*" Türë's shaking voice asks. My eyes flick back to him and it's not fear that is rattling through him. It is anger.

At me.

"What he won't suspect. He thinks I am some waste of a queen. Some purring kitten that will mewl and step aside." I lean forward, even as I feel the flames of my fury at last pouring out of me. I don't have to look towards the window to catch my reflection to know I am surrounded in a blue cocoon of flame. "I think our enemies, as well as my own people, need to be reminded of *that*." He catches my pointed words, a spear at him, and he snarls.

"If you are doing this because of what I said—"

I laugh coldly, a cruel and foreign sound to my ears, and to his apparently, as he straightens in surprise. I settle back into the throne and tap my finger slowly again as I speak. My words each as sharp as the drakonbone dagger strapped to my side. "You presume much that I would start a war because of your pathetic words, General Türe." I feel the other's eyes on me. Ivrik's as cold as mine, Patryk and Ilithyia's confused and worried. "You told me how I wasted an entire town because of a massacre upon the Creatures of the Forest. How are you *possibly* surprised that I would seek retribution for another kingdom taking one of my cities?" I try to stop my voice as it rises, but only manage to stop just short of yelling. I take a few calming breaths, reining my fire back into a shell around my body. I let the flame's warmth try to warm my chilled soul, icy with my anger and hurt. I can see he doesn't believe me. He still refuses to see the Queen I was trying to be, one who would ruin herself before failing her people. But still a different queen than he wanted.

"You know what would happen if we told your little secret." He gestures at the others, who all tighten at the implication of where he is going with such a statement. I stare at him blankly before laughing loudly. Even Ivrik winces at the noise. "You are not in your right mind. We could tell everyone. It would take nothing to get you to step down from your rule." Türë tries to talk over my laughter.

"Türë!" Patryk snaps, his own temper bubbling over, clearly ashamed of his friend. His brother.

"No, no—" I interrupt Patryk, waving on Türë encouragingly. "By all means, let him continue to admit to treason."

Türë's jaw tightens even more. "I think I have said all I need to for my point to get across."

"Great. Now it is my turn." I smoothly stand from my throne and slowly prowl closer to the man I had considered a good friend, who I thought I had begun to care for. "You threaten me, Türë. Not out of malice, but from a place that somewhere deep down does care about what happens to my people. I cannot fault you for that. What I do fault you for is your threat against *me* and your betrayal of trust. Who we are now and who we used to be are different. For the love and trust we used to share, I will look past this." I pause, letting the fire fill my eyes with their flame. "Once." I hear three held breaths release in a whoosh behind me as I stand before Türë now. I lower my voice, and try to not let the pain I actually feel inside my heart show. "I understand your story may be different now, the choices you had to make have shifted you. But just because you decided to be the hero of a different sort, doesn't mean you can decide my life—my choices." My words crack as I say them and pray he listens to me. "Don't become the villain in my story." I reach forward, taller than him from where I stand on the stairs leading to the throne dais, and my hand snaps out to grip his chin, forcing his eyes to lock onto mine. He tries to avoid it, but fails as my nails dig into the sensitive flesh. When his dark gaze at last meets mine, he blanches at the silent promise that can be easily read in them. My eyes pin him as I promise. "You won't like what happens to the villain."

Quiet fills the throne room as we all wait for his decision. *Please don't push this.* I silently pray to Jera as I watch him closely. Should he decide to make another move to displace me, after all he had gone so far as to voice such a thing to two of my Underkings, I would have to kill him for that treason. I nearly collapse in relief when he drops to a knee, head bowed in submission.

"I am truly sorry, Evara. I don't know what I was thinking!" He reaches out for my hand, but I step up, out of reach. *He dare?* Thankfully, Ivrik seems to sense I am out of words at the moment and need help.

"You may address her as Your Majesty, or *Queen* Evara, General. But I would suggest keeping silent for now." Ivrik's voice is calm, and he looks at Patryk, silent words passing between them I can't understand. I take the reprieve to return to my throne, my legs beginning to shake beneath my skirts, and it takes all my control to sit gracefully.

"My orders are this: General Türe will be joining Ivrik at the Charobi fortress, as will as a host of soldiers to help strengthen its walls. Together they will monitor and report on Mirinth's next movements." I force myself to return my stony gaze to Türe who stares at me in dismay. "You will be on probation, General. Any steps out of line will be reported to me and will be dealt with swiftly."

"Please, Evara—" Türe starts, trying to stand and approach me. To my surprise, though I manage to conceal it, Patryk steps between us. Ivrik also places himself in front, holding a firm hand out, stopping Türe from getting any closer.

I continue, trying to appear unfazed. "Should you prove that you are *not* a traitor and are still worthy of your position, then over time we may move on from this betrayal." He jolts back at the word. *Betrayal.* As if it only occurred to him as I said it aloud that what he had done was indeed a betrayal. "Until then, Patryk please find the gladiator Ionel and his *owner*." I scoff at the word. "And inform him that he is being drafted into Her Majesty's service until further notice and will need to move into the castle as soon as possible to be on hand." Patryk nods, though his back remains facing me, his attention doesn't leave Türë.

I look from Patryk, to Ivrik, then down to Türë. He lifts his head from where it had been hanging in sorrow to look back at me, as if he had been able to feel my gaze. "I didn't want to do this." I whisper, knowing he can hear me still. I press my eyes closed, fighting the desire to pull it all back, to change my mind and forget all of this ever happened. But what I had told Ivrik was true, as I unloaded my plan to him at the castle gates, there was no more trust. I force my heart to harden.

I could not count on him remaining in the castle and not try to control me or manipulate my feelings for him to use to his advantage. Since the day I had learned that he had kept Mirinth's possible attack a secret from me, the worry had been planted that this is where we would end up. I decide to tell him my truth, to confess what I had been hiding from *him* because of the fear of what he would do to keep control. "I can't trust you, Türë. You say you don't trust me to be Queen, and you have an idea of who *you* think I should be. But that won't let me be who I *want* to be. You said I am not the woman you love, how she is gone for good. But I have started to *remember*. I remember you." All four pairs of eyes snap to me, disbelief and shock rippling through all of them at my words. "I remember the words I told you that night in the garden." He looks confused a moment, trying to place what I mean. *"Every time I feel like I am missing something, know that it is you. It will always be you I am looking for."* I repeat from the dream, the memory. Picturing the dark archway, the kiss that felt like the answer to every question I ever had, and the rich scent of mint and cypress as I say them. In my mind, I see the bright green eyes that seems to examine every part of me without hesitation or judgement.

Wait.

His chestnut eyes narrow and I suddenly feel like I missed a step as my head grows fuzzy. Green not dark brown. And Türe smells like the forest, not... I feel like the breath has been sucked from my lungs. "That wasn't you." I whisper.

"No. That wasn't me." He snaps. My head continues to swirl as I try to picture more, to pull more from the memory that had come to me the previous night as I had stood over the drink table in Ivrik's room. The man had been in shadow, but I had thought it was Türe, after the feelings I had. But... *Someone else... who?* I realize everyone is still staring at me and I force myself back to the present. I don't let this change of perception sway me, even as I consider what Türe might know about it. His treason had not changed. I shake myself.

"You will be joining Ivrik when he departs early in the morning. I wish you both safe travels and will be looking forward to your reports." Ivrik and Patryk both bow deeply at me, before turning and, gently, yet insistently, pull Türe along with them. Each giving me a kind look that says everything I need to know. They would stand by my side no matter how hard. *I* have their loyalty, not Türe.

I don't bother to set a guard on him. I knew in my heart he had truly regrets all of his actions from today, and his intentions had only been instinctual from his hurt. If I had thought for a moment he would flee, or hell even be a danger to anyone in this castle tonight, then he was lost to me for good and I should demote him and lock him up. As it was, I had no plans to rid myself of one of the best weapons we had going into this war.

My mind drifts back to the memory I had been so sure was Türe. Until we had finally shared the kiss and it fell flat—then all of his actions afterward.

Not Türë. My mind returns to that as the doors swing shut behind the three men, leaving just Ilithyia and me. She sinks onto the step in front of me and, using the throne's base as a backrest, leans her head against my leg, heaving a loud, dramatic sigh.

"Well, that was a hell of a day!"

thirty-nine

I spend the few hours of sleep I do manage to get enduring tumultuous, fractured dreams and rise for the day with a churning stomach. Ivrik, Türë, and two of my best trained regiments of soldiers were going to be departing shortly after dawn. Once there was enough light to see the road clearly. Ivrik and Patryk both had come to my room shortly after I had left the throne room. To see if I was okay, as well as to warn me that I had until dawn to change my mind. I don't regret my choices from the night before, but I do regret having to make them. I had lost one of my closest confidants, and now my kingdom was definitely at war. Not that there had been much to doubt it before. What else was my choice after Mirth took one of my cities? But now it was declared. It was real. But as much pressure as it places on my heart, it also brings a sigh of relief. Before, it had felt as if we all had been holding our breath, waiting for the other shoe to drop. Now that it had, we could act.

I sigh and roll out of bed, resolving myself to function yet again on a grand total of two hours of what could barely be considered as sleep. I slowly tug on my robe with a yawn and shuffle to the wardrobe that had been relocated into my new room across from the study. The rest of my things would be moved from the other end of the castle over the next few days, but until then I had the necessities waiting neatly for me in the near seven foot tall carved wooden wardrobe that takes up a corner of the room. I pause, my hand on the handle. Taking a step back, I look at the design and see the same tree carved into it that I continue to picture in flashes. *Jera*. I smile at the comforting sight, tracing a fingertip across its trunk, before tugging the door open and getting dressed for what was going to be a very long day. A soft tap comes from the door and I pause to take a steadying breath before moving to unlock it. I had promised both Ivrik and Patryk I would keep my door shut and locked whenever I was alone in here. It seems like an unnecessary pain, but I oblige them. It is Ilithyia's pale, still sleepy face that pokes around the door.

"Tea?" She asks, a hesitant smile bringing some light to her eyes. I sigh in relief and wave her into the room.

"Yes, please!" This deep in the castle it got much cooler and, on a rainy day like today, it was especially chilly. She enters with a tray filled with a steaming teapot and a plate of biscuits and jam. I delay my dressing, deciding that a warm mug of chamomile was just what my icy soul needed right now. I hug the mug closer to my chest, my heart beginning to ache at the not long ago memory of Türe having a morning similar to this. "Did I do the right thing?" I whisper into the steam. Ilithyia freezes, a biscuit held midway to her mouth. She sets it back down and looks at me closely.

"May I speak openly, my friend?" I nod and swallow against the hard lump in my throat.

"I have known Türë for a long time. He has always been one who pushed his limits on what is proper, but what he did last night was not acceptable. He *never* should have spoken to you, threatened you, in the way he did. I do not think there was another choice you could have made. He is not the King. No matter what he thinks about himself." She clinks a nail rhythmically against her tea cup as she thinks. "I do not know all that happened between the two of you in the training pit yesterday, and I do not need to. But I think that, whatever it was, broke something in you, something valuable that you had given him. The only way for that wound to be healed, at least in my experience, is time and distance. If you are meant to be together again, you will be."

My eyes water with tears at her reassurance and belief in me. "Thank you for your words. I sometimes just feel like I am drowning in it all. And up until now, I thought for sure that Türë had been the one pulling me up for air. But yesterday, I began to wonder if he was the one who had been holding me under all along."

"He has changed. Since the Awakening he has been *different*. I can't help but wonder if maybe he just saw this as his opportunity for you to at last make him High King."

I think on that. "What was our relationship before? He never did truly tell me." I realize with irritation how blind I had been.

I see her own annoyance at Türë flash across her face. "He alluded that he told you. You two were as close as siblings. I believe he had tried courting you multiple times, ever since he stepped foot on the continent. I don't believe he ever stopped, even after you told him you would not be more than friends." She grimaces in apology.

"He tried for that long?" I shake my head and stuff a biscuit into my mouth, trying to fathom it. "Why didn't I pursue him? He is attractive and successful, and…" I break off blushing. Ilithyia doesn't seem bothered however.

"Oh, he is. And he knows it. I truly do think he was a friend of yours, but ambition and opportunity made him see a way to the throne, being finally able to win your heart was a bonus after star-cycles of lusting after you."

"So why didn't I? I admit I have feelings for him now, so there must have been a spark at some point that I just never acted upon." I remember the man from the garden, his face still fuzzy and out of reach, aside from his eyes. Though his scent now fills my nose with such potency that I glance around the room. I could not believe that I thought it was Türë. Maybe I had just wished it was, and shoved away what I knew in my heart to be true. There had been nothing, but a sense of wrongness, when I kissed him that first time. Ilithyia sinks back into the red velvet chair and fans her face dramatically.

"It is dreadfully romantic actually. You were—are— already married. That was right after the second Awakening. You met a mortal man and fell in love. On your wedding day, it was revealed by the Priestess that you two were actually soul-bonded. She declared your love would transcend both of your lives and would forever find each other. No matter which lifetime, you would be drawn together again and again." She sighs dazedly. "He was your one and only King. When he died, you swore you would never marry another and would always be in search of King Donovan." I stare at her in shock, my now cold tea forgotten. She leans forward, her eyes sparkling with delight. "I think that is why you decided to go through the Awakening this time. So you could find him again, and be together once more." She whispers to me her theory.

"Do you think that is—" I start, something clicking inside me.

"—who you were remembering when you thought it was Türë

in the garden?" She completes my thought, nodding her head enthusiastically. "I did some poking around last night." Ilithyia blushes, as if suddenly realizing how many lines of propriety she crosses with everything she has shared with me. Not the facts of my history, but *her* ideas and musings.

"Please continue!" I encourage her. "I order you too." I wink at her, though my heart thunders in my chest. She laughs, but does as I request. Both of us sit up on our knees, excitement filling the air.

"Okay. This wing of the castle was the one you shared with King Donovan. I think that is why you are so much more comfortable down here, and also why, umm..." She hesitates again. "I think it's why Türë wanted you moved to the new rooms."

I mull this over, along with everything else. I only end up more confused and heartbroken. Was it all true? Had Türë only been after the crown? Was anything real? There was no true explanation. Part of his choices could be seen as trying to help or protect me. But this... I look to the window, where the honeyed light of sunrise begins to fill the room.

"Why did you all go along with it?" I ask. She blushes and I reach out to reassure her that the question was not one of anger. Not at her.

"He told us this is what you wanted us to do." She says. "We trusted him to do right by you. I am not sure if this is what you requested or not, but regardless, he needed to also respect your decision now.

"I need to see him before he goes." I say, shooting to my feet and tugging on my boots and the dress I had grabbed from the wardrobe. Ilithyia watches me with a frown.

"What are you going to say to him?"

"I don't know." I try to restrain a snap. "I just need to see him. I don't want our last contact for a while to be everything last night.

And I need to know the truth. If this is what I really wanted. I will drive myself mad if I don't speak to him." She nods sympathetically and follows me without another word as we rush to the gates where they would be departing. I pause, despite the need to hurry, and turn to face Ilithyia, who follows me closely out of the room. "It was Türe you were trying to warn me about in the bath that day, wasn't it?" She doesn't answer, but I know anyway, as she dips her chin, averting her gaze.

We manage to make it just as Türe pulls himself onto his familiar onyx stallion. He catches the sound of our hurried steps, his attention immediately locking on me. Agony is the only word I can think comes close to the look on his face. I try to catch my breath as we make it to the group waiting to see off those departing this morning. Patryk, Athene, Isos and a few other friends wait nearby. The bulk of the soldiers wait outside the castle gates, already having said goodbye to their loved ones before coming here for their final training. Ivrik nods in greeting at me, but eyes Türe with caution. None of us were sure how Türe would react today. And after my talk with Ilithyia, I wasn't sure if I knew what to expect from him at all.

"May I have a word, Türe?" I manage to ask, voice calm despite the tightness in my chest. Relief ripples across his face and he immediately dismounts. I know he thinks I have changed my mind about sending him as he closes the distance between us and reaches for me. I step back, silently rejecting the embrace. Hurt replaces the relief and his hands drop limply to his sides, reality clanging through him once more.

"What can I do?" He whispers, pain clear on his sharp face.

"I don't know, Türe. I don't even know if everything about you was an act." I don't hide my pain, showing him just how much he has ripped into my mind and made me question everything.

"Yesterday, I don't know why I said that in the training pit. I just was frustrated and am still trying to adapt. Can't you give me that break? I *love* you, Evara. You. No matter what memories you have or don't have."

"And last night in the throne room? What is your excuse for that?" I bite out as he pales, suddenly unable to meet my eyes.

"I was angry. You left and denied me any chance for explanation! Then summoned me to do so in front of the others. I felt attacked and fought back like anyone would have."

"You threatened to reveal my secret and take my kingdom from me." I say flatly. Remorse shows clearly on his face, but even now I don't know whether it is genuine or an act. He reaches for my hand again. This time I allow him to take it.

"It was a *mistake.* You know I would never do that. They were words said in anger. Though it doesn't excuse them, I know, it is what happened." He pulls my hand into his chest, where I can feel and hear his heart thumping steadily. "Please, don't send me away." Türë pleads.

"Why did you hide King Donovan from me?" I ask, coldly. His face only flushes deep red and I pull my grip from his, suddenly clammy and cold. I..." I look past him to where Ivrik has now dismounted and stands beside the others. Each of their faces show pity, but other than that reveal nothing of their opinion on the matter. This decision was mine, and mine alone. "I can't trust you anymore. Not now." I manage to force my words through the tears. My voice is soft, though I still see Türë flinch back as if I had screamed them.

Shattering my heart even further, he drops to a knee and grabs for my hand again, raising my palm to his cool forehead. Though he hides his face, I still spy the tears as they begin to fall. But genuine or an act, I can't tell anymore. "I am so sorry, Evara. All I can do now is to prove to you that your trust in me was never folly. All I can do is hope that someday I will win back your heart that I so foolishly took for granted. No matter how long it may take. I will never stop trying to be the man you deserve, and that you thought I was. I am so sorry I have failed you. Please forgive me. We have time." He doesn't wait for any answer, only lifts his head long enough to press my palm to his lips. He then stands and returns to his horse. He looks back only once before mounting and riding through the gates and out of the castle to wait with the rest of the soldiers.

Ivrik takes a deep breath, and releasing it with a long whistle. "Jera help me, he is going to be grumpy the whole trip." He mutters, earning an elbow to the ribs from Athene. Ivrik scowls at her before throwing an arm around her shoulder and tugging her in for an awkward side hug.

"Take care of her, alright?" Ivrik says to her and Patryk. He tries to say it quiet enough so I won't hear, but thanks to my Sidhe advantage, I still do.

"You take care of *yourself*, okay?" I reply. Concern for my friend churns my stomach. I pull him in for a hug and breathe through the tears that surface. I wish he could just stay. *Was I making a mistake, sending both him and Türë—sending anyone—closer to Mirinth?* But I didn't have a choice. We were at war and our borders had to be defended.

He nods, but I see his own fear glinting in his eyes. Squeezing me tighter one last time, I am shaking by the time we both pull apart. Ivrik sniffles a bit, his own unshed tears stuffing his nose. Then he pulls Patryk in for a hug. The two brothers, in all but blood, clap each other on the back and exchange a few words of support before Ivrik marches to his horse. Before any of us can stand it, he too vanishes through the gate and into the morning mist.

forty

The chill of Umna has completely fallen across Alessandra and the mountains to the east are painted white with a heavy blanket of snow before I can finally knock Ionel on his ass with only my fist and own wits. I stare down at him, one foot atop his chest, keeping him down. My eyes widen and I gasp for air. The fog of my breath that clouds in the frosty morning. Ionel laughs loudly, a sound that still makes me pleased whenever I hear it. Applause patters around the two of us from the crowd that had gathered, in spite of the freezing early morning. Ionel had been transformed since coming to live in the castle full time. His training regimen had been promptly added to Türë's old one, and he had fallen into fast, easy friendship with the other guards who he had taken over training. I help him up and notice how his eyes dart to Ilithyia, who stands on the sidelines, chatting with Isos.

After the war had officially begun, and after considering how easy it had been for Mirinth to infiltrate the castle, I had asked Ilithyia if she would be comfortable learning some self-defense.

Just in case. She had agreed enthusiastically, eyes sparkling with the challenge. Ionel had agreed with little care or a second thought if he would mind adding another personalized training session to his schedule. But then his jaw had dropped as he watched her sashay into the pit like she was entering a royal ball. He had promptly recovered, but I still noticed how often he would stumble over his words when she was tight in his arms in a hold, or how his eyes would track her as she walked away. I also realized pretty quickly how much more he smiled when she was near. I had made a vow to myself to stay out of it, but even with the vow, I tried my best to find convenient reasons for them to interact. Delivering messages to him, inviting him to dinner, and extra training sessions for both Ilithyia and me. If she was or wasn't interested, I couldn't really tell. She was a vault where romance was concerned, and I would still occasionally catch her flirting openly with Isos.

The war now is truly beginning to show an effect on my kingdom, so I probably shouldn't give their love lives as much thought as I do. Young men and women from across the kingdom had begun to arrive at the castle, enlisting in the guard to protect their land and families. Alessandra had gone from a large city to one bursting at its seams, giving me and Patryk an extensive list of seemingly unending things to attend to. But watching Ilithyia and Ionel, it suffices as a harmless distraction, and a necessary one for my sanity. If I could help two people I cared about find love in this horrid time, then all the better.

I shake loose the thoughts that constantly swirl through my mind. Even sleep still rarely serves as an escape. Dreams—nightmares—plague me nightly. Only on the days where I run myself so ragged and exhausted do I maybe get a few hours of undisturbed sleep. The dreams had begun their constant assault the night after Türë and Ivrik had departed, and I had no reprieve since.

I snap back to reality as Ionel rubs his jaw where a bruise already begins to form from where I had connected.

"Sorry!" I wince and call to a nearby weapons assistant for a wrapped block of ice for him.

"No, that was a good hit!" Ionel grins widely in spite of the surely sensitive skin that tugs. "It is an honor to get such a mark from someone widely regarded as a lovely lady." He teases and I smack his arm.

"You swear you didn't let me win?" I ask, lowering my voice so only he can hear. His eyes glimmer at my question as it does every time I ask it.

"No, Vara! You kicked my ass thoroughly without any assistance on my part." His mouth quirks up at the corner, as does mine. He is the only one who calls me Vara, and for some reason, it makes my heart soar every time. He was one of my closest friends now, and it was a relief to have him. I could always count on him to be honest. Sometimes painfully so, but it was nice to know that the option for the truth was always there. After Türë, I tried to not second guess *everyone*, but sometimes I can't help the doubt that still flares up. "You did very well. Now go get water and ready yourself for blade training." His attention is pulled to Ilithyia who approaches us.

"Is she interrogating you again?" She scowls at me.

"Of course."

"Such trust issues..." She teases with a roll of her eyes. "Is it my turn yet?" Ilithyia playfully punches his arm, making his cheeks flush.

"Ready whenever you are, my lady."

"Ugh... don't call me, *my lady*! You make me sound so old." She whines, but winks at him before turning to enter the sparring ring.

He watches her walk away, and I raise my brows at him. All I earn is a glare before he turns and stalks into the ring to join her. All business.

I stifle a laugh and do as he said, I chug a full glass of the ice water as I watch the two begin. It is Arne who joins me at the tank, sparring sword in hand and a cocky grin on his face.

"I won't let you win like Ionel did." He pokes at me with its dull end. I bat away the sword with a scowl at him and grab mine, swatting him lightly with it.

"He did not!" We bicker back and forth as we move to one of the other empty rings. It had been another large change, combining the Nefriti weapons training with that of the castle guard and soldiers. A change I had to fight for. The Nefriti were a proud bunch, rightfully so, and ones who liked to keep to themselves. However, it had been hard to fault the logic when I pointed out all needed to have the upmost training if the battle came to our gates. It wouldn't matter if the person who had saved your life was guard, soldier, or Nefriti, you would just be grateful they were well trained. Despite their conceding to my request after many hours of disagreement, they had made it clear that they were not happy about it, and would still keep their traditions to themselves. I had fought a sigh, but agreed. Cheers sound and we turn to find that Ilithyia had just pinned Ionel, who grins up at her from where she sits on his chest.

"I think he *likes* getting knocked on his ass by her." I give Arne a light shove before raising my blade. We both enter the calm mindset required for sparring. It is harder than it looks, shutting out everything other than the opponent in front of you, but also keeping an edge to your consciousness in order to prevent actual damage to each other. Just twenty days ago, I had accidentally snapped a guard's arm by losing my focus and bringing the wood down too hard in a strike. Thankfully, we had been using the sparring swords and not true metal, or else the understanding guard would have found himself in an even worse situation. I had not used a real blade since I had first fought Ionel all those moon-cycles ago. Though with the threat of Mirinth continuing to loom around us, it was only a matter of time before I would have to hold steel rather than wood. That thought is enough to make my control slip.

Pain roars through me, my insides flaring with fire. I drop to the ground, crying out at the agony that spears through me. Immediately Arne shouts to the others in alarm and kneels beside me, eyes raking me for any sign of what was wrong. He hisses in surprise and pain as his skin blisters where he tries to touch me. Ionel, Ilithyia and others that train around us rush over to help, but Isos, who also runs forward, shouts for them to stop. He grabs Arne, who cradles his arm, pulling him back.

Agony is all I can focus on, though I do note the others rushing to clear everyone away from where I kneel smoldering in the sand. I try to catch my breath, but all I taste is ash and flames. *Water. I need water...* I try to picture the cooling sensation it brings but it is only shoved aside by the wave of heat that ripples out from me. I hear the others shout and dive for cover from the pulse. I see nothing but the white hot ball of flame that surrounds me. I try to shove it down. Praying to the wind, the rain, to Jera herself, for control. I plead for reprieve from the element that is burning me from inside out. I hear the crack of lightening, but am unable to see the flash as it strikes nearby, my eyes are screwed shut as I try to wrestle my control. My tenuous control that had slipped its leash for the first time in a moon-cycle. I hear cries of fear all around me, and I pull even harder on the power that threatens to take over me completely. Suddenly a bucket of water douses my skin for a half a second. Its icy temperature the barest bit of relief against the inferno. Though it almost immediately turns it into steam, it gives me the pause I need to wrestle back myself. I call upon the rain from the clouds gathering above.

A minute passes, then two, as I beg the rain to fall. I use the downpour and icy wind to cool the still burning heat inside me until at last I am able to shove the flames, still roaring like an inferno, deep down into the cavern where the monster I keep locked in its cage lives. At last I throw the lock on the door that holds it all at bay. Heaving in a breath of air, I kneel in silence as I catch my breath and the pain begins to recede.

I finally open my eyes and look up. Where dozens had been, either training or observing, now only Ionel, Ilithyia, Arne, and Isos stand, pale and shaking. Ionel holds an empty bucket and I realize that had been the source of the water that gave me the chance to pull back. I also notice that they all stand in front of Ilithyia. Should the worst have happened they had been willing to protect her. *From me.* Because from the stubborn look on her face as she elbows her way past them toward me, I knew she refused to leave when she should have. When they all should have. I swallow the bile that rises at the realization of what could have happened. I look down in shame, only to see a reflection of myself. I scramble backwards, confused. But instead of the rough grains of sand I feel something foreign and smooth. Suddenly I realize why. My fire had been so intense it turned everything for a dozen paces to glass. My friends stand at the edge of the demarcation line, concern filling their faces. But I only stare back in horror.

I had no words of explanation or reassurance.

And Türe was no longer here to tell me how to stop it.

I sit in the gallery, now war room, and pour over all the maps and the latest information on Mirinth's movements. Isos, my constant shadow, stands in the corner. I feel his eyes on me, though I ignore them. We had not spoken of what happened during training this morning. I had nothing beneficial to say to them, anyway. After an hour passes, I sigh in irritation and look up to meet his heavy gaze, opening my mouth to snap at him. A wave of relief washes over his face when a messenger suddenly appears, bowing at me, before handing over a thick sealed envelope. I recognize Ivrik's seal and take a steadying breath before ripping into the letter.

"Ivrik says Mirinth's forces are gone. No longer within sight of Charobi like they have been since the start of the star-cycle." I look up at the map spread out across the table. "Why would they move? They haven't abandoned Dulen, so it's not like they have changed their mind…" I talk aloud, though I learned a while ago Isos wouldn't answer me. *Not his place,* he had said, quite firmly, when I finally asked him one day why he never commented. I rub my sore temples, a headache growing from the exhaustion of another sleepless night, coupled with the depletion that comes from releasing as much energy as I had this morning. I had been serious when I told Türë I was going to cease practicing magic, so the toll of this morning seemed to be extra heavy. I glance towards Isos. He is a seasoned enough soldier to be the Captain of my personal guard, and he understands warfare. Even if he wouldn't weigh in. Worry shows on his face for a few breaths before he catches me looking and he shifts back to a neutrality that has me gritting my teeth. As many issues as I had with Türë, at least he gave his opinion. I could call for the Lords and leaders of the military that still remain here in Alessandra but, most of the time, that just led us in circles. Usually we would all leave more confused and frustrated than before, accomplishing nothing but wasting time.

I read the letter again, but see no mention of Türë. It was always a blessing and a curse when Ivrik took careful steps to ensure he didn't mention the General. I appreciated the steps he takes to maintain the distance I sorely needed.

Time. I need to give us both time to learn who I am apart from him, and what I can do on my own. I hear a knock and it startles me enough to drop the missive. It is Patryk who enters and I shoot him a grin, but my body goes icy at the grim look on his face.

"Isos, would you give us a moment, please?" Patryk says, his voice portraying a calm that his shaking hands give away as false. Isos looks wary, but does as asked with a quick smile of reassurance at me before slipping through the door and pulling it shut behind him.

Patryk slumps in the chair beside mine. Like all the energy has drained from his body. "A Mirinth scout was just found in Vante. He was caught writing a message giving the all clear to a legion of two thousand Mirinth soldiers that will overtake the city in a matter of days."

My blood chills and my eyes drop to the map again. *Well that explains why they are not outside of Charobi anymore.* "Shit." I curse aloud and Patryk nods in grim agreement.

"Should I call for—" he hesitates, unsure if he should say *his* name aloud. "—the General?" I think on it for a moment. The legion of soldiers we had sent to Charobi would take forever to get assembled and up river in time to help Vante. And with as much movement as Mirinth seems to get away with so secretively, I wasn't sure we should leave the south border vulnerable for any matter of time.

"How were they even able to *get* this close to Vante without detection?" I ask, running my fingers through my hair in frustration. Patryk shrugs.

"According to the captured scout, they found a way through the Cliffs and then across the plains." My attention catches at that and I shove to my feet and begin to pace. The movement helps me think.

"Has there been any sign of these soldiers? Or just the scout and his word that this is what is coming?" I was not making any plans on the information without its confirmation. Patryk grimaces.

"Let's just say it wasn't of his free will nor was he willing to part with the information without... necessary enticement." I hate the idea of torture, but this is war. There was going to be more pain and death than just one scout by the time this was done. I stop and brace my palms on the table, staring down at it as if hoping that a different vantage point would make some miraculous answer appear. I stare until my vision blurs and I sigh loudly, rubbing my bloodshot eyes.

"Shall I call for the General?" He asks again, this time gently.

"No." An idea—a crazy one—hits me. "Send a letter to the others about what is going on, but tell them it is being handled. Nothing more." Patryk looks at me in confusion.

"There is no one else—" He starts, but lets the sentence drop at the determined look on my face. "You are not thinking that—"

"I will lead them." I state, not leaving room for his contradiction. "I have been training, I have the Nefriti here. Only two thousand troops will be easy enough to handle with the forces we have here when we join the others stationed at Vante. I will take fifteen hundred of the soldiers and warriors from here and meet up with Eivan's forces in Eri. We will pin them between the Cliffs and the fortress walls of Vante and stamp them out. We would be able to get there in two days if we leave tomorrow morning. The calvary alone is three thousand strong here, so I will leave half and we can ride through the day tomorrow."

Patryk mulls this over, and though he still looks uncertain. He can see the logic and advantage of this move over calling in Türë to take care of it.

"Are you sure you can lead this? What about Ionel, or even Isos?"

"We need them here to continue training the new recruits. They can't afford to be lost."

"Neither can you." Patryk's soft voice cuts in, his eyes sad.

"I do not *plan* on failing, nor do I have the desire to. This is something I have to do. And something I *can* do." I sit again before reaching out and taking Patryk's clammy, quivering hand in my own, trying to ignore the pale sheen of sweat that washes his face grey. "The people need to see their Queen fighting for them, or else I am nothing but a figurehead hiding out in a glittering castle."

"My castle doesn't *glitter*. It *shines*." He mumbles, after a pause, in faux irritation. I laugh, breaking the tension. "I will let the calvary know, and send letters to the others as you asked." He concedes and gives my hand one more squeeze before leaving me to my thoughts. The door shuts with a hollow click and I stare down at the table filled with notes, maps, and books.

"I will not fail." I say to the empty room, my voice echoing thanks to the far away ceilings. Even to myself, though, it sounds like a lie. "I *cannot* fail."

forty-one

"*Fuck* it is cold!" I rub my hands together in a feeble attempt to generate heat. Even with them wrapped in my fur-lined gloves, the wind is biting cold. My cloak whips around me and Afina knickers in annoyance as it spins up and connects with her face in a loud thwack. "Sorry, Afina! Almost there." I reassure her with a few loving strokes along her frosty neck. The snows had hit last night, dumping enough of the white fluffy crap to be a real pain in my ass. Tucking my cloak as tightly as I can around my shivering body, I try not to complain too much. I look back over my right shoulder and wince in sympathy at the line of ice cold soldiers that follow us. There had not been a single word of complaint coming from any of them, so I could not do so without feeling horrid. Thankfully, the calvary and Nefriti warriors whom I had brought plow ahead of us, making as much of an easy path for us that they can and taking the brunt of the blowing wind and ice. While the snow had slowed our pace considerably, it was not as bad as if we had all been on foot. I squint at the horizon line in the limited light that filters through the heavy dark clouds. I lower my voice so that those closest to us cannot hear. "Shouldn't we be able to see the city, or at least the castle towers, by now?" I mutter to Arne, who is completely enveloped in his fur-lined cloak, letting his own horse lead the way without an ounce of shame. A clench of worry wars with the ache of exhaustion, chill, and hunger that has sat in my belly the last two days. We had eaten, of course, but nothing close to the delectable meals the chef in the castle had cooked for me each day. For one, it too was cold. But I had fought down the hard, ancient bread that tasted like dust, and the jerky that apparently was not beef, but some type of ground squirrel that runs rampant in the plains. Against my better judgement, I had swallowed it all, then excused myself to my tent, where I held my aching stomach and tried my best to sleep through the cold and hunger.

"Not in this weather. We will be lucky to see it when we come within a mile of its gates." Arne scowls at the sky, emerging briefly from his bundle. He had agreed immediately when I asked him to accompany me to this risky battle, even though he had not yet completed his training and was not technically a full Nefriti yet. Only a half of a moon-cycle away, the elders of the Magnar had conceded that they would make the exception of his absence. Arne was no stranger to battle. He had apparently served many star-cycles in the guard before being selected as a member of the honored Nefriti. I had wanted to weep at his feet in gratitude, all while shoving aside the fear of the danger I was placing my friend in. I had sent some of my limited stock of magical balms to heal the burns I had inflicted on him during my meltdown. Within the day, the burns had all but vanished, but the guilt lingers still. I also know, from how closely he watches me and never leaves my side, he had been tasked by Isos and Patryk with being my shadow. If they were not able to join me, they made sure Arne would fill their shoes.

After he accepted, I managed to compose myself before going to Isos to request he choose who would be best to accompany us in our assist of the soon-to-be-besieged Vante. I had quelled against the thought of him having to pick which of his friends would follow us into their death. Because some, likely many, would die on the walls and fields that surround Vante. But he was also my most obvious option for choosing who would give us our best shot. I glance back again at the silent, blurred, line of emerald green that stands stark against the snow. As horrid as the situation was, I take the moment to appreciate the beauty of the uniform of the Tesindren set against the snow. Deep emerald green with ebony buttons and trim, they looked both elegant and deadly. *And freezing.*

I nervously look up at the sky again, praying to Jera that we will make it by nightfall. We all needed, at the very least, a semi-decent nights sleep before the expected strike from Mirinth. With the thick cloud cover blanketing the sky, it was impossible to see where the sun was positioned, and therefore how long we had until complete darkness. At that point we would have to make a choice. Either make camp at wherever we were and have to haul ass tomorrow, praying we would make it to Vante in time. Or we could try and push on in the dark and risk the chance that we would be lost, miss out on sleep, or even worse get surprised and attacked by Mirinth's forces before we could help.

"There!" Arne sudden shout startles me and I turn to find him pointing slightly off to the left of the road we had been attempting to follow.

"What?" I say, after a moment of not seeing what he is so excited about.

"That slightly grayer shadow in the distance. That is the fortress tower!" He says, animated and speaking loud enough for those behind us to hear. They pick up the cheer, relief giving them some color back to their cheeks. Even the horses' steps quicken, understanding from the attitude shift that their journey is about to end.

"Okay, let's make it to that dip in the valley." I squint around us, then point off to the right a slight distance away. "That should conceal our group for the night, and then it will be a quick ride in the morning to the gates." Arne nods and nudges his wary horse forward, to convey the decision to the rest. I stare into the distance, trying to make out more of the castle than just the slightly darker blip far in the distance. I blink back the sting of dry eyes and decide to give up on that when it only gives me more of a headache. While my eyes had adjusted slightly to the solid white expanse that I had been staring at all day, the additional strain, coupled with the soreness of riding the last two days, had burrowed knives into my head and back. I roll my neck and shoulders, trying to provide some relief, to no avail.

Arne returns to my side with a grin. "A good night's rest, and a decent meal will give this lot the pep in their step that they are going to need." I nod, trying to share his optimism about the situation. The little, flickering bit of confidence I had when I first made the decision to come to Vante's aid myself was dwindling with each step Afina carries me closer to its gates.

Yes, I had been training almost constantly since the Awakening. Not just my body, but my mind, too. Various strategies, battle plans, and movements of Tesindren's previous military. But now that I stood on the brink of it—my strength begins to flicker.

Arne somehow seems to sense this as he raises a brow at me. "Too late to turn back now." He chuckles and bumps me with an outstretched leg. "You can do this." He says quietly, an understanding smile on his pink, wind-chapped face. "There is no one else I would follow into battle without hesitation. Tomorrow you will find a new side of yourself, but maybe you will meet a piece of your old self, too." I manage a half smile in thanks at him before I nudge Afina a little faster to keep up with the new pace.

*****

Everyone is so eager to be out of the cold and wind, it took barely any time before the tents were up and the campfires roar, thawing our icy bones. I couldn't help but feel guilty that I could have kept all of them warm this entire time, with only the slightest depletion of my power. But that was followed by a giant list of *ifs*. If I had been continuing my practicing. If I had any true control over it. And the one that kept me awake at night—if I didn't incinerate everything around me again the second I tapped into the heavy weight of unused power.

I knew that my meltdown in the training pits, only a mere three days ago, weighed heavily on all of my friend's minds. But I was doing a better job at keeping it stifled. Well, I was doing as best as I was able with the amount of pressure I currently struggle under. Twice I had tried to loosen the reins, just a bit. The resulting wind that had cascaded down upon us had nearly blown us off the road. Nobody but Arne had been suspicious of the second sudden gust. Though he had glared at me in suspicion, thankfully he hadn't said a word. Only when all the tents were erected did I finally retreat to my set up in the middle of the camp. Stepping through its flaps, I nearly melt at the immediate reprieve from the icy wind. Though my tent was quite a bit larger and nicer than the rest of the encampment, it was still simple. To the left of the flap of cloth that functioned as a front door was another sectioned off part of the tent. Hidden behind that second 'door' was the thick bedroll, a stool with a single candle atop it, and a washbasin. In the main part of the tent was a simple table with enough chairs for ten, with a larger one at its head that functioned, I suppose, as my traveling throne. At the center of it all was a large fire whose heat already was filling the space with its delicious comfort.

"There are usually shelves, couches, and more comforts than this." One of the Nefriti had explained that first night we had set up the tents. "But since we will be taking it back down in the morning, we won't put it all up just yet. That usually only is done at your request, or when you will be staying somewhere for a longer period of time." Apparently, in the past, I had always traveled with a company of Nefriti, though normally my fellow Tomyris warriors. To their disappointment, I had asked that they, along with the Magnar, remain in Alessandra. Every one of them was itching for a fight, and as the elite band of warriors in my kingdom, asking them to stay behind was insulting. Until I explained that in my absence, they were needed to protect the capital should I fall. They would be our final chance. My honesty had sobered them. So many still viewed me as the unbeatable, immortal, infallible queen. The thought that I could be lost, leaving the kingdom truly vulnerable, it shook them enough that they agreed. Allowing a few Nefriti, and in Arne's case, a Nefriti initiate to ride with me in their stead.

I discard my soaked cloak on a post within the range of the fire, hoping its warmth would dry it more quickly. Moving to the area sectioned off as my bedroom, I begin to pull the gown off that was no more dry than the cloak. I tug on the simple white nightdress that had been packed for me and sigh at the touch of something blessedly dry and warm. I pull back the rough sheets before pausing at their milky white color. Looking back down at myself, I take in the dirt caked under my nails and painting my skin, before glancing at the washbasin filled with clean water with a sigh. I decide to just get it over with before I could change my mind, despite the exhaustion that makes my body shake. A bath would be heavenly, and while this wasn't the kind of luxurious bath I had grown used to, maybe I could pretend.

I dunk my hands in and hiss at its frosty bite. Scrubbing as quickly as I can, I splash my face and parts of my chest that are visible before patting them dry with a nearby towel. *Now just my feet.* I nearly decide it wasn't worth it, but then realize that after tonight I wasn't sure when I would have the chance for even a barely respectable bath like this one. So with a grunt at its weight, I tug the large bowl off the stand it sits on and hold my breath as I dunk, scrub, and dry each foot. Surprisingly enough, the cold actually feels wonderful here. I hadn't realized until now how stiff and blistered my feet had become from the long, exhaustive days of travel. I notice a bottle of oil that Ilithyia had thoughtfully packed for me. Sitting on the edge of the mattress, I take my time, massaging it into the tired sore muscles of my feet, and then up my legs. I inhale its soothing lilac and mint scent and have to bite down on a sob that threatens to burst out. I stare at the canvas walls that surround me and realize how much I truly love and miss my castle. My home. But I cannot remain hidden and cowering behind its beautiful walls, I remind myself. No. All of Tesindren was my home, really. And even though I had not yet seen it since the Awakening, I was glad I was at last getting to see more of it. I only wish the circumstances were different.

I grip the sheets beneath my fingers, the suffocating magic beginning to rise at my lowered mental walls. I was exhausted, emotionally and physically. I breathe through the siege of its hammering against the cage I desperately keep it locked inside, praying it will hold out. If only until the battlefield. There I could release myself freely. If I took Mirinth's soldiers with me, so be it. Better for it, actually. But I would not allow it to hurt my own. I use this thought to stiffen my resolve. I picture the bandages that had wrapped Arne's arms after I had burned him. I take long soothing breaths and try to think of anything else.

Against my better judgement, my thoughts wander to Türë. Even after all that had happened between us, and the uncertainty and distrust he had caused, I still missed him. Or at least who I thought he was. I groan in irritation before flopping back into the mattress. I snort a short laugh at my confused heart before flipping my back to face the fire that warms the tent, then force my eyes closed.

Thanks to the long, cold days, my body finally finds sleep without trouble.

✳ ✳ ✳ ✳ ✳

The acrid taste of smoke fills my mouth and lungs.

I try to scream, but the sound is lost among the rest of the hurt and dying. It is all around me. Agony. Death. Every part of me aches, but I barely can feel it among the pain that surges through my heart with each beat it struggles to take. I stare, my heart frosted as ice, at the corpses scattered around me, looking back from eyes that will never flare with the spark of life again. I look for someone, but all I see are unmoving bodies. Miles of them, it seems. My world has been reduced to making myself breathe, when all I want to do is lay down and join them. That will make this pain in my soul stop. The stone castle walls stand scorched behind me, ominous and dark in the blood-soaked night. Without even a moon or stars to give some glimmer of light, all that illuminates the field churned around me is burning grass and death. I feel bile rise and join the burning scorching my throat.

"Evara!" I hear a terrified male voice screaming my name, and I sob in relief. Spinning around, I try to find something of the voice, but see no sign of him. Only death. "What are you doing?" His voice is filled with panic, but still I can't find him. I try to scream again through my raw throat.

An icy but gentle wind cuts through the smoke and caresses my face. It makes my breath catch with its contrast to the surrounding scene. Even so, I feel lighter at its touch. I breathe in its calming scent. *Mint and cypress.* I gasp at the familiar scent, a familiar stranger that had filled my dreams. "Donovan!" I shout, and suddenly I am on a different battlefield, looking for my love after we had been separated. I take off at a run, yelling for him, but my eyes snap open and that world of smoke and fire is gone. I am back to the hell waiting to be unleashed outside Vante.

And I am freezing.

I look around, my teeth chattering, and realize I am sitting in a snowbank. Steam rolls around me and I blink a few times, trying to reconcile what is real and what is not. It takes a few minutes before I both hear and see Arne crouching beside me, calling my name again and again until I look at him finally.

"What in Jera's name are you doing?" He asks, his voice cracking with emotion. In this instant, a concerned friend rather than a warrior addressing his Queen.

"I—" I look around, my mind still trying to understand myself. "I'm not sure. I think I had a nightmare, but how I ended up here..." I look around again. "Where is the camp?" I ask, panic setting in when I see nothing around us.

"A ways back that way," Arne says waving over his shoulder. "Dreaming indeed. I was just getting into bed when someone came running to tell me you were seen leaving camp unattended in nothing but your nightdress." He sighs in exasperation. "Everything okay?"

"Yeah. I just—" I look around at the snow that drifts down around me. "I think my nerves got the best of me." I force a laugh, but Arne only looks back at me.

"The magic is overtaking you again, isn't it?" He asks, gently. I don't bother pointing out the inappropriateness of him questioning or even seeing his Queen this way. We were far past that.

I tuck my knees into my chest, shivering. He notices this and immediately shrugs his own cloak off, wrapping it around my shoulders with a careful, cautious gesture. Not that I blame him. The last time he had tried to intervene during one of my outbursts, I had burned him badly.

"I don't know what to do about it." I confess, knowing my friend won't hold it against me. "The more I stifle the beast inside, the more it aches to get out, but when I do release it, well, you have seen what happens." I try to fight the self pity that rushes up as I hold up my hand, watching it catch on fire. "I will figure it out, though." I stick my hand in a puff of snow and wait until the steaming stops before I reach it out to Arne. To his credit, he takes it without hesitation and helps me up.

"I have an idea." He admits, looking slightly nervous. I eye him, my curiosity peaked. "Did...the General..." He drifts off and I shoot him an annoyed look.

"You can say his name! I am not that fragile." I snap and he winces, embarrassment flushing his already wind-chafed cheeks even more crimson.

"Right. General Türe did tell you about the massacres of the Creatures of the Forest long ago, right?" I nod, wondering where this could be going.

"If you are suggesting finding one of them to teach me, I don't think any exist anymore." I say, even as my mind flicks to Eganël. *Maybe that actually is an idea. Türe had a conflict of interest and minimal powers. Maybe Eganël would be willing to help me with Türe now gone.*

"Actually, I was thinking the opposite." A particularly harsh burst of wind batters us, and we both begin to push through the nearly knee high drifts of snow towards the encampment. "In the village I grew up in, there was an old tale about an herb that was used to nullify the creature's magic. If we were able to find that and you drank it in your tea or something like that—" I stop in my tracks and spin, smiling at him. He starts at my sudden movement, and looks worried until he sees the wide smile of relief on my face.

"It would nullify mine, too." I whisper, almost worried that if I say it too loud that fate would hear it and somehow prevent me from the destiny of suffocating under my own power. "Do you remember what it was called?" I rack my brain for some recollection if Türe had ever mentioned it.

"I don't. But General Türe definitely should, and I bet if none of the other Underkings do, King Noran at least will be able to track it down. He is well known as a resource for the Nefriti for historical information, and something so important as that would be recorded somewhere. If only in your private documents that he would have access to. Or maybe the Elders know something. You could ask Elder Dakar." Arne seems to pick up on my enthusiasm, relieved that his idea had not backfired and made me more upset.

The rest of the way to the camp, we stay silent, lost in our own thoughts and memories. Arne trying to recall the herb's name, while I just tried to imagine a day without the constant pain and exhaustion from battling the power battering at its cage. At last we make it to my tent and the look Arne levels at me has me raise my brows in surprise.

"Do I need to sleep outside this tent, or will you promise me you will stay inside for the few remaining hours of the night?" I roll my eyes at him.

"I will do my best to not allow my unconscious self to wander uncontrollably." He chuckles, bowing deeply as I pull his cloak off and pass it back to him.

"Goodnight, Your Majesty."

"Arne—" I stop him before he can turn away. "Just call me Evara. I think we are past any attempt at formalities by now." He grins back at me, eyes dancing with humor, before bowing once more and turning, disappearing into the line of tents spread out around me.

I duck inside and sigh at its warmth, even though the fire is barely cinders now. Returning to my bed, I slide under the sheets, ignoring my dirty feet this time, and pass out again. Before sleep claims me, the dream I had hits me and I sit up. I tug my knees to my chest as I try to pull up every second of the dream I had, realizing now it was actually a memory. Even as I breathe a sigh of relief at the realization that another memory had come to me, it is overpowered by the horrid vision of the battlefield, making my fear of the next day surge. I force myself to lie back, staring at the roof of the tent as it buckles and flaps in the wind.

At least I knew what to prepare myself for. All I could do was hope that Jera would not abandon us tomorrow, when we would need her the most.

forty-two

A horn's call sends me shooting up in bed. A bed much smaller than I am used to, my surprise sends me flailing to the floor with an *oof.* I groan as my tailbone sings from the impact and I turn to locate the source of laughter that comes from the center of the tent. Arne had entered to find me on the floor rubbing my ass. I scowl at him.

"Morning." He greets me with a wan smile. "You ready for today?"

I pull myself to my feet. "Is anyone really? What in Jera's name is that horn for?" None of the other mornings had brought about such a horrible way of waking us. His smile falters at the question.

"Our scouts have spotted the Mirinthians." He says, and my blood chills. Immediately, I lunge for my battle suit. The drakonskein glitters in the low light, but even its beauty cannot pull my focus from the upcoming day ahead.

"How far?"

"They will be at Vante's walls by tonight."

"Exactly as the scout said. Was the information about their numbers accurate?" My second question really two parts in one. *How truthful had the captured scout been? Were we walking directly into a trap, and one we would not walk away from?* The images from my nightmare the night before flashes in my mind before I shove them away.

"They are." My shoulders slump in relief.

"Okay, we need to send our messengers to Eivan, though I am sure he, too, knows they are approaching. We will wait to pin them between our forces and the walls as we planned." Arne nods and disappears through the flap. Without ceremony, I slip on my battle dress, and begin to struggle, attempting to braid my mess of chestnut hair back from my face, when Arne steps into the tent again.

"That is done."

I shoot him a grateful smile, even as my fingers shake with anticipation and nerves. He watches me closely.

"How is the beast inside doing?" He asks, trying to make light of it, for my sake.

"Sleeping in its cage. For now." I admit. Thankfully, it was the truth. Unsure if it was because I was distracted, or if it is simply biding its time. He only nods. His understanding and trust in me feels like a warm embrace. "Are the others ready?"

"They are assembling south of the camp. We will be ready to march within the hour." *An hour.* My head spins with the speed of it all. Days of traveling and anticipation, and suddenly it is here. I look for the weapons belt and the sword Ilithyia had grabbed for me from the castle arsenal. "Wait." Arne stops me. "I was told to deliver something to you, courtesy of Isos." I watch him curiously as he reaches beneath his cloak and pulls out a shining scabbard inlaid with emerald and moonstone. My breath catches as he holds it out to me. "He apparently took the liberty of persuading

Yessin Arboff to make haste in finishing this for you." I take it, open mouthed, and am immediately surprised at its weight. Or lack there of. It was lighter than even the pine training swords that beginners use. I marvel at its intricate design and grasp the handle. The blade glides free of the oiled scabbard without a sound. Glimmering a pale gold hue, its layered steel creates a design that looks like waves. Its handle is designed in the shape of a lily, appearing uncomfortable, it fits perfectly into my hand, as if it has been made from a mould of my palm. It looks more for decoration, rather than the horror of battle. *Deadly masterpiece, indeed.* I swing it, testing its balance. It sings as it slices the air and feels like a mere extension of my hand rather than a separate piece of metal. No, this was a weapon of war, not meant for a glass case. It begged to part bone and flesh.

"It's beautiful." I whisper before returning it to its sheath.

"It is one of Eganël's finer pieces, I will say. Even with the shorter than normal timeframe given." Arne eyes the weapon with affection and unveiled jealousy. "I had only heard stories." He shakes his head, appreciatively.

"Tell you what, if I die, the blade is yours." I tease him as I attach it to the weapons belt along with *Nehtarûmarth*.

To his credit, he laughs. "And should I, you can have mine." He responds, with a wink, as he pulls his common warrior's blade free of his own scabbard slung at his hips.

"I would treasure it always." I smile back at him, while also making a note to commission a blade for him from Eganël should we both survive this ordeal. "Well," I look around the tent. "I think that is all." My cloak is now merely damp rather than soaking like it was last night. I pull it around my shoulders and take one last deep breath in preparation of exiting the tent.

"Actually," Arne stops me suddenly, hand held aloft. I stop, frowning at the sudden shift in his demeanor. "There is something we are required to do first." My confusion must be clear, but he doesn't explain, merely opens the tent flap and waves someone in. I recognize the woman immediately. One of the Tomyris Elders, I had felt her eyes on me during my trainings and the few times I had met with the Elder Council. Elder Ygrette, I remember after a moment. Apparently, though only in about her forties, she was one of my warriors who had enlisted as a soldier the moment she was able, and was quickly selected to become Nefriti. The *Ynyra* lines that stripe her arms, neck, chest, and face do not detract from her beauty. Instead, it only illuminates it. Each is a display of her immense strength. Though my country had not been at war for centuries, the Nefriti still follow their ancient traditions of marking their bodies with each victory. And with various pirate infiltrations at the ports, poachers who came up from Mirinth, and defending their places in the Nefriti rank, there were still plenty of opportunities to earn the honored marks. If I survived tomorrow, I would begin my collection again and Arne would receive his first.

The woman doesn't bow or return my smile. I glance at Arne, who nods subtlely, a show of support, even though I can see he is nervous too. "I am here to prepare my sister and brother for battle." She says, her voice surprisingly light and youthful. I try to hide my surprise. Though unexpected, I am still incredibly touched. Ever since my Awakening, I felt half a part of them, and half like a stranger looking in from the outside. When I was told she would be accompanying us, I had truly been surprised at the gesture. My supposedly 'fellow Tomyris' had been anything but welcoming to me. Without further discussion or waiting for prompting, Elder Ygrette strides across the tent to where a locked trunk sits in the corner. I had seen it the night before, but not paid any proper attention to it. She slides a key free from a chain at her waist and unlocks the box without ceremony, pulling a selection of items I can't immediately identify from it. She turns around and orders us, with a snap of her fingers, to kneel. Neither of us argues. Beginning a chant in a language that rings familiar from my time in Nefriti training, only the words and tone are different. The songs chanted during training were that of perseverance and strength. Though I can't make out each word, the ones I do make out are those of ferocity, protection, ruthlessness, and honor. With a sharp and sudden movement, she throws a handful of something into the fire that still flickers in the middle of my tent. Whatever it is, it ignites with a loud hiss and crackle, throwing a scented smoke in the air. I inhale deeply, and don't notice for a moment the sound of drums that begin to echo around us, the surrounding soldiers of my military also readying for what was to come. Her voice mingles with the smoke and the beat, filling my spirit with the encouragement it needs to face the coming battle. I feel her moving next to me, where Arne kneels, and after a few moments, her attention turns to me. Startlingly soft hands brush over my eyes, indicating I should close them before they delve into my hair. After a few brushstrokes loosen the knots and ragged braid I had thrown my hair into this morning, she begins an intricate braiding pattern until my hair is woven into numerous plaits that pull the cumbersome hair away from my face. Elder Ygrette's chanting again changes to one of harsher tone, speaking of death to my enemies. Of vengeance. I hear Arne startle slightly next to me and prepare myself for what comes. It is not what I expect, but thankfully I manage to not jump as the icy touch of fingers coated in something cold and wet brush a pattern across my forehead, cheeks, nose, and eyelids.

The Elder's words finally come to an end, though the drums outside continue to grow in tempo and volume. I open my eyes slowly, and turn to look at Arne. He stares back at me, though he looks completely different. Face painted with lines and dots of green, black, and white, he wears the intimidating mask of a warrior. Even his hair is pulled free of its normal trainee bun atop is skull and braided in a long strand, like I had seen the Elder Magnar wear to council meetings. From the look on his face, I must appear the same to him, only the Tomyris version. Smaller braids woven with leather from each of my temples, down the back of my ears with one larger plait decending from my crown down my back and decorated with feathers. Both of our eyes are lined with thick black lines, and I must admit it makes Arne look intimidating. The stories I had read about past Nefriti did not lie. We would be fearsome to behold on the battlefield. I spy the pride gleaming in his beneath the paint. This was the first time in history a trainee of the Nefriti was given full battle honors and preparation like this. I turn to thank Elder Ygrette and find her painting on the last line of her own face adornment.

"You will fight with us?" I ask, shocked. I had asked the Tomyris and Magnar to remain, in the capital, but here she was readying to fight. I had, apparently incorrectly, assumed that she was unable to fight and protect, which was the reason she had been chosen to come with us. From the smirk she levels on me, I know Elder Ygrette knows my thinking. Tugging a gigantic axe free from where it hangs at her side, she slides a thumb down the head of it, slicing the pad open. I gape at the deep burgundy blood that shines there as she takes the blood and paints one final line from crown to chin in her own blood.

"I am here. I will fight." She merely says before shoving the axe back to its holster at her side and strides from the tent. Arne and I share a look before grinning to each other, nerves beginning to resurge, and follow her out of the tent.

Sunshine beats down on my face and my lips tug into a smile at the sensation. At least if I were to die today, it would be in the sunshine rather than the gloom. Afina stands outside my tent, already saddled and ready. I don't give myself any more chances to think about or to rationalize what I was doing here. My hands shake as I grip the saddle horn and pull myself up. Arne does the same beside me and together we join the waiting calvary. I send a thanks and a prayer to Jera for my friend. I know he was trained as a soldier and now a Nefriti warrior, but it is a different feat to ride into battle without qualm beside a Queen who had never truly experienced battle. At least not in this memory.

My heart nearly stops when I take in the sight of the group waiting for me. Rows of emerald and navy, lined up in trained precision, make me fight against the tears of pride and sorrow that prick my eyes, even as the booming war drums fill the air and set my blood thrumming.

How many would walk off the battle field today? Would I even be one of them? I swallow hard and try to look as calm as they would expect from their renowned warrior queen. Arne and I make it to the front of the column of soldiers to cheers and the thunderous banging of shields joins the drums. My blood thrums in excitement at the sound, in spite of my nerves. I feel the thrum of the beat shake my bones, the same sound I know has graced the battlefields of Tesindren for a millennium. We lead the regimen, along with Elder Ygrette who joins us at the head of the formation. As a fellow Tomyris, it was her rightful place. We set a fast pace, nudging our horses and the calvary behind us into a swift canter. With the clouds now lifted, we crest the hill we had spent the night concealed behind and into full view of the glowing white walls of Vante's castle that gleam in the sun and snow.

Surrounded by three exterior walls and a monsterous cliff, the castle seems to float atop a large hill. Not as tall as the mountains that border the western edge of Tesindren, but enough for a military advantage, as well as a magnificent sight. I try to count the flags painted with the crest of the kingdom that whip in the wind atop each peak and tower, but lose count after sixty two.

Spread out around the protective walls was a city just slightly smaller than Alessandra. It was breathtaking.

Then I see the black mass smeared in the distance, marching on Vante. It stands between our group and the castle. *Just as we had planned.* I release my breath and feel a glint of optimism. I glance at Arne, and see a similar look to what I would guess my own is. *Don't let down your guard. Things can still go terribly wrong if we misstep or miscalculate.* I send another silent prayer up to Jera as we watch the mass of soldiers arrive at the borders of the city, blowing past the meager gates with barely any resistance. It was to be expected. The city was not meant to withhold a force of any number. The castle walls is where the outcome would be determined. Whether our messenger we had sent ahead to alert them had arrived in enough time for everyone to make it safely into the castle's protection, we wouldn't find out for sure until afterwards. But I took no sound of screaming or people running amok as a positive sign.

I fight the urge to push Afina and the others faster. I knew the horses would probably love to be released, but we needed to conserve their energy for the battle itself. We *all* needed to pace ourselves. I am immensely grateful we had the night to relax after pushing hard. It would be a waste to drain us all now.

"Evara." I hear Arne call out. And I turn my face to him, though don't slow Afina. He meets my gaze, his face and demeanor more serious than I had ever seen. "Jera bless you, protect you, and take you into her arms." I blink at the words, even as I realize they are being exchanged between the few Nefriti who had joined us, all painted as we were, who ride at my back. *A battlefield prayer. And some of the last words many of us all will hear.*

"Jera bless you, protect you, and take you into her arms, Arne." I repeat back to him, and my eyes water some as an understanding passes between us. A silent goodbye should the worst happen.

The angry shouts and screams now reach our ears. As one, we rush through the city gates and empty streets until at last we reach our enemies who stand between us and the castle protecting the citizens of Vante.

forty-three

The world blurs as I slip my sword free from its scabbard. My heartbeat suddenly feels deafening. Though I can't be sure if the pounding in my ears is my racing pulse, or the thousands of hoof beats that fill the air. The army at my back releases their battle cry as we unleash ourselves upon the unsuspecting Mirinthians. I don't think of restraint as my arm falls again and again, taking a life with each stroke. My muscles burn with each swing of the blade. Even with its lightweight, I fight to lift my arm as the minutes—hours—pass. I don't count how many I fell. Each one fades into another until we at last stand amid unmoving and bloody bodies. I don't remember dismounting Afina or could even guess when I lost track of Arne. I look around the field again in a panic, the similarity to the memory from the night prior flooding me. Scanning frantically for his familiar face and my mount. I gasp for breath, spinning around in preparation for another attack, another coming blow. But nothing.

There is no one left to fight against.

I feel a surge of pride and vindication mingle with the horror at the death spread out in front of me. For every soldier dressed in my colors laying among the dead there are ten in Mirinth ruby and black. I stumble slightly, my legs catching up to the exhaustion. I hear cheering through the ringing in my ears. *We did it.* I gape around again. *We beat them.* Elation and relief surge through me at the realization. My legs buckle fully this time, and only swift, steady hands catch me from plunging face first into the blood-soaked slush and mud. *Arne!* I realize, distantly, as my head spins, taking in the familiar, though gore splattered, face.

Relief is clear on his own face and I realize his mouth is moving, asking me something I can't make out. I shake my head, trying to clear my mind. "Are you hurt?" I at last make out. I ponder that question, looking down at myself before answering with a giggle that bubbles out.

"I don't think so." *Why am I laughing?* I can't help myself as the giggle turns into full on laughter. Arne frowns at me, concerned at my reaction. "Why am I laughing?" I ask, not feeling humored by the situation at all, yet unable to stop the harsh sound. The laughter mingles with tears.

"I think you are in shock." He says gently. "Can I take you into the castle?" I look around at the limp forms that cover as far as I can make out.

"What about them?" The question sobers me, a heavy melancholy taking over. We won, but at the cost of how many lives?

"We will take care of them. Just come with me." He looks me up and down. "Can you walk?"

"I don't know." I admit. My whole body is numb. I am not sure if I can even tell if I was missing a body part at this moment. My brain does not seem to be functioning properly at all. Suddenly one of my first cohesive thoughts hits me again. "Afina! Where is

Afina?"

"I had her taken to the castle after you jumped off of her." He says, looping a supportive arm below my knees and pulling me into his arms.

I don't remember that.

I don't even bother to fight against his help. I hadn't lied. I wasn't sure if I could walk or if I was hurt at all. I knew nothing but the desire to sleep.

I tell myself to look away, but I still find my eyes drawn to each of the pale, unseeing faces of those we pass. I shut my eyes and lean into Arne's chest, trying to shove away the images before they could burn into my mind fully. *Coward.* My inner voice spits a me before I can silence it. Tears of shame fill my eyes, but I still don't look. It feels like only breaths before the sound of his footsteps shift from soft pads on dirt and hay, to the solid beat against stone floor.

"Is she okay?" I hear a frantic male voice that sounds slightly familiar call out to us.

"Yes, just needs a bed." Arne grunts, adjusting his grip on my limp form. I tune out the rest, focusing all my energy into listening to the rhythmic pulse of his heartbeat, rather than the cries of pain from the wounded we pass. Thankfully, where ever the man leads us, it is through some door and into a silent hallway.

A door creaks just as the man says, "Here. Her chambers are further away, but this is private enough and closer to healers for now." Huffing a thanks, Arne sets me down gently into a feather soft mattress. I cry out as pain spears through my back. I try to pull myself up, but I'm too tired. The man with the familiar voice and Arne each grab me and curse loudly. From the pain that incinerates my back, I guess that I must have a wound after all. Arne holds me up as I gasp for breath, barely able to hear the words he says to me through the pain. I hear a soft woman's voice join the panicked conversation, but where theirs were rushed and overwhelming, hers is tense but calming.

"This is going to hurt, Your Majesty. I'm sorry. But try to breathe through it." I do as she says as the pain grows even more intense. Stars burst in my eyes and I hear a hiss of pain from Arne. He doesn't say anything, but I realize suddenly that I have dug my fingers into the arms holding me up. Hard enough they pierce through his clothing, drawing blood.

"I'm sorry." I manage through my tears, trying to ease my grip. He only mutters something reassuring that I don't quite catch. My attention is too focused on the healer's voice who talks to someone under her breath. Worry filling the words I manage to catch.

"—embedded in the ribs—tip poisoned so she isn't healing—don't know how she is alive—have to yank it out now before it pierces her lungs—best chance—"

"Just do it." I yell, making Arne jump in my arms at the sudden noise. The man who had been arguing with the healer falls quiet, and I feel soft pressure behind me on the bed.

"Be ready to catch her." She instructs the two men from where she has kneeled by my back. Then to me, "Take a deep breath."

I do so.

Then I can't stop it any longer.

I scream.

My tongue feels glued to the roof of my mouth when I drift back into consciousness. I tug open my crusty eyes to an unfamiliar room. The only light comes from a small flickering fire to my left. I try to sit up and feel a burst of pain radiate up my back. I groan, but note that as bad as it was, it did feel less than when I last was awake. A creak from a nearby chair draws my attention across the room. A man sits there, watching me with a kind smile worn on his face. A face I had seen before, only once in person. *King Eivan.* That is when I realize why the man from earlier sounded so familiar. It was Eivan.

"Don't move too much." He says gently, a flicker of worry dancing in his eyes. "Can I get you anything?"

"Water, please?" I ask, my voice a rasp, torn raw from screaming. "What was it?" He quickly pours me a glass and I take it as gingerly as I can.

"An arrowhead, but not a normal one." He explains, observing me closely for any sign of lingering pain or danger. Now that he mentions it, I vaguely remember breaking off a piece of an arrow shaft in the midst of battle. My mind begins to revolt though as other memories of the fight start to emerge, so I pull my attention back to the present.

"I'm better." I reassure him. "At least as far as I know." I frown down at the various cuts and scrapes I now notice pepper my hands and arms. "How long was I asleep?"

He understands my full question. "The battle was yesterday. You have been out for about fourteen hours. It was a solid victory. Thank you for coming to our rescue. Though I must admit, I am furious at you for putting yourself at risk." I was a few millennia older than the man, yet the look he leveled at me was one of a concerned father or older brother.

"And the ones lost?" I force the words out.

"Around two hundred of our own. The official count has not been made yet. But not one of Mirinth's force survived."

I gasp. "The count was nearly two and a half thousand

Mirinthians! Not *one* survived?" I feel sickened at the thought, and try to convince myself that they gave us no choice.

"Arne? Where is he?"

The door creaks open as I ask. "Right here." He steps into the room with a cautious grin. "How you feeling, sunshine?" Eivan shoots him a dangerous look and I huff a laugh. "Oh—I mean—Your Majesty!" He snaps into his Nefriti facade and shoots me a nervous, wide-eyed look.

"Oh, please!" I wave my hand and cautiously lean against a pillow with a half smile. "You can call me whatever you wish at this point. I have both burned you and dragged you into battle in the last week alone." Eivan relaxes slightly, though his brows shoot up at that. "Long story." I say, hoping to save myself a lengthy explanation that I had no energy for. Luckily, he doesn't push the matter. I sit up further and smile at my friend. "I am *so* relieved you are okay. When I couldn't find you at first, I began to worry."

"I am going to go find the healer." Eivan says before bowing at me and vanishing through the door. Arne takes the king's place beside the bed and I catch him trying to get a glimpse of my back. I sigh, annoyed at both of them treating me with delicate gloves.

"Will you look and tell me how bad it is?" His eyes flick to mine in relief before nodding. I lean forward and he steps closer to see better in the soft light. The resulting hiss he makes tells me everything I need to know. A quick clip of heels sounds from the hall and the healer marches into the room. She only drops a quick curtsy before pushing past Arne to examine my wound. She makes a low hum, but says nothing else. "What? What is wrong?"

"Its healing, but...slowly. Much too slowly for someone of your power. Being Sidhe you should be much further along. Even accounting for the poison coating the blade, your hands at least shouldn't still have all of those wounds. Something traumatic is happening with your magic. Was there anything before the battle yesterday that felt off? Were you hurt recently?" I share a wide-·eyed look at Arne, before donning a look of innocence. I don't answer, which only makes the woman make the humming noise again. "Well I can give you a special salve for you to coat the wound twice a day. It should help it go a little faster until you figure out *whatever* is the cause." I appreciate her respect of my privacy. "Let her sleep when she needs to boys. And if it starts to pain you more, call for me and I will bring you a draught for the pain." She gives me a warm smile. "I believe you will recover just fine, Your Majesty." The woman pats my hand kindly before leaving me in the care of Eivan and Arne.

The moment I determine she is out of earshot, I pull off the sheets, shoving myself out of bed. The two men jump forward in alarm and try to maneuver me back into the warm sheets. I wave them off with a glare.

"I need to be seen, alive and well, or else this victory will mean nothing. The whole reason we are in this war at all was because they viewed me as vulnerable. I cannot seem weak now. Now leave so I can dress." I shoo them out. I look to the wardrobe I had spotted when I first woke, taking a guess that these were the rooms set aside for me when I visited. I hoped that also meant I had fresh clothes, other than the nightdress I wear. I could send for my things left with the campsite we had set before the battle, but right now everyone was busy. They didn't not need to be bothered with my clothes. I groan in disappointment as I don't find what I had hoped.   I dress in a everyday linen dress. Decorated with embroidered lilacs, its pale blue color was much too cheerful for the circumstances. But since I couldn't find anything close to my normal clothing, my options were this or a full ball gown. I dress as quickly as I can while ignoring the agony that thrums down my back with each movement. I sift through various containers of what appeared to be makeup before finding a cloth that I dampen, managing to scrub the war paint that is now intermixed with sweat and blood. Finally I deem myself mostly presentable, my hair still somehow tightly woven into its braids, only a few feathers are missing or frayed. I frown at my still sore and torn hands, and the healer's words resurface. Was my refusal and struggle with my magic also affecting my healing? There were so many other questions that arise, if that was the truth. With that reasoning, it could even be effecting my immortality and I wouldn't know until it was too late. I shove these worries aside, along with all of the other things piling up in my already tired mind. I have enough to focus on today. Most importantly checking on my likely very afraid people.

At the door, I pause, my attention catching on something leaned against the bed. The blade I had wielded yesterday that had taken so many lives, yet also saved many more. I grab it and sling the scabbard belt around my waist again. Somehow even with the soft, cheerful dress, the sword and scabbard compliment it. I was just thankful to whoever cleaned the gore off for me.

"You should name it." Arne's voice in the hall stops me and I pause, looking at him in confusion. "The sword. You need to name it." Eivan grins at me, crossing his arms across his chest.

"Please do something better than '*peace* maker' this time." Eivan says, chuckling as he tugs at his beard. I roll my eyes, but a word flickers into my mind. *Skuldskapare.* I murmur it to myself, pull the sword out examining it. I repeat it, louder, and feel a smile tug my healing split lip.

"Which means?" Arne prompts. I frown at the comprehension that my mind had been able to pull a word from the old language. *Another thing to think on—at a different time.*

"It means *Fatemaker.*" I say, sheathing the blade again, even as a tingle of what feels like acceptance ripples through the sword.

"Of course it does." He mutters with exasperation as Arne burst into laughter. "I think *Peacemaker* even sounded more intimidating." I shoot a glare at him, before taking one last steadying breath. Bracing myself for whatever was happening outside of the room, I pull the door shut behind me and step out to see Raefus Castle for the first time.

forty-four

I memorize each face I pass on my way through the castle, the look of reverence and joy that shines from them heals each of the cracks in my heart, little by little. By the time we reach the point where the Tesindren soldiers who had fallen were laid out, I don't feel what I expected.

I am filled with overwhelming sadness, guilt, and sorrow for each person who makes up row after row of men and women who had given their lives. But I am not as destroyed as I would have been if I had come to see them first. Instead, I saw all the lives saved by their sacrifices. The people who they had given up their lives for. This is what we had ridden for days through snow and ice to come and save. If this was the cost for the safety of the women who had passed me their babies, so I might see the future generations we had spared from a horrible death. Or the fathers who had thanked me on their knees for sparing their young sons from having to pick up the sword and take lives that they were not prepared to take. This was our sacred duty. To protect the innocent and rain hell down upon those who threaten them. For the first time, I grasp what Türë had tried to tell me when we had argued about my actions of ruthless revenge at Dothsmerna. *Those who show no mercy deserve no mercy.*

I fight the urge to throw my arms around Elder Ygrette's somber form when I come across the Elder at last. I certainly wasn't expecting it when she suddenly drew her dagger and, before I could react, sliced the upper part of my left bicep about halfway around. Dress and all. It didn't nick the muscle beneath the skin, or really even hurt compared to my back, that still sings with each step I take. The small scream that I don't manage to clamp down on is more of surprise, but loud enough that everyone in the room surges forward until I hold up my hand to stop them. Arne beside me, receives the same cut, twin to mine and the still bleeding cut I spy on Elder Ygrette's own arm. *Ynyra* lines, I realize. I watch with mingled curiosity and apprehension when she withdraws a pouch dangling from her waist belt and scoops a small handful of what appeared to be colored powder and divides it between her two palms. What does hurt like a bitch is when she slaps a handful of the cobalt blue powder onto each of our cuts and grinds it into them. The excerpt regarding this history Noran had sent me to learn flashes in my mind. *Cobalt for victory in battle. Red for victory against a challenger. Black for victory in defense of home. White for death of a loved one.* I hear Arne's matching sharp intake of breath against the pain as Elder Ygrette shouts first in the ancient tongue, then in the common language for all those around us who watch with awe and curiosity.

"You have looked death in the face and have overcome it. For the honor you bring the Nefriti with this victory, you are marked." I am not sure what we are supposed to do next, so I glance at Arne, who just stares in elation at the slice that would scar and color, marking him permanently as a Nefriti. A day, he had told me, he had been praying to Jera for, preparing for, since he was eight star-cycles old. Elder Ygrette bows at us both, and we return the action, before she spins and strides from the room. We exchange a grin as we examine each other's marks.

"Mine is bigger." I tease as we continue through the castle to find some dinner.

After such a long day, I was ready to take my supper alone in my room. There is so much to think over and, after the long day on my feet, my back screams in pain. Though I wouldn't admit it aloud. There were many others I pass with missing limbs or more horrible wounds than I was dealing with. Instead of retreating to the warm bed that beckons, I join the others in the Great Hall. Many of the city dwellers, those whose houses had not been destroyed or were at least livable, had returned to them. But together we all still convened in the castle for dinner, at King Eivan's request. We had much to celebrate, and much to morn. But we would do it together, and rise again.

Seeing Eivan with his people and hearing him address them with such conviction, it was easy to see why I had chosen him. My taste had been impeccable, in all of my Underkings. I grin to myself as I sip at my stew. It wasn't fancy in the slightest, but it was the best meal I had ever tasted. I refused my throne, and instead sat among the people on the ancient wooden benches. At first, they had been shy and reserved, but as time passes and more ale is consumed, soon they laugh and tease me as freely as any of my friends in Alessandra. It is Arne that drags me away eventually. Insisting he had seen me limping, he gives me the choice of either getting into bed of my own volition or he could summon the healer to make me. I give in without much fight. I am exhausted and the pain was getting too great to hide. So with many waves and good nights, he helps me up the stairs.

"If I may say—" He says, kneeling over the fireplace in my room, igniting it himself after I refused to summon a maid to help. "You handled today admirably." I smile at him from beneath the covers I had snuggled deep into. I can't help but feel lighter at his praise.

"You really think so?" He nods, face somber.

"The people *adore* you." Arne dusts his hands off on his pants, standing as the fire successfully flickers into life. "I know it might not be my place, but as your friend, I am proud of how you handled all of this. And after Türe, I was worried for you. We weren't as close as we are now, but I could still see how it affected you. You have come a long way since our first training together where you, we," He corrects himself at my look. "could barely run around the castle." He grins at me, suddenly shy after his little speech.

I sit up slightly to see him better. "Did you know me? Before?"

"Not like I do now. You were kind—don't get me wrong— but I was just another training initiate. You were much more reserved from what I could tell." He admits. I don't know how to respond. Or what that means about how different I was now.

"Thank you for your honesty, and even more for your friendship." He bows low.

"I will see you in the morning. Call for me, or the healer if you need anything." He stares me down until I nod, even as my eyes begin to fall shut. I hear the closing squeak of the door, and drift into a warm sleep.

❋ ❋ ❋ ❋ ❋

A beam of light shines hot on my face, pulling me from my

dreams of screaming soldiers and weeping children. I groan and pat about blindly for the pillow, wanting to tug it over my face and avoid the day. I pry open my eyes to look for it, and my stomach drops. I am not in the bedroom. Or even in a castle. The vibrant emerald of foliage fills my vision as I realize I am back in the Forest.

"Umm..." I sit up slowly, looking around for some clue as to how I got there. There is no way I could have walked that far, not in the snow, and not without *someone* seeing me. That, coupled with the pain no longer radiating with my movement, I conclude this is a dream. Though I still am cautious of each noise, everything feels too real, and if this was Jera's involvement, I could really be here. I sit, waiting for something to tell me why I am here suddenly. The soft chirping of birds, the rustling leaves in the full treetops, and the skittering of little feet of creatures that scamper across the forest floor fills the air. Then something else catches my attention. I stand as a familiar humming tune grows, beckoning me forward. I hesitate a moment, then decide to follow. With each step, I relax more into the sounds and feel of the nature around me. I step into a meadow I recognize immediately. Across its open space stands a large, but still young sapling. I can't help the smile that blossoms on my face, because I know that tree.

"Jera!" I breathe and suddenly find myself running towards her.

"Have heart, my daughter. I have taken them into my arms." A sad woman's voice calls out to me, a brilliant light illuminates the tree from behind. "Evara, you must find me." My heart skitters, but no matter how hard I run, hand up to shield my eyes from the painful brilliance that fills the meadow, I remain always too far away. "You must come to me. You must reclaim yourself."

"Jera!" I cry out for her even as I trip, her words muddling my brain. "I am trying, but I can't get to you!" A sob racks through me when I look up to see I still have not managed to move any closer, despite my efforts.

"Come to me." She says again, her voice fading into the wind that suddenly whips through the meadow and yanks me from my dreams.

forty-five

I gasp awake, shooting up to sitting, before my back roars at me in anger at the abrupt movement. Feeling my tight stitches pull and crack against my skin trying to heal, I curse under my breath and squint around the room, trying to guess what time it could be. My confused mind is stuck halfway between the meadow and the foreign room I wake in. It is still dark outside, the logs in the fire Arne had assembled for me are mere embers now. I rub my temples, trying to gather the fragmented remains of my dream. A loud bang comes from the door, and understanding clicks into place. That was what had pulled me from my sleep. I stare, unmoving for a moment. The stubborn part of me begs desperately to pretend it wasn't happening. That it would go away and Jera's message in the dream would fade into the dark, rather than obviously being a dark omen. Again it comes though, someone knocking frantically at the door. I shake myself, and throw back the sheets just as I hear Arne's startled voice call out to whoever was at my door.

"Do you have any idea what time it is?" He growls in irritation. "What business have you with the Queen at this hour?" I hesitate on the other side of the locked door. If Arne is suspicious, I need to be careful.

"I cannot find King Eivan, but I must speak with either the King or the High Queen immediately." I ponder this a moment before deciding the raw desperation in the man's voice is genuine and throw open the door. The man, a lower guard of Raefus Castle.

"What is it?" I take in his pale, shaky demeanor, and my stomach drops.

"There is a man who just arrived who insists he speak with you. He doesn't have long, Your Majesty. He may already be dead." The guard rushes out, turning to run back the way he came, bouncing on his feet in impatience, waiting to make sure I follow. "You need to hear and ask questions from him, but I have no further time to explain! Please understand." He begs. I glance at Arne. He looks unsure, but nods, following after me as I start to run alongside the man. As we sprint to the castle gates, where the guard said the man was waiting, I try to think of what it could be. We arrive before I can prepare myself and I see the proof of the guard's words. Only a hand holds in the man's innards. I shove away the urge to vomit and kneel beside the panting, grey man.

"What happened to you?" I ask, trying to adopt the healer's calm demeanor that I had noted and appreciated when I was in pain. He gulps down air and his eyes shine with misery. "Get a healer!" I snap at the guard, who takes off running again. I debate with myself if it is worth the gamble of using my magic and healing it myself, but a subtle head shake from Arne makes me stop. He is right. I was too on edge to provide any real help right now. And I was not versed enough in healing magic to not accidentally seal up his wound with his insides still out.

"I—I'm so sorry, ma'am—I mean—shit— Majesty." I force a half smile and pat his shoulder.

"Don't you mind about that. And what are you sorry for?"

"Charobi—its been taken." He grunts in agony, a cold sweat trickling down his forehead. I thought I had known fear before, but it wasn't anything close to this. Jera's words resurface as the world around me begins to spin and flicker. *Have heart, my daughter. I have taken them into my arms.*

"Was anyone able to make it out?" I hear myself say the words, though my mind is wrapped in a fog. "King Ivrik? General Türë? What of them?"

"I'm sorry—I—" The man takes a few short wet gasps before he stills. I stare back into his unseeing eyes. So many questions and answers now stolen from me. Gone with this man's life.

✳ ✳ ✳ ✳ ✳

I hear Eivan's voice first, bellowing and confused, trying to understand what was going on. He arrives right on the heels of a beautiful young woman I know immediately is a healer. She takes stock of the situation and, without a blink, drops to her knees beside me, hands running over the man expertly. Even as she drops to her knees beside me, I don't bother to tell her it is too late. Part of me hopes that she can perform a miracle and revive the limp, silver-haired man. *I should have saved him while I still could.* In a daze, I hear Arne telling Eivan what the man had said. I slowly bring my eyes up to meet his and see his own sorrow and terror there. He had known Ivrik since his childhood and Türë his entire life. Türë had been one of his teachers and a role model, and Ivrik was a fellow Underking.

And another city lost. A fortress. One that had stood for

hundreds of star-cycles without anyone so much as breaching its walls. But now... I look back at the man growing cold in front of me. It was clear from his worn, yet maintained clothing he wasn't a soldier. A farmer maybe. *Had his wife patched this shirt, now stained with his lifeblood? Was she too lost in Charobi? Or his children?* I push onto my feet and take off at a stumbling walk. Though I do my best to retain my composure, I hear everyone around call out, concern clear in their tone, but I disregard it. I need to think.

To be alone.

I should have sent the calvary to Charobi. Or Türë here. Or... All the possibilities clamor in my head uselessly. Only filling me with more *maybes* or *should have beens*. I find solace in the warmth of an empty stable. Well, empty aside from the horses who quietly pass the night in their beds of sweet smelling hay. I tuck myself into the darkened corner of an empty but fresh stall. I try my best to catch my breath and quiet my thoughts, to no avail. For the first time in many moon-cycles, I feel nothing from the magic that normally wakens due to emotion. It is silent. As if its will had broken alongside my heart.

I take the time to work through each of the various options and where those roads would have led. It helps me. Somewhat. Nearly every option continued to take me to this same choice, or a worse one. But if Ivrik or Türë had been lost... Or, Jera help me, both of them. No. I wouldn't think about that. Not until we had heard more information. More than likely they are being held or, with their abilities, they could have escaped. If they *had* been caught, there was a higher chance that they would hold someone of their rank for ransom or manipulation. I try to convince myself, but Jera's words echo on repeat in my mind. The sun has begun to rise when I at last dry my tear-stained cheeks and emerge from the stable. The castle and city still sit silent, not yet awake to spread the word of the blow Mirinth had landed to the kingdom. I stare blankly around me and can't help but wonder how long until those grateful, hopeful people who had called out to me just yesterday would look at me with bitterness and disappointment.

I hear a soft cough, and sigh in annoyance before I even turn around— already knowing who I will find. "You are taking your promise to be my shadow a little too seriously."

"It's not your fault." Arne says, ignoring the bite of my tone. Thankfully, I see no pity in his eyes, only grim understanding.

"It doesn't matter if it is or not. I still will forever hold the blame for this in my heart." I reply dully.

"I know." He pushes off the nearby wall he leans against. "King Eivan sent a band of scouts to try to find out what happened and what can be done for Charobi." I nod, knowing I should go find him and figure out what to do next. Sorrow swells up and I feel the tears begin to trickle out again. "Hey..." He says gently, stepping up to me without any hesitation, pulling me in for a hug, and breaking the control I had regained over my emotions. I sob openly into his chest, and his grip around me doesn't slacken, despite the long minutes that pass.

Eventually, the tears dry up, until only an empty hole stands gaping in my aching heart. I had no idea what all to even mourn yet. I needed to gather my wits, or I would fall apart completely. Everyone would look to me, and I needed to handle this the way everyone is expecting me to.

I hiccup a few times before pulling away. "Sorry, I—think I stained your jacket." I admit sheepishly. Arne chuckles a bit before rubbing a thumb gently under each eye and brushing away the drops that cling to my cheeks.

"We all need a good shoulder to cry on sometimes, and I have been told mine are unequal." I shoot him a grateful look before taking a deep breath and squaring my shoulders.

"I need to find Eivan." I say and notice then Arne's eyes shift to something behind me.

"Perfect timing then." I turn to follow his gaze and find him walking towards us. Arne bows low to the both of us before excusing himself.

"I'm sorry I fled like that. I'm still trying to balance my emotions with my duties." He shoots me an incredulous look and we begin to walk in the direction of the castle. "What?" I ask, my brow furrowing in surprise at the slightly humored glint in his piercing blue eyes.

"I don't know if this makes it better or worse—but you have always been this way." He chuckles a bit, then his smile fades as quickly as it had come. "You feel things much more strongly than anyone else I know. But that is good! The kingdom is wonderful because its queen has the biggest heart and uses it to embolden her people. You inspire empathy and kindness, over profit or ego." His words bring a lump to my throat and I blink away the tears that fill my eyes again. *Just when I thought I had none left.*

"Thank you. That does actually help." We pass a snow filled garden, its skeleton trees poking out above the drifts and benches. I shoot him a confused look, now unsure of where we were actually going as we deviate from the main castle path.

"I figured since everyone was beginning to wake that you would want to avoid the main part of the castle. There is a back gate around the next corner." Eivan explains. I nearly wilt with gratitude.

"So what are your suggestions on what to do next?" I ask, though every bit of my heart fights against thinking about it, let alone talking about it.

"I think you need to return to Alessandra." He says after a minute. Surprise at his answer must show on my face, because he begins to explain without me having to ask. "It is the safest place in the kingdom, and where the kingdom will look to now for reassurance. It will also be the first place Türë or Ivrik will return to if they escaped. You won the battle here. Do what you need to do now. Mourn and think about what you will do next. But promise me you will not forget that you led us to victory and saved this city. Don't let King Tanth take that from you." He pauses, eye growing hard and darken with a solemnity that seems to age him. "I worry about the dark days ahead for us all. But you are smart and brave. You will figure it out. You always have. That is why we all follow you. Why we support and have your back." This time I am not able to stop the tears that fall and I pull Eivan in for a tight hug.

"I am grateful for you." I say simply, and he coughs, blushing a bit when I pull away. "I know we have spent hardly any time together, but I do want you to know that whatever happened with Charobi—" My voice breaks slightly over the word. "—I do not regret my choice in coming to your aid."

"Have you thought that maybe—" He stumbles over the words I had been horrified to think about as he reaches to open the hidden door.

"This was all a distraction while they moved on Charobi?" I finish for him. "Yes." I say, admitting with a sad half smile. "But I would still come here to save these people. To save you. Other things I might have done differently. But not that."

Eivan bows low to me, blinking hard against his own watery eyes, promising to stay safe and send word of any further information that he hears, before excusing himself. I linger outside a bit longer, letting the sun warm my face, chasing away the cold chill of the wind that blows in from the sea only a few miles south.

I had nothing to pack before leaving. None of my items had been brought in to the castle yet, other than the sword and dagger

I sling around my hips again. I was ready to go home. I say a few goodbyes to those I pass, but as word begins to spread, the castle grows quieter. The looks becoming more somber and reserved.

It is noon when Arne and I lead a band of calvary—those unhurt and well-enough to ride— back through Vante to cheers of farewell and thanks. I send a prayer up to Jera for warm weather to melt the snows and grant us a fast, safe journey back to Alessandra. I pause at the city walls, turning to wave one last time at Eivan who sits atop a large red and copper stallion at the castle gate. I take in the prairie surroundings one more time before rejoining the line of soldiers that merrily chatter of home. All of us push the pace, and none of us even mention stopping to camp for the night. Though I would not speak it aloud, I wish with every beat of my tired heart that Türë and Ivrik will be waiting for me when I walk into the castle. This vision pushes the thought of sleep away until at last the spire of Yvonya Castle appears far in the distance. I repeat Eivan's guiding words in my head and they echo alongside Jera's from my dream.

I had much to do, and enemies were closing in fast.

forty-six

I should be dead asleep. We had ridden far into the night and what little sleep we had gotten was in turns on horseback. At this point, I would probably fall asleep here at my desk, but I didn't really care. I wasn't even doing anything of note, merely staring dully at the leather spines of the books that line the wall. I just couldn't bring myself to treat myself to any sort of comfort when we still had no word of Ivrik, Türë, and the rest of Charobi. My dream that they would be waiting, safe and sound, was in vain. A useless waste of time, energy, and hope.

I swirl my ruby-red wine around the nearly empty bottle, staring at it until my vision blurs. Rubbing at my exhausted eyes, I sigh and pick up one of the many papers that piled up on my desk in my absence. Patryk maintained everything for his territory, Telor, as well as Alessandra. But anything relating to the entire kingdom, the war, or its military was all my responsibility—now that Türë wasn't here to help.

Again, my thoughts return to him and Ivrik. Even with Patryk's reassurance that he was positive they were fine—thanks to their immense skill in both weapons and survival. I didn't believe him. I couldn't shake the heaviness that fills my chest. But it was clear that he was doing everything in his power to reassure himself. I certainly wasn't going to shatter the fragile illusion that was keeping him going. The city bell tolls again amid rumbles of thunder from the storm that rolls in. Thankfully, once we passed out of Erit and moved north, the snow had been washed away by some winter rain. Of course, the freezing rain ended up almost being worse than the snow. A knock at the door startles me from my thoughts and Patryk pokes his head in.

"Can't sleep either?" He asks, stepping in fully.

I shake my head before draining the remaining mouth full of wine. "I just keep hoping—" I shake my head again, and catch the understanding look Patryk shoots me as he plops down heavily onto my sofa.

"That any moment they will walk in." He finishes for me. "Yeah, I keep praying for the same thing." I reach into the bottom drawer of my desk where I had discovered a nearly full decanter of amber scotch on one of my earlier investigations. Pulling it out, I grab the set of glasses alongside it and pour two knuckles full for each of us before joining Patryk on the sofa. I nudge his foot that is propped up on the other end. He moves enough to make room for me as I juggle the two glasses, though it's a tight squeeze for us both to fit. He sits up a bit and clinks the glass I pass him against mine. "Tell me, how was Eivan? Grumpy? Grey?" I laugh quietly into the glass as I take a large swallow of the burning liquid.

"He was well. Considering everything that is happening. He is settling down with a young healer, if you believe the rumors." I remember the woman who rushed in with him to help the man who had told us about Charobi and wonder now if that had been her. "I didn't get to spend nearly enough time there, getting to know him or the people." I stare at my reflection in the glass and notice the dark shadows beneath my eyes. I worry distantly if they are going to be permanent, they are so deep set. "He suggested that I return here quickly, but now I wonder if I should have stayed longer. If only to help them rebuild what was lost in the battle. Maybe that would have kept me distracted enough, rather than just sitting here all day and night mulling over it."

"Do you begin training again tomorrow?" He asks, draining his drink and setting the glass aside before lounging back fully onto the sofa.

"I told Ionel that I would need the next few days off. My back is still stiff and the healer I saw this morning made me swear not to push my luck." I huff a laugh, propping my own legs up so each of us were able to lay across the too small sofa. Patryk makes a face at my feet and their close proximity to his face, making me laugh again.

"I can't believe you got wounded that badly." His voice softens, trying to hide the wash of fear. "That could have been really, really bad Evara."

"I know." I admit. "Thankfully Jera's blessing shone upon me again and spared me from death. There were many—too many—others who were not so fortunate."

"I'm glad you are okay, though." He says after a few minutes, his voice growing thick with emotion. Pinching a bare toe between his fingers, he gives my foot a wiggle. I smile sleepily at him before squirming deeper into the comfort of the soft cushions and my friend's comforting presence. Silence, aside from the relaxing rumble outside, surrounds us.

"Patryk?"

"Hmm?"

"Can I ask you something? I know you said you would tell me anything that you knew if I asked you." He stiffens, but doesn't reply. I continue anyway.

"I don't need or want to know everything. At least not right now. But—" I continue to stare at the ceiling and think over my question that I had been warring over ever since I had first sent Türë away. *Do I truly want to know the answer?* "Do you think—or know—Did he ever truly love *me?* Or was it all for the crown?" I force out at last. I flick my eyes down the sofa to Patryk when I still get no answer, and find him staring blankly at the ceiling, too. He blinks so I know he is still alive, and awake, so I just decide to let him think over whatever it is he needs to say.

After several long minutes, he sighs deeply. "Do I know for sure that the crown wasn't an influence on some of what he did? No. I don't honestly know that, nor can I say one way or another. But Evara, he loved you. He still loves you. Of that, there is no question in my mind. He may have said some horrible things, but we all make mistakes and sometimes do stupid things. I think he grew worried that who he had known for centuries was gone and the Evara who you are now wouldn't feel the same about *him.* Fear is a horrible creature. One that makes monsters of us all." I think this over and realize how much I had needed to hear that. The reassurance that I was not a total fool who not only had been manipulated into losing both Dulen and Charobi, but also into giving away her trust to someone who did not truly deserve it.

"Thank you again for your honesty. I wasn't sure what all to think, even now, about it all. Everyone has their own opinion as to how I should have handled it and how I did. I hope you do not think the worst of me for it. If it settles anything in your mind, I truly regret that I sent him away to that fortress. I basically dared Mirinth to attack it." I groan and press the back of my hand to my eyes. "But then I end up telling myself that there is no place Türë would have rather been. Though I am not sure if that is the truth, or just what I continue to try and convince myself." I know I am rambling now, but Patryk is such a quiet listener, it is so easy to talk to him. But as breaths pass, and then a minute, and no answer comes, I remove my hand and sit up to look at him. I have to bite down on a laugh when I find him fast asleep and drooling steadily on my velvet pillow. I lay back down and stare out at the lightning that flickers through the window. I feel its electricity call to my magic so strongly, I have to force my eyes shut to fight its allure. Jera's words echo with the thunder that shakes the floor only a second after the flash. *You must come to me and you must reclaim yourself.*

Over and over, I had tried to think of what that second part could mean. *Reclaim myself.* I didn't even know who *I* was! How could I reclaim that? And that first part, even with me wanting to go to her, I couldn't. Not now that my kingdom was in turmoil, my borders were falling, and Ivrik and Türë had not been heard from in days. I huff a sigh and gently remove myself from the sofa without disturbing the now snoring Patryk. I slip through the door, but don't cross the hall to where my warm, empty bed waits for me. I slip silently through the shadowy halls of the sleeping castle. I end up standing at the door to the garden, just far enough inside that through the open door the rain peppers only my bare toes. I pull up the bottom of my skirt to feel the chilly wind and droplets the storm raging above brings. Instead of giving into the allure of stepping out into what I can see is a torrential downpour, I retreat a step and pull the door closed behind me. The garden makes me think of Türë, and now the mysterious Donovan more. It is not the place of peace that I desperately needed right now. I wander through the castle and somehow end up outside a familiar door. Ivrik's. Where the garden had made me sad, the room beckoned to me. Though I know he more than likely locked it before departing, I still try the handle. To my immense surprise, the knob turns and the door swings open to a dark room. Void of his lounging frame across the settee, it is horribly empty. I step inside, feeling like an intruder, until I catch Ivrik's scent of soap and leather. I breathe it in deeply, letting it calm me. Exhaustion and sadness sweep over me and I find my steps leading me to the giant bed. I fight a sob as I crawl underneath the crisp sheets, filling my mind with the one night we all had here together before everything fell apart. My head sinks into the pillow that smells so much like my friend, and I fall asleep at last.

✽ ✽ ✽ ✽ ✽

"Evara!" Ilithyia's sharp voice wakes me, and I sit up, looking around, confused at first where I was. I remember then. Ivrik's room. "We have been looking everywhere for you." The worry mixed with relief in her voice has me grimacing with guilt.

"I'm sorry, I didn't even plan on coming here I just—ended up here."

I yawn and glance at the window for some hint as to what time it is. But with the shades pulled tight, it was impossible to tell. It could be high noon without a cloud in the sky and I wouldn't know. "What time is it?"

"Two in the afternoon." She huffs with pretend irritation. "Patryk has been on my case all morning to find you. He says you left him with a crook in the neck, letting him sleep on the sofa like that." I have to hide my smile. Ilithyia returns with one of her own, though cautiously. I immediately feel bad. Yesterday, when I had arrived, she had been on the receiving end of my gloom and misery. Rather than being happy at seeing her safe and well, the lack of news had dismayed me, and I shut myself into my study. She had even been excited to show me my room that she had finished redecorating in my absence until she had all but wilted in disappointment when I had refused to see it.

I reach out and grasp her hand. "Will you show me my room? I am ready to see it now!" Her smile widens, and she nods quickly.

"I had to beg Ionel to come help me move some of the furniture down, but with his help I could make it *perfect.*" In spite of myself, I feel my attention peeking at the mention of my handsome trainer and glance sideways at her, catching the slight touch of blush on her cheeks.

"I'm glad he was able to help! Did you two spend a lot of time together while I was away? You know, training?" I prod for more information from her, but she dodges my attempt, tugging me along with her as we leave Ivrik's room and return to the hall where mine is.

"Just the usual amount of training. We did catch up a little on how he is adapting to the new role here, though." She says off hand with a shrug as we arrive in front of my door. "Okay, close your eyes!" I shoot her an impatient look, but obey. Her excitement, coupled with a few hours of good sleep I had at last gotten, works wonders on my lingering dark mood. I hear the familiar soft squeak of the door hinges and she pulls me into the room. Immediately, even with my eyes closed, I relax. This space was mine. I could feel it already. Smelling of lilies and lemons, I inhale deeply.

I feel Ilithyia's hands leave my forearms after leading me into the center of the room. A burst of light flares against my closed eyelids and I hear the whir of curtains sliding open at Ilithyia's direction.

"Okay, open them!" She orders, excitement filling her voice. I obey and take in the transformed room. I had given her permission to redecorate for me, and she had not held back in the slightest. Everything was either emerald leafy green, the same hue of the bright yellow lemons that hang from the four lemon trees she had somehow fit into the room, and the dark warmth of the walnut wood that makes up the floor, woodwork of the doors, window sills and wardrobe. The curtains are each hemmed with a thick velvet green ribbon and embroidered with an intricate floral pattern in gold thread that shines in the sunlight beaming in through the windows. What had been a cave of dusty browns and blues, now is full of color and warmth. But unlike my rooms I had before, I liked the changes here even better. It had all the things I *did* enjoy about my suite of rooms in the new part of the castle, but now with the coziness of the wood. It had familiarity, where the new rooms had been foreign and cold. While the marble throughout the castle was glorious, it was not what I preferred for my bedroom. Much too cold and hard. Wood had character, stories, and a breath of life to it.

I realize suddenly I still had not spoken and Ilithyia is eyeing me anxiously, her hands clasped to her chest as she monitors my reaction closely. "It is *amazing!* Ilithyia, you are a blessing..." I approach the lemon trees, so tall the bottom branches leaves brush my head as I walk under them. "I see why you needed Ionel's help moving these!" I laugh and pluck a ripe lemon, pulling it to my nose to inhale deeply. "What a fantastic idea!" I shake my head in wonder again at her before moving on to examine the rest of the small treasures that I hadn't even noticed yet. Lilies and greenery hang or sit on almost every other surface, giving the space more of an earthy greenhouse feel, filling the room with the most amazing aroma.

"The lemons I thought would be perfect, since you like them in nearly all of your drinks. Now with your tea or water you can have fresh ones whenever you like. And I noticed you always lingered to smell the lilies whenever you are in the garden, but above the bed I have hanging lavender instead. I know you sometimes have trouble sleeping and lavender is supposed to help relax you." She explains, nearly buzzing with joy. I cut her off suddenly though, throwing my arms around her and squeezing tightly.

"Thank you. *Thank you!* It is beyond my wildest dreams, and just what I needed." Pulling away to look around at the bright colors and nature she had brought in for me. I shake my head in disbelief and admiration. Somehow she had known just what I needed. "You are a true friend, and I appreciate you taking so much time and effort to do this for me." She beams and reddens, shuffling her feet with sudden bashfulness.

I sigh, this time with contentedness and stare with longing at the bed, even though I had just woken up. Now that I had stepped foot in the room of my dreams, I longed to fall into it. To sleep, and sleep, and *sleep*. My long days and restless nights were catching up to me at last.

"I even had your clothes brought down!" Ilithyia starts, suddenly remembering. I look around but see no sign of them or even a closet. "There is an empty room next door that I had them just move it all to." She grins widely. "It's even bigger than the closet you had upstairs, which I admit is a feat in itself. And it took a little convincing but I got them to chisel a door into your bathing chamber.

"Would you go pick out something for me?" I look down at the filthy, wrinkled dress I had now traveled and slept in. "I do believe I would enjoy a bath and some fresh clothes." We both jump at the sudden sound of water splashing in the bathing chamber off to the left. Ilithyia stares a moment at the clearly empty room, then her eyes slide to me in confusion. We both tiptoe to the door and poke our heads around the corner to see the large tub filling itself. I laugh in amazement and hook my arm in hers as I lead her into the room, deciding to let her in on the secret.

"Has anyone told you about how this part of the castle was built?"

forty-seven

I had spoken true. Ilithyia was a wonder and a gift from Jera, as magnificent as my magic. Her chattering and fussing as she helped me bathe and dress in something fresh and beautiful pulled me from my worry, filling my heart with light again. If only a thimble full—it was more than I had in days. All quarter even. Emerging from the bath into a forest of leaves, flowers, and golden lemons was like a refreshing wind on the hottest of summer afternoons. Only her insistence and tugging prevents me from falling into bed for the rest of the day. But like a concerned and finicky mother, she insists that I would sleep better tonight if I got up and did something with my day. I had grumbled but begrudgingly agreed and, somehow, I ended up in the stables brushing down Afina.

The mare nibbles lovingly on a loose strand of my hair as I scratch her velvet nose. I know she is technically Ivrik's, but since he had left her here, I had come to think of her as mine. She was always who I requested and, I admit, I dote on her relentlessly.

She whinnies and bumps my elbow hard enough that the brush in my hand flies to the ground. I scowl at her, knowing well enough now to tell that she wants one of the shiny fresh apples from the barrel I had brought to the stables. I had spent the glowing afternoon beneath one of the trees in the city garden. I had been astonished to know it produced fruit for eating at any point of the star-cycle. Vernas, Aurá, Umna, or Frë, it did not matter if it was covered in snow, or roasting in the heat. As a previous gift of mine to the citizens of Alessandra, it was, of course, magically grown to produce such an achievement. "You have to wait a minute." I chide her. "I am nearly done, and *then* you get your treat." I bend over to pick up the brush and she bumps my back, knocking me to my knees. I spin to face her even as she whinnies loudly again, this time bobbing her head in what clearly is a laugh. "You little —!" I start, but end up laughing. Scooping up the brush, I scowl without anger at her.

"Are you alright, Majesty?" A timid voice comes from the stall door and I turn to find a young boy watching me, wide-eyed and wary.

"I am indeed. Thank you, sir!" I dip a curtsy and smile at the boy, only around six star-cycles old, trying my best to ease the nervousness that shows on his round, rosy cheeks. He grins shyly before looking up in awe at Afina. "Would you mind helping me?" I ask, noting the look. "Afina is a bit peckish and won't let me finish brushing and braiding her. Would you come give her some treats and distract her for me?" Before I can finish, the boy nods vigorously, joy sparking in his eyes. I point to the barrel of apples and the pile of carrots sitting beside it on a stool. "Will you grab some of those and give them to her?" Suddenly nervous, the boy hesitates. I smile gently. "She is very kind, even if she is an impatient pain." He slowly edges forward, gaining confidence with each step until he reaches her head. I show him her favorite places to be scratched and how to feed her without getting nipped fingers in return. The smile that shines brightly from the boy fills me with happiness. "Have you ever ridden?" I ask, returning to brushing Afina now that she is distracted.

"No, Majesty. My family doesn't have a horse. But I like to watch the soldiers on horses practicing every day!" He says, puffing out his chest. "I am going to train hard and be one someday." Then he wilts suddenly. "My brother says it is a waste of time though. He says I will be nothing more than an innkeeper like my pa." I frown with my back turned as I trade the brush for a comb.

"And who is this brother who knows so much?"

"He is the barkeep's runner next door." He perks up some. "He sometimes lets me come with to watch him, and I can sneak away to look at the horses, like today."

"I see." I turn back and watch the boy, whose carefree smile fills his face. "Well, there are always going to be people out there who will try to reason you out of your dreams. But don't listen to them. If you work hard and believe in yourself enough, you will accomplish whatever you set your mind to." The boy beams.

"Would you let me be a soldier in your army, Majesty?" He asks, excitement sparkling in his baby blue eyes. For a second, the image of the battle field blooms in my mind, the numerous dead and wounded, and I try to not picture the little boy's face in their place. I swallow hard.

"What is your name?"

"Jeron, Majesty."

"Well, Jeron, if that is what you so desire, it would be an honor to have you in my army." Excitement rushes through him and he puffs his chest out again.

"I will practice my sword fighting every day until I am old enough!" He promises.

"Well, if you want to be a member of the calvary and ride a horse, you better practice that too." I pretend to think hard a moment when I see his shoulders droop as he realizes that not having a horse might make that difficult to do. "I know!" I snap my fingers in the air. "You may practice on one of *my* horses." I pretend to scrutinize him, walking around him in a circle. "I think you will be a worthy investment, and these horses need the exercise." I poke a finger into Afina's round belly, who chomps loudly on her third apple, unbothered and wholly content. Jeron giggles and my heart threatens to seize in my chest. "As you can see, they are spoiled. But you must get your parent's permission. I don't want this practicing to get in the way of your schoolwork or chores at home. My soldiers must be intelligent too, you know." The chubby-cheeked young boy bounces up and down with excitement.

"I will, I will! Thank you, Majesty. I will go ask them now!" He drops a quick bow at the door, remembering his manners suddenly, before running off. I laugh a little to myself, and finish grooming Afina with a smile on my face.

Before returning to the castle, I stop by the stable master's room to inform him of the young boy who will be assisting with and learning how to ride the horses. A rare smile transforms the aging man's usually stern, lined face. Any argument or disapproval regarding my request I had been prepared for never came. The stable master tells me he had never been blessed with any children, but had always longed for the opportunity to pass along his experience and training. My heart soars at the knowledge I had at least made two people happy today.

I return to the castle as the sun sets, a beautiful soft rosy hue. The barely tolerable temperature drops along with the sun itself, but I don't rush. I reflect on how different my mood was from yesterday at this time—even from this morning. A stark contrast. I decide to seek out Ilithyia again. I needed to thank her, for the millionth time, for pulling me from the darkness I had felt creeping into my heart. The castle and the city gates across the entire kingdom now remained locked at all times with a full guard set atop the walls. Any comings and goings now were questioned, aside from mine, of course. Those keeping the evening watch spot me and have the gates open by the time I reach them. I beam at them, recognizing a few from our previous nights at the local tavern. A shiver writhes up my spine when I note how their eyes immediately shutter, averting their gazes instantly. My breath catches as I look at each of them closer, noting the lack of smiles, and finding only pale, alert faces.

"What is it?" I begin to ask, but one of the Captains hurries to meet me as the portcullis drops back into place behind with a metallic clank. He bows low, a fist to his chest.

"Your Majesty, they have been looking for you. Your presence is requested in the gallery immediately." I feel as if my chest is going to burst, my heart thundering, and I get overwhelmed with a sudden rush of vertigo. I nod at him, unable to speak, and swallow my trepidation. Whatever we had learned, or what new information had come in, it was not good.

My legs carry me to the gallery of their own accord and I enter to find only Patryk staring blankly at the map strewn table. Relief sweeps across his distraught face when he sees me and he shoots to his feet. "Where the hell have you been??" I notice then how red his eyes are, and the streaks of not yet dry tear tracks mark his ruddy cheeks. I take a single step back, and shake my head, already feeling my own tears sting my eyes. I didn't want to know what had shaken the guards and brought my friend to tears.

"Don't. Please." Anguish flares in his eyes, and he sinks back into the chair with a broken sigh.

"I have to say it. And *you* have to hear it." He says, voice breaking a bit with surprising anger. "You want to be Queen? This is part of it."

I blink at his unusual bite, but realize it is the truth. In this moment he needs me to be strong. I straighten my spine and slowly make my way to my usual chair at the head of the table. I do my best to take slow, deep breaths as my panic begins to make my magic roil in its cage. I could hold it together.

For Patryk.

"We heard word from the troops Eivan sent to Charobi. The fortress and everything within fifteen miles is under Mirinth's control. They—" He swallows down a sob. "Lost a few men getting the information they did." Patryk turns his full attention to me, his eyes free of their spark. He looks like he had aged ten star-cycles from last night. "Ivrik is dead." He says dully. And I feel his words hit me like a wall.

"What?" I whisper.

"He was killed in the battle, protecting the children they had hidden in the fortress." Any bit of the hope and happiness I had reclaimed that day is doused with each word he says. "Thankfully, it appears the children he died to protect all live, though they are now captives of Mirinth." He glances at a sheet of paper that rests unfolded on the table in front of him. "We have not received any ransom demands for them, but they sent a list of who they have in their capture. All the children, along with one General Türë, and a few of the Captains that were stationed in Charobi." I lean forward, bracing my forehead and arms on the table as I feel the tears and sobs overwhelm me.

Before now, it had been the not knowing one way or another that had been eating me up inside.

Now that I had the truth, it destroys me.

forty-eight

"King Ivrik had no equal. Sharp and unyielding when it came to defending what and whom he cared about. And he was good. Protecting his home and his people to the last. I was fortunate enough to claim him as my friend. When he came to me as a child, he knew immediately that Tesindren was his kingdom and we all were his people—his family. I will dearly miss his wit, love, and kindness every single day until we meet again in the Afterworld." My voice breaks, and I nearly lose my fortitude to finish. "The great Goddess Jera told me herself that he now rests in her loving arms." I hear sniffles come from the hundreds that had assembled for the funeral ceremony held for Ivrik. This was the three hundred and ninety-second, and final, ceremony I presided over in the last week. One for each Tesindren life confirmed to be lost between Charobi and Vante. As horrible as it had been, I forced myself to do each one. All hard in their own weight, but Ivrik's rang differently in my heart. The other men lost were not ones I had known in life, and while I mourned their loss, it was Ivrik's face that still tore into my heart. The attendance of the other ceremonies were not sparsely attended by any count. But Ivrik's was a clear testament to his reach in life. We had taken one look at the approaching crowd and filled streets, and moved the ceremony out into the city gardens. The only place large enough for everyone who came. There was no body. I didn't want to think about what had happened to it. A letter from King Tanth had been delivered with the names of those who had perished. He had cruelly mentioned it had been compiled with help from General Türë. Another heartless and tactical jab at me from the enemy king, who now held two strong footholds on the southern border of my kingdom. I had ordered each of the cities and fortresses to bar their gates, take extra precautions, and to sound the alarm immediately should Mirinth be spotted on the move. The loss of an Underking had compromised the entire foundation of my kingdom, and two of Paith's most well defended strongholds. Though fourteen days have passed since Charobi's fall, we had yet to identify how they had gotten past the walls and gates that had stood strong for centuries. "For all of Tesindren, for Paith, for Charobi and Dulen and all of those lost, we must stand unified. For Ivrik. For Jera. For each other, we must not falter." I shout into the crowd, trying to muster my strength to endure the rest of this ceremony.

"For King Ivrik, for Jera, for King Patryk, King Noran, King Eivan. For Tesindren. For the High Queen!" The crowd shouts in unison. These words send a shiver down my spine, and I raise my chin higher, trying to remain standing under the weight of their continued support in me, and their love for Ivrik and the rest of my Underkings. Trying to be worthy of them all.

I exit the raised platform in the garden and slowly return to the castle. It was a sunny day, though even with the sun's rays, it was far from a warm day. Winter was truly here, and with it, all of the usual problems are made worse by the strain and threat of war. While I didn't have the heart to ask Ilithyia to strip my room of everything she had just worked on, I did have her pull anything of color from my wardrobe upon hearing of Ivrik's death.

Black would be my color until this war was complete. Though I did allow one other hue to remain.

A single battle dress of blood red.

That, I would wear to King Tanth's execution.

My black lace veil catches in the wind that picks up as I approach the castle. I hear the wailing of mourning songs start up from the garden. According to Patryk, they would continue for the next three days. During which none would eat even a crumb of bread. Only a solitary glass of water was allowed at sunrise. After the three days passed, the songs would change to those of celebration. I had bristled at first hearing that. But he explained it was a celebration of what his life had been, and for Ivrik now, being in paradise with the Goddess. This mourning parade was not just for Ivrik though, it was for all whose ceremonies had been held this week. It was going to be a loud, long few days. With the amount of people in attendance, the songs could no doubt be heard for miles. But those lost deserved nothing less.

Tonight I was to attend a private ceremony with the mourning Nefriti. As custom dictated, for Ivrik, a previous warrior, he would receive full death rights and the ceremony that accompanied it. I flex my almost completely healed arm, feeling the fresh skin from my first *Ynrya* line stretch with the movement. Every morning while dressing, I still couldn't help but stare with a mixture of pride and nausea at the solitary cobalt slash. I would possess two marks by this evening's end. Though it was uncommon for a *Ynrya* line to be marked for the death of someone not blood-related or married too, none of the Elders had argued with my request to be marked by Ivrik's death.

I had wanted to participate in it all—but Patryk had pleaded with me not to. He needed me now. With two of our number now either lost or captured, there was much that needed done. Too much for me to be out mourning and not sleeping or eating with the rest. I hear slow, tired footsteps following me and turn to find Patryk returning to the castle, too. His head hangs heavy and shoulders slump from grief. He is so lost in it, I doubt he even realizes I am only a few feet ahead of him.

"Hi." I greet him with a soft voice, trying not to startle him. He raises his head, but has no smile for me. Not even an attempt at one. I had done my best to step forward since we had heard about Ivrik's death. I had wanted the start of Umna to be not just a change of seasons and quarters, but also to use it as an opportunity to step forward more. But not this way.

I had taken over all of Patryk's normal duties and given my friend the break he both deserved and needed. Thankfully, Isos had finally broken his vow to stay out of courtly business and stepped in to help with his surprisingly considerable knowledge about the kingdom as a whole, as well as each of the various territories.

I don't ask Patryk how he is, or anything at all. I already know the answer because of the wound in my own heart. While I had *technically* known Ivrik longer, Patryk had many star-cycles of happy memories with a brother who was suddenly no longer here. It would take him and the others a long time to adapt. Not heal. It would never heal. He could only learn how to live with the grief and loss until it no longer took up every breath or waking thought. Instead of talking, I loop my arm through his and together we silently return to our home. The songs of old echo off the walls that surround us as we endure the grief that threatens to swallow us whole.

✽ ✽ ✽ ✽ ✽

I stare up at the moonless, black sky and tug my woolen shawl tight across my shoulders. It rubs horribly against the *Ynrya* line another Elder had placed on me at the beginning of the ceremony. To my astonishment and heartbreak, I notice multiple others being marked as well. Each and every person here had known, loved, and respected Ivrik, but I never had guessed at the extent. Remorse for the time I had not spent just *being* with my friend before I lost the chance forever hurts more than any pain from a blade. The giant bonfire in his honor flickers its light and warmth upon all the Nefriti gathered, as the voices of the Tomyris and Magnar pour out over the castle and into the city. A city that has fallen silent and still to listen. It was rare a Nefriti warrior fell, let alone in battle. So this extensive ceremony was one, I am told, that has not occurred for over a century. The Nefriti death wails for Ivrik fill the air with its rough, emotionally raw tune. I don't have to hide my tears here. The sorrow that I feel is reflected in each of my shield brothers and sisters. None try to hide their raw and heart wrenching anguish. Here our sorrow was embraced. The only other warrior I had noticed receive a *Ynrya* line of white across his heart for Ivrik steps up beside me. I had seen his face before, but never learned the name. His grief is as potent and clear as mine. His tears freely fall, dropping onto his chest, bare despite the cold, and mixes with the blood that drips from the mark. I did not know who he was to Ivrik, but I knew he felt my pain. I reach out and take his hand, stiff at first, then relaxing into the simple reassurance that I was here with him.

The keening cry of the ancient songs of the Nefriti reflects the screaming agony in my soul.

They sing of how he had died a warrior's death, defending the children in Charobi.

It was how he would have wanted to go. I know this.

But still, my friend is gone.

I don't know all the words, but my wailing joins theirs as we mourn the loss of Ivrik as one.

✾ ✾ ✾ ✾ ✾

The songs that have been sung for two days now ring through my head, and thankfully, the third and final day has begun. I rub my tired eyes and tug on one of my curls, now pulled back with a simple solid black ribbon. I knew my monochromatic attire and lack of care for my appearance was beginning to wear on Ilithyia, but I didn't care. She wisely didn't comment on it, only made a face every morning at the different onyx dress she pulled out for me each day. At least my drakonskein battledress was technically black. Only when it caught the sunlight did it shimmer like spilled oil. Not that I spent much time in the sun these days. Winter had truly set in, so Ionel had relocated all of my training to an empty room in the guardhouse. Even if we had been still training outside, we were up and finished before the sun rose, and I was at this desk by the time the rooster crowed. I hear a knock at the door and look up to find Patryk, solemn and dressed similarly in black.

I don't waste a forced smile. He wouldn't give back one, anyway. We didn't bother to pretend with each other. At least not yet. I knew the day would come that I would have to pull his shattered pieces back together. But that would be done later. Now I would let him mourn his brother.

"You asked for me?" He greets me without any emotion.

"I did." I set down the quill I had been writing with and turn my full attention to him. "I apologize for having to pull you from your mourning, but this couldn't wait any longer." He slumps in a chair beside mine with little fanfare. "I am leaving for Naro in the morning." Slowly his eyes raise to mine, but he doesn't say anything, so I continue. "I will have everything taken care of as far as business, so don't worry about that. I will return in three days' time. I just wanted to inform you of my absence."

"Why are you going to Naro?" He asks finally. I hesitate, trying to choose my words with care. I didn't want to tear open the still healing and sensitive wound.

"I have to name Ivrik's successor." I admit carefully, now unable to meet his blank gaze.

"So soon?" His voice cracks with emotion and I squeeze my eyes shut tight, as if that will stop me from hearing the betrayal in his voice.

"It has been twelve days—and I know it doesn't seem like enough. I'm sorry, Patryk. Believe me, I am. It just—"

"Can't wait any longer." He nods weakly. "I understand." I can see the truth. He may not like it, but he understood the position I am in. That territory was extremely vulnerable right now with Ivrik's loss, and the threat to Naro was growing by the second. To be honest with myself, I didn't see how we would stop them if they wanted to take Naro right now, capturing the full territory. "May I ask who?"

"I still have not asked him yet, but I hope he will accept. You know him well." I come around the desk and sit in the chair opposite Patryk. "It is Isos." I say with a heavy sigh, already missing my friend, but not knowing what I will do should he refuse. Patryk huffs loudly and I realize with a start that was the closest I had gotten to a laugh, or even a smile, in far too long.

"I never thought of him before, but now that you say it, I could not picture a more fitting successor." I reach for him and grasp his hand. His tired eyes raise to meet mine.

"I hope you know how much I abhor having to find someone at all, but Ivrik would not have wanted the last of his territory to fall because I, we, were too stubborn to move on." The glint of tears shine in Patryk's eyes, but he nods sharply with a short laugh, blinking away the ever present tears.

"He would make fun of us for going to this extent of mourning too." My heart flutters at the sound, grateful for the first step towards healing. No matter how small it may seem. "Did Jera truly tell you that?" He asks softly. I know immediately what he is referencing. I had debated mentioning it at all in my eulogy, but decided in the end it would comfort people to know that Jera was still present, still active among us. Even if we didn't understand why this was happening.

I nod. "Yes. She came to me in a dream that night. I didn't understand what it meant until I was awoken by the soldier who carried news of Charobi's fall. We will see him again." I squeeze his hand tightly as a tear spills down my cheek. Patryk nods again, then coughs, trying to cover the emotions that war within him.

"Well, I will pray for your safe travels and will see you when you return." He stands and bows with his fist to his chest before giving me what was meant to be a smile. Though it didn't reach his eyes, I appreciated him trying.

The door thuds shut and I find myself alone again. "Now all I have to do is convince Isos to take the job." I mutter to myself, pushing back from the table and going to seek out the Captain of my Guard. If he didn't reject, or outright laugh at me, then I would have my next Underking of Paith.

forty-nine

I pass door after door of guards, all who launch to their feet when they realize who strides down the hall. I could have had Isos sent for, but that seemed—I don't know—like a waste of someone else's time, I suppose. I was perfectly capable walking across the castle grounds to the guardhouse. It was big enough to be its own castle, complete with its own training facilities, kitchen, gardens, and stables. And the sheer number of rooms astounds me. I was fully aware of the large number of soldiers in residence at Alessandra, either training or living here full time, but seeing it in person was different. The amount of doors I pass, each leading to a room that two or three of my guards called home, it seemed crazy. I had somehow only been into the training portion of the immense building until now. I look down hallway after hallway after hallway, and realize I am completely lost and should have sent someone, or at least *brought* someone, to help me find Isos. I blush after I accidentally poke my head through one door to find a communal shower. One filled with men. A few of them turn beet red, diving for various towels, pants, or really anything that would cover their total nakedness. I try not to laugh at the complete horror on a few of their faces, but hurry on. While none of them had been horrible looking, they weren't nearly enough to tempt me. Even if they had been, intimacy was the *furthest* thing from my mind right now. At last, I come across a, thankfully, fully clothed soldier who offered to lead me to the Captain. In two turns we arrive at the closed door and I lift my fist to knock, pausing to send a prayer to Jera that he would accept. He was the best candidate for it. Plus, he was already well known and loved by the other Underkings.

Before I can knock, however, I hear a familiar giggle and freeze. I don't have a chance to react or even consider hiding as Ilithyia pulls open the door across the hall. I stand stock still, fist still raised to the door, watching as she laughs brightly before leaning in to give a quick, yet sweet, kiss to whoever stands just out of my view. It doesn't take much to guess, his accent easily identifiable even if I hadn't spent so much time listening to his barked daily orders. I drop my hand and turn to face them head on, raised brows and my hands on my hips. Both Ilithyia and Ionel freeze when they spot me, standing there with a huge smirk on my face. They stammer, unable to come up with anything to say, but I just shrug and turn back to face the door. I knock on Isos's door, flashing a wink over my shoulder.

"About time, you two. I was running out of ways to push you together." Isos opens his door, and looks as surprised as Ilithyia and Ionel had been to see me standing in his hallway. He looks back and forth at the three of us, before inviting me in. I wave at the silent and bewildered couple, a smile starting to tug at their mouths again, before I enter Isos's room.

Unsurprisingly, his rooms were as spotless as his character and reputation. Only a smidge bigger than some of the other rooms I had spotted on my search for him, they were still smaller than my bathing chamber. His status as a Captain at least did earn him the luxury of not having to share a room, but still the space was expertly laid out to squeeze in a small two person table, a sofa, single bed, kitchenette, and a desk. I sit on the sofa, and after clearly debating whether it would be inappropriate to sit on the sofa too, he decides to play it safe, sitting on the small bed across from me.

"Is everything okay?" Isos fidgets with his comforter nervously, and I feel suddenly slightly sorry that I invaded his space without letting him know I was coming.

"Yes, everything is fine." I try to reassure him, then grimace. "Well not everything... But you know, I am fine. As I can be." I sigh and laugh under my breath at myself. I did not seem like a Queen appointing her next Underking, that was for sure. I can almost feel Ivrik rolling his eyes at me—and I had no doubt he did, if this was how I had asked him. "Sorry, I am just tired." I say in feeble explanation. Isos only smiles kindly, understanding everything that the word encompasses. Because *tired* was only the brim of the overflowing barrel of emotions I was dealing with lately. "I came here today to ask you something." Always wanting to help, he leans forward, bracing his elbows on his thighs as he waits for me to get to whatever my question was. I try to sit up taller, trying to convey the unswayable confidence I had in my choice. "I have decided on who to appoint as Ivrik's successor."

"Oh—" He sits up in surprise. "I guess I knew it wouldn't take you long, with everything going on. But that has to be hard to choose. I can be packed within the hour and ready to go by tonight if you wanted to start off today." I blink in surprise. I had been prepared to argue with him. I had even prepared a speech to tell him why he was the best choice. What I had not been prepared for was to have him agree to it without my even having to really ask him.

"I— I guess I thought it would take you longer! I am planning to leave by the morning, or afternoon tomorrow at the latest." I look around at the organized yet still full room with a frown. "Are you sure you will have everything you need that quickly?"

It is his time to frown at me. "Well, how long are you planning on staying in Naro?" Then it hits me.

"I apologize, I think we have two separate thoughts happening. I should be more clear. Isos, it is *you* I want to become Underking of Paith." His face goes blank, the confusion dropping away to shock as he tries to digest my words. Then he throws back his head and laughs. Loudly. I stare back, brows lifted and wide-eyed, and just decide to wait for him to finish.

"You have to be joking." He finally catches his breath and says in a rasp. I shake my head no, and wait for him to laugh again. Instead, he stands and begins pacing across the small room, waving his hands as he speaks. "I know nothing about ruling a kingdom! The others, at least, were trained as children, and came from nobility. I was a slave, Evara. I know nothing about the royal... stuff."

I raise my hand to quiet him, and thankfully, it works. *At least I get to use my speech.* "You have proven not only to me, but to everyone who knows you, that your blood and lack of royal history have nothing to do with your future. As far as knowing nothing, well, you have proven the opposite of that. Especially this quarter, and these last days, it has been a lot, but you have helped me more than I ever could have expected. You know what you are doing. To go even further, you have heart and you will give Paith your all. I am learning too, so I know how hard it can be. But of anyone, I believe you are our best chance. The others agree with me as well." I had sent word days ago to the other Underkings, to both prepare them and give them a chance to oppose if they did not agree. Every single one had been supportive and excited to welcome him into their ranks. "They are all eager to have you join their brotherhood. And I know that even stubborn Ivrik would admit that you are what Paith needs right now." I swallow the urge to cry at the look of comfort that my words bring him, softening his furrowed brow. "They need *you*. In spite of the hand you were dealt in your youth, you have risen to your rank purely on your own merit and dedication. And I, for one, trust you implicitly." Isos opens his mouth a few times to speak, but every time, it snaps shut again before he can speak. "I will let you think on it. But please consider it, Isos. The kingdom needs you." I stand and squeeze his shoulder before I slide past him to the door. I pause in the doorframe with a quick glance over to where he still stands silent. "Can I ask you one thing?" His faraway stare lands on me and he nods. "Is there anything I can do to convince you that you are worthy of such an honor?" A hint of a smile tugs at his lips.

"No. The fact you even considered me is more than enough. Now its just trying to convince myself, and wrap my mind around if it is something I can handle." Isos considers a moment before speaking again. "I never in my wildest dreams saw this path for myself. I always saw myself growing old and training the other guards with Türë. Or protecting you for the remainder of my days. The thought of taking on such a role—such a responsibility. I just need to make sure that I am truly the best person for the kingdom, even with your faith in me." I smile sadly, but understand completely the pressure that he suddenly finds himself under. A pressure he had never looked for.

"Well no matter your choice, you will always have my respect, friendship, and a place in whatever castle or city you choose." I drop into a bow with my fist pressed to my chest. When I raise my gaze again, I see the tears sliding down Isos's cheeks, as he stares at me in silent reverence. He knew the honor it was for a Queen to bow to anyone. And for the first time, I could see him realize that he was more than just the boy I rescued from a slave ship. So much more.

✳ ✳ ✳ ✳ ✳

Walking back to the castle, I can't help the warmth that fills my heart. The uplifting music that now wafts from the city garden, the last hours of the mourning period, finally replaces the wails and crying. That coupled with my conversation with Isos, I begin to feel not as lost and helpless. Though the atmosphere is lightened somewhat, the grief still makes my heart ache with each beat. I meet Patryk on my stroll and call out to him. He turns, waiting for me to catch up, and takes in my relief and lighter steps.

"He accepted?" Patryk asks, as pleasantly surprised as I was. I nod as he joins me on my walk to the castle. "Did he at least keep you on the edge of your seat?" I blink back a sudden pang at the sense of normalcy that hits me with the snap of a whip.

"He certainly did." I smile and loop his arm in mine. "What are your thoughts on cake?" Frowning in confusion, he looks down at me.

"Cake?"

"Yes, there is much to celebrate and I think I might request the cook to whip us up a cake in honor of Ivrik and the celebration of Isos's acceptance." Patryk swallows hard and I see the light that had begun to spark in his eye gutter. I wince at my misstep. "I'm sorry, it is too soon." I start to say, but he stops, pulling me to a halt along with him, shaking his head.

"No, we should have cake. Lemon cake. It was Ivrik's favorite." He smiles sadly, eyes glazing over, lost in some memory. "Life goes on. I know that he would be frightfully angry if we didn't celebrate in his name, or for Isos." Together, we start our stroll again in comfortable silence, our steps unhurried, drifting through our own thoughts as the uplifting music continues to fill the city. "Would you mind if we each said something tonight for Ivrik? A story, or something in his honor. I know we had the chance to speak at the ceremony, but that was addressing a crowd." I nod before he can even finish speaking, squeezing his arm tightly.

"I think that is a fabulous idea." We reach the castle gate and each split off. I head to the war room, and Patryk continues to his room. I catch a maid in the hall who promises to pass along my dessert request to the cook before I sit back down at the table with a long sigh. "Okay, Isos taken care of. What next?" I mutter to myself. While his acceptance solved a half dozen issues, it created another dozen. For one, I needed to find and appoint a replacement for his current position of Captain of the Royal Guard. I scout about the table for a stray quill and begin yet another list of things I had to do before departing tomorrow, and then everything after.

I hear a knock at the door standing open. Though usually shut, I had them propped open that morning so I could at least get a glimpse of the sunshine—if only at a distance. I had spent so many hours shut away with only fire and candlelight for days. It was beginning to give me what I feared would be a permanent headache. I look up to find a guard standing beside a young man I had never seen before, shifting back and forth uncomfortably in the doorway.

"Yes?" I ask, setting down the quill and giving my full attention to the unusual pair. The man looked road-worn, but still relatively put together. He is not dressed in any uniform and, from the aged mud that cakes his boots, I make a guess that he is a farm hand or someone who worked the land for his living. Why he now stood at my door, I could not guess. The guard shoots me a look of annoyance.

"Apologies, Queen Evara. The man insisted he had something that he must give to you personally. He swore on the Goddess herself to do so. He would give to no other."

"And what is this *something*?" I ask, narrowing my eyes at the man. My suspicions rise at the strange man's true intentions. He blushes at my attention and stammers out an apology.

"I tried to hurry, but the roads were not kind. Mighty far from Charobi too. And my horse was hurt ya see. But I swore to 'im."

I inhale sharply at the mention of Charobi and catch a similar look of shock on the guard's face too.

"I take it he didn't inform you of that tidbit, did he?" I chuckle and wave the man forward. The guard glares at the young man.

"He failed to mention that, yes." He snips, and the man winces.

"I knew that you would ask too many questions. But the Queen needs to hear what I have to say and get what I swore to bring her." It is clear that, though the guard didn't appreciate it, he understood the truth of that. Anyone with information on Charobi would have been stopped and questioned in depth for a lengthy time. No known survivors had been heard of after the city fell, so we desperately needed any and all information.

"That will be all, Jerrik." I say with a glance at the name embroidered on the lapel of his uniform. Even though the guard, Jerrik, did not look pleased to leave me with the man, he bows before leaving the room with a worried glance back at me. I, however, was not worried. The poor man stands, quivering with fear and exhaustion. And I knew my guard was well trained enough that if he *had* possessed any weapons, Jerrik had taken them all. Because of that, when the man reaches into his pocket, I don't tense. Should he be stupid enough to pull something as risky as that, I had little doubt I could take on the young man, maybe only nineteen or twenty star-cycles old, without much fuss. Not to mention the eight Royal Guards that stood out in the hall beyond. Instead of a weapon, however, the young man pulls out a thick envelope. I frown in confusion.

"I was in Charobi when it fell. I was helping shoe King Ivrik's horses when the Mirinthians slipped through and lifted the gate." Thankfully, I was still sitting, or else I would have collapsed right then.

I swallow, "Do you know how they got in?"

"I only know what I heard, ma'am—I mean—Majesty." I ignore his stumbling and encourage him with a wave of my hand. I take a few eager steps towards him, but part of me worries that if I get too close, the man will combust, he shakes so violently. "The ones who raised the alarm shouted something about the sewer, but by the time anyone understood, the Mirinthian devils had made it to the gate tower and locked themselves in so they could raise it." I scramble for a map of Charobi's layout and follow with my finger to the sewer lines and hiss at the unexpected hole in the defenses that they had exploited. The flaw that had cost me so much.

"Shit." I mutter, then return my attention to the man who looks now like he might fall down. "Please, sit." I force myself to remember some etiquette, even though deep down I just want to shake the man until he tells me everything. He still had not explained the bundle of parchment in his hand.

He doesn't sit, but instead advances a few steps before dropping to his knees. "I was with the General and the King when the attack began and I rushed out with them to find out the ruckus. Well, its still pretty fuzzy from all the panic around, but I remember the General yelling at King Ivrik to get to the castle. The King, he grabbed a few of the stable kids to get them to safety too. But the

General, he grabbed his sword and fought. I tried my best to follow him, but he wouldn't let me. He said I needed to swear to him I would do something instead and handed me this letter. He then made me swear in Jera's name that I would bring this to you and no other." He extends out the letter, which I take with shaking fingers and pull into my chest. "I tried to fight. I should have stayed and died with them." The man's voice breaks with a sob. "The General told me this was more important, so he got me an opening and I ran for it." The tears flow steadily now down his dirty cheeks and he grasps his hair in dismay, revealing missing and cracked fingernails. "I could hear the screams for *hours*. I still hear them at night when I try to sleep. Forgive me, Majesty. I wanted to stay and fight with them. My family, my friends—" My heart feels like it cracks at the poor man who is torn with guilt and shame. Even though it goes against everything in me, I set the precious letter aside for the moment and I sink onto my knees beside the now wailing man.

"You did so well. I know this won't ease the pain, but if you had not listened to General Türë, I would not have gotten this very important information. I thank you for your sacrifice in bringing this to me. It will not be forgotten. I know firsthand how horrible it is to hear those screams, and I wish I could take that from you, though I cannot. All I can say is that you have my deepest gratitude and I will do whatever I can to help you in repayment." I slowly rub circles across the young man's back as his cries turn to gasps of air. He slowly catches his breath and looks up at me.

"Sorry..." He mutters, wiping his runny nose on his filthy sleeve. "I just had been focusing on getting to you and I guess didn't realize until now, when it all hit at once, how horrible I felt." He croaks miserably.

"What is your name?" I ask.

"Beven Toleil" He says.

"Well, Beven," I smile gently at the bleary eyed man. "Let's go find you a room and get you washed up. I think a few hours of well deserved sleep will serve you wonderfully. If you would like, I can have a sleeping draught made for you too." Beven nods enthusiastically to it all and I help him back to his feet, leading him to the hallway where I find Jerrik still waiting, a hand on his sword in case he heard me call for him.

"Jerrik, please take this man to the North Wing and have him choose an empty room. He will be staying here for the night." The man's brows raise in surprise but his hand drops away from his side as he nods at me. I turn to another guard standing nearby and smile shakily when I find Rhodie, who grins back. "Would you find Ilithyia and ask her to bring a sleeping draught to Mr. Beven in the North Wing please?" Rhodie agrees and sets off as Jerrik and Beven disappear around the opposite end of the corridor.

I feel my stomach clench, now that I no longer have anything to draw my attention away. Türe had a letter for me. One that was so important he made a poor farrier swear on Jera's name to cross the kingdom and deliver it to me and me alone. I return to the gallery and pull the doors shut behind me and, with a firm heave, push the lock into place.

fifty

I sit staring blankly at the unopened letter until the bell tolls six times, informing me I am going to be late for dinner.

"Shit." I mutter to myself, tucking the bundle into a pocket hidden in a seam of my black and grey gown. I had wasted an hour, maybe even two, struggling with myself and trying to find the courage to open Türë's letter. I had no idea what to even expect from its contents. Knowing Türë, it was some sort of military plans or information pertinent to the war. At least, that is what I hoped for, at the same time of hoping it isn't. I wasn't sure what I would do if the letter contained anything regarding his feelings toward me. With him being in the situation he was in, I didn't dare dream that I would see him again, and after how we left things between us... It was all just too intense for my exhausted mind and heart to dissect right now. But on the other end of the spectrum, if it wasn't something personal, well, I could honestly use some of his wisdom that I had relied upon so heavily in my first moon-cycles. The support and encouragement I missed so much.

I pull the lock back from the door and emerge in darkness. Not unlike the rest of my days spent entirely shut up in the room trying to work and plan for, well, everything. I sigh and aim for the large dining room. The throne room was reserved for formal dinners, hearings, and other ceremonial events, and the ballroom was, obviously, for balls and holiday celebrations. But the dining room was just for a smaller, more intimate group. Apparently, it was usually where my Underkings and I would eat together, back in the days when it was safe enough for them to leave their castles to come here. Capable of fitting ten, the six of us would fit comfortably enough. Tonight it would be Patryk, Isos, Athene, Ionel, Ilithyia, and myself. I had not spoken yet to Ilithyia after our run in at the Guardhouse but she had apparently asked Patryk if Ionel could join us tonight, since it was obvious their secret interlude was up. I wonder distantly if Isos had known the whole time, and then how long it *had* been going on. I had been orchestrating run-ins since they had first met. Had they already been together when I thought I was being clever? I snort a laugh and the guard standing closest to me glances over, worry in his eyes. *Great. Now everyone is going to think I am going mad.* Then I consider a moment. *Maybe I am going mad... who knows for sure.*

I reach the dining room and already hear the chatter of familiar voices inside. I pause and deftly touch the letter through my pocket, my heart aching with the memory of those who should be here tonight, but weren't. One of whom never would be again. I remember suddenly Patryk's suggestion for us each to say something in Ivrik's memory and smack my forehead a few times in frustration at myself. In my distraction of receiving the letter, I had neglected to write anything. I guess I was going to have to improvise. A nearby guard pulls the door open for me and I nod at him in thanks. Distracted by my racing thoughts, I don't realize until I am in the room that a large painting of Ivrik stands in the corner, draped with a shimmering black veil. I freeze and stare at the familiar blue eyes, the cocky smile and his pale gold, slicked back hair. The room quickly quiets when they see my reaction. My ears start to ring and my vision blurs. *No, no, no, no!* I yell inside my head. *I can't loose control.* The friends filling the room aside, I could not let loose any of the magic I had been stifling. If not for their sake, or the guards standing out in the hall, then for the fragile paper bundle in my pocket that I could not risk losing. It had somehow made it across my kingdom to me in the hands of an unexpected carrier. *If it made it all this way to burn to ash in my pocket...*

I feel hands on me before I can tell them to not touch me for fear of burning them. But their touch remains, though they feel like ice on my heated skin, I must be keeping enough of a leash on my power that no flames slip free. I don't let myself acknowledge any relief at that fact. My magic would jump at any opportunity to slip through the bars of its cage. Instead I look up at my supporter, and find Isos. Brave, kind, *foolish* Isos. Though he had seen first hand the damage a single touch could inflict when I lost control, he still had approached me and touched me to try and help. I taste sparks and feel a jolt of lightning coat my tongue with its spicy smoke. I thankfully yank my grip free as it surges, clearing Isos just in time before I can light him up. I hear his sharp inhale, but he still doesn't retreat. I have my jaw locked tightly against the power that tingles through my body. I wonder if I open my mouth, if I would spew fire like the images I had found of drakons. Strangely, this thought calms my rolling power slightly. Enough so that Isos dares to grab me again, this time to get my attention. Feeling like my mind is swarming with a million bees, I struggle to focus on him. I feel something press into my palm. A small bit of bread, or cake? I look at him with confusion, until I make out the word he mouths. Or maybe he does speak aloud, I just can't hear him over the insistent buzzing that fills my head. I shove the bite sized loaf into my mouth quickly, scared that if I left it open too long the flames and lightening would escape again, this time hurting all my friends who have gathered around me. *Too close.* I want to shout at them. I swallow the sweet bread and gasp.

The effect is instantaneous.

Like a campfire doused with a bucket of water, my inner flame gutters. The tendrils of power flee into the cage where it now cowers in a corner, growing still until it seems to sleep at last. I regain awareness to find myself on all fours, just as my elbows collapse and I fall the rest of the way to the ground. I shudder at the foreign feeling of the now empty space the magic had occupied. Where it felt as if it had been carving my will away, piece by piece. Slowly the muttered voices of the others begin to return to me and the ringing subsides. I sit up, wincing at the cold sweat that coats my back.

"What did you give me?" My teeth chatter as I realize how freezing I am, now that my inner fire had truly been doused.

"I didn't get a chance to tell you this afternoon, but that idea you and Arne had on the way to Vante, well I figured out the herb and had an exceptionally discreet healer friend of mine mix it into some bread for you." I gape at Isos in disbelief. "I was only planning on telling you. I wasn't sure how much everyone else knew, or how much you wanted them to know, but I didn't have a choice right then." He says, lowering his voice so only I can hear him. "I have all of the herb hidden in a safe place though. Even the healer had never heard of it before. I made her swear in Jera's name that she would not speak of it and the herb to anyone but you or me. I had to take the risk in telling her who and why I needed it. The risk of giving you too much and poisoning you was too great for me to mislead her." He grimaces in apology, but I reach out and grip his hand.

"Thank you, Isos." I breathe, my voice horse from the flame and lightning that had scalded my mouth and throat. "It is gone, at least for now." I smile, though weakly. My body aches as it adjusts to the lack of constant strain that had come with fighting my magic every second of every day. Even those days that it had been more docile. Now it was like my entire body was a sore muscle. "And it is okay they know. I trust each of them with my life." I smile at the concerned faces that surround me. Ionel reaches out a hand to help me up and I take it gratefully, standing shaky legs. I shoot him a grateful grin. Taking a rattling breath I turn to face the others with what I hope is a calm smile. "I am fine! Please let us start dinner, I am *starving!*" That I don't have to fake. I am suddenly ravenous, as if the magic had been sitting and filling up my stomach the entire time. I eye the large glazed ham and giant pot of mashed garlic potatoes steaming beside it, and my mouth waters.

"Sorry, I should have warned you about the painting." Patryk mutters with an apologetic grimace. I reach out to take his hand, noticing it is shaking. My heart seizes with despair at the fear I had caused my friends. *Fear of me.* I shove that thought aside for later contemplation. Tonight was about Ivrik.

"It was just a shock. I apologize for my reaction." I say to him, then raise my voice to the others who now sit around the table, kindly pretending to not listen to Patryk and I. "I apologize to all of you for any fear I caused."

"I want to be clear, it wasn't fear *of* you. It was fear *for* you." Patryk reassures me, and his hand squeezes mine before I pull away. I shoot him a grateful smile, but no matter how hard I try, my heart cannot be convinced of it.

"Shall we eat, then each say our Ivrik story, or vice versa?" Patryk asks us all.

"I vote we eat!" Ionel nearly shouts, then immediately blushes with embarrassment. We all burst out laughing at his enthusiasm. "Sorry, it just looks so delicious." Ilithyia stares openly in adoration at him, patting his hand.

"Isn't it so cute when his accent gets thicker the more embarrassed he gets?" Patryk snorts a loud laugh that he tries to cover with a cough at the even deeper blush that coats Ionel's face. Athene smacks his hand in playful reprimand. My heart soars at the sound I had not heard in weeks.

I purse my lips, trying to not laugh, and find my gaze drawn to the still smiling portrait of Ivrik. My court follows my gaze and the laughter trickles out. Without an inkling of what I am going to say, I remember another reason we were celebrating. A cause for celebration that I did not want to get overshadowed, nor displace Ivrik's portion of the evening. I stand and clink my wine glass with my knife officially, even though they were already looking at me. I let the clear pealing tone ring out before speaking. "Before we get into the food, and the memories of our beloved friend, I have an announcement to share with you all." Out of the corner of my eye, I see Isos straighten with pride. Though I had already told Patryk, he plays along like a true thespian. Gaping in confusion and exchanging wondering looks with the others. He shoots me a wink and I have to bite down another surprising laugh. "I am so pleased to tell you that I have contemplated, decided, requested, and now *appointed* the new Underking of Paith." I let their impatience linger.

"Well, who the hell is it??" Athene breaks in after my lengthy silence. It is Patryk's turn to swat at her now.

"I am happy to announce for the first time, King Isos of Paith." Gasps and then the patter of enthusiastic applause fills the room, along with shouted congratulations and a loud whooping, courtesy of Patryk. He claps his newest brother on the back, and

Isos beams at the genuine excitement filling the room, as well as hearing his title officially for the first time. I could tell from the relief, replacing the hint of nervousness in his eyes, that he did not fully believe that he would be so welcomed. "Ivrik was, and is, forever beloved by his people. And I have no doubt that Isos shall be as well." A silver shimmer of tears glints in Isos's eyes and he suddenly looks down at the table. "To King Isos!" I say, raising my glass in salute as the other do as well.

"To King Isos!" We all call out.

I sit back down amid the chatter of my friends and court and smile to myself. *Maybe everything will be okay.* I sit forward and turn my attention to Ionel, who, though still animatedly talks to Ilithyia, keeps his hungry eyes locked on the glistening ham. "Ionel?" He jumps slightly at his name. "Would you do the honor of carving the ham, please?" He nearly overturns the table trying to do so, setting off yet another round of laughter.

All of us groan with a hand on our full bellies. We had each eaten more than our fill, watching in disbelief as Ionel reaches for a third, and then even a fourth helping. At that point, we could only watch him devour every bite with silent awe. Finally setting aside his fork with a satisfied huff, he seems to suddenly become aware of all the eyes on him. "Was a good ham!" He explains, wiping his mouth oh so daintily before sitting back in his chair with a content grin.

My attention flicks towards the portrait that stares down at us all. "Now we have all eaten more than our fill, I think it is time to speak of our lost friend. Who no doubt is watching over us with constant sarcastic comments and judgement." This makes everyone smile, even as the sadness returns. "Patryk, would you like to start since this was your fantastic idea?" He nods, even as his throat bobs. I give him a reassuring grin. We all knew how hard this was going to be, each of us dreading and also looking forward to our turn.

He turns to face the portrait of Ivrik and I notice tears already glint in his eyes. "Ivrik, you were my brother since the day I met you. Though you weren't Tesindren-born, you were born with the heart of a Tesindren. You never faltered in your belief in this kingdom, in our brotherhood, and in me." His voice cracks on the final word and he pauses to regather himself. "Always quick of wit, you were even quicker to forgive and help. That is something I always envied in you, and now will miss more than ever. I could always count on your guidance when I was unsure, and your support should I ever need it—which I frequently did." He chokes a tearful laugh, sniffling some. "I will miss you forever, my brother. There is not a day that will go by I will not think of you and wonder what you would have done in my place. I—" A sudden forceful knocking comes from the door and we all jump to our feet, startled to the point of being defensive. Indeed, Ionel now stands with a dagger in hand, Ilithyia pushed behind him, and Athene peers out from behind her husband. Isos too stands ready with a sword stretched out toward the door.

"Majesty!" A voice calls as the person knocks again. I recognize the voice of Jerrik, the guard who had brought Beven to me earlier.

"You may enter." I call out, and the door is pulled open to reveal indeed the pale-faced Jerrik. I suddenly am washed with exhaustion, though thankfully the magic doesn't sear my insides for the first time in many moon-cycles. It was never good news to be interrupted by a guard, especially these days. Let alone one that looked as shaken as Jerrik did.

"Your Majesties—" he pauses slightly to give obligatory bows to both Patryk and I. "I fear I bring bad news." My heart sinks as my mind races through each of the horrible possibilities. Türë had been killed, or even Eivan or Noran. Or Jera forbid—all three.

"Well what is it?" I ask impatiently as the man hesitates.

"Eludar is under siege." He manages to get out. I feel like I take a punch to the gut as all the air rushes out of me with a huff. I sit with a heavy thump into the chair thankfully still behind me. A single thought rolls on repeat in my mind.

Shit. Shit.

Shit!

fifty-one

"Under siege, but not fallen." I say aloud and look up to Jerrik in confirmation. He nods sharply. I inhale deeply, trying to settle my thoughts filled with a confusing mixture of relief and fear.

"The messenger said it began three days ago, and he was dispatched to let you know immediately. None had been killed when he left, but the city was surrounded on all sides. From what he said, the castle is prepared for such attacks. Though they are usually seafaring. They can last for at least half of a star-cycle before things get dire—so long as they are not breached." My mind flashes to what Beven had told me, and I immediately look around for a quill and paper.

"Is the messenger still here?" I snap.

"Yes, resting. He is exhausted."

I chew my already sore lip as my mind tries to come up with something. "They are getting in through the sewers. At least, that is what they did in Charobi. They are—"

"The only things not blocked off in a siege." Isos finishes for me, eyes wide in sudden understanding. I nod and I send a silent thank you to the man, Beven, for bringing us this information that was our only chance of standing against Mirinth, and to Türë for ensuring the man came to me. I feel my hand drift to the sealed envelope. Was there other crucial information that I was denying us all because I was too cowardly to open a letter?

"We need to tell them to either station guards at each sewer entrance to stop whomever comes through, or collapse them entirely. Otherwise it won't matter how long they think they can last, it won't be more than a week." I shove to my feet and begin to pace. "But how can we let them know in time? Even a messenger riding through the night won't be able to get back into the city—not without being caught and killed." Suddenly, an idea hits me. "Yessin Arboff." I thankfully remember to use his pseudonym, not wanting to invoke his wrath by revealing his true name. "Get me the blacksmith!" I snap at Jerrik, who takes off without a second of hesitation, spurred by the ferocity of my insistence. I feel a pulse of appreciation for the man, but then my attention returns to the group around me and the plight at hand. Before I can address them, though, I hear hurried footsteps approaching from the hall. I can tell by their different cadence that they are not Jerrik's. I frown in their direction as a mud-covered, sweaty man steps into view, immediately blocked by three guards who step into the doorway.

"Your Majesty, I am the messenger from Eludar." He explains. I wave him into the room, and the guards begrudgingly let him pass. "I am afraid the man at the gate heard only part of my message before he took off to find you." My brow furrows at that, and I try to prepare myself for the next inevitable blow. "Before the Mirinthians arrived in full force, they sent a party to talk with King Noran. Their intention was to get his surrender. You see, they brought along with them the body of King Ivrik as a threat, disguised as a boon." I force myself not to look at the portrait draped in black across the room and again feel a swell of gratitude for Isos and Arne for the absence of magic. If not for his actions, I would have incinerated this entire castle by now. Yet the man continues, either oblivious to the horror that thunders in my mind with each word or he just wants to be done with his duty. "The party also *gifted* King Noran with the heads of all those that had been lost at Charobi. As I said, a threat disguised as a boon. But they also carried a message from King Tanth." The man has to fight the urge to spit at our enemy's name in his mouth. An urge I am thankful he does not give into, since we were inside.

"And what was this message?" I ask, in a voice so fueled with anger that I don't even recognize it myself. He swallows and glances at the rest of my court, standing pale and silent as ghosts behind me.

"General Türë will be executed in five days time." He says finally.

I swear my thudding heart turns to stone at this words, and only pure numbness keeps my legs from collapsing out from under me. I sway, trying to collect myself. "Thank you for this information. Is there anything else you know?"

"I only know that King Noran told them to go fuck themselves." He admits, then his eyes widen at the words he had just said to the Queen. But I barely notice, only nod and dismiss him. He bows quickly and then is gone. I stare at the dark empty doorway, before striding through it and down the hall. I can hear faintly the worried whispers and footsteps that rush out after me. My friends trail me briefly, obviously distressed. I can't comfort them right now though, so I just leave. I didn't have words, or strength for anyone else.. Thankfully they don't follow me past the corridor, even though they watch me stumble down it in a daze. I didn't know where I was going, I just needed to be alone.

Everything is falling apart, and I have no idea of how to pull it all together again.

I end up in my garden, again and again drawn to this place. It dawns on me, thanks to my most potent memory, that it is King Donovan, the man I loved so strongly it transcended lifetimes, that I was truly drawn to. As if our time here had leaked into the stone path and called incessantly to me. This garden was a last piece of him. That seemed to be all I had left, pieces. Pieces of my kingdom. Pieces of my control. Pieces of my friend being delivered to another.

Pieces of my soul being traded bit by bit for my people.

Since we learned Ivrik had been killed, I had not let myself feel hopeless. Yes, my doubt had simmered in the back of my mind, but I had not given up hope that I may fail everyone. I refused to let these thoughts in. Or maybe in truth it was just the heat of my anger that burned them away before they could take root in my mind. Either way, the flood now bursts through the gates and I end up on my knees beside the bubbling fountain. Even in the middle of winter, the fountain flows. Another piece of magic I assume was built into the castle. Its rhythm does not heal my aching heart however, but at least keeps me company.

"I don't know how to do this! I don't know how to be what my people need. Each time I feel like I am finally making even a hairsbreadth of progress, I am shoved backwards twenty thousand paces." I cry out to the night air, the wind snatching up my words to carry them to Jera. "Please help me... I am so lost! I am being tugged in so many different directions I don't know which to choose. Do I go to you, as you have called me? If I do, I abandon my people. If I go to Eludar to help them, I leave Türë to die. If I go to Türë, it is doubtful I could make it to Eludar in time, and many more will die there." I grasp frantically at my hair, my cries turning to wails. I rest my head on the cool marble lip of the fountain pool and try to let its smooth stone soothe me. But there is no comfort. Not while my heart and mind are so weary and ravaged.

I don't even have a guess of how long I sit there, a puddle of grief and tears. No one bothers me, if they even knew where I was. But I didn't honestly care. I had let Patryk grieve. I had let my people grieve. But myself? I had not given myself the chance to acknowledge the gaping wound, and in turn it had not healed —only festered away. My sobs slowly turn to hiccups and sniffles as I begin to regain my self-control. It was a lovely reprieve to not have the suffocation of my power trying to claw at me, but now I felt truly alone with my thoughts. Unable to find anything to distract me from them, I have to face them head on. I acknowledge them fully, letting myself feel their sharp pain until it begins to dull and lighten. Along with my inner pain, I also acknowledge the heavy weight that I have been pushing off all afternoon. The weight that still sits in my pocket, unopened and drawing up innumerable unanswered questions. I inhale and exhale deeply as I pull it out. Before I can talk myself out of it any more, I break the thick navy wax seal and pull out its contents.

For Queen Evara,

My love, my heart, my friend. I beg your forgiveness for my words, my actions, and at the root of it all—my deception. All I wanted, in truth, was and is your happiness and to try to help you in whatever way I could. In the end, I failed you miserably and I will regret such a horrible thing for the remainder of my life.

I wrote this in the fear that I will never get to see you again and tell you in person all the things I have to, when death finally separates us after so many centuries together. But also in the hope that when that day comes, this will make up any of the pain I have caused you. Whatever happens, I want to ensure that everything I need you to hear will survive and make it to you. I will carry this letter around with me as a fail safe should things with Mirinth do not go well and I am lost. I left you today with a promise that everything I do will be in atonement for my sins. And this letter resting heavy in my pocket will be a constant reminder, as constant as your absence, that I can feel with every breath I take. My desire is and will always be that you will find it in your heart to somehow forgive me and call me home. But if you are reading this letter, well then I should assume now I suppose that day will never come. Hence, this message, since I can no longer tell you in person.

I can assure you, if I have perished, do not hold yourself at fault. It is and will always be my greatest desire to greet death as a warrior in defense of your people. Of my people. You followed your heart, sending me away, and I will never fault you for that. Your heart is one of the many things I do so love about you, Evara.

Every day I have seen you since the Awakening, I have watched you struggle with finding out who you were, and how it lines up with who you want to be now. I am a coward who so horribly feared that I would not be good enough, or blessed enough, to win your heart. I fear I have forced my own view of who I thought you are, rather than allow you to discover her yourself. Even after you came to me and confessed your feelings, I did not let myself hope that it would last, and instead shut you out even more. Then, in despair and anger, even went so far as to say what I said in the training pit. I am so sorry for that. The moment the words left my lips, I prayed you knew that it was not you I was saying them to. But to myself. I was the one who changed in the Awakening. You left and I was transformed into a man I did not care for. My fear tainted my character and it is something that fills me with regret each morning I wake without you beside me.

When you receive this letter, if I am gone. I pray you know you are not alone. Jera is with you always. That is what I wanted to tell you all along, but again, my cowardice overtook me. I wanted to be who you relied on. In the end, it is Jera, the Goddess who personifies balance is who is truly your strongest ally. Do not give up your magic, my Queen. I beg you. It is part of who you are. To be yourself, you have to embrace all of yourself to find your balance. You will forever be adored by me, by your court, and by Jera. Do not fear her. Embrace her. Only then will you be your strongest.

I wish I could have told you all this in person, but that fault rests with me. I only pray that my death will be in your service and make a difference in the tide of this war. Even when some things come to light that I know you will despise me even more for, please know I did it for you. I pray in the end you know I loved you until my dying breath, and will do so even in the Afterworld.

Forever yours,

Türë

I read the letter thrice before folding it up carefully and returning it to my pocket. Something about the writing seems familiar, though I struggle to place it. Hard as it was, each read through heals another crack in my fragile heart, even as my list of questions I have for him grows.

I believed his pain. It was impossible for me not to. What reason would he have to lie if he wrote it in preparation to be his last words? I stand, using the fountain lip to brace myself. I shake with exhaustion and grief. Now that I allowed myself to feel it, it was an ache that lingered in my muscles and bone more than the fatigue had after the battle at Vante. I stare up at the full moon overhead.

"Thank you for getting the letter to me." I whisper to Jera. There was not a doubt in my mind that she had been the only reason the weaponless Beven had made it safely from the battle at Charobi and all the way to me unharmed. Though I didn't understand what the plan was, I knew she would guide me down the right path if I let her. In all my studies with Noran, that had been clear. She would never force anyone to come follow her, but she was always waiting with hope that they would. "I will come to you. I swear it. But first I have to save Türë. Eludar can hold out. For now. Türë cannot. I know I am going to need him before this is all over." A surprisingly warm wind brushes across my cheek, like the caress of a finger. I smile and lean into the touch of the Goddess herself. Her blessing on my decision.

I spin on my heel, feeling the strength of decision filling me up, and head back into the castle to find my friends. I hope Eganël has already arrived. We had work to do, and not much time.

"You call me here, but then don't have any clue to tell me *why* you needed me?" I hear Eganël's voice from down the hall, reasonably angry and confused.

"As we have been trying to tell you, the *Queen* is the one who summoned you, but as of this moment, she is occupied. I am sure she will return shortly and be able to answer all of your questions." I hear Patryk use his fake friendly voice, clueing me in to the fact that he had probably said this numerous times without any solution. If he was confused why I had summoned a blacksmith, he didn't give any hint.

"I am here." I say, coming down the stairs into the hallway where they argue, raising my voice above whatever Eganël was beginning to snap back. "Apologies, Eganël. We received some news and I needed a moment to process it." I flash a winning smile and do my best to ignore the stunned and confused faces of my friends. I could tell from their immense surprise at my reappearance that they were not expecting me back anytime soon and were trying to come up with what exactly to do about that. They also didn't understand why I referred to the blacksmith they knew as Yessin, as Eganël. But I don't have the time to explain that or to apologize for my slip up.

Though he obviously was annoyed, and rightfully so, Eganël sweeps an elegant bow at me. "What can I help you with, Your Majesty?" I notice that he fails to offer any condolences for Ivrik or Türë, both of whom he had known. But then I realize with a pang that he probably was so accustomed to death after his own long star-cycles of life, it no longer phases him. I wonder distantly if that was how I had been before the Awakening, remembering Ivrik's stance on my memory removal being a gift to me.

"Türë told me of your attempt at fire bracers. Have you continued to imbue your magic into your weapons like that any more?" I decide to bypass the bullshit and ask him directly. I had a feeling that as far as mind games went, Eganël would be willing and eager to play the long game. His brows slowly rise and he blinks a few times, clearly not expecting that question.

"Why, of course not, Majesty! It is *illegal* after all." I roll my eyes at him, before staring him down pointedly, making it obvious I didn't believe him for a moment.

"Fine. If you want to play it that way—I need you to do it for me again." He again blinks a few times as he processes my words. Patryk looks back and forth between us, as if just realizing the blacksmith I now call Eganël was the *same* Eganël who he had certainly heard the tales of after we caused the fire centuries ago.

"Apologies. I am going to need you to repeat that and elucidate a bit more please." Eganël says, stunned.

"If you were able to fuse wind magic, for example, into a metal bird like contraption, could you control it and send it cities away?

Hypothetically." I ask. Eganël's eyes flash with excitement as his mind races. Like putting a puzzle together, I can see his mind whirling with the various possibilities.

After a few minutes of silence, his eyes refocus and land on me. "I do believe you might be on to something there, Your Majesty." He grins widely. "And how soon would this need to be figured out? Hypothetically." He flashes a wink at me.

"Tomorrow." He blanches, then pales when I add, "Tomorrow morning, preferably. Either way, as soon as possible."

He throws back his head and laughs, loud and hard. None of us even flinch as we wait for him to collect himself. "Tomorrow morning... You really are something, Your Majesty! You..." He trails off taking in all of our solemn faces and his humor falters a bit. "Are you *serious?* It is already past ten! You need something in twenty-four hours?" He gapes at me.

"Or less." I add.

"What?"

"Twenty-four hours *or less.*" I correct him. Then watch the blood drain from his face as I explain what we had learned about the sewers and the siege now happening at Eludar.

"Damn." He rubs at his forehead and paces back and forth a few steps before facing me again. "I will do everything I can to hurry. But I might need your help with the magic. I don't possess wind power myself. So if I try to imbue it I don't know if it will listen to me or just be chaos. But with your power over the element, it might work. We will have to try a few times to make sure we get it right." I shoot a silent questioning look to Isos, uncertain as to how long the bread he gave me to stifle my magic would last. He thankfully understands and nods yes. It would be out of my system soon enough to help Eganël.

"I can help, but you should know my control is not what it once was. I... struggle greatly with it actually." Eganël looks me up and down uncertainly.

"Well it looks like we are both going to have a challenge ahead tonight." I nod, and bid a grim farewell to my friends. It was going to be a long night indeed.

fifty-two

I yawn so hard my jaw pops and I wince. The sun is beginning to rise and Eganël and I are on our sixth attempt at making an object fly and navigate on its own. My magic had begun its reappearance about an hour ago, blessedly, slowly rather than in full force. While we waited for it to reappear, Eganël had made a few models. Each trial we had tweaked certain elements, but still each failed epically. The first one even started a decent size fire after it hit a nearby building and exploded. Thankfully, after a substantial amount of cursing on my part, and laughing on Eganël's, we had put it out and smoothed things over with its occupants. The second had completely ignored any instruction or direction and, actually, we honestly had no idea of what happened to that one after it drifted into the sky and out of view. The third, well... we don't want to talk about that one. In fact, a pact was made, both of us swearing to not mention it ever again. The fourth had actually made decent progress. Until it passed out of my view and nose dived onto the street. The fifth hadn't even lifted from the table before Eganël had glared at it and threw it into the fireplace with a jumble of muttered angry curses. We were running out of time and my energy was fading. After this sixth attempt, we would only have two more metal birds assembled and our time frame to warn Eludar was dwindling fast.

I pray to Jera. *Please, I need your help. If this is the right thing, please show me that this is it. We are running out of time and I don't have any of it to waste. Please Jera… show me the correct path.*

Then a word is whispered in my ear, so clearly I spin to see who snuck up behind me. *Together.* I hear again, and understanding snaps through me.

"Eganël, come here. I need you to hold my hand while we both add the power. Together." His eyes narrow, thinking it through until he nods and steps forward. Until now, he had made the small bird like contraption, and I had added my power at his instruction. But it was his gift to imbue power to objects and my power of wind that needed to be fused together. It was obvious upon retrospection.

I place my fingertips of my left hand upon the cool metal, and take Eganël's into my right. I gasp at the glow that shines from where our hands connect. For the first time, Eganël looks awestruck, and a spark of hope gleams back at me from his sapphire eyes. "Do it!" He whispers, and I return my attention to the form in front of me. With a mental push and silent prayer, I shove my wind into the object. For the first time, the metal warms comfortably beneath my fingers. Not hot enough to burn, but hot enough to notice a change. I grin and watch breathlessly as the small metal bird now glows a bright blue. *Now for the actual test.*

"Fly to Patryk." I whisper my hopeful command and the bird doesn't hesitate before launching into the sky and disappearing toward the castle. Neither of us breathes as we wait, still holding each other's hands. We are too excited and distracted to care. Five minutes pass, then ten. But each of our eyes stay locked on the sky that minute by minute grows brighter with the tangerine sunrise. When still nothing appears and we drop hands, disappointment and desperation fills the workshop. I rub my eyes with the back of my hand. "Okay, well, that one made progress. What else do you think we need to change?" The look on Eganël's face makes my heart sink, though. It was one I had not yet seen before on him. Blank. I knew then that he was out of ideas.

"Evara!!" I hear my name being called from a few streets away. I frown and turn toward it. *What could it be now??* Then I see Patryk running towards us, a wide grin on his face. "It worked!" He shouts and then skips. The King of Telor actually skips a few steps, he was so happy. I blink, not understanding yet, my head is throbbing with exhaustion. Then it clicks as I spy the small bit of metal clasped in his hand.

"It *worked?*" I spin to Eganël who stares wide eyed at Patryk too. "But it didn't return."

"I tried to send it back, but it grew still and cold." He skids to a stop beside us, breathless but ecstatic. "What did you tell it to do?"

I think back. "I told it to fly to you."

"Maybe it is in the orders. Perhaps for a return you needed to say *Fly to Patryk, then fly back to where he orders* or something like that!" Eganël says, pacing his shop as he tugs at his growing scruff. Frankly, his appearance and shaky demeanor make him look like a madman. I try to not laugh and focus on the task. I am sure I did not look much better, all covered in soot and sweat.

"I need a piece of paper." I look around for a scrap to use. Our mingled excitement thankfully gives me enough of a jolt that I think I can try one more time. "Can I see the bird?" I ask Patryk as I scribble on a piece of dusty paper with a scrap of charcoal. I hear the clunk of metal as the apple-sized metal bird is sat on the work table again. I roll the scrap up and insert it into the hole Eganël had bored for this during its creation. "Okay, ready Eganël?" I ask and smile as I extend my hand to him again. I see my own tired exhilaration mirrored on his face as he takes it. I take a deep breath and tug one more time on my wind. "Fly to Isos, then wait for his direction and obey." I say once the sapphire glow again lights up the tiny figure at my touch. Once more, the bird launches into the air and we wait, now Patryk joining our vigil as the minutes pass. Three minutes pass before Eganël lets out a cheer and points into the now bright blue sky. Sure enough, the little messenger bird returns, landing on the table with a surprisingly hefty thud before it stills and the glow fades. With shaking fingers, I pluck the scrap of paper from the hole and unfurl it to see Isos's scrawled response.

It worked!

Together we all cheer so loudly that people nearby emerge from their homes to find their king, High Queen, and local blacksmith all laughing, shouting, and dancing in the street.

We try it twice more before finally feeling confident that it will arrive at Eludar as intended. By the time we are preparing to send the actual letter off, Isos has joined us and together we three draw up a letter to explain the additional threat that hides within the fortress itself. When the bell tower tolls nine times, I stand ready with the metal bird, so tiny despite its great importance, held carefully in my palm. Its letter already rolled and set securely in the carrier hole, all that was left was to bring it to life and give it directions. Now well practiced, Eganël and I clasp hands again, but this time I pause before sending the wind into the metal bird. Instead, I include a prayer to Jera.

"I ask you now to protect and guide this message as swift and sure as you can. Please help it get into helpful hands and let Eludar be saved." I bow my head and murmur. Then, with now practiced words and thoughts, I command the wind. "To Eludar, to King Noran, then wait for directions and do as they bid." Suddenly, the weight in my palm vanishes and I follow the small dot of metal until I can no longer see it against the bright rays of the sun. I look at the others who stare after it, too. "Well, that is all we can do for now. We just have to wait." With my task done and the excitement of success subsiding, I feel my overwhelming exhaustion set in and I sway on my feet. I had not used that much magic in a very long time. Only now that my focus is not drawn elsewhere do I realize that, even with the herbs now completely out of my system, I am able to maintain control. I do not even feel like it was a risk to myself or those around me to use it. The realization makes me feel almost giddy with relief. But that also could be in part because of draining of so much magic and the sleepless night.

I sway again, but this time feel hands of all three men grabbing my arms to stop me from falling face first into the dirt. "I can take her." I hear Eganël say and realize that they had been trying to decide how they were going to get me back up to the castle. Along with being taller than average, I was heavier than I appeared, thanks to my sculpted muscles I had earned in my training. I was heavy enough that, coupled with the distance uphill to the castle, it would have been too far for either Isos or Patryk to carry me. But Eganël, with the advantage of being an elf, a secret I didn't think either man had gleaned yet, he could carry me with no problem. I might have to deal with his complaining the whole way, but right now, I was so tired and relieved that I didn't even care. With zero warning, I feel weightless as he scoops me into his arms, winning the battle of wills. "That was quite a display, miss. But when you regain yourself, I am going to need you to explain exactly *why* Captain Isos is dousing you with abalmas root." I smile softly as I lean against his chest with a sigh.

"Do you know everything?" I mutter. He chuckles, sending a tingle of vibrations across my cheek. I hear the steady crunch of his footsteps, but no others. We were alone. Patryk and Isos either staying behind or running their own errands in the city. I remember suddenly that Isos and I were supposed to be leaving for Naro today. I groan to myself at the thought of doing anything right now, and feel Eganël tense with worry. "Sorry, not you." I mumble, just loud enough for him to make out.

"You know, you can talk to me." He says softly, as he shifts me in his arms carefully. "I know I'm all sarcastic and rude sometimes, but I *am* one of the few people who understands some of what you are going through. And I will do my best to remain unbiased and non-judgmental." I smile and force myself to open my eyes and look up at him. I find him looking back down at me, a surprisingly genuine look on his face.

"Thank you, Eganël. I will remember that." I say before my exertion overwhelms me again and I have to rest against his shoulder.

"Maybe I am overstepping things, but I also want you to know that I am sorry about what happened between you and Türë." That comment makes my eyes snap back open, exhaustion or no. "Okay, I don't know *exactly* what went down, but I have known you both long and well enough to be able to assume what happened. It was something bad enough for you to send him away, after all." I hesitate. This man was Türë's friend, or at least I think he was. Friendlyish, at least. I didn't want to taint his opinion, of either of us. But as he pointed out, he might be one of the *only* people who would have an unbiased opinion on the matter.

"It was bad. But even though it bordered on treasonous, I still regret sending him away. Especially since it appeared to be to his death." I admit quietly.

"Bordered on *treason?*" Eganël hisses in my ear, obviously not expecting *that* to be the cause of Türë's banishment.

"Well, it was actually outright treason, I suppose." I wince and both feel and hear Eganël stumble a step.

"Okay now you *have* to tell me." I sigh with fatigue, but tell him the summary of what had happened. He doesn't answer, even as we approach the castle gates and I hear the guards cry out in alarm at the sight of me being carried to them in the arms of the local blacksmith. Or who they all *thought* was just a local blacksmith. It still surprised me how well Eganël was able to hide in plain sight, among those whose ancestors had tried to kill his people, along with the other Creatures of the Forest. Though I didn't think the people would have any prejudice against him now, I also didn't blame him for preferring to remain safe in the shadows as Yessin Arboff.

Eganël doesn't speak as he carries me the rest of the way to my chambers, led there helpfully by one of the particularly worried guards. This had been the compromise to letting Eganël continue to carry me into my room. Even after I had reassured the guards I was okay, the middle-aged man who was the highest rank present had only furrowed his brow and insisted on escorting me through the castle himself. In spite of my aching bones and drained energy, I felt a trickle of affection run through me. My people were good people with big hearts. Like anywhere there were bad eggs, but the Tesindrens as a whole were well known for their generous, kind spirits, and steadfast loyalty and resolve. This guard was just a singular example of that.

I was so proud to be their Queen.

I smile at the guard in thanks as we enter my room, and his tense expression softens somewhat. Eganël places me gently on the bed and begins to tug at my laces to remove my filthy, soot covered boots. Part of me wanted to argue that I needed a bath before I crawled fully into bed, but the other half just wanted to close my eyes, the desire to sleep winning out in the end. I sigh in relief as the first boot is pulled free, and then the second. Eganël laughs softly at me before I feel a pressure on the mattress at my feet. I pry open my eyes to find him sitting at the foot of the bed, watching me. I glance to the door and still find the guard standing there. Not directly watching, but I knew he was aware of Eganël's every movement and, at the slightest hint of my discomfort or danger, he would be at my side. My heart warms again and I make a mental note to ask for the man's name. I still needed a new Captain of the Royal Guard in Isos' place, and this man was a definite promising possibility.

"I will say this in his defense, simply for the sake of our previous and lengthy friendship." Eganël's sudden voice makes me jump slightly, but I don't speak and instead let him continue. "In his heart he is convinced that you are his soulbonded. But something with Jera's blessing, coupled with your long life, has made it so that he is not *yours*. I know not if he believes to be the reborn High King Donovan, he never confided *that* much in me. But he believes with every breath in him that you are the missing piece of his soul." He sighs and runs his dirty fingers through his equally grimy hair, eyes darkening with emotion when they land on me. "I lost my soulbonded. Long, long ago. So I can imagine, if that is what he feels about you, he would be desperate to prove himself. Not just to you, but to himself." I realize how close Türë's confession in the letter came to what Eganël was telling me now. "He is a good man, I will say that. But I also will tell you this. If he has threatened, hurt, or disappointed you in any way, then no matter what *shit* he is dealing with, it does not excuse what he did. As my mother said a forever ago, *it serves as an excuse—not a reason.*"

"I just wish I knew what was real and what was not. The others tell me he, and my old self apparently, are keeping things from me. Things I wanted withheld for a reason. But how do I know that is the truth. I didn't even know I was *married* before the morning I sent Türe away and Ilithyia spilled." Then a thought hits me.

"Wait—did you know Donovan? You said you and I knew each other before Türe and I did." He pauses, eyeing me thoughtfully before nodding slowly.

"They were keeping that from you?" Eganël's angry concern finally makes me feel not as crazy for my own reaction. "I don't see why they were trying to do that. Unless—" He trails off.

"Unless?" I prompt.

"Unless that was Türe trying to slip in and maybe make a claim as your soulbonded. If you didn't remember Donovan, then maybe he saw it as a chance that the heartbond would occur between you two." He looks disturbed by this. "I see why you sent him away. Treason or no—if someone tried to take the place of my Nelope, I would be furious." The permanent hardness I now recognize as grief softens just slightly at his soulbonded's name. "And yes, I knew Donovan. He was the only mortal I truly liked. I was sad to see him die." I knew that he *had* died, obviously, but I had never thought of him *dying* before now.

"How did it happen?" I ask through the lump in my throat. My sleepiness has not gone, but it recedes behind my intrigue.

"A battle. An arrow actually, straight to the chest." He grimaces. "You had sixteen beautiful star-cycles together before that horrible death. The entire kingdom mourned for a decade. King Donovan was a good and honorable man. But he also took no shit." He grins slightly at my husband's memory. "He was someone I truly considered a very close friend, and you two were incredibly happy together. Even though your time was cut horribly short. You know he is buried in the castle garden, don't you?"

I sit up with a gasp. "What did you just say?" I manage to ask, even as the guard darts into the room, startled by my noise and sudden movement. After reassuring him I was fine, he retreats to the door again, though with a warning glare at Eganël.

"Child!" He mutters under his breath at the guard. And I bite down on a laugh at Eganël's indignation at the man who was, in comparison to our ages, still a child. "Yes, there is a bench that you insisted be carved out of the tree that marks his resting place." He takes in my speechless stare and shakes his head with a furious growl. "Nobody really told you where your husband is buried?" I see a glint of his flame spark in his eyes and if I wasn't so tired, I am sure my fire would be visible now.

"Maybe they didn't know?" I say, though it comes out more of a question.

"Türë knew." Eganël says pointedly, and my shoulders droop.

"I have spent so many hours in the garden. Before this room and my study, it was the only place I felt comfortable. I had no idea why." I picture the bench I had sat on nearly every time I had been in the garden. It was where I had gone my first night in the castle. There had been an inscription in the stone, but it was faded enough I couldn't make it out. I confirm this with Eganël and he nods.

"That's it. If you trace your finger along the line, it will reveal a set of stairs that will take you to the mausoleum." I gape at him.

"How do you know that?"

"I put it there. I was the one who made the tomb." He admits, crossing his arms across his chest and looking proud. I shake my head in astonishment.

"Can you just confirm something for me? It is odd but... what did the King *smell* like?" He raises a brow at me, but doesn't seem to be too thrown by the unusual question. Eganël thinks a moment on this.

"I guess I would say like... fresh rain." I feel my hope slip, and I bite my cheek in frustration."And mint, maybe a little like pine or cypress too." Eganël adds, not seeing the whiplash my thoughts had just had. I choke back a sob, relieved tears filling my eyes.

"It is him then!" I whisper aloud, though mostly to myself.

"What do you mean?" Eganël asks.

"I have been having a few memories resurface." I admit to him under my breath, shooting a glance at the guard. But the man seems anything but concerned with the conversation we are having. Focusing down the hall and even humming to himself. I realize in surprise that he was doing this on purpose to tune out our conversation and give us privacy. I like this man more and more. I see Eganël follow my stare and nod approvingly at the man too. *If Eganël is impressed, that is saying something.*

"You think they are of Donovan?" He asks, somehow unfazed by this.

"I didn't know for sure until you confirmed it. I can't see his face, it is shadowed, but I do remember his smell. Mint and cypress. I thought it was Türë at first but..." I trail off, but Eganël understands anyway.

"Interesting... I thought nothing was supposed to remain after each Awakening. But now you are telling me that your powers are resurfacing faster and stronger than before, and you have some memories returning. I am guessing you have no idea what that means either." I shake my head no and he sighs dramatically. "Well I suppose I will think on it as well and see if I can come up with any reason." He swings his legs back to the floor and stands with a deep stretch. "You, however, are far past due for some sleep. As am I." He heads for the door and the guard, whose attention has returned to the tall, graceful man, lowers his head almost imperceptibly at the guard, but pauses. Turning back, he wears a sad grin. "It may not be my place, but try and give Türë the benefit of the doubt. I can swear to you on my life that nothing he did was with malice. Not from his point of view, at least. It sounds like he may have gotten carried away, but he would do *anything* to help you, even if it meant giving up a piece of his soul. Literally." My brow furrows in confusion, but the mysterious elf only dips a bow at me once more, before slipping past the guard and out of my sight. Disappearing before I could ask him anything more.

In spite of my racing mind, I smile gratefully at the guard who nods sharply at me, then pulls the door shut before I can think to ask his name. Too tired to get up and go after him, I lay down and at last fall fast asleep to the smell of lavender and lemons.

fifty-three

I stir and stretch, feeling each of my muscles twinge. Not from swinging a sword like normal, but from the ache of exerting as much magic as I had yesterday. I groan, sitting up slowly. Blinking at the sun sitting low in the sky in confusion, rising in the wrong direction, until I realize that I have slept all day and night was fast approaching. My stomach growls and I grab at it before forcing myself out of bed. Food. I needed to track down food before my stomach began to eat itself. I stumble to the wardrobe for where my robe hangs and tug it on. Even with hours of blessedly uninterrupted sleep, I still am filled with bone-deep exhaustion. If not for the cramping in my stomach that demands sustenance, I would have rolled over and gone back to bed. I pass a mirror and balk at my appearance. My hair, a tangled mess of curls that sticks out in all directions, is nothing to the pillow creases and bloodshot eyes that stand stark on my face.

There is no way I am going to leave my room like this. With a groan of disappointment, I flop onto the nearby sofa with a huff, then stare at the unusually full tea table set in front of me. My heart soars with appreciation for whichever of my friends had the foresight and care to do this. Because set up in front of me was a pile of snacks and treats to feed me three times over. I squeal with glee when I lift a silver dome to find a tray filled with my favorite pastry: sugar-covered donuts. I immediately stuff one in my mouth and groan with satisfaction when I discover they are still warm.

I explore my way through various cheeses, breads, crackers, jams, and pastries until I am so full I could not fathom taking another bite. I lean back and look around my room. It is amazing the different feeling I have here as opposed to the rooms I had been staying in upon first arriving at the castle. I notice that Ilithyia had finished moving the last of my items in and my attention catches on a small leather-bound book that had been placed on the side table. I rack my mind for where it came from until my memory snags on the day that I had been late for my first day of training with Ionel. I had been dressing in a rush and the book had flown out from where it had been hidden among my clothes.

Hidden.

I frown and grab for it, flipping through a few pages. It's a journal. My breath catches and I flip excitedly back to the first page. I realize the treasure it is as I see the name elegantly scrawled across the golden name plate.

My journal.

I stare at the date marking the first entry, the air frozen in my lungs. Third Vernas, First of Third Tesria.

Holy shit. This journal was one I started right at the beginning of my last Awakening. I slam it shut and press my forehead against the embossed cover. Despite the treasure I knew it to be, I wanted to throw it into the fire. Did I want to read this? Truly? Or would it only make me doubt every choice I had made since this Awakening had begun? Would it only give myself more things for me to compare myself to? I take a deep breath and sit up straight again.

No. I needed to read this. For whatever reason, someone, perhaps even my past self had hidden this for me to find. I had to know why, this of all things, had been placed aside and not destroyed like Türe told me they had been.

I open the book again, tucking my legs underneath me and settling back into the pile of pillows.

I remember nothing.

Do you have any idea how annoying that is?? Why the hell would I do this not just once but multiple times?? I feel empty, like a shell that has been scooped out. That unfairly attractive soldier, Donovan, who found me in the forest insists that this was what I wanted. But how do I know he isn't tricking me? This all feels like some joke. There is no way I am anyone's Queen. The idea is laughable. Especially in this condition. I am as useful as a newborn babe now. If they hadn't come to get me, I would still be wandering around the forest trying to guess my own name! What a joke.

I can't help but laugh aloud at the truth of her words. My words. Relief floods through me at the recognition that my initial feelings had not been unfelt by me before. There is something astoundingly comforting in that. In my head, I had always pictured myself as powerful, controlled, regal. This picture painted in just a few sentences feels familiar and a lot less intimidating of a person to emulate.

Smiling widely, I look back down at the page. My joy is replaced with a stone dropped in my gut as realization floods me. Horror turns my bones to ice. I scramble off of the couch, barely noticing when my knee bumps the table partially filled with what was left of my dinner, sending water and crackers flying. I don't care though as I dash across the room, still holding onto the precious book with shaking hands. I cradle it to my chest with one arm as I yank open the nightstand drawer and pull out the rolled parchment that had been hanging from Ladir's neck.

I stare dully at the words before my sluggish mind makes sense of it all.

The handwriting on the scroll doesn't match the journal.

I push the door to Patryk's study open slowly, numbness filling every part of me. I have my suspicions, but needed confirmation. If I was right... well, everything would change.

"Evara! What are you still doing up? Aren't you leaving for Naro early tomorrow?" He greets me with a smile, one that quickly melts from his face into concern as he takes in my demeanor. "Evara?" He stands slowly, as I ease gently onto one of the chairs in front of his desk. His study was similar to my own, though filled with much newer furniture and much less dust. I find I cannot speak, so I just hand him the journal. He takes it cautiously before flipping it open, then gasping in surprise. "This is amazing! Where did you find—?" Patryk glances at me, brow furrowing again in concern when he realizes my reaction was not of joy. Not what he would expect from the discovery of an old journal of mine.

"The handwriting, do you recognize it?" I ask at last, my voice dull and rough. He looks back down at it before nodding slowly, wholly confused by my reaction.

"It is yours." He confirms. With still shaking hands, I hold out the scroll to him. He unfurls it, and he realizes immediately what I am so upset about. "But isn't this the letter—" His eyes flash to me. "They don't match."

"That was supposed to be written by my past-self for me after the Awakening." I nod, seeing his thought pattern following the same path mine had gone. He pales, returning his attention to the scroll. I wait for him to examine it as my thoughts race. I had never had a comparison of my handwriting from before to even make me think that the letter could be a fraud and had never thought to show it to anyone else. It came down to two questions that play on repeat in my mind. First, why would someone go to the lengths of faking the letter instead of just destroying the original? If there was even one I wrote myself to begin with. Second, what would that someone gain by doing it?

Patryk inhales sharply and spins away from me, setting the precious journal carefully aside before digging through the piles of paper stacked neatly on his desk. He must find what it is he is looking for, because he suddenly goes still. I stand and walk up beside him to see what he had discovered. Pinned beneath his hand is a correspondence he had received a few days before Charobi had fallen. My breath catches when I see it beside the letter.

The scrawl matches perfectly.

Cheeks flushed red with anger, Patryk heaves in breath after breath as he works through what it means. I already know, but I have to see the concrete proof. I gently pry his palm up from where it blocks the signature of the writer.

General Türë.

We stare at it together, as if we could change it. As if we could make it go away.

"Fucking hell, Türë!" Patryk growls suddenly and flops down into the nearest chair. "*He* wrote the letter? Why?" He asks the question aloud, though he knows I don't have the answers. I pull the letter from where it had furled up again on his desk and re-read it for what must be the hundredth time.

"Did I ever mention I was leaving a letter? Did this replace one that I had left, or was the whole thing made up by Türë?" I add to the questions that continue to hang in the air unanswered. Patryk shakes his head.

"You never mentioned anything to me, but Türë was the last one to see you before you left. So I don't know for sure." He moans, rubbing a hand across his forehead.

"I don't understand." I confess, my voice low and thick, as tears fill my eyes. "Why would he *do* this to me? Is it truly all for a crown?" A moment passes before Patryk slams his fists down onto the arms of his chair, standing with such urgency, I jump in surprise.

"Fuck this, and fuck him." He says, more to himself than me, as he strides to his desk and yanks open a drawer with a fury I had never seen in him before. He lifts a key so I can see it and I look between him and the obviously ancient, ornate key. "I am going to tell you everything."

✱ ✱ ✱ ✱ ✱

I stand behind Patryk, hands clasped together so tightly that the white of my knuckles stand out, even in the dim light of my study. I would ignite the torches, but in my current condition of despair and distraction, I don't dare. Instead, I test the bars that hold the monster of my magic in its cage deep within me. It seems to writhe with satisfied glee at my distress, but thankfully it remains, for now, under my control. Despite that, I decide to find Isos soon for another piece of the abalmas root bread.

We stand before the locked door in my study. The door that had bothered me from the first time I had tried the handle with no success. Turns out my intuition had been right about this being something more. It turns out my intuition had been right about *many* things. I trace my eyes over the delicate carvings set into the bronze handle and my heart leaps as the *thud* of the key unlocking it seems to echo in my chest.

"Wait!" I shout suddenly, leaping forward and grabbing Patryk's arm before he can push it open. "I thought you all said I didn't want to know these things, whatever it is you are going to show me. That I wanted these secrets kept for my own good." A muscle jumps in Patryk's jaw as he works over how to respond.

"Those wishes were conveyed to us by Türë." He states, spitting out the words with his still building rage. I was not the only one Türë had betrayed. Each of those he had called his brothers, those he had known for decades, he had manipulated as well. I mull this over. It should have been obvious. Of course Türë had lied to them about this too. He lied in the letter, he lied to my face. He lied about everything, apparently. And like a fool, I had fallen for it.

We all had.

"Okay." I nod, releasing his arm and wincing with guilt as he has to shake his arm out as the blood rushes back to his hand from my too tight grip. "I am ready." I whisper, even as I try to convince myself.

He glances back at me, and I can tell from his narrowed eyes that he doesn't believe that for a second. But the door swings open anyway. He steps aside, letting me enter first. I ease the door open the rest of the way and take a few tentative strides into the large room. I spin on a heel, my fists clenching in rising anger.

"Is this some sort of joke?" I yell out at Patryk.

"What do—?" He enters the room now, and from the sudden paleness that washes his face grey, I know that he is just as thrown as I am. "No. No!" He spins around in a frenzy, tugging at his copper hair until it stands on end. "There were dozens of boxes of items and paintings. Books and—and journals!" His voice rises and falls in disbelief until he turns to face me again, arms falling limp at his side. "It's all gone." His voice breaks on the last word, and I know his dismay is genuine. I sink onto the dust covered ground, and catch a glimpse of the outlines, the ghosts, of everything he said was here before. I have no more tears to shed for treachery.

Then I see a flutter from the doorway. Patryk catches the movement too and strides over to it, scooping up a single piece of paper that had fallen from where it had been tacked to the back of the door. A sour taste fills my mouth as the words from Türë's final letter to me rings in my ears. *Even when some things come to light that I know you will despise me even more for, please know I did it for you.*

I watch his eyes scan the page. Once. Twice. Thrice. Then he silently passes it over to me, before turning and marching through the door.

I take a few breaths before looking down at the single line of words scrawled in the familiar penmanship of Türë.

It is for her own good.

fifty-four

I stroll through the newly built castle halls, deeply inhaling the soft scent of the baby-blue dahlia that I had found resting on my pillow this morning. The continuous sound of hammers banging away as they worked on expanding the old castle had become my usual morning ambience. If my powers were not still dormant, I would have assisted them. Even if to only imbue the stones like I had when I built the original foundations. I would miss the ever present magical presence that made my castle come alive at my command. Oh well. I wasn't going to wait for the next hundred star-cycles for it to return. Not when my husband had convinced me to move the entire seat of my kingdom here. We could only sleep in tents for so long.

Husband.

Humming quietly with a smile wide on my face, I make my way to the empty field of dirt that had been set aside for the Nefriti to train on. It had been their one request when I asked if they would follow me to my new home. I had been relieved and astounded when they, at last, decided to begin training anyone who wanted to come and learn the ways of the warrior, rather than keeping it in the family lines or among their magical kind. It had taken star-cycles, but I had convinced them at last to share their knowledge—with those who earned it. Thankfully, those who had signed up and been selected had been eager and, so far, hardworking and patient. They also hadn't minded living in the feeble tents until we finished the castle and guard house.

I pause at the balcony overlooking the bodies that already drip with sweat and dust, despite the sun rising not even thirty minutes ago. While I missed the view of the ocean, being more centered in the kingdom was reasonable enough to make me move to a barely established town farther in the northeast than I had originally desired for my capital. I glance below for the face that makes my heart leap, no matter how often I saw it.

I find him immediately. My eyes landing on my soulbonded as if my mind had always known where he was. Even across the castle. I rest my chin on my palm as I lean against the railing, examining each muscle and bead of sweat that drips down his shirtless, sun-tanned torso. He lunges and parries without flaw, though when a cocky grin spreads on his face, I know that he knows I am watching him. I close my eyes and send my desire for him down our heartbond so suddenly and strongly that for the first time he misses a step. The warrior he duels with seizes his opening, smacking him solidly on his upper thigh and laughing openly at him. I snap my eyes open and find my husband scowling across the courtyard at me for my purposeful distraction. Though I know he can only see my form and not my expression with his human eyes, I still smirk and laugh as I push back from the rail, making my way to the stairs that lead down to the training field.

"You looked a little distracted there, my love. Did you have something on your mind?" I grin up at him as he meets me halfway.

He towels himself off and chuckles his devious growling laugh that makes my toes curl. Reaching for me, he pulls me in and nuzzles at my ear. Even all sweaty and dirty from his morning exercises, I can still smell the soothing scent of his cypress soap mingling with the mint tea he insists on having every morning. I can't help the breathless moan I make as I lean into his lips and tilt my neck back for better access. He chuckles alluringly, and I feel his desire grow too. Not from the bond, but from the sudden pressure that grows from where his waist presses against me. I pull his face to mine and give a slight teasing nip at his bottom lip. It is his turn to groan.

We had been married now nearly two moon-cycles, but still could not get enough of each other. Though our castle was in the beginning stages and there weren't many rooms yet, we had tested out each and every one of them so far. As well as a few of the storage closets and hidden hall alcoves.

"Come with me." Donovan breathes, his mouth still on mine as he takes my hand and leads me with a near run into the newly planted gardens that already were sprawling and beautiful. Every plant encouraged by my tending and by the guidance and care of the florenta. He finds a decently hidden spot beside the large white marble fountain and lowers himself on top of me, giving me a kiss so passionate my heart thunders in my chest. "I love you, my soulbonded. My wife. My Evara."

Before I can respond, everything suddenly darkens and I am surrounded by ash and smoke. I cough at the rancid air and squint, trying to place myself. I call out for my king, but he is gone. A helpful gust of wind blows away enough of the smoke to reveal a massive dark grey expanse of stone, blackened by the once incinerating heat of some fire that leaves tendrils of black veins snaking up its side and out of sight. Though I have never been here before, at least not since the Awakening, I know this place instinctively. Charobi.

I inhale slightly in shock, then regret it immediately as a cough racks through me. My lungs reject the tainted air. I lift my arm up to make a cover across my nose and mouth. But my horror only continues to grow as my eyes adjust to the sharp contrast of the black moonless night stark against the bright red flames that still smolder in various spots in the vast open space. I frown at my surroundings, not remembering this in the images and maps I had seen of the fortress. I rack my brain but don't recall any sort of empty field of this size within its walls. Then I realize what it is, and what keeps the separate pools of fire kindled. It was the city itself. The houses, the shops—all of it burned to nothing more than a few burnt posts and stones discarded here and there. A sob chokes out of me and I fall to my knees among the cinders. I hear hollow snaps beneath my legs and, upon closer inspection, realize it was not sticks but human bones cracking beneath me.

"Jera, why do you show me this?" I cry out, then break into another body wracking cough.

"To show you what will be, if you do not find a way in." A woman's voice answers, and it seems to come from all around me. Jera.

"If I knew how to do that, I could save them. But I don't know how!"

Only silence answers me, then finally, "How did your enemy?" The voice asks, echoing, before I feel her presence suddenly fade and I find myself alone once again, staring at the remains of Charobi.

"How did—?" I think this over and suddenly realize. "The plumbing, but—." Understanding shoots through me like a lightning bolt. According to all of our information, nobody from Charobi or its fortress had survived or escaped that night Mirinth had snuck in and overtaken it. Nobody besides Beven. **Something they don't know about.** *I thank Jera, and, despite my fury at the moment, Türe for that gift that had been delivered to us. Not just now for Eludar's hopeful survival, but also for our success in the coming battle. If*

Mirinth has no idea that we had learned how they had gotten in, they wouldn't have closed off the plumbing.

The key to their success would now become our own.

I gasp awake, sitting straight up in bed. Nearly colliding with Patryk, who curses and jumps back from where he had been bent over, trying to shake me awake. The air scrapes against my bone dry throat and I swear the ashy taste of burnt wood and flesh still lingers on my tongue. Coughing hard, I rasp out, "water." Thankfully a fresh, still ice filled pitcher of water sits atop my bedside table. I drain the glass Patryk quickly pours me without taking a breath. Fortunately, the horrible taste is washed clean from my mouth.

I feel the ominous pressure in my gut, the familiar telltale ache that informs me my magic had refilled itself during my sleep. Stirred by my tumultuous dreams, it now teasingly scrapes a talon down the door of its cage. It purrs contented inside me, as if genuinely pleased at my recent use of it. The only reason it had not burst out of me during my panic from the dream. Not a dream. A vision, I realize. Less of a gift, and more of a warning from Jera. Time was running out. But I now have a plan.

I swing my legs out from the covers and jump to my feet. Ignoring Patryk's confusion, I rush to my bathing chamber, I grab the clean dress Ilithyia had set out for me, finally shucking off the clothing I had put on two days ago. Covered in soot from the forge, and sweat from both my dreams and the exertion of creating the magic that animated our messenger bird, it is filthy. I debate whether it would be best to simply toss it in the hearth to burn, rather than have a laundress waste her time trying to clean it. I shudder, stepping into the tub, not waiting for the water to warm up before splashing some on my face. The icy sting is refreshing and much needed to pull the last fog of exhaustion away. I slip on the fresh clean dress with a relieved sigh.

Running back out to my room where Patryk waits for me, impatient and befuddled, I tell him my good news. "I know how we are going to save Türë from his execution. He may deserve punishment, but first he owes me—us—answers. Not to mention, we need him to find out where he put my things. I refuse to believe he would destroy them. Let's go to the gallery. We are going to need the maps. And we need Isos, Elder Dakar, and Ionel to meet us there, too." I chatter excitedly, tugging Patryk after me through the door. Though I can tell he was surprised, Patryk just adapts calmly, as always, following after me into the hallway without a further question or comment. When we come across the first guard, we send them off in pursuit of the three men I need. I step into the breeze of the open air hallway that connects the old castle to the new seamlessly, and only then realize that the sun is rising. I should be preparing to depart for Naro with Isos. But I shut down any of the guilt before it can surge and distract me. It was important we have an actual *plan* if I was going to make any attempt at liberating Charobi. And with the rough ideas forming in my mind, many of the people I would need were here.

Reaching the war room, I send for some sandwiches and tea. We were going to need sustenance and none of us were going to leave this room until we had a firm solution to win back Charobi, and spare Türë from his scheduled death. With Patryk's help, I purge the large table, covered in its hundreds of maps, figures, and various information regarding the kingdom and its defenses, until only a large depiction of Charobi is left. By the time Isos arrives with a bleary-eyed Ionel, and a scowling Elder Dakar in tow, only the items regarding Charobi remain on the table ready for us. Realizing I need to take the edge off my magic that begins to grow agitated at my stress, I send a tendril of my wind magic to tug on the door and pull it shut behind the three men that join Patryk and I. I fight the urge to cheer when I am successful at, not only that, but at ensuring that tendril was all that slipped free. Maybe I *could* keep control.

"What is the matter now?" Ionel groans, snapping me back to the problem at hand.

"Jera spoke to me." I say bluntly, squaring my shoulders and turning my full attention to the men gathered around the table. Ionel pales, Isos stares back with an impressed grin, Patryk heaves a sigh, and, I swear, Elder Dakar somehow scowls harder. "She helped me realize a way to get in and take back the city, as well as take back Türë." All four jaws drop at that.

"Okay, tell us!" Ionel says eagerly, waving his hand with impatience for me to continue. The others sink into their seats, ready to absorb the information and create a cohesive plan.

"It is simple really, once I realized it. They went to extreme lengths to ensure how they got in would not reach us. Either capturing, or killing those in Charobi who knew. With one exception." They all look confused back at me, not quite understanding. It was only then I realize I had never told any of them about Beven and the letter Türë had insisted he deliver at all costs. They had no idea how I had gotten the vital information about the sewers. I blink in surprise, struck silent by their unlimited faith in me. *They never even questioned me on it.* I shove that realization aside for now, and explain as quickly as I can about Türë's request of the farrier and the origin of the information that had bought us precious time in Eludar. I exchange a look with Patryk, effectively silencing him from mentioning anything about Türë's deception and the items missing from the locked room in my study. It was going to be hard enough convincing the others to allow me to lead the fight in Charobi. I didn't want to add the discussion of if it was worth the risk to save a betrayer.

"Okay. I see why they didn't want us to know their mode of infiltration, but how does that help us get to Türë and the others held in Charobi?" Isos asks.

"They don't *know* that we have that information. We can assume they haven't blocked off the sewers, confident we won't think to enter that way." Patryk mulls aloud.

"Until they hear of our defensive change at Eludar." Elder Dakar adds, sending a shiver of apprehension down my spine. I had not thought of *that*. They would indeed figure out that we knew they were infiltrating through the plumbing if we blocked them that way in Eludar.

"Shit." I mutter to myself. "How long do you think until word can get back from the Mirinthian soldiers outside of Eludar to their men still at Charobi?"

"I would say, assuming they don't have any sort of special messaging system like what we now have, they would have to send it either by boat or by a rider over land. So... five days by rider, three by boat." Isos answers, then blushes as we all turn our attention to him. "Sorry, its still weird to have a say." He chuckles a bit. "I'm used to being the guy in the corner." I smile in understanding at him, and Patryk pats him on the back reassuringly.

I rub my temple, trying to get my disconnected, jumbled thoughts to align. "Okay, so assuming my letter has arrived in Eludar and Noran is adjusting accordingly—" I do the math. "Shit." I say again, and look up at the others who have a matching grim look on their faces. "The latest we can leave to make it in time is tomorrow morning. And that is pushing it."

"I would say so. But it will be hard to ready that many soldiers that quickly. And to push the entire calvary that hard again, and with an even longer distance... You know how long it took you all to arrive at Vante. Charobi is over double that distance." Patryk says with a wince, leaning forward to brace his palms on the table over a map of the city.

"You forget your own shield-brothers and sisters, Your Majesty." A gravelly voice interrupts my thinking and I turn my attention to the Elder.

"Pardon?"

"The Nefriti too are here to serve and protect your kingdom. We have been content to remain behind these walls for too long. Even our Queen, one of us, has forgotten our original purpose—to protect, free, and serve those who cannot." His rhythm of speech always is alluring, slow and pointed, each word serving a purpose.

I feel shamed, and rightfully so. I *had* forgotten the Nefriti. The Tomyris and Magnar alone were worth a hundred well-trained soldiers. In everything that had happened in the last quarters, I had neglected my place among them. I decide to make re-earning my place an absolute priority when, if, I returned. I bow my head in remorse. "I apologize, Elder Dakar. How would you suggest we utilize their skill here?"

"Take them with you." He replies simply.

I look down at the various notes and figures. It made the most sense, actually. They were always ready to go at a moment's notice, and were trained for all kinds of missions, including stealth. Plus, it would be great to have the cohesive unit of the Tomyris and Magnar at my back. Because I was personally going in after Türë, no matter what the others said. I chew my lip, thinking hard, re-strategizing now to account for the Nefriti elite.

"I will send another of the messenger birds to Naro to have their calvary mobilized and ready. It will be less distance to push their rested horses and soldiers, and give them ample time to prepare. We will be able to move much more quickly and arrive in a much better position than if we took the soldiers from here."

The others nod, and I rush over to a ledge where the few metal birds had been placed for safekeeping until we needed them again. Eganël and I had even charged them, so they were ready for use.

"Wait. Are you sure we should deplete the numbers at Naro? Should the worst happen, and your attempts at freeing Charobi fail, they could turn around and seize the opportunity to strike the then vulnerable Naro." Isos interjects.

"Or it could be a trap, allowing them the chance to possibly even slip past Naro entirely and aim for Alessandra." Ionel says, scratching his rough stubble and scar covered cheek.

"Well then, I will take a few of the Nefriti, so we won't have to pull so many soldiers from Naro, the ones capable of riding hard and fast. Them, plus a few from each the Tomyris and Magnar, should leave plenty of warriors and soldiers both here and at Naro. You are right, this very well could be a trap, and I don't want to pull too many from anywhere right now." I say, beginning to pace as I work through the various downfalls and options.

"We are *all* capable of riding hard and fast, Your Majesty. Just say the number and I will have them ready in the hour." Elder Dakar chimes in. I mull this over.

"In reality, we shouldn't *need* an overly large force. Just a skilled one. One small band to slip in through the sewer and open the gate. Once we let the rest in, I can't imagine it would be difficult to retake. We can do them together in one fell swoop. And if we are lucky, timed well enough, we can get those still held behind the wall to turn on their guard. So fifteen Nefriti and four of each of the Tomyris and Magnar." In a safe room, miles away, I could almost convince myself that it wouldn't be messy or risky. But realistically, I knew nothing was that easy. And if it was, it was a trap. "Thoughts?" I ask, looking around at the men who I can tell are running through it all in their own minds. They exchange a wary look, yet nod between each other.

"It is risky, very risky." I say, before any of them can.

"But it is the best plan we have." Patryk says with a heavy sigh.

"Are you willing to risk it all for your General?" Elder Dakar asks, bluntly enough that both Patryk and Isos wince at his brutal, but necessary question. "Should you fail, that could be the end of Tesindren." The fact that the others neither interject, or object, to what the Elder says, reveals their own worries about it.

"Would Türë want you to take such a risk on his behalf?" Patryk asks as gently as he can.

I force myself to think on it, rather than just reply instinctually. That reply would be *absolutely, it is worth any risk*. But I had my entire kingdom full of people to consider, not just one I had so many questions for. One that had many answers owed to me. I close my eyes, and the vision of Charobi burnt to ash fills my mind, and I swear I can smell the smoke again. "It is not just Türë I do this for." I reply finally, my voice low with the anger that begins to rise up at the image Jera had shown me twice now, mingling with my own rage at the General for his choice in taking mine away. "I have seen what Mirinth does to my cities, and will do to Charobi if I do not retake it. I will not tolerate it any longer. Taking back Charobi is for more than just Türë. It is for the people whose bones lay burning among the ash of their homes that Mirinth burned without remorse. It is for Ivrik's memory. Rescuing the General is definitely a factor, but if it were for him alone—as much as it tears at my soul to admit—no. I would not take this risk to go after just him. But for Charobi. For the others who remain their prisoners, and for the fortress that we will desperately need in this war, it *is* worth the risk to me." I see pain clear in each of their returning gazes, and I look back at it without faltering. For I could not falter now. There is too much on the line. But I feel Jera pushing me in this direction, so I cannot ignore the call. Once I returned safely, I would go off in search of her, as she had requested. I had ignored, or denied, the summons until now. But if I truly was to continue being her hand in this world, I needed to listen to her better. I realize that, painfully, now.

At that same moment however, I feel the warm caress of an invisible hand brush against my cheek. I tense slightly in surprise, though don't pull away. I know immediately, it is Jera. Both accepting my unspoken apology, and giving me her blessing for what was to come.

fifty-five

I squint at the last glimpse of the silver bird carrying a message of our upcoming arrival to Naro, glinting in the bright early morning sun, and send a prayer of success along with it. Mirinth choosing to take Dulen and Charobi, well, they were expected and obvious targets. Eludar was a genuine surprise, being the farthest point away from Mirinthian borders in my kingdom. I didn't have time to think on it fully at the moment, but I had shared my concern with the others. Tasking them with mulling over that puzzling ineffective strategy while I focused the next few days on the task at hand. I jump, suddenly startled from my vigil by Patryk's shout. Surrounded by the specially selected Nefriti to join Isos and I on our rush to Naro and then Charobi, Patryk slows his hurried gate with a flush of embarrassment as we all turn to look at him in surprise. A wide grin of relief remains on his face, however, and Isos and I share a look of anticipation.

"What is it?" I ask, a bit concerned, even though his joy is clear to see.

"Our message reached Eludar in time!" He manages to force out between heaving breaths. He must have run all the way through the castle to find us.

"What?!" I gasp, so overjoyed and relieved, I have to clutch onto Isos to keep standing.

"The bird arrived just in time!" He explains, bouncing on his heels with his own relief and excitement. "From the time and date mark on the returned message, they received the bird by that evening." I gape, trying to fathom such a thing, and for the little magic bird to have already returned, it must have been flying impossibly fast. I send another prayer of thanks to Jera, as well as my wind, for achieving such an amazing feat. A giant weight lifts off my shoulders. I had now managed to protect two of my cities from a seemingly inevitable defeat. *Now if I could reclaim one. Maybe we can save the kingdom.* I reach out and pull Patryk in for a hug. He goes rigid with surprise for a breath before wrapping his arms around me and returning the embrace. "Be safe and come back in one piece, okay?" He says into my ear, his voice low and rough with sudden emotion.

"I will." I say, pulling back and grinning at him with what I hope is a reassuring smile. I take one last look around at my castle, my gaze lingering on the stairs and balcony I had seen in my dream. I had felt so much better in those days. Was that the actual reality, or just skewed by the dream? Or had it been the presence of the man I now knew was my husband and soulbonded? Or maybe it was the utter absence of my clawing magic. I hadn't forgotten Eganël's revelation, even if I had not had a chance yet to return to the garden. The resting place of my lost love. But I would see it. Once I returned, I would go to see the man who had captured my heart—even if all that remained of him was encased in stone. I turn away from the gleaming white balcony and pull myself onto Afina. I notice suddenly the cheery face that holds her reins. I smile in joyful surprise at the boy who beams up at me. "Well, if it isn't Mister Jeron!" Sure enough, it was the young boy who had told me of his greatest desire to ride horses and someday be a trained soldier in my guard. "I see your parents accepted your training with the Stable Master."

He nods his head vigorously and scratches Afina, so expertly under her chin, that she knickers loudly in satisfaction before nibbling with affection at the boy's hair. "Yes, Majesty! I have already learned how to trot, and how to brush and saddle the horses. But I also learned how to clean out their poo." He says this last part with a wrinkled nose, before blanching and saying quickly, "I don't mind it though. Even if it is a bit smelly. Master says to win a horse's love and respect, you have to do it all." He boasts, his chest stuck out with pride.

"I am so very glad to hear of it, Mister Jeron! Keep up the excellent work and I will come visit you to see your progress for myself when I return." Jeron hops from foot to foot with glee as he hands me Afina's reins, stepping back before dropping a quick bow, as if just remembering that was what he was supposed to do. I laugh, and shake my head. It was a reassuring sight to see, the pure happiness of the child. *This is who you are fighting for. Whom you are to protect until your final breath.* The thought sobers me a little and I look to Isos and the other warriors who wait for our departure. I grin widely when I spot both Arne and Helene in their ranks. They had completed their initiation ritual with flying colors and at last became true Nefriti. They return the smile and I turn forward again, feeling a sudden surge of anticipation of the battle to come. The slice of vengeance I might be able to finally level upon King Tanth. "I must go, Mister Jeron. Be well!" I nudge Afina in the direction of the castle gates that begin to groan open. But then a silent tug has me hesitate and I instead move Afina over to where Patryk stands nearby. Confused, he meets me part of the way. "See that young man there?" I incline my head to where Jeron waves enthusiastically at each of the warriors that pass him. Patryk follows my line of sight, finding the boy, before nodding. "I would like you to take over his studies. I want him trained as you and Ivrik were." I say, quietly enough so only he can hear. It takes a few breaths before full understanding of my intention makes his brows shoot upwards in surprise. He again turns to look at Jeron. This time with a different eye.

"Absolutely." Patryk says, finally with a soft smile. "It has been too long since we have had a child in the castle. Athene will be thrilled."

"Do what you can to keep it quiet. I don't want pressure falling on the boy until he is ready, and of course, with the threat of enemies—" Patryk stops me with a raised hand.

"I understand. I will speak with his parents and, if they are amenable, I shall take him in as my own, as my mentor did with me."

I nod in thanks and with one last goodbye, and a final wave at Jeron, I leave Yvonya Castle. But this time I don't look back.

Isos is *furious* with me. I sigh in exasperation at my glowering friend, but don't back down. We had made it to Naro quickly and without anything wild happening. Thank Jera for that. With about an hour remaining of daylight, I am doing all I can to get Isos established and settled in Whitich Castle before I had to leave. I had been somewhat prepared for a semi-large force to be waiting for us when we arrived, but then been thrown and impressed when Naro's steward had informed us that a slight adjustment in the plan had been made in order to usher us along to Charobi even more swiftly. As stubborn, antagonistic, and somewhat flippant as my King of Paith had been—Ivrik was *adored* by his people. His death had each of them roaring for revenge. Indeed, the elder steward, Edar Blois, was quivering with rage as he explained what little they did know about the falling of Charobi and Dulen. Thankfully, he had welcomed Isos warmly, and promised to help his new king adjust. The appropriate ceremonies and celebrations would have to wait for now, however, but Edar assured me that he would spread the word about the new appointment and help the transition go smoothly. In exchange, I had to promise him I would water the dust with the blood of every Mirinthian soldier that now held Charobi. I was partly awed, and partly horrified at how bloodthirsty the aged man was. But it again only illustrated the love and loss, now felt by the entire kingdom for my friend. After a bit of meandering and distracted rants, I manage to pull Edar back to the matter of the soldiers that were meant to be waiting, and what he had meant by an adjustment. With a sly grin, he explained that he had the floating barges pulled up to the docks. The ones normally used to transport large amounts of livestock up and down the rivers throughout the kingdom.

"That way it will ship you, the army, and the horses down the river through the night. Now you can sleep, eat, and then de-board and continue on horseback the remaining length, rather than staying here through the night." I stare at the man in awe, before laughing and thanking him profusely for his helpful strategizing. He only blushes and ducked his head, suddenly bashful. "I am glad you are not angry with me for taking such liberties and moving them there. I only aim to help, you see. Those bastards took my King." The old man tears up, unabashed as they well over and flow down his cheeks. He waves off my feeble attempts at comfort and bustles us along through the castle.

The difficult part now? I had to make sure Isos remained here, rather than coming with me and the warriors to Charobi. And it was not going well. Up until about fifteen minutes ago, I had begun to say goodbye, as casually as I could. I had been managing to avoid any mention of the tiny detail of the plan where he would *not* be accompanying me to Charobi.

"Isos," I start, rubbing my temples that throb incessantly from stress. "Can't you see? Tesindren can not lose another King." My voice is soft, but clear enough that he falls quiet. "My people are strong—of mind and heart— but that is a loss that I am not sure they can take. Look at Edar, if you do not believe me. Look at the people in the streets that are dressed in black." Indeed, nearly every house and person we had passed upon our approach to the beautiful city and looming castle standing above the silvery blue lake were dressed or draped in the deep black of mourning. "Look at me." I whisper to him as I gesture down at myself and the colorless attire I worn since learning of Ivrik's demise. "If this does prove to be a trap, or if we fail, I need you *here*. I need Paith's King to be in Naro. Or everything along this river, including Alessandra, will fall. Swiftly."

I can see I have made my point as Isos's shoulders slump in surrender and he sits heavily into a nearby chair. Edar had brought us to a sprawling set of rooms, ones so big that Isos had immediately looked uncomfortable. I picture the small home he had made of his Captain's barracks back in Alessandra and stifle a laugh. They were not Ivrik's rooms. No, I had been clear in my request that Isos would require a *new* suite. Eventually Ivrik's things would be removed, and we would all have to move on. But not yet. And knowing Isos, he felt the same about such matters. "Swear to me." I start. His sudden intensity breaks into my wandering thoughts. "Swear to me you will return and you will not ride to your death—even if it means forfeiting Türë, Charobi, and the others." I swallow hard and suddenly find it near impossible to meet Isos's unwavering gaze. This was not a request from a King to his High Queen. This was from one friend to another. In the request I can see his own grief from the loss of Ivrik, and with a pang, I belatedly realize probably many other friends that had fallen in the recent battles. It hadn't occurred to me until now that he had likely known all of them. After all, every soldier passed through Alessandra for training at some point or another. Though he was not draped completely in black, he was carrying his own weight of grief that I had not truly seen until now. And he too could not lose another person close to him.

It was that realization that has me speaking the words with vehemence. "I swear I will return. I will not die at Charobi." With that vow made, he hangs his head, before breathing deeply and standing. Suddenly taller than I ever remember him being before. I realize with heart wrenching pride, that he has truly accepted and stepped into the role of King. The figure he told me he never expected, or dreamed, he would be.

"Well then, you better go." He smirks suddenly before adding, "Or I have no doubt Edar will gladly lead the charge tomorrow." I snort a laugh that is definitely not very queenly.

Looping my arm in his, we leave his rooms and make our way through the nearly empty castle. "Yes, I am quite surprised he hasn't somehow already slipped through into Mirinth and slit King Tanth's throat himself!" I try to remember the way to the stables, where Afina waits for me. It had been a struggle to take her, now feeling like she was my last gift from Ivrik. One I was terrified to part with. But in the end, I couldn't bring myself to leave my trusted mare. It seemed somehow fitting that she would be there with me, to assist in leading the charge to win back the city her original master had loved so dearly.

"I hope you don't mean *me?*" The bemused voice of Edar comes chuckling from a darkened hallway that we pass, making both Isos and I jump and shriek in surprise, then laugh and apologize in embarrassment. For our reaction, and for the comment we had made before that which had been overheard by the brilliant steward.

He waves off our apologies with a humored smile before he winks at Isos and responds with a glint in his eyes. "I would never kill that horrible man myself. No, I would just truss him up like a pig and deliver him to Her Majesty to do with as she pleases!" Isos and I purse our lips together to stifle our laughter, even as Edar spins on a heal and takes off back down the hallway toward the stables. Isos and I share a quiet snicker before following after the surprisingly quick paced man.

Isos gives me one last embrace before our somber parting. I try not to think too much about his pale face, tinged the color of watered down pea soup, as he watches me and the handful of Nefriti drift away. Sitting on the barge now, I watch the sky grow darker by the minute until the pinpricks of stars begin to speckle its navy canvas. In spite of what is coming, I can't help but feel somehow relaxed for this moment. Rather than filled with nervousness that will certainly come tomorrow, I feel more serene. Probably because, for once, there was nothing more I could do at the moment. I lean my head back against Afina's warm side. She had not been overjoyed at boarding the barge, but once on, she had quickly found a spot against the boat's stanchion and laid down with an exhausted huff. I had pushed her far and hard recently, and like the gift she was, she did so without complaint. Well, some complaints, but she still did whatever I asked. I scratch her neck and she leans into my attention with enthusiasm. I smile at her, reaching for a bag of apples I had brought aboard for the horses. A tasty bribe should the need arise to distract a nervous mount. Even though Afina looks at me with tired eyes, her ears flick with excitement at the apple I hold out to her. After crunching it happily, she bends back and nuzzles my cheek before returning to her original position and falling asleep quickly.

"She is like a big dog." A nearby Nefriti comments, humored by my horse's personality. I laugh softly and nod. He lounges against the port rail across from me, helmet gleaming in the light of a lantern. I squint to get a better look at his somewhat familiar face. Suddenly, it hits me. It was the same man who had stood outside the door, worried for me when Eganël had brought me to my room nearly unconscious.

"I know you!" I blurt out. "I thought you were one of the castle guards?"

The man nods, a heavy frown on his face, made even darker by the shadows cast by the lantern as it swings in the wind. "No, Your Majesty. But I can see why you would think that. I have been stationed in the castle since we joined the rotation to help the castle guards. But I requested Captain Isos—er… King Isos and Elder Dakar, to let me come with the group leaving today. I—I have family in Charobi. A sister, her husband, and all five of their children." He grimaces and suddenly finds the helmet in his lap extremely interesting.

"I am so sorry." I say miserably. It is all I really can say. There is no reassurance I can give him. Everyone here had been told what we were walking into. We had calculated that the risk of the information getting out to be less than the shock of all these men coming upon the ashy remains of a city they had all, no doubt, spent time in. And in this case, had family in. They needed to be aware of what exactly we were going to be walking into beforehand. While I had seen the remains of the city, I had no idea what to expect of the fortress' condition.

"I am sorry for your loss as well, Your Majesty."

"Please call me Evara." I ask with a smile and shake of my head. "I am not so formal or fancy. The man nods, though doesn't look so sure. "What is your name? I meant to get it earlier, and to thank you for watching out for me—but I fell asleep." I admit with a light laugh.

"Yantley, Eryn Yantley, Maj—Queen Evara." He corrects himself.

"Well, Viktu Yantley, it is a pleasure to meet you, though I wish it were under better circumstances." His mouth tugs up with a hint of a smile, a half-hearted one that doesn't reach his eyes.

"Aye, but it is said that hard times come to those who can handle it. Gotta just hope that Jera has given us enough to get through it." He replies.

I hesitate. "I don't mean to pry, but I remember seeing you at King Ivrik's death ceremony too." It hadn't dawned on me before now. He nods and sighs deeply, fidgeting with a strap hanging beside him. "How did you know him?" Before I can help it, my gaze is drawn to his chest where the now concealed *Ynyra* line for Ivrik is hidden. He smirks, knowing the truth behind my question. The real one that I was too polite to ask.

"You want to know why I was marked for Ivrik?" He asks bluntly. I swallow, but shrug.

"I know who he was to me, but to no one else. I never thought to ask him before, and now..." *Its too late.* Thankfully he doesn't seem offended and nods with understanding.

"Ivrik was my partner, back when he was Nefriti. We trained together, fought together, and bled together." He pauses looking up at the night sky. "I had all sisters, but Ivrik, he became my brother. It seemed only right that he be marked as such. I will never forget him." He says, voice somber and weary, before leaning his head back against the sun-bleached wood and closing his eyes. Even with the topic of conversation taking a sad turn, one word he said still lingers in my mind, even as his snores begin to fill the barge.

"Hope." I mouth to myself, before leaning back into Afina's rising and falling side and shutting my own eyes, waiting for sleep to come.

fifty-six

Against my will, I gag loudly—even though I had just reprimanded one of the five Nefriti with me for doing exactly the same thing. I flinch at the echo the sound makes and grimace apologetically at the man, who smirks back at me. Those I'd chosen to join me for the task had declared they were honored. Until I informed them we would be infiltrating through the sewer. I attempt to take a centering breath, but immediately abandon *that* when I remember exactly what was in the air.

I am going to need one hundred scalding baths to remove any part of my skin that came into contact with this horrid place. In all my planning and thinking of going in through the sewer pipe, for some reason, it hadn't occurred to me that we were going to be traipsing *through a sewer pipe.* I hear another dry heave come from behind me and I grit my teeth. It was taking forever, much longer than I had ever wanted to spend among rotting refuse and waste. Every sound and footstep echoes a thousand times, so we move extremely carefully to ensure there is no sign of our approach. We didn't need to give them any time to prepare for what was coming. The grand total of six that makes up our party were more than I originally wanted, but even I couldn't expect King Tanth or his military leaders to be *that* foolish to not station someone at the place where they had slipped in. So I had begrudgingly agreed that more would be necessary to ensure that, even if something went wrong, the entire attack at least would not fail.

Something squishes beneath my boot and I tense, frozen in horror at the list of unspeakable things it could be. Another heave rises against my will and I shudder. One positive thing about having to endure this disgusting path was I certainly wasn't thinking about what would happen next. Or even who would die today. It could be me. It could be all of us, if this was all a trap.

Which it probably was.

I feel a tap on my shoulder and catch a scream before it can slip out and give us all away. Turning to the others, I see something had distracted them in an off shooting pipe we had just passed to the right. Frowning, I join them and immediately the reek of the sewer and innumerable questionable liquids that now clings to every bit of skin and cloth are immediately forgotten. Not one hundred paces from where we look out of the ground level grate sits a shackled and obviously beaten Türë. Aside from being tied to a post, he appears to be in one piece still. The execution had not yet occurred, thank Jera.

"The General!" Arne hisses, gripping the bars as if he could pull them apart to get to Türë.

"Quiet." An older man, a superior to the others, reminds him. Arne closes his mouth with a snap and retreats a few paces back into the shadows beside us. We were far enough into the darkness of the pipes that we couldn't be seen. Not unless someone dropped to their knees and stared directly in, but still close enough we could see the overall scene of the courtyard beyond. Too many people linger nearby to try to get out here.

"We need to go." I breathe, but my insistence is only half-hearted. I suddenly felt that if I stepped out from view of him, Türe would disappear once more from me.

The older man, Viktu Paden, if I remember right, nods in agreement and steps up to touch each of the other Nefriti. Pulling their attention back to him and I. Firm, yet understanding, Viktu Paden risks a whisper to the other four men who face us. Viktu's Jarvis, Aleri, and Boath, I recall from the quick morning introduction. I see the conflict I feel reflected in their own eyes. Türe had trained each of these men personally before they had been selected to join the Nefriti. Though I had my own issues with him, their dedication to the General was hard to overlook or begrudge. It had been the reason there had been so many volunteers for this task.

"—get him out. But we have to do it the right way, or it will all be for naught." Viktu Paden concludes. Turning their attention back to me, I nod at them, and hope they know how much it pains me to leave him behind, too. Though for different reasons. That thought drives my steps faster as I turn and resume our trek through the filth to the grate that should not be barred. This one is supposed to lead to what should be an empty alley beside the central gate house. That was our target. The full might of the company of warriors and soldiers we had brought with us now waits, hidden just out of sight from the scope of Charobi's wall. All we needed to do was raise the gates as quietly as we can and barricade ourselves in the gatehouse. I had tasked the Tomyris and Magnar with leading the charge. With inflicting their wrath upon the Mirinthians inside.

A shiver of recognition had wracked my body when I had joined them this morning for the battle preparations. Though I had experienced them not long ago outside of Vante, it was a foreign, yet familiar, experience with twenty-four of us. Aside from Arne, Helene, and myself, all the rest had many *Ynrya* lines slashing down their arms from their previous victories. It was in the air, a feeling I had not entirely felt through my training. Not until now. I was in the presence of ancient warriors. Even if they were younger than I was, their spirit and that of the ceremonies that tethered us to our predecessors were tangible. I did not fail to notice how even our own soldiers had shifted nervously when we rejoined them, intimidating and terrifying with our painted masks of war. This time it had been the other Elder Magnar and Elder Makal who performed the ceremony. As eerie as Elder Ygrette's voice had been, the baritone growl of Elder Makal had set a different tone. This time we were not to be the saviors. We were the warriors of deliverance. The hand of wrath and vengeance.

My steps falter, as does the men who follow closely behind me. The grate that should be unblocked and unbarred now is completely closed off by a combination of newly set thick metal bars and a wall of piled stones. Well, there goes the original plan.

Fucking hell.

Had they already heard from those outside Eludar that we had figured out the cause of their success? Or were they just smarter than we had given them credit for? My mind races, trying to adjust our plan that now appears to be falling apart by the second. The knee high 'water' standing in the pipe sloshes as I shift my weight and suddenly I inhale sharply as an idea hits me. An instinct I immediately regret.

"Freeze. Stop moving." I whisper, hands fluttering with nerves as the others obey immediately. Either because they were well trained, or because my tone was shocking enough that they obliged without a thought. I look down to examine the liquid that flows back the way we had come. As disgusting as it is, there was a barely detectable current that moves through the sludge. It had to originate somewhere other than where we stand. Possibly another way out. I set off in the direction the current flows and, in a few minutes, find another opening. This one too is barred, but at least it isn't barricaded off completely. If I could somehow get the metal bars out of the way, it would still be big enough for us to get through. But I would have to somehow bend or melt the metal bars, each one as thick as a pike handle. We were running out of time, and every moment we lingered here, we risked two main things. One, the army outside would assume we failed and adapt accordingly. That plan risked many more lives, if not all of us. Two, the longer we stand here at the mouth of this tunnel, the more we risk being spotted by a passerby.

For the first time since entering, I contemplate doing what I had promised Isos and myself that I *would not* do.

"Go around the corner and stay out of sight." I order, barely above a whisper, but still loud enough I flinch at the echo before scolding myself for the misstep. They do as I say and the second they are hidden, I delve into my magic. Nervous and shaky to give myself over to my volatile fire, I close my eyes and picture Türë. I use him to draw my focus and control. My anger. Calling on the countless hours he had patiently worked with me, all while betraying me. Even if it had led to disaster, it is those thoughts that center me now as the bars a few paces in front of me begin to glow red hot.

❃ ❃ ❃ ❃ ❃

We emerge, blessedly, onto an empty side street. Each of us taking a deep, relieved breath of the fresh air before remembering the need for stealth. We slip again into the shadows and try to figure out exactly where we were now. Of course, it is a little awkward when I ask who had spent the most time in Charobi and knew it the best. They all had looked at me, obviously not thinking of the fact that my memories of Charobi were wiped clean. Instead, I delve deep into my mind, trying to conjure up something from my hours of staring ceaselessly at the blueprints and maps of the fortress we now stand in. I look up to count the towers that border the closest outer wall. *Six towers. Okay, that is the east wall...* I turn to the wall that connects it. Sure enough, eight towers sit atop it. I grin to myself, making each of the men exchange nervous glances.

"That is the north wall that we need to aim for." I point it all out for them. "But we need to go down this street, south, to reach Türë." I chew my lip, contemplating something extremely foolish. My gut tugs and I know it is Jera, giving me a sign. I would have to make some adjustments. "You five get to the gatehouse and raise it. I am going after the General." They immediately protest, as I expect, though more forcefully than I could have predicted.

"Absolutely fuckin not." Viktu Paden snaps at the same time Arne does, obviously so surprised by my words that any sense of propriety of what to say to their queen goes out the window. If we weren't in the situation we were, I would laugh at their reactions. But when another, more urgent tug pulls at me, I know my time is running out.

"There is no time for this." I huff an impatient sigh, mostly to myself. "Look, I am not asking. Either you will obey your Queen's order, or you will commit treason." I cross my arms over my chest and stand tall, daring them to push the matter. "What will it be?"

I know I have succeeded when they each shake their head in exasperation, but give no further argument. Viktu Paden glowers at me fully, but doesn't protest further.

"What are you planning to do, if you don't mind me askin?" He asks.

"I have to find the General and free him. Fast. I have a bad feeling that if we don't get him out beforehand, he will be the first put down. But we also still *need* to get that gate open. I will do what I can to give you some distractions while I'm at it, too." Viktu Paden's brow furrows, and he starts to say something. I cut him off. "Don't worry, they won't know it is me." I call upon the fire that jumps to the surface at the slightest thought. I stifle my wince of fear at that, and the realization that my melting of the iron bars hadn't depleted its strength. Not at all. Rather, it had only served to awaken it. *Well, I need it. So I am just going to have to roll with it.* Thankfully, the reminder of my power reassures them, or at least stifles any remaining arguments. Only Arne stares me down. I knew he was going to be harder to shake. Smothering the flame with my other palm, like I would a candle, I gesture with my chin to the wall I had pointed out as the north. "Wait until you seal yourself in the gatehouse before setting the signal and lifting the gate." I remind them, before I take off down the adjoining street and vanishing. I send a silent prayer for their success before turning my full attention to the pull that now yanks incessantly at me. I hear another pair of steps behind mine, and don't have to look to know who it is. Nobody else would so openly disobey an order. I don't stop though. I don't have time to argue. I turn down street after street, looking for Türë. He was here! Somewhere. I had *just* seen him. The fortress is nearly empty, much to my surprise. I had expected Mirinthian soldiers patrolling the streets, or at least there to be *some* presence. I at last come across the post where he had been tethered. The post that now stands empty, aside from a large metal ring set deep into it, showing the still fresh blood from Türë's numerous beatings. I hear Arne curse in frustration behind me. Fear twists my insides, then suddenly I hear it. Cheering. I walk in a daze for a few steps, trying to make some sense of what I was walking into. Then I take off at a sprint again when I hear the cheering screams intermixed with chants of *Kill! Kill! Kill!* I get as close to the crowd as I dare, then gape at the scene in front of me. Like Alessandra, Charobi Fortress had its own training pits and dueling arena. But in the days that Mirinth had claimed the stronghold as their own, they had taken the initiative to build up the walls surrounding it, filling them with benches. After meeting Ionel, I had read up on the histories of the kingdom before Tesindren. They hosted week long tournaments and games they referred to as gladiator fights. But unlike the ones Ionel participated in, where death was a rare occurrence and not the desired outcome—this arena played by different rules. These battles were to the death.

Bloodied and near stripped of their clothing, men in the center ring fought for their lives. I didn't have to know their names to know that these were my people. The ones who had been left to do whatever they could to survive. Apparently in Mirinth's mind, that was to bludgeon each other to death for their entertainment. I choke on a sob, one more from rage than sadness. I at last find him. Chained at the feet, with despair filling his eyes, he fights against the very soldiers he had trained and known for star-cycles. My heart shatters, forgetting the betrayal and the lies in that moment. I had to get him and the others out of there.

Now.

I take a steadying breath through my furious tears and look for the perfect source for a distraction. I scan the makeshift stadium and map the quickest route to Türe, who ducks a swing a little too slowly, clear evidence of his exhaustion and dwindling will. I feel the breaths flying by, way too fast, as what little time I do have is chipped away with each breath of hesitation. I get as close as I dare before placing a shaking palm onto one of the support beams that holds a large section of the spectator benches aloft.

"What are you doing?" Arne whispers impatiently, eyes flicking from me back to the spectacle in the pit. I ignore him, trying to focus.

"Please Jera." I beg, and I dip a finger into the pool of magic that surges upwards. Suddenly the feeling of a fresh, cool stream washes up my body and cools the inner fire that had begun to surge. I let it douse all but a little thimbleful of a spark. It catches almost immediately and I pause only long enough to make sure it doesn't flare out. Instead, I grin wickedly at the flames that begin to worm their way up the post towards the men who sit screaming for blood above me. *Thank you, Jera.* I send up before I am on the move again. Leaving Arne behind, I take off at a run in the direction I had planned. Heading back to Türë and the others. To get them free and stop whatever blade would fall when they realized that Charobi's rightful inhabitants had come to reclaim what was ours. The jeering shouts of heartless Mirinthians fill the air. No one is looking as I slip into through the crowd and end up at the shoulder high wall that blocks me from the pit. I take it at a running sprint, and feel the power of my Sidhe body surge. Another gift I had not appreciated or even thought of much until now. Pushing off the nearest bench, I vault over the stacked stone barrier before catching myself in a practiced roll, then onto my feet. The men fighting in the pit all turn to face me, bleary-eyed and obviously confused. They take in the lines of paint and my warrior braids and their eyes flare with recognition and exhausted hope. Around us, the crowd hasn't even noticed the newest addition to the fighters, let alone realized that I am heavily armed. Their attention instead is drawn to flames that now lick up the stands and across their seats.

Adorned in a solid iron battle crown, and still reeking of the sewage that cakes every inch of my legs, I don't look away from my people, who lower their weapons once they realize who it is that has come for them. Then *he* steps into view, the clanking of his chains seem deafening.

Türë.

I stare him down. Now that I am face to face with him again, all my thoughts swirl in a frenzied jumble. I want to scream at him with one breath, but then in the next I want to wrap him in my arms and tell him I forgive him. I don't look away, my sword hanging limply in my hand, worried that, if I even blinked, the spell that had been cast in the space separating us would break. He rubs his eyes, hard enough to hurt, and blinks rapidly as if he didn't believe that it was truly I that stands in front of him. Then a horn sounds, echoing ominously off of every surface and the entire crowd stills and silences. Now I grin viciously as my gaze turns to the Mirinthian's, who suddenly stare down at me as a different kind of cheering fills the air. A single word is shouted from someone atop the wall before an arrow punches through his throat and chaos erupts.

Nefriti!

Orders are shouted and a flurry of armed men rush towards the fighters, who still stand gaping at me in disbelief. But they still don't fully realize that an armed, trained, and frankly, *royally pissed off* queen stands among them. And not just any queen. The Nefriti were already here.

I was already here.

Death and vengeance had come for them all.

I raise my sword just as the first Mirinthian soldier runs for me. His eyes flick first to my body, confused that a woman now was among what had been exclusively male fighters. Then they land on the spiked band of cold iron that graces my brow and, when they drift down my horns to the sharp black stripes that line my face, he pales and pisses himself with fear. Understanding too late who and what I am. I still grin devilishly as he dares to reach for his sword. Too late. I snap into fluid movement and the man's head flies ten feet from his limp body, just as the rest of the soldiers that remain in the area surge towards us. To their credit, my men, even exhausted, beaten, starving, and armed with only wooden clubs, give a roar of defiance and they rush to aid their queen. Together, we collide with the Mirinthians.

I fight towards Türë. My sense of urgency skyrocketing. He was still chained and, even with his own advantages of being a Sidhe, he was increasingly vulnerable at the moment. Just the few glimpses I had of him, now and from back in the tunnel, it was clear he had been through hell. Mirinth knew he was my General and confidant, and they had treated him accordingly.

I am too distracted looking for Türë, and a soldier I spot too late launches a deadly pointed spear at me. I move to lift my sword to block, but not fast enough. I shudder as a shock floods me and I clasp at the stinging in my side. I gasp for breath and brace for the agony, trying to catch my breath, waiting for the full pain to hit me. Two Tesindren's closest to me dive to my side, but I can only barely make out their words as my ears ring. I pull my hand away from where it had been holding the source of my pain —prepared for the grievous amount of my life blood sure to be staining it.

Instead, there is only the barest scratch on the exterior of my drakonskein battle dress. Probably a bruise beneath, but nothing like it should have been. In a daze, I look down at the two shirtless and bruised Tesindren's who kneel beside me with open anguish. They turn to the others, shouting for help. I understand then, as their bodies shift to the side. Time seems to freeze as I at last find him.

Türë lays in the dirt, the thick silver spear sticks through his stomach and out of his back. I fall to my knees beside him, my hands fluttering over his body. I realize then he had seen the blow, and intercepted it. The only wound I received from what should have been a killing blow was from the mere tip of the blade that had gone through Türë. *I need to heal him.* The thought shudders through me as I think of how much of a toll this wound will take on my energy. It had taken nearly all of me to heal Ionel's skin deep injuries the first day I had discovered the healing side of my power. And that had been after working with my magic *every single day.* I feel my stomach drop at the thought of how difficult it will be to heal this complex of a wound. My attention is pulled from this however as the man who delivered the blow laughs with an undeniably evil cackle, his eyes flashing a solid black, before pulling out another sword from a corpse laying near him.

"Mine." I growl, shoving to my feet, my hate for this man boiling over as I look at Türë who pants in clear agony from where he lays on the ground. I would heal him. I had no other choice if I wanted answers from him.

First, however, I am going to kill this man.

fifty-seven

"You." I raise a hand and level a finger at the man who had stabbed Türë in my place. Some part of my mind notes the man's finery and the lengthy line of medals that are pinned on his uniform. I consider his use. Whether it would be worth the effort to *not* kill him, but to take him alive and use him as a bargaining chip. As they had used Türë against me. But when I look again at Türë, who begins to shudder and cough, my rage surges and my self-control flickers. He spits a glob of red-colored saliva into the dust.

"Get him out of here." I bark at the Tesindren's closest to me. They hesitate, but then after a pointed glare, they join the rest who surround Türë and begin to carefully lift him onto a nearby plank of wood as a makeshift gurney. Türë groans miserably, and he starts to say something to me. I can't make it out though before the men close in around him, disappearing from the fighting ring and into the fray filling the fortress. I know Arne is somewhere around here, and I hope he too makes it out okay. But I have to block it all out now. The Mirinthian man, not ten paces from me, now steals all of my focus. I cock my head, returning his mad grin, before he takes the first step. Surprisingly, the man fights well for a human. It was clear he was well-trained and ruthless. He had to be, to get an upper hand on Türë as he had, even with the cowardly blow he had dealt. There is no honor in killing someone with their back turned, which was exactly what he had been trying to do.

Nevertheless, this man was a master. That was clear after the first few blows are exchanged. Each whistle of his sword through the air was quick and precise. Each step planned and meticulous. But I had my anger and my Sidhe blood roaring through my veins. Not to mention the knowledge and weight of all those counting on me to walk away from this. I think of the vow I had made Isos and I pray to Jera that I would not break it. That stiffens my resolve and I unleash on the man, each blow ringing through our bones. After the first hit, I see the glimmer of realization flicker in his eyes.

It was then he realized that today was the day he would die.

I feel eyes on me, and risk a glance out of the corner of my eye to its origin. To my elation, Arne, as well as a crowd of Tesindren soldiers and Nefriti, stand at the edge of the arena, watching their Queen whip through the air with the lethality and grace they had only heard of. A few had seen me in training, but only Arne had seen me on the battlefield. I had looked when I had returned to the castle and the final numbers had been tallied. That day, four hundred Mirinthians had fallen to my blade outside of Vante. Today, I would add another dozen here at Charobi. Including this man.

We had taken back the city, I realize with relief, when I see the watching crowd rapidly grow. It was the only explanation for the large group's unhurried demeanor. I spy over half of the Nefriti watching me, stone-faced, and I realize that this was my opportunity to prove to them as well as myself that I *did* deserve my place as a Tomyris. I was no fool. I had heard the whispers among them that I was no longer worthy to even be a Nefriti. This gives me even more strength than my anger had. From then it only takes a further five blows before the man's blade is knocked free from his quaking hand and it skitters into the dust fifteen paces away.

Rather than cheers of victory, an eerie calm spreads through the spectators. The man drops to his knees, breathing hard with rage tight across his chiseled face. I lower the tip of my blade to his throat.

"I wouldn't kill me." His voice is surprisingly pleasant, opposite of his disposition.

"And why the hell is that?" I ask with a rough, sarcastic laugh.

"I am valuable. Much more so alive than dead." I examine him, and see the truth in his cocky gaze, one he returns without a flinch.

"Do you know who was *valuable* to me?" I whisper, leaning down until my face is even with his. He pales at the monster he sees writhing inside me. "King Ivrik. The man who you killed and whose body you then tried to use as a *fucking bargaining chip* for Eludar's surrender. Oh, and the man you just ran through, not more than a few minutes ago. That man has been at my side for *centuries*." I snarl at him, and for the first time the man flinches with pure terror. I admit, it gives me the barest bit of satisfaction as I see him begin to shake with blood-chilling fear. "Tell me. Do you still think you are more valuable to your King than they were to me?"

He gulps nervously before answering. "I am the King's eldest son, the Crown Prince."

Fuck.

He *is* valuable. I sigh, and it takes every ounce of my self control, but I slam my sword into its sheath. Irritated that I cannot kill him, but satisfied with the fact that we had indeed succeeded today, I turn to go. We had secured a valuable bargaining chip. That was another victory I would take gladly. I turn on my heel to ask the soldiers still watching from the side to take him away. But then I catch the cocky, victorious grin that spreads wide across the Prince's face. White-hot rage explodes inside of me and, before I can stop it, the Crown Prince of Mirinth bursts into flames with a scream of pain I will never forget.

I know it should probably matter more to me than it does that I had just killed a man without truly meaning to. Especially since that man had ended up being the son of the King waging war against my kingdom. But truthfully, I am so worried about Türë, and thrumming with adrenaline, that I simply can't bring my focus back to the foul-smelling human pyre that I leave behind.

It still burns, but it no longer screamed.

I pass through the city to cheers from both the liberated and liberators as I pass. I do my best to smile and wave, but even with my half hearted excitement, the crowd's energy doesn't falter. It only takes a few minutes. My steps quick and my mood obvious enough that it stops those who would approach me. All I knew was that I needed to see him. To talk to him, honestly, for once, and maybe have a chance to fix all the pieces that still lay broken around us.

I spin at my name being called—somehow able to distinguish it from the rest of the people. Only later do I realize it is because of its tone. The helplessness, the fear, and the urgency. My eyes land on Viktu Yantley, the Nefriti I had spoken with on the barge that had carried us here. I was glad to see him in one piece, though slightly bloodied. I rush to him, and thankfully he answers my question before I can even voice it.

"Not good, Majesty. I don't know how he is still alive—but he has maybe minutes." His voice is choked from running through the dust as he tells me the opposite of what I want to hear. "The healer here says it mostly just went through muscle somehow, but it did nick his left lung. They say they cannot heal him." He tells me as I follow him, both of us breaking into a run towards where Türë lay dying.

I can't lose him, not now that we were finally so close to rescuing him. Not before I learned more. The tears drop thick and relentlessly down my face and I push through every heavy breath as I try to make it to Türë. I am so tired. Emotionally and physically. I wasn't ready for this, but if the healers couldn't help, then what I had left in me had to be enough. I could do it. I had to. Viktu Yantley turns off of the central street and barrels into a small, but newly built building that must be the sick house. Inside there stands rows of empty beds and walls filled with shelves of ointments, bandages and jars of herbs. At the end of the row, a small crowd of people gathers.

Not all the beds are empty. The crisp white sheets where they had placed Türë are now painted with bright red blood, so light it is nearly pink. The sound of wet coughing can be heard even over the cheering that comes from the street outside. Everything blurs and my vision fills with a white spotty film that I can't blink away. I reach out and grab for the closest thing—Viktu Yantley. He steadies me with a mumbled curse of surprise.

"I can't—" I whisper to him, my desperate gaze landing on his face, worn with his own grief that seems to age him. Tears form in his eyes and he blinks to clear them. I remember then what he had told me on the barge. He had likely lost a sister, brother-in-law, nieces and nephews here, as well as friends he had trained with. All in addition to Ivrik.

I am not the only one struggling with loss.

"You must, my Queen. You will regret it if you don't. Trust me." He rasps, and I nod after a moment, knowing that truth for myself. I had been denied a goodbye with Ivrik. I wouldn't lose that chance with Türë. Not when I was mere steps away. I give Viktu Yantley's arm a squeeze, hoping to convey both my thanks and my sympathies, before standing tall and moving to Türë's side. I take one look at his pale face, muddy hair, and blood-covered chest and lips before shoving it all down deep. I would lose it later. Right now, I needed to be present with my General, my friend. The one who had betrayed me, but also who had helped me.

I sink onto my knees beside the bed, ignoring everyone else gathered around. Their talking stops when they see me, but I don't care. One by one, they drift away, leaving us together in his final moments. I reach out and take Türë's hand, making his eyes fly open in surprise. They had been pursed shut tightly in pain, but they soften when they see me. In spite of that pain, and the hand of death that moves ever closer, the fool tries to sit up.

"No, no, stay where you are!" I stammer, and place a hand on his shoulder to keep him laying down.

"Let me— I need to kiss you—just once more." He chokes out, and blood specks spatter his lips. I bite down on a sob so hard that I taste my own blood.

"No, you are not going to talk of *once mores*. You are not going anywhere. We are going to go home, and you will be fine." He smiles at me with such sadness, before wincing in a pain that makes him gasp, then break out into a coughing choke. "Someone please! Come help him!" I shout in a desperate scream to the others who stand by the door. But none come to help.

There was nothing that could be done.

I turn back to stare into his familiar eyes, bright with agony and remorse. Shaking, I rise to my feet and bend down over him. I ignore the blood, and instead focus on his scent, his warmth, his love. I press my lips to his, just as I feel him still and give one last rasping breath.

I shove back, terrified and shriek at the eyes pressed shut and the chest that no longer rises. The hand now limp in mine.

"No!" I scream at Türe, slamming my palm into his chest. "You *do not* get to die. Do you understand?? I am going to heal you! You don't get to just *die!*" I hear the others running at me, and a firm hand grips me back, tugging me away from Türe. "No." I scream again, and feel only a hint of remorse when my despair shoots a spark of electricity into whomever holds me. The hand yanks back and I am again at Türe's side. "Jera— help me do this. Please!"

I have already given you everything you need. The familiar sad voice calls out in my mind. *What? A long life? Power I can barely control?* I can't help but feel unfounded anger to the Goddess who has given me more than I deserve.

Power you can control. Jera whispers before her presence vanishes again from my mind, as quickly as she came.

Another hand dares to grab at me, and I spin shouting at them, my fury and grief unleashed. "Get out!" I snarl. To not much surprise, they do. And fast. Maybe a minute has passed since Türe had ceased breathing, though it could be a star-cycle, the way time seems to flow. I turn back to his still body, raising my hand and sending one final thought to Jera for her help.

I call down each of the elements. Every one a gift from Jera and they pour into the room. Wind swirls, tugging at the blood-soaked sheets and Türë's loose hair. Flame sets each of the candles blazing and a sweat breaks out on my forehead as the temperature spikes. Lightning sparks in the air, crackling with life and energy. Water spills out of the pitcher that sits on the bedside table, cleansing the blood from both of our lips as it swirls around us. With one last scream that shreds my throat, I beg—no, command— them each to heal Türë. Water to soothe, refresh, and heal. Flame to bring the warmth back into his body. Wind to fill his lungs with air again. And lightning to spark energy back into his heart.

To bring him back to me.

fifty-eight

I wake, screaming and thrashing, looking around for the source of the pain. Begging for someone to help me. A voice curses voraciously before repeating my name as some attempt at calming me. It works, though the pain persists. But I recognize Isos, who lights a nearby candle and approaches me cautiously.

"Isos?" I croak, looking around and trying to place myself.

"You are in Naro." He says, only half of the explanation I need.

"Naro? How? And—" I wince at the roar of pain that wracks my body again as I clasp my hands into tight fists. "What happened?" I ask, slowly breathing through the agony until it is manageable, trying to piece any of my memories together.

"Well—" Isos begins carefully, sitting on the edge of the bed. "How much do you remember of the battle and aftermath?" I think on it silently, pushing my throbbing head far past its limits as I try to reorganize my scattered thoughts.

"I remember traipsing through the sewer as planned, and then finding out the tunnel we were looking for had been barricaded, so we rerouted to another entrance. We had spotted Türë down in the—" My heart stops suddenly. "Türë! Is he—?"

"He is alive." Isos says, though a strange look flashes across his face, trying to calm me before I can really lose my mind. I don't believe it. I can't. *He was dead when I—* "Please continue, then I will tell you all that *I* know." Isos pleads with me, pulling my mind back on track.

"Fine." I decide to give the quickest summary I can, but end up derailing as soon as everything begins to flood back in. "We had seen Türë a little earlier on our way through the sewer, so when we got into Charobi, I—um—" I shift, suddenly embarrassed and longing to apologize to those men. If there were any that still lived. "I ordered them—" I start, miserably. But Isos cuts me off.

"They told me about that little tantrum you threw. Go on." In his eyes, I see the irritation of the man who had been the head of my protection and Royal Guard for the last six star-cycles. But I also saw in them my Underking, who now understood, at least a little, of how it felt to be constantly followed and fussed over.

"It wasn't a tantrum! It was not the time nor place for a debate on whether I needed babysat. Things needed to happen, and they required us splitting up. Either way, Arne followed me. Despite my threat." I straighten up, defensive of my decision, even if I still felt ashamed for threatening the men who simply cared for their Queen.

"Go on." Isos prompts again with an exasperated eye roll. It is then I see the deep shadows beneath his eyes, so dark they are the hue of a day old bruise.

"When did you sleep last, Isos?" I chide, suddenly worried about my friend.

"More than an hour? When you arrived here unconscious six days ago."

My jaw drops at that. "Six days?"

"Yes. Now please continue, so I may tell you what I know and finally get my ass to bed." He bites, even as a yawn punctuates his point.

"Well, the men took off to the gatehouse so that we could still let the others in. And I followed the pull that kept tugging me to what I knew was Türë." Isos's eyes raise in surprise at that, but he doesn't interrupt. "When I found him again, they had a group of our captured soldiers, along with Türë, in a fighting pit. They were their *entertainment*. All our men had were clubs and their fists. Türë was even still chained at his feet, bloody and beaten." I shudder at the memory of how horrible it was, to be so close yet unable to run down there and free them straight away. "I knew I had to play it smart, so I set fire to one of the posts and once people started to see the smoke, they were no longer paying attention to the fighters in the pits. So I slipped right in. I was in by the time the men on the walls sounded the alarm about our troops." I clench my eyes shut. "This is where it gets blurry." I try to explain as well as I can about Türë's mortal wound and then dueling the man who had stabbed him. I *fail* to mention the identity of the man or the fact I had accidentally set him ablaze. I decide to keep that information to myself. At least for now. Mostly because I didn't want the lecture, but I also didn't want even Isos to know how the deadly the slip of my control had been. Not until I can think on it. I explain how I had found Türë, fading quickly, and then how he had died. The tears from my sorrow still fall, even though Isos had told me he was somehow alive. *Alive.* "That is all I remember, then I woke up here." I conclude with a deep breath, sitting back against the oak headboard with a hiss of pain.

"Well, now I suppose it is my turn." He launches into a story that happened, parallel with my own, told to him by both Viktu Yantley and Viktu Paden. "The men who accompanied you into the fortress made it to the gate house, relatively unharmed. One took an arrow to the thigh, but got a healer to it in time. They barricaded themselves in, as you ordered, and raised the gate without any alarm being sounded. It wasn't until our force was nearly at the walls before a sentry realized what was happening and sounded the alarm, as you heard. From what I understand, our warriors and calvary swept in and found little resistance. The ones who did try to stop us were quickly cut down, and then they went to go find you. They arrived just in time to see the others that had been captive carrying away Türë, who was pouring blood, and then watched as you brought your revenge down upon the man. Whoever he was. They said they didn't dare interfere, and instead could only watch as you leveled the Mirinthian, then talked with him for a minute or so. They said it looked as if you two came to an agreement. But then he smiled. All *prickishly,* was the word they agreed upon. Then you stiffened, blinked and the man went up in flames." Isos' piercing eyes stay locked on me.

Fuck. Well there went that secret. He already knew well of my struggles with magic, but still I felt ashamed. I know he wants me to admit I did not have the control I thought I had gained after using it with Eganël to create the messenger birds. Instead I can only return his gaze without comment. I was not in the mood to be chastised right now—even if I deserved it.

He only sighs before continuing, running a hand through his hair and leaning forward onto his elbows. "The group carrying Türë made it to what had been Charobi's infirmary." My attention catches on the *what had been,* but I don't interrupt. "There it was clear that he had mere minutes, between his weakness from starvation and torture, losing so much blood from the wound, and the blade having pierced his lung. Even his advanced healing could not keep up. So they set out to find you, because that was what he kept ordering. Even on his deathbed, the General was quite ferocious and insistent, apparently." He chuckles, though unenthusiastically. "I guess Viktu Yantley was able to find you, and that is where your stories join. From his account, I can now fill *you* in." We both inhale slowly, before huffing a laugh at our harmony. I knew this next part—Türë surviving or not—was going to be awful. Even through the blur and numbness that surround the flickering bit of memory I did have, I could still feel the sharpness of despair that suffocated me. "They said he died in your embrace... and that upon realizing that, you lost your mind with grief. You started screaming and wailing at Türë, at Jera, at everyone—in an unfamiliar language, they said. When they tried to intercede, you ended up lighting up the poor fellow who grabbed you." I flinch at that and the foggy events beginning to resurface.

"Is he okay?" I whisper, remembering the poor man who had tried to hold me and calm me.

Isos laughs, though it doesn't reach his exhaustion glazed eyes. "Yes. He shocked anyone he came into contact with for about four days afterwards, and a bit of his hair is prematurely grey now, but his children got a great laugh out of the trick." I feel the barest sliver of relief, then wave him on before wincing at the pain from my bandaged arms—which he had not yet explained. After all, I was supposedly fire proof. His eyes flick to my arms at my flinch, but continues on. "You demanded everyone leave, and then suddenly it was like a great whirlwind came in and it shoved everyone out. A few dared look through the window, but were thrown back when a bolt of lightning struck the building and caught it on fire. Everyone began to panic and tried to get to you and Türë, but it was no use. They could only watch, with the other horrified soldiers who gathered, as the infirmary burned down with their Queen and General inside. It was to everyone's great surprise that, when the smoke finally cleared, there remained a solitary trundle bed with a somehow breathing

General and a blistered and burnt, nearly to a crisp, Queen." He shakes his head in annoyance. "I was summoned immediately to come help. They knew I was your previous Captain of the Guard and knew best how to *handle* you. You were shocking, and scorching anyone or anything that came near. A few daring men were able to slip in and carefully shuffle Türë away, but no one risked coming too close to you." Isos sighs, and yawns again. "I apologize, but—" He grimaces with a look of shame. "I probably shouldn't have, but I didn't know what else to do. Please forgive me, but I had to inject you with abalmas root to negate your magic so we could help you." I probably should feel upset, or at least nervous that even one person had the ability to knock out my magic so easily. Even if it was someone I trusted implicitly. But I felt so relieved that he had the means and the right judgment to do so when he felt it was required.

"Isos, thank you. You do not need to apologize. I trust you when you say there was no other way. I would rather it be this way than someone get hurt due to my lack of control." Relief floods his tense, weary face.

"Before you go ahead and forgive me, you should know it had other effects this time." Again his gaze flicks down to my bandages. "In exerting so much power in reviving Türë— however you did it— it either drained your energy so fully that your body couldn't heal itself or—" He cuts off, looking unsure.

"Or what?" I prompt.

"Or it was payment for the revival. The power that they said you summoned that day... everyone says they had never seen anything like it. Even hardened Nefriti admitted they were both awestruck and terrified of such a display."

"Payment." I sigh and look down at myself. "Well if it was payment, it was worth it if it worked. He truly lives?" I ask, softly.

"Yes. He lives. He is very weak, and the healers say it will take time before he is back to his full strength. But he lives. They also say that your blisters will heal once the dose I gave you is out of your system, but—" Isos trails off, not meeting my eyes.

"Just tell me." I plead.

"It is likely the scars will remain. Whether from the dose I gave you and it allowed them to set permanently in your body, or if it truly is the mark of your payment—I don't honestly know. But they will remain. All the healers say so."

I think this over, and repeat. "If it worked, it was worth it." Because to me it was. The pain, the scars, the fear—if that was the cost of keeping Türë alive then I would gladly pay it again. At that thought however, a silent warning rings through my heart, warning me coldly against ever trying it again. I shudder at the sensation, and it takes a moment to recollect my bearings.

"Can I see him?" I ask after a minute.

Isos hesitates. "I think you need some more rest. It is extremely late." My heart sinks with disappointment, but I give in. Even though I was worn out already, it was more for Isos's sake that I let it go. For now. It was clear he was ready to fall asleep right where he sat and was certainly in no state to help me wobble to wherever they were keeping Türë. "In the morning." He promises with a gentle smile and a tender pat on a foot hidden beneath my sheets. I nod and shuffle down further into the blankets, feeling the lure of their comfort, though I have to breathe through the sting of my blistered arms. My eyes flutter shut as I hear the squeak of a nearby bed and they fly open again. I sit up a moment and squint through the darkness to see Isos stretching out in a cot I had not noticed before. Placed only a few feet to my right.

"What are you doing?" I ask into the silence.

"Sleeping. Shhh." He grumbles at me.

"In here?" I ask, surprised. This castle had nearly as many rooms as Yvonya Castle in Alessandra.

"Yes. Because I don't trust that *you* will stay in bed once I leave." He snips, and I snicker. *Damn it. He knows me to well.* Because that was exactly what I had planned to do. "Goodnight Evara." He whispers, drifting into sleep. And I knew I could sneak out as soon he fell into deep sleep, but I decide to not betray my friend's obviously limited trust in me. Instead I lay back down. Even with my mind racing about what I had done, and Türë's miraculous recovery, sleep overtakes me just as Isos begins to snore.

fifty-nine

I groan awake, my arms stinging again as my movement cracks and stretches the delicate skin. I squint, bleary-eyed, at the rays of sun that stream in. Though meager, they were my first light in apparently now six days. Seven, if today counted. I hear a thud to my left and turn to find Isos pulling on his boots. Though he still had severe shadows under his eyes and an exhaustion that sits heavy on his shoulders, it was somewhat lessened then when we had spoken late last night.

"Good morning." He rumbles in his familiar cadence. At least that was the same. I have to remind myself that for most of his time going forward, he would be here in Paith, the territory I had given him. He would not be joining me on my trip home. A slice of regret cuts into me at the burden I had placed on him. And even though he sits in front of me, I already miss my friend. His next words shake me from my stupor, however. "I assume that you still wish to be taken to Türë." That makes me sit up straighter and I nod, trying to conceal the pain that radiates through my body. His eyes narrow and he pulls a chain beside the bed. I frown at him in confusion when nothing happens, then I hear the quick, light patter of hurried footsteps approaching before I realize he had called for a healer. The elderly woman steps in after a gentle knock, then beams at the sight of me sitting up in bed.

"Your Majesty! It is so good to see you awake. You have been worrying the King and your people something awful." She scolds me, though playfully, making me smile and blush, even with the pain.

"Apologies, apparently I was more tired than I thought!" I try to pass it off a joke, but it falls flat. The woman is kind enough to laugh politely, but Isos only groans in exasperation. I glare at him over the woman's shoulder, who begins to examine what feels like every inch of my slowly healing body.

"Good, it appears the um... *medicine* you were given is beginning to leave your system." She eyes Isos warily and I appreciate her tact at keeping my secret.

"He knows everything." I assure her, then flinch as her finger prods painfully at my lower back, where I had been struck at Vante. She relaxes a little, though the muscle in her jaw feathers in anxiety. "What is that pain? Did I burn there too?" The pain differed from the burning in my arms, but still just as harrowing. Especially as she pokes at it again. This time I feel the pain deep in my bones and I take a sharp breath in. She clucks her tongue in frustration as I writhe, not at me, but at the resistance she meets. I realize then, with a start, she is using magic. I glance, wide-eyed, at Isos. But he seems unaware of this, or at least unsurprised. My eyes flick up to the woman, and she flashes a wink at me.

"Well it appears that this scar is not going to heal either. The skin and nerves seem to have already realigned to accommodate the scar tissue." Her attention moves from my back to my arms, both of which are still completely wrapped in thick, cream rolls of gauze from fingertips to shoulders. "Let's check these. Then I will apply more salve to help with the pain before fresh bandages." I nod enthusiastically and the woman chuckles again.

"May I ask what your name is?" I ask as she begins to unroll the tight gauze wrapping my arms, starting with the left. I turn my head to look at Isos instead, not ready to see the aftermath that burns even hotter as it touches the air. I grit my teeth against its pain and her hands move more quickly.

"Of course! How rude of me. I am Patrycia, the head healer here in Naro."

"And have you also been taking care of the General?" I ask through shallow breaths. Her motions slow briefly and I tense, uncertain at her sudden demeanor change.

"I have, Majesty. He is doing much better than when he came in." She says, shortly. Not angry, but distracted.

I am still watching Isos when his attitude also suddenly changes. His eyes widen in alarm before schooling them back to blank. "What??" I ask, unable to force myself to look at my arms even still.

"The scars," Patrycia hesitates. "I have never seen anything like this before." She murmurs, then moves to begin unwrapping my other arm. I gather up all of my courage as Isos watches silently. The only sign of his true feelings—whether they be anticipation or horror— is the growing speed of his breathing. I take a deep breath and hold it in as I turn to see the cost I incurred at saving Türë.

It puffs out in a rush, and I am so shaken I barely feel the pain as my other arm is subjected to the air as well. I look down at both of my arms. I had been prepared for red and purple, bloody and bruised blisters. From their reactions, so had been Patrycia and Isos. Instead, thick bright blue veins trail up from the center of my palms, climbing up each forearm and vining up past my elbow and past my shoulder to where I can no longer see. From the subtle throb down my back however, I know that if I lifted my tunic off, I would find them continuing down my back to the base of my spine, ending in the spot Patrycia had prodded so painfully with her magic not minutes ago. I also knew what they were.

They were indeed the payment of what I had done. They were the marks from where my lighting had traveled through me and into Türë's heart. The marks of bringing life back into him.

They were a beautiful cost, and a permanent reminder.

"They are pretty, somehow." Isos murmurs solemnly. "Are they very painful?" I shake my head no, and was surprised to find that it was the truth. Even as I examine them, the burning pain begins to fade. My body, it seemed, had at last healed, sealing in the marks.

Both begin to protest, but I ignore them as I shove to my feet. My head spins slightly, but that was more from hunger than any pain. "May I please be taken to Türë now?" I ask, in a way that let them know that I wasn't truly asking. Food could wait. I needed to see him with my own eyes.

Isos sighs and exchanges a knowing look with the healer, who seems still entirely thrown by my recovery. "There is something I did not share last night with you, mainly because I didn't want you to worry until you were well enough. But also partly because I wanted to finally get some damn sleep."

I glower at him. "What?" I knew he had been keeping *something* from me.

"He is still... asleep. He has not woken since you revived him." I stare at Isos, trying to understand what he means, my arms going limp at my sides. "He is healing, but slowly." He looks to Patrycia for help.

"General Türë's body went through a lot. It is going to take time, but all of my colleagues and I believe that, once his mind recovers from the shock, he will wake. It is just taking a little longer than expected." She tries to reassure me, but it only does the opposite.

Oh Goddess...

Did I do it wrong?

Did I bring back his body, but not his soul?

"I must see him. Now." I demand.

✹ ✹ ✹ ✹ ✹

I stare at Türë. His normally summer-tanned face is pale as death, though all traces of the blood that he had coughed up was gone. I touch my hand to my lips. It's as if I can feel him breathe his last below me all over again. I grip his limp hand, mentally wailing at him to wake.

"I am so sorry I did this to you. Please wake up." I beg, pulling his hand in mine to my chest, trying to will some warmth into his body. He was alive. They hadn't lied. But only just. His heart beats so slowly that when I first listened to its pause between its pulses, I nearly screamed when it didn't thud when I expected it to.

I knew what this was. As clear as if it had been shouted into my ear. A message. A reminder of what I had to do. Of the promise I had made. I stare down at the vibrant pattern that now is tattooed onto my body. After all, I had made a vow, and now Jera was holding me to it. I feel the familiar flutter of my magic returning, stretching its limbs sleepily.

If I wanted answers, I needed to fulfill my end of the bargain. Or else the location of where my things had been taken would be lost, along with Türë.

I knew what I had to do.

I was alone, aside from the unconscious General. The others, kindly giving me a moment of privacy with him, had shuffled out when it became clear I had no immediate questions about his condition. I notice a pad of paper and quill sitting nearby on the healer's table and grab it, hands quivering violently. I flip to an empty sheet and scrawl two letters before folding them carefully, and setting them each where they were sure to be found. I step up to Türë's bedside again and stare down at the immobile figure.

"I'm going to bring you back, and then you will answer for your crimes. Even if you saved my life, you still owe me that." I whisper, before turning to where the pane of glass blocks the steady breeze from Lake Naro. Before I can falter, I push open the window, slipping through it and, using the crevices in the wall as hand and footholds, I maneuver down the wall to the ground.

Then I run.

sixty

My father never asks for me.

So when he does, I know to be afraid.

I walk through the cold castle as quickly as I can, though I dread each step I take. Something must have happened to put him in the mood to summon me. I tug my fur-lined cloak closer around me, as if I could make it a permanent layer to my body. One to cushion the blow that was inevitably coming.

It was never *abuse,* what my father did in his moods. No, that was too vulgar of a term for a king. It was simply *discipline.* It did not matter if I had done anything to deserve it or not. Most of the time, I just try to stay far, far away from the horrid man. But when he calls for me, like today, it was expected I arrive promptly. No matter what I was doing.

I pause at the iron doors that stand between me and my father. I stare up at them, fighting the urge to snort. One of the previous Kings had them installed centuries before, stuck on the idea that iron could keep magical creatures out. What a load of shit. But here they still stand. I reach for the handle, pushing past the cold radiating from their metal surface. I pray to the forgotten Goddess that they have frozen shut, sealing my father inside forever. No such luck. It glides open on oiled hinges.

My father, King of Mirinth stands, silhouetted against the roaring fireplace, his back to me. *Always cutting the intimidating royal figure.* I enter as quickly and quietly as I can, hoping to avoid detection right away. He almost *oozes* rage. I swallow hard. Bracing for the inevitable. Only a barely discernible tilt of the head lets me know that he is aware of my presence.

I take my usual spot against the wall, wishing for the thousandth time that my brother, Maccormak, had not been sent to war. When he was here, he usually was able to provide a buffer. Favorite son and heir had earned him the right to grow up both unblemished and unfailing in the eyes of our father. We had a sister, apparently. Though we had never seen her. Both our mother and the newborn had been shuffled off in the night to some hidden corner of the kingdom. Our father had no use for girls and, with two sons, our mother had fulfilled her purpose.

My father turns to face me, and for the first time in my life, I see the silver glint of tears in his eyes. My heart stutters.

"The time to actually do something with your existence has come, Prince Conri." My father's low baritone seems to swell, filling up the room. I ignore the insult, as I have always done. In my head, however, I recite the words I wish I could scream at him. *I am one of the highest trained soldiers in your military. Your Generals come to me for advice and planning. I have trained as a scholar and a warrior my entire life. But yes, I know it is not good enough.*

"The savage Queen in the north has slaughtered your brother." The words land, interrupting my inner monologue, and my world turns grey, tilting on its side. I huff out a breath, feeling like I was just punched in the throat. I fight every realization in that moment that hits like a spear and turns my entire life upside down. My focus catching again and again on the one thing that matters above all else.

My brother is gone.

No. Not just gone. Taken. Stolen from me by the monstrous queen who had torn apart my family for decades. I grit my teeth and make myself feel every ounce of grief that spirals into my aching heart.

"How?" I choke out.

"She burned him alive." He answers, fist tightening around the letter clenched in his hand. King Tanth turns back to face the fire. "You know what you must do now. Go and do it."

I pause, wanting to fight against the order, because this was not supposed to be my fate. It was the deal. I was so close to being free.

But there is no other option now.

Maccormak is dead and I am now next in line to be King.

I wish he would just beat me instead. "Father, I—" I start, my voice rough with grief. Grief from Maccormak's death, and the death of the life I had wanted. He spins towards me, fury making his eyes somehow grow so black the whites are nearly imperceptible. The only physical sign of cost of his agreement. The cost of *possibly* winning a war with the famed warriors of the North.

I rub my aching chest and the scar that blemishes the skin above my heart. There was never a rhyme or reason when it would begin to throb. The numerous healers I had seen throughout my life, at my mother's insistence, couldn't even explain how I had been born with such a gruesome birthmark, let alone why it would pang randomly. Only a foreign priestess that my mother had snuck into the castle one day star-cycles ago had an explanation. She claimed it was my death mark from a previous life. Maccormak and I had laughed for hours after that load of crap.

"Do you not wish to avenge your brother?" He hisses at me with rage, and against my will, I take a step back in fear.

"I do!" I almost shout, then collect myself. "I do." It was the truth. My brother was the one good thing in my life. My best friend. I straighten up, deciding then I would do what needed to be done to make my brother's death worth it.

"Then go, Prince Conri. Hell shall rain upon them for what they have done. See it is so." King Tanth dismisses me with a wave of his hand, and I take the opening to flee for the doors. They slam shut behind me and I barely make it to the window before throwing it open and vomiting out of it.

When my stomach is finally emptied and the tears have stopped burning my cheeks, I sink to the ground, bracing my back against the wall.

I would make the Queen pay for the life she had taken. And then I would become King and become what my brother wanted to be. A different King than the brutal monarch they had become accustomed to. *My brother would have—no. I will follow through on the future he had seen for the kingdom and make a new Mirinth.*

For Maccormak.

But first, I would kill the Queen of Tesindren.

Acknowledgements

First, and always, thank you to my amazing husband, Slade. Without your support, encouragement, and cheerleading, I would never have embarked on this wonderful journey—let alone finished. There were so many times I wanted to scrap this whole book and move on. But you continued to believe in me, even when I didn't believe in myself. I am so grateful for all the times you helped me work on a plot hole out loud, and for being the first to hear the story. Thank you for being my guiding star on the darkest night and being the extraordinary man whom I absolutely love and cherish.

My Aurelia, this book finally enters the world as you now take your first steps and begin your own life story. You have been the most understanding baby, enduring my writing and editing sessions, and listening with a smile on your face as I talked to you about this world and these characters. I pray you continue to find the joy in the world and fill it with your imagination and adventure. This book is for you, my darling daughter. To show you that you can do anything if you persevere and set your mind to it. After all, this story was one that I began when I was only fifteen. Who knows when you will find your own story?! No matter where your path takes you though, I will always be with you, cheering and supporting you like you have done for me.

To my friends and family who helped me edit, prepare, and complete: Ron Fowler and Sami Stratton. I appreciate you more than you know! Thank you for your help, this book would not be the same without you!

And finally, thank you, reader. I am forever indebted to you for choosing my story to read. To risk plagiarizing the airlines—I know you have other options, so thank you for choosing *Among the Forgotten*. I hope you will continue to join me on Evara's journey! It is going to get wild…

J.R. Molt is a passionate author and voracious reader who enjoys fantasy, espionage, historical fiction, and action writing. Their work focuses on seizing hope, conquering evil, and overcoming obstacles.

J.R. Molt has been writing for over fifteen years, with her debut novel, **Daughter of Stone** getting published in 2021. When not writing, J.R. Molt enjoys painting, camping, obsessing about books, and yoga.

She grew up in Kearney, Nebraska, and currently resides in Wyoming with her husband, Slade, daughter, Aurelia, and their dog, Odin. You can find out more about J.R. Molt and her work on Instagram or Facebook.

Follow her on Instagram, Facebook, and Twitter

@jrmoltauthor

Previous Works:

The Stone Trilogy

Daughter of Stone (Book 1)

Son of Steel (Book 2)

www.ingramcontent.com/pod-product-compliance
Lightning Source LLC
Chambersburg PA
CBHW010018200726
48283CB00015B/2960